## St Raphael's Catholic Primary School.

The Year 3 Book Prize Award is awarded to:

## Adriana DeAzevedo

You have been chosen for the book prize this year because you have worked consistently to a high standard as you have always tried your very best. You have been a delight to teach as you are always enthusiastic and curious to learn about new things and it has been wonderful to observe your confidence grow over the course of this year. Adriana, you already have a love of books and I really hope you have fun reading about the famous five's famous adventures. You should be really proud of yourself – Congratulations and happy reading!

Miss Donnelly.
3 Simeon.
July 2009.

*Enid Blyton*

# The
# Mysteries
## Collection

# EGMONT

*We bring stories to life*

*The Mystery of the Spiteful Letters* first published in Great Britain
in 1946 by Methuen & Co Limited
*The Mystery of the Missing Necklace* first published in Great Britain
in 1947 by Methuen & Co Limited
*The Mysteruy of the Hidden House* first published in Great Britain
in 1948 by Methuen & Co Limited

This edition first published in Great Britain in 2008 by Dean,
an imprint of Egmont UK Limited,
239 Kensington High Street,
London W8 6SA

ISBN 978 0 6035 6342 3

7 9 10 8 6

Printed and bound in Spain

# CONTENTS

BOOK ONE

# The
# Mystery
of the
# Spiteful
# Letters

BETS and Pip were waiting impatiently for Larry, Daisy and Fatty to come. Bets was on the window-seat of the play-room looking anxiously out of the window.

' I wish they'd buck up,' she said. ' After all, they came home from boarding-school yesterday, and they've had plenty of time to come along. I do want to know if Fatty's got any more disguises and things.'

' I suppose you think there'll be another first-class mystery for us to solve these hols,' said Pip. ' Golly, that was a wizard one we had in the Christmas hols, wasn't it ? '

' Yes,' said Bets. ' A bit too wizard. I wouldn't really mind not having a mystery these hols.'

' Bets ! And I thought you were such a keen detective ! ' said Pip. ' Don't you want to be a Find-Outer any more ? '

' Of course I do. Don't be silly ! ' said Bets. ' I know you don't think I'm much use, because I'm the youngest and only nine, and you're all in your teens now—but I did help an awful lot last time, when we solved the mystery of the secret room.'

Pip was just about to say something squashing to his little sister when she gave a yell. ' Here they are ! At least—here are Larry and Daisy. Let's go down and meet them.'

They tore downstairs and out into the drive.

Bets flung herself on the boy and girl in delight, and Pip stood by and grinned.

'Hallo, Larry! hallo, Daisy! Seen Fatty at all?'

'No,' said Larry. 'Isn't he here? Blow! Let's go to the gate and watch for him. Won't it be fun to see old Buster again too, wagging his tail and trotting along on his short Scottie legs!'

The four children went to the front gate and looked out. There was no sign of Fatty and Buster. The baker's cart drove by. Then came a woman on a bicycle. Then up the lane plodded a most familiar figure.

It was Mr. Goon the policeman, or old Clear-Orf as the children called him. He was going round on his beat, and was not at all pleased to see the four children at Pip's gate, watching him. Mr. Goon did not like the children, and they certainly did not like him. There had been three mysteries to solve in their village of Peterswood in the last year, and each time the children had solved them before Mr. Goon.

'Good morning,' said Larry politely, as Mr. Goon came by, panting a little for he was plump. His frog-eyes glared at them.

'So you're back again, like bad pennies,' he said. 'Ho! Poking your noses into things again, I suppose!'

'I expect so,' said Pip cheerfully. Mr. Goon was just about to make another crushing remark when there came a wild ringing of bicycle bells and a boy came round the corner at top speed on a bicycle.

'Telegraph-boy,' said Pip. 'Look out, Mr. Goon, look out!'

The telegraph-boy had swerved right over to the policeman, and it looked as if he was going straight into him. Mr. Goon gave a yelp and skipped like a lamb out of the way.

'Now then, what you riding like that for? A public danger, that's what you boys are!' exploded Mr. Goon.

'Sorry, sir, my bicycle sort of swerved over,' said the boy. 'Did I hurt you, sir? I'm down-right sorry!'

Mr. Goon's temper cooled down at the boy's politeness. 'What house are you wanting?' he asked.

'I've got a telegram for Master Philip Hilton,' said the telegraph-boy, looking at the name and address on the orange envelope in his hand.

'Oh! Here's Pip!' said Bets. 'Oooh, Pip—a telegram for you!'

The boy propped his bicycle by the side of the pavement, its pedal catching the kerb. But he didn't balance it very firmly and it fell over with a clatter, the handle-bar catching Mr. Goon on the shin.

He let out such a yell that all the children jumped. He hopped round, trying to hold his ankle and keep his balance too. Bets gave a sudden giggle.

'Oh, sir, I'm sorry!' cried the boy. 'That dratted bike! It's always falling over. Don't you be angry with me, sir. Don't you report me, will you? I'm that sorry!'

Mr. Goon's red face was redder than ever. He glared at the telegraph-boy, and rubbed his ankle again. 'You deliver your telegram and clear-orf,' he said. 'Wasting the time of the post-office, that's what you're doing!'

' Yes, sir,' said the boy meekly, and gave Pip the orange envelope. Pip tore it open, full of curiosity. He had never had a telegram sent to him before.

He read it out loud. It was from Fatty.

' SORRY NOT TO SEE YOU THESE HOLS. HAVE GOT A MYSTERY TO SOLVE IN TIPPY-LOOLOO, AND AM LEAVING BY AEROPLANE TO-DAY. ALL THE BEST ! FATTY.'

The children crowded round to see the telegram. They couldn't believe their ears. What an extraordinary telegram ! Mr. Goon could hardly believe his ears either.

' You let me see that,' he said, and took it out of Pip's hand. He read it out loud to himself.

' This is from that boy Frederick Trotteville, isn't it ? ' he said. ' Fatty, you call him, don't you ? What does it mean ? Leaving by aeroplane for Tippy—Tippy—whatever it is. Never heard of the place in my life ! '

' It's in South China,' said the telegraph-boy unexpectedly. ' I got an uncle out there, that's how I know.'

' But—but—why should Fatty go—why should he solve a mystery out there—why, why . . .' began the four children, absolutely taken aback.

' We shan't see him these hols,' suddenly wailed Bets, who was extremely fond of Fatty, and had looked forward very much to seeing him.

' And a good thing too,' said Mr. Goon, giving the telegram back to Pip. ' That's what I say. A jolly good thing too. He's a tiresome nuisance that boy is, pretending to play at being a detective—and using disguises to deceive the Law—and poking his nose in where it's not wanted. Perhaps we'll have a little peace these holidays if that interfering boy has gone to Tippy—Tippy—whatever it is.'

'Tippylooloo,' said the telegraph-boy, who seemed as much interested as any one else. 'I say, sir—is that telegram from that clever chap, Mr. Trotteville? I've heard about him.'

'*Mr.* Trotteville!' echoed Mr. Goon, indignantly. 'Why, he's no more than a kid. *Mr.* Trotteville! Mr. Interfering Fatty, that's what *I* call him!'

Bets gave a sudden giggle again. Mr. Goon had gone purple. He always did when he was annoyed.

'Sorry, sir. Didn't mean to make you all hot and bothered, sir,' said the telegraph-boy, who seemed very good indeed at apologizing for everything. 'But of course we've all heard of that boy, sir. Very very clever chap, he seems to be. Didn't he get on to some big plot last hols, sir, before the police did?'

Mr. Goon was not at all pleased to hear that Fatty's fame was apparently spread abroad like this. He did one of his snorts.

'You got better things to do at the post-office than listen to fairy-tales like that!' he said to the eager telegraph-boy. 'That boy Fatty's just an interfering little nuisance and always was, and he leads these kids here into trouble too. I reckon their parents'll be pretty glad that boy's gone to Tippy—Tippy—er . . .'

'Tippylooloo,' said the telegraph-boy obligingly. 'Fancy him being asked out there to solve a mystery, sir. Coo, he must be clever!'

The four children were delighted to hear all this. They knew how the policeman must hate it.

'You get along now,' said Mr. Goon, feeling that the telegraph-boy was a real nuisance. 'Clear-orf! You've wasted enough time.'

'Yes, sir; certainly, sir,' said the polite boy. 'Fancy that fellow going off to Tippylooloo—by aeroplane too. Coo! I must write to my uncle out there and get him to tell me what Mr. Trotte-ville's doing. Coo!'

'Clear-orf!' said Mr. Goon. The boy winked at the others and took hold of his bicycle handles. The children couldn't help liking him. He had red hair, freckles all over his face, red eyebrows and a funny twisty mouth.

He got on his bicycle, did a dangerous swerve towards Mr. Goon, and was off down the road ringing the two bells he had as loudly as ever he could.

'There's a boy that's civil and respectful to the Law,' said Mr. Goon to the others. 'And he's an example to follow, see!'

But the other children were no longer paying attention to the fat policeman. Instead they were looking at the telegram again. How surprising it was! Fatty *was* surprising, of course—but to go off by plane to China!

'Mother would never let *me* do a thing like that,' said Pip. 'After all, Fatty's only thirteen. I can't believe it!'

Bets burst into tears. 'I did so want him to come back for the hols and find another mystery!' she wailed. 'I did, I did!'

'Shut up, Bets, and don't be a baby,' said Pip. 'We can solve mysteries without Fatty, can't we?'

But privately each of them knew that without Fatty they couldn't do much. Fatty was the real leader, the one who dared to do all kinds of things, the real brain of the Find-Outers.

'Without Fatty we're like rabbit-pie without any rabbit in it,' said Daisy dolefully. That sounded funny, but nobody laughed. They all knew what Daisy meant. Things weren't nearly so exciting and interesting without Fatty.

'I just can't get over it,' said Larry, walking up the drive with the others. 'Fatty off to South China! And what *can* be the mystery he's solving there? I do think he might have found time to come and tell us.'

'That telegraph-boy thought an awful lot of Fatty, didn't he?' said Bets. 'Fancy! Fatty must be getting quite famous!'

'Yes. Old Clear-Orf didn't like him praising up Fatty, did he!' chuckled Larry. 'I liked that boy. He sort of reminded me of some one, but I can't think who.'

'I say—what's going to happen to Buster?' suddenly said Bets, stopping still in the drive. 'Fatty wouldn't be allowed to take his dog with him—and Buster would break his heart left alone. What do you suppose is happening to him? Couldn't *we* have him?'

'I bet Fatty would like us to have him,' said Pip. 'Let's go up to Fatty's house and ask his mother about Buster. Come on. We'll go now.'

They all turned and went back down the drive. Bets felt a little comforted. It would be something to have Fatty's dog, even if they couldn't have Fatty. Dear old Buster! He was such a darling, and had shared all their adventures.

They came to Fatty's house and went into the drive. Fatty's mother was picking some daffodils for her vases, and she smiled at the children.

' Back for the holidays ? ' she said. ' Well, I hope you'll all have a nice time. You're looking very solemn. Is anything the matter ? '

' Well—we just came to see if we could have Buster for the hols,' said Larry. ' Oh, there he is ! Buster, Buster old fellow ! Come here ! '

## 2    FATTY REALLY IS SURPRISING

BUSTER came tearing up to the children, barking madly, his tail wagging nineteen to the dozen. He flung himself on them and tried to lick and bark at the same time.

' Good old Buster ! ' said Pip. ' I bet you'll miss Fatty ! '

' It was a great surprise to hear that Fatty has gone to China,' said Daisy to Mrs. Trotteville. Fatty's mother looked surprised.

' In an aeroplane too ! ' said Larry. ' You'll miss him, won't you, Mrs. Trotteville ? '

' What exactly do you mean ? ' asked Mrs. Trotteville, looking as if she thought the children had gone mad all of a sudden.

' Gracious—Fatty can't have told her ! ' said Bets, in a loud whisper.

' Told me *what* ? ' said Mrs. Trotteville, getting impatient. ' What's the mystery ? What's Fatty been up to ? '

' But — but — don't you know ? ' stammered Larry. ' He's gone to Tippylooloo, and . . .'

' Tippylooloo ! What's all this nonsense ? ' said Mrs. Trotteville. She raised her voice. ' Frederick ! Come here a minute ! '

The children turned breathlessly to the house —and out of the front door, stepping lazily, came Fatty ! Yes, it really was Fatty, as large as life, grinning all over his plump face. Bets gave a loud shriek and ran to him. She hugged him.

' Oh, I thought you'd gone to Tippylooloo ! Didn't you go ? Oh, Fatty, I'm so glad you're here ! '

The others stared. They were puzzled. ' Did you send us that telegram ? ' said Daisy suddenly. ' Was it a joke on your part, Fatty ? '

' What telegram ? ' asked Fatty innocently. ' I was just about to come down and see you all.'

' This telegram ! ' said Pip, and pushed it into Fatty's hand. He read it and looked astonished.

' Somebody's been playing a joke on you,' he said. ' Silly sort of joke. And anyway, fancy you all believing I was off to Tippylooloo ! Gosh ! '

' You and your jokes ! ' said Mrs. Trotteville. ' As if I should let Frederick go to China, or wherever that ridiculous Tippylooloo place is. Now, if you want to go and talk to Frederick, either go indoors or go for a walk.'

They went indoors. They still felt very puzzled. Buster danced round, barking in delight. He was overjoyed because the whole company of Find-Outers was together again.

' Who delivered this telegram ? ' asked Fatty.

' The telegraph-boy,' said Pip. ' A red-haired chap with freckles and a cheeky kind of voice. He

let his bike-handle catch old Clear-Orf on the shin !
You should have seen him dance round ! '

' Hm,' said Fatty. ' There's something queer
about that telegraph-boy, *I* think ! Delivering a
telegram I didn't send ! Let's go out and look for
him and ask him a few questions ! '

They went out, and walked down the lane
together, Buster at their heels. ' You go that way,
Larry and Daisy, and you go the opposite way, Pip
and Bets,' said Fatty. ' I'll take this third way.
We'll scour the village properly for that boy, and
meet at the corner by the church in half an hour's
time.'

' I want to go with *you*, Fatty,' said Bets.

' No, you go with Pip,' said Fatty, unexpectedly
hard-hearted. He usually let Bets have her own way
in everything. Bets said nothing but walked off
with Pip, feeling rather hurt.

Larry and Daisy saw no telegraph-boy at all,
and were waiting by the church corner in twenty-
five minutes' time. Then Pip and Bets came up.
They hadn't seen him either. They looked up and
down for Fatty and Buster.

Round the corner came a bicycle, and on it was
—the red-headed telegraph-boy, whistling loudly.
Larry gave a yell.

' Oy ! Come over here a minute ! '

The telegraph-boy wobbled over, and balanced
himself by the kerb. His red hair fell in a big lock
over his forehead, and his uniform cap was well on
one side.

' What's up, mate ? ' he said.

' It's about that telegram,' said Larry. ' It's all
nonsense ! Our friend Frederick Trotteville hasn't
gone to China—he's here ! '

' Where ? ' said the boy, looking all round.

' I mean he's in the village somewhere,' said Larry. ' He'll be along in a minute.'

' Coo ! ' said the boy. ' I wouldn't half like to see him ! He's a wonder, he is ! I wonder the police don't take him on, and get him to help them with their problems.'

' Well, we *all* helped to solve the mysteries you know,' said Pip, beginning to feel that it was time he and the others got a bit of praise too.

' No, did you really ? ' said the boy. ' I thought it was Mr. Trotteville that was the brains of the party. Coo, I'd like to meet him ! Do you think he'd give me his autograph ? '

The children stared at him, thinking that Fatty must indeed be famous if telegraph-boys wanted his autograph.

' That was a dud telegram you brought,' said Larry. ' A fake, a joke. Did *you* fake it ? '

' Me fake it ! Coo, I'd lose my job ! ' said the telegraph-boy. ' Look here, when's this famous friend of yours coming ? I want to meet him, but I can't wait here all day. I've got to get back to the P.O.'

' Well, the post-office can wait a minute or two, I should think,' said Pip, who felt that none of them had got very much information out of the telegraph-boy, and was hoping that perhaps Fatty might.

A small dog rounded the corner, and Bets gave a yell. ' Buster ! Come on, Buster ! Where's Fatty ? Tell him to hurry.'

Every one thought that Fatty would come round the corner too, but he didn't. Buster trotted on towards them alone. He didn't growl at the tele-graph-boy. He gave him a lick and then sat down beside him on the kerb, turning adoring eyes up to him.

Bets was most astonished.  She had never seen Buster adoring any one but Fatty in that way.  She stared at the little black dog, surprised.  What should make him like the telegraph-boy so much ?

Then she gave a loud squeal and pounced on the telegraph-boy so suddenly that he jumped.

'Fatty !' she said.  'Oh, Fatty !  What idiots we are !  FATTY !'

Pip's mouth fell open.  Daisy stared as if she couldn't believe her eyes.  Larry exploded and banged the telegraph-boy on the back.

'You wretch !  You absolute wretch !  You took us all in properly—and you took old Clear-Orf in too.  Fatty, you're a marvel.  How do you do it ? '

Fatty grinned at them all.  He removed his red eyebrows with a pull.  He rubbed off his freckles with a wetted hanky.  He shifted his red wig a little so that the others could see his sleek black hair beneath.

'Fatty !  It's the most wonderful disguise ! ' said Pip enviously.  'But how do you manage to twist up your mouth to make it different and screw up your eyes to make them smaller and all that kind of thing ? '

'Oh, that's just good acting,' said Fatty, swelling a little with pride.  'I've told you before, haven't I, that I always take the chief part in our school plays, and this last term I . . .'

But the children didn't want to hear about Fatty's wonderful doings at school.  They had heard about those too often.  Larry interrupted him.

'Golly !  Now I know why the telegraph-boy

praised you up so ! Idiot ! Calling yourself *Mr.* Trotteville and waiting for your own autograph ! Honestly, Fatty, you're the limit ! '

They all went to Pip's house and were soon settled in the playroom, examining Fatty's cap and wig and everything.

' It's a new disguise I got,' explained Fatty. ' I wanted to try it out, of course. Fine wig, isn't it ? It cost an awful lot of money. I daren't tell Mother. I could hardly wait to play that joke on you. I'm getting awfully good at disguises and acting.'

' You are, Fatty,' said Bets generously. ' I would never have known it was you if I hadn't noticed Buster sitting down looking up at you with that sort of adoring look he keeps for you, Fatty.'

' So that's how you guessed, you clever girl ! ' said Fatty. ' I call that pretty good, Bets. Honestly, I sometimes think you notice even more than the others ! '

Bets glowed, but Pip did not look too pleased. He always thought of Bets as his baby sister, and thought she ought to be kept under, and not made conceited about herself.

' She'll get swelled head,' he growled. ' Any of us could have spotted Buster's goofy look at you.'

' Ah, but you didn't,' said Fatty. ' I say— isn't it great that old Clear-Orf thinks I've gone to Tippylooloo ! That *was* a bit of luck, his happening to be with you when I cycled up this morning. Didn't he jump when I let my bike fall on his shin ! '

They all stared at Fatty in admiration. The things he did ! The things he thought of ! Bets giggled.

' Won't he be surprised when you turn up ! '

she said. ' He'll think you've come back from Tippylooloo already ! '

' What a name ! ' said Daisy. ' How in the world did you think of it ? '

' Oh, things like that are easy,' said Fatty, modestly. ' Poor old Clear-Orf ! He just swallowed that telegram whole ! '

' Are you going to use that disguise when we solve our next mystery ? ' asked Bets, eagerly.

' What's our next mystery ? ' said Pip. ' We haven't got one ! It would be too much to expect one these hols.'

' Well, you never know,' said Fatty. ' You simply never know ! I bet a mystery will turn up again—and I jolly well hope we'll be on to it before old Clear-Orf is. Do you remember how I locked him up in the coal-hole in our last mystery ? '

Every one laughed. They remembered how poor old Mr. Goon had staggered up out of the coal-hole, black with coal-dust, his helmet lost, and with a most terrible sneezing cold.

' And we sent him some carbolic soap and found his helmet for him,' remembered Daisy. ' And he wasn't a bit grateful, and never even thanked us. And Pip's mother said it was rather an insult to send him soap and was cross with us.'

' I'd like another mystery to solve,' said Pip. ' We'll all keep our ears and eyes open. The hols have begun well, with you in your new disguise, Fatty—taking old Goon in as well as us ! '

' I must go,' said Fatty, getting up. ' I've got to slip back and change out of this telegraph-boy's suit. I'll just put on my wig and eyebrows again in case I meet Clear-Orf. Well—so long ! '

A WHOLE week went by. The weather was rather dull and rainy, and the children got tired of it. It wasn't much fun going for walks and getting soaked. On the other hand they couldn't stay indoors all day.

The five of them and Buster met at Pip's each day, because Pip had a fine big playroom. They made rather a noise sometimes, and then Mrs. Hilton would come in, looking cross.

'There's no need to behave as if you were a hurricane and an earthquake rolled into one!' she said, one day. Then she looked in surprise at Pip. 'Pip, what on earth are you doing?'

'Nothing, Mother,' said Pip, unwinding himself hurriedly from some weird purple garment. 'Just being a Roman emperor, that's all, and telling my slaves what I think of them.'

'Where did you get that purple thing,' asked his mother. 'Oh, *Pip*—surely you haven't taken Mrs. Moon's bed-spread to act about in?'

'Well, she's out,' said Pip. 'I didn't think it would matter, Mother.'

Mrs. Moon was the cook-housekeeper, and had been with the Hiltons only a few months. The last cook was in hospital ill. Mrs. Moon was a really wonderful cook, but she had a very bad temper. Mrs. Hilton was tired of hearing her grumble about the children.

'You just put that bed-spread back *at once!*'

she said. ' Mrs. Moon will be most annoyed if she thinks you've been into her bedroom and taken her bed-covering. That was wrong of you, Pip. And will you all please remember to wipe your feet when you come in at the garden-door this wet weather ? Mrs. Moon says she is always washing your muddy foot-marks away.'

' She's a spiteful old tell-tale,' said Pip sulkily.

' I won't have you talking like that, Pip,' said Mrs. Hilton. ' She's a very good cook and does her work extremely well. It's no wonder she complains when you make her so much extra cleaning—and, by the way, she says things some-times disappear from the larder and she feels sure it's you children taking them. I hope that's not so.'

Pip looked uncomfortable. ' Well, Mother,' he began, ' it's only that we're most awfully hungry sometimes, and you see . . .'

' No, I don't see at all,' said Mrs. Hilton. ' Mrs. Moon is in charge of the larder, and you are not to take things without either my permission or hers. Now take back that bed-spread, for goodness sake, and spread it out neatly. Daisy, go with Pip and see that he puts it back properly.'

Daisy went off meekly with Pip. Mrs. Hilton could be very strict, and all five children were in awe of her, and of Mr. Hilton too. They would not stand any nonsense at all, either from their own children or from other people's ! Yet they all liked Mrs. Hilton very much, and Pip and Bets thought the world of her.

Daisy and Pip returned to the playroom. Mrs. Hilton had gone. Pip looked at the others and grinned.

' We put it back,' he said. ' We pulled it this way and that, we patted it down, we draped it just right, we . . .'

' Oh, shut up ! ' said Larry. ' I don't like Mrs. Moon. She may be a good cook—and I must say she makes marvellous cakes—but she's a tell-tale.'

' I bet poor old Gladys is scared of her,' said Daisy. Gladys was the housemaid, a timid, quiet little thing, ready with shy smiles, and very willing to do anything for the children.

' I like Mrs. Cockles the best,' said Bets. ' She's got a lovely name, I think. She's the char-woman. She comes to help Mrs. Moon and Gladys twice a week. She tells me all kinds of things.'

' Good old Cockles ! ' said Pip. ' She always hands us out some of Mrs. Moon's jam-tarts on baking day, if we slip down to the kitchen.'

Larry yawned and looked out of the window. ' This disgusting weather ! ' he said. ' Raining again ! It's jolly boring. I wish to goodness we'd got something to do—a mystery to solve, for instance.'

' There doesn't seem to be a single thing,' said Daisy. ' No robberies—not even a bicycle stolen in the village. Nothing.'

' I bet old Clear-Orf will be pleased if we don't get a mystery this time,' said Fatty.

' Has he seen you yet ? ' asked Bets. Fatty shook his head.

' No. I expect he still thinks I'm away at Tippylooloo,' he said, with a grin. ' He'll be surprised when I turn up.'

' Let's go out, even if it *is* raining,' said Pip. ' Let's go and snoop about. Don't you remember how last hols I snooped round an empty house and found that secret room at the top of it ?  Well, let's go and snoop again.  We might hit on *some*thing ! '

So they all put on macks and sou'-westers and went for a snoop.  ' We might find some clues,' said Bets hopefully.

' Clues to *what* ! ' said Pip scornfully.  ' You have to have a mystery before you can find clues, silly ! '

They snooped round a few empty houses, but there didn't seem anything extraordinary about them at all.  They peered into an empty shed, and were scared almost out of their wits when a tall tramp rose up from the dark corners and yelled at them.

They tramped over a deserted allotment and examined a tumble-down cottage at one end very thoroughly.  But there was absolutely nothing queer or strange or mysterious to find.

' It's tea-time,' said Fatty.  ' We'd better go home.  I've got an aunt coming.  See you to-morrow ! '

Larry and Daisy drifted off home too.  Pip and Bets splashed their way down their wet lane and went gloomily indoors.

' Dull and boring ! ' said Pip, flinging his mack down on the hall-cupboard floor.  ' Nothing but rain !  Nothing to do ! '

' You'll get into a row if you leave your wet mack on the ground,' said Bets, hanging hers up.

' Pick it up then,' said Pip, in a bad temper. He hadn't even an exciting book to read.  His mother had gone out to tea.  He and Bets were alone in the house with Gladys.

' Let's ask Gladys to come up to the playroom

and play cards,' said Pip. ' She loves a game. Mrs.
Moon isn't in to say No.'

Gladys was only too delighted to come and play.
She was about nineteen, a pretty, dark-haired girl,
timid in her ways, and easily pleased. She enjoyed
the game of Happy Families as much as the two
children did. She laughed at all their jokes, and
they had a very happy time together.

' It's your bed-time now, Miss Bets,' she said
at last. ' And I've got to go and see to the dinner.
Do you want me to run your bath-water for you,
Miss ? '

' No, thank you. I like doing it myself,' said
Bets. ' Goodbye, Gladys. I like you ! '

Gladys went downstairs. Bets went to run the
bath-water. Pip went off whistling to change into
a clean suit. His parents would not let him sit up
to dinner unless he was clean and tidy.

' Perhaps it will be fine and sunny to-morrow,'
thought Pip, looking out of the window at the
darkening western sky. ' It doesn't look so bad
to-night. We might be able to get a few bike-rides
and picnics in if only the weather clears.'

It *was* fine and sunny the next day. Larry,
Daisy, Fatty and Buster arrived at Pip's early, full
of a good plan.

' Let's take our lunch with us and go to
Burnham Beeches,' said Larry. ' We'll have grand
fun there. You should just see some of the beeches,
Bets—enormous old giants all gnarled and knotted,
and some of them really seem to have faces in their
knotted old trunks ! '

' Oooh—I'd like to go,' said Bets. ' I'm big
enough to ride all the way with you this year.
Mummy wouldn't let me last year.'

'What's up with your Gladys?' said Fatty, scratching Buster on the tummy, as he lay upside down by his chair.

'Gladys? Nothing!' said Pip. 'Why?'

'Well, she looked as if she'd been crying when I saw her in the hall this morning,' said Fatty. 'I came in at the garden door as usual, and bumped into her in the hall. Her eyes looked as red as anything.'

'Well, she was quite all right last night,' said Pip, remembering the lively game they had had. 'Perhaps she got into a row with Mrs. Moon.'

'Shouldn't think so,' said Fatty. 'Mrs. Moon called out something to her quite friendly as I passed. Perhaps she's had bad news.'

Bets felt upset. She went to find Gladys. The girl was sweeping the bedroom floors. Yes, her eyes were very red!

'Gladys, have you been crying?' asked Bets. 'What's the matter? Has somebody been scolding you?'

'No,' said Gladys, trying to smile. 'Nothing's the matter, Miss Bets. I'm all right. Right as rain.'

Bets looked at her doubtfully. She didn't look at all happy. What could have happened between last night and now?

'Have you had bad news?' said Bets, looking very sympathetic.

'Now just you heed what I say,' said Gladys. 'There's nothing the matter. You run off to the others.'

There was nothing to do but go back. 'She *has* been crying,' said Bets, 'but she won't tell me why.'

'Well, leave her alone,' said Larry, who didn't like crying females. 'Why should we pry into her private affairs ? Come on, let's go and ask about this picnic.'

Mrs. Hilton was only too glad to say that the children could go off for the day. It was tiring having them in the house all day long, especially as Pip's playroom was the general meeting-room.

'I was going to suggest that you went off for the day myself,' she said. 'You can take your lunch *and* your tea, if you like ! I'll get it ready for you, whilst Fatty and the others go back to get theirs.'

It was soon ready. Mrs. Hilton gave them the packets of sandwiches and cake. 'Now just keep out for the whole day and don't come tearing back because you're bored,' she said firmly. 'I don't want to see any of you till after tea. I've got important things to do to-day.'

'What are they, Mother ? ' asked Pip, hoping he was not going to miss anything exciting.

'Never you mind,' said his mother. 'Now, off you go and have a lovely day ! '

They rode off on their bicycles. 'Mother seemed to want to get rid of us to-day, didn't she ? ' said Pip. 'I mean—she almost *pushed* us out. I wonder why ? And what's so important to-day ? She didn't tell us about any Meeting or anything.'

'You're trying to make it out to be quite a mystery ! ' said Bets. 'I expect she's going to turn out cupboards or something. Mothers always seem to think things like that are very important. Hurrah, Pip—there are the others ! Come on ! '

With a jangling of bicycle bells the little party rode off. Buster sat solemnly in Fatty's basket.

He loved a picnic. A picnic meant woods or fields, and woods or fields meant one thing and one thing only to Buster—rabbits !

## 4   MR. GOON'S GLOVE

THE children had a lovely day. It was warm and sunny, there were primroses everywhere, and the little bright mauve dog-violets made a carpet with the wind-flowers.

' This is glorious,' said Daisy. ' Thank goodness the weather's changed at last. Let's lay out our macks and sit on them.'

Buster went off happily. The children watched him go. ' Off to solve the great Rabbit Mystery ! ' said Fatty. ' Where is the rabbit-hole that is big enough to take a dog like Buster ? That is the great problem Buster's always hoping to solve.'

Every one laughed. ' I wish we had a great problem to solve,' said Daisy. ' I've sort of got used to having something for my brains to chew on each hols. It seems odd not to have anything really to think about.'

The day passed quickly. It was soon time to go home again, and the five mounted their bicycles. Buster had with difficulty been removed from halfway down a rather big rabbit-hole. He had been very angry at being hauled out, and now sat sulkily in Fatty's basket, his ears down. Just as he had almost reached that rabbit ! Another minute and he'd have got him !

' Buster's sulking,' said Pip, and laughed. ' Oy, Buster ! Cheer up ! '

' I wonder if Mother's done all the important things she said she had to do,' said Bets to Pip. ' Anyway she can't say she's been much bothered with us to-day ! '

They all parted at the church corner to go their different ways. ' We'll meet at Larry's to-morrow ! ' said Fatty. ' In the garden if it's fine. Cheerio ! '

Pip and Bets biked down their lane and into their drive. ' I'm jolly thirsty,' said Pip. ' I wonder if Gladys would give us some ice out of the frig to put into a jug of water. I feel like a drink of iced water, I'm so hot.'

' Well, don't ask Mrs. Moon,' said Bets. ' She's sure to say no ! '

They went to find Gladys. She wasn't in the kitchen, for they peeped in at the window to see. She wasn't upstairs either, for they went up and called her. Their mother heard them and came out of the study to greet them as they ran downstairs again.

' Did you have a lovely day ? ' she said. ' I was pleased it was so fine for you.'

' Yes, a super day,' said Pip. ' Mother, can we have a drink of iced water ? We're melting ! '

' Yes, if you like,' Mrs. Hilton said. They shot off to the kitchen. They peeped in. Mrs. Moon was there, knitting.

' What do you want ? ' she said, looking unexpectedly amiable.

' Just some iced water, please,' said Pip. ' But we weren't going to ask you for it, Mrs. Moon. We were going to ask Gladys. We didn't want to bother you.'

' No bother,' said Mrs. Moon, getting up. ' I'll
get it.'

' Is Gladys out ? ' asked Bets.

' Yes,' said Mrs. Moon shortly. ' Now, take
these ice-cubes quick, and slip them into a jug.
That's right.'

' But it isn't Gladys's day out, is it ? ' said Pip,
surprised. ' She went the day before yesterday.'

' There now—you've dropped an ice-cube ! '
said Mrs. Moon. ' Well, I'm no good at chasing
ice-cubes round the kitchen floor, so you must get
it yourselves.'

Bets giggled as Pip tried to get the cold slippery
ice-cube off the floor. He rinsed it under the tap
and popped it into the jug.

' Thanks, Mrs. Moon,' he said and carried the
jug and two glasses up to the playroom.

' Mrs. Moon didn't seem to want to talk about
Gladys, did she ? ' said Pip. ' Funny.'

' Pip—you don't think Gladys has left, do you ? '
suddenly said Bets. ' I do hope she hasn't. I did
like her.'

' Well—we can easily find out,' said Pip. ' Let's
go and peep in her bedroom. If her things are
there we'll know she's just out for a while and is
coming back.'

They went along the landing to the little room
that Gladys had. They opened the door and
peeped in. They stared in dismay.

Every single thing that had belonged to Gladys
had gone ! Her brush and comb, her tooth-brush,
and the little blue night-dress case she had embroidered at school for herself. There was nothing
at all to show that the girl had been there for a
month or two.

' Yes—she *has* gone ! ' said Bets. ' Well, why didn't Mother tell us ? Or Mrs. Moon ? What's all the mystery ? '

' It's jolly funny,' said Pip. ' Do you think she stole anything ? She seemed so nice. I liked her.'

' Let's go and ask Mother,' said Bets. So they went down to the study. But their mother was not there. They were just turning to go out when Pip's sharp eyes caught sight of something lying under a chair. He picked it up.

It was a large black woollen glove. He stared at it, trying to remember who wore black woollen gloves.

' Whose is it ? ' asked Bets. ' Look—isn't that a name inside ? '

Pip looked—and the name he saw there made him stare hard. On a little tab was printed in marking ink, five letters : ' T. GOON.'

' T. Goon ! Theophilus Goon ! ' said Pip, in surprise. ' Golly ! What was old Clear-Orf here for to-day ? He came here and sat in this study, and left a glove behind. No wonder Mother said she had important things to do if she had old Clear-Orf coming for a meeting ! But why did he come ? '

Bets burst into a loud wail. ' He's taken Gladys to prison ! I know he has ! Gladys has gone to prison, and I did like her so much.'

' Shut up, idiot ! ' said Pip. ' Mother will hear you.'

Mrs. Hilton came quickly into the study, thinking that Bets must surely have hurt herself. ' What's the matter dear ? ' she asked.

' Mother ! Mr. Goon's taken Gladys to prison, hasn't he ? ' wept Bets. ' But I'm sure she didn't steal or anything. I'm sure she didn't. She was n-n-n-nice ! '

' Bets, don't be silly,' said her mother. ' Of *course* Mr. Goon hasn't done anything of the sort.'

' Well, why was he here then ? ' demanded Pip.

' How do you know he was ? ' said his mother.

' Because of this,' said Pip, and he held out the large woollen glove. ' That's Mr. Goon's glove. So we know he has been here in the study—and as Gladys is gone we feel pretty certain Mr. Goon's had something to do with her going.'

' Well, he hasn't,' said Mrs. Hilton. ' She was very upset about something to-day and I let her go home to her aunt.'

' Oh,' said Pip. ' Then why did Mr. Goon come to see you, Mother ? '

' Really, Pip, it's no business of yours,' said his mother, quite crossly. ' I don't want you prying into it either. I know you all fancy yourselves as detectives, but this is nothing whatever to do with you, and I'm not going to have you mixed up in any of your so-called mysteries again.'

' Oh—is there a mystery then ? ' said Bets. ' And is old Clear-Orf trying to solve it ? Oh Mother, you might tell us, you might ! '

' It's nothing whatever to do with you,' said Mrs. Hilton firmly. ' Your father and I have discussed something with Mr. Goon, that's all.'

' Has he been complaining about us ? ' asked Pip.

' No, for a wonder he hasn't,' said his mother. ' Stop howling, Bets. There's nothing to wail about.'

Bets dried her eyes. ' Why did Gladys go ? ' she said. ' I want her to come back.'

'Well, maybe she will,' said her mother. 'I can't tell you why she went, except that she was upset about something, that's all. It's her own private business.'

Mrs. Hilton went out of the room. Pip looked at Bets, and slipped his hand into the enormous black glove. 'Golly, what a giant of a hand old Clear-Orf must have,' he said. 'I do wonder why he was here, Bets. It was something to do with Gladys, I'm certain.'

'Let's go up and tell Fatty,' said Bets. 'He'll know what to do. Why is everything being kept such a secret? And oh, I do hate to think of Clear-Orf sitting here talking with Mother, and grinning to think we were not to know anything about it!'

They couldn't go up to Fatty's that evening, because Mrs. Hilton suddenly decided she wanted to wash their hair. 'But mine's quite clean,' protested Pip.

'It looks absolutely black,' said his mother. 'What *have* you been doing to it to-day, Pip? Standing on your head in a heap of soot, or something?'

'Can't we have our heads washed to-morrow night?' said Bets. But it wasn't a bit of good. It had to be then and there. So it wasn't until the next day that Pip and Bets were able to see Fatty. He was at Larry's, of course, because they had all arranged to meet there.

'I say,' began Pip, 'a funny thing's happened at our house. Old Clear-Orf went there yesterday to see my father and mother about something so mysterious that nobody will tell us what it was! And Gladys, our nice housemaid, has gone home, and we can't find out exactly why. And look—here's a glove Goon left behind.'

Every one examined it. ' It might be a valuable clue,' said Bets.

' Idiot ! ' said Pip. ' I keep telling you you can't have clues before you've got a mystery to solve. Besides, how could Goon's glove be a clue ! You're a baby.'

' Well—it *was* a clue to his presence there in your study yesterday,' said Fatty, seeing Bets' eyes fill with tears. ' But I say—it's all a bit funny, isn't it ? Do you think Goon is on to some mystery we haven't heard about, but which your mother and father know of, Pip, and don't want us to be mixed up in ? I know that your parents weren't very pleased at that adventure we had in the Christmas hols. I wouldn't be a bit surprised if there isn't something going on that we children are to be kept out of ! '

There was a silence. Put like that it seemed extremely likely. What a shame to be kept out of a mystery when they were such very good detectives !

' What's more, I think the mystery's got some-thing to do with Gladys,' said Fatty. ' Fancy ! To think there may have been something going on under our very noses and we didn't know it ! There we were snooping about in barns and sheds and all the time there was a mystery in Pip's own house ! '

' Well—we'll jolly well find out what it is ! ' said Larry. ' And what's more, if Goon is on to it, we'll be on to it too, and we'll get to the bottom of things before *he* does ! I bet he'd like to do us down just once, so that Inspector Jenks would pat him on the back, and not us, for a change.'

' How are we going to find out anything ? ' asked Daisy. ' We can't possibly ask Mrs. Hilton. She'd just shut us up.'

' I'll go down and tackle Goon,' said Fatty, much to every one's admiration. ' I'll take his glove back, and pretend to know lots more than I do—and maybe he'll let out something.'

' Yes—you go,' said Pip. ' But wait a bit—he thinks you're in China ! '

' Oh, I've come back now after solving the case there very quickly ! ' laughed Fatty. ' Give me the glove, Pip. I'll go along now. Come with me, Buster. Goon isn't likely to lose his temper with me quite so violently if you're there ! '

## 5    THE 'NONNIMUS' LETTER

FATTY rode off on his bicycle, Buster in the basket. He came to Mr. Goon's house, and went to knock at the door. It was opened by Mrs. Cockles, who cleaned for Mr. Goon, and for the Hiltons as well. She knew Fatty and liked him.

' Is Mr. Goon in ? ' asked Fatty. ' Oh good. I'll come in and see him then. I've got some property to return to him.'

He sat down in the small, hot parlour. Mrs. Cockles went to fetch the policeman. He was mending a puncture in his bicycle, out in his back-yard. He put his coat on and came to see who wanted him.

His eyes nearly fell out of his head when he saw

Fatty. ' Lawks ! ' he said. ' I thought you was in
foreign parts ! '

' Oh—I solved that little mystery out there,'
said Fatty. ' Didn't take me long ! Just a matter
of an emerald necklace or so. Pity you didn't come
out with me to Tippylooloo, Mr. Goon. You'd
have enjoyed eating rice with chop-sticks.'

Mr. Goon was sure he would have enjoyed no
such thing. ' Pity you didn't stay away longer,' he
grumbled. ' Where you are, there's trouble. I
know that by now. What you want this morning ? '

' Well—er—Mr. Goon, you remember that little
matter you went to see Mr. and Mrs. Hilton about
yesterday ? ' said Fatty, pretending to know a great
deal more than he actually did. Mr. Goon looked
surprised.

' Now look-ere,' he said. ' Who's been telling
you about that ? You wasn't to know anything,
any of you, see ? '

' You can't keep things like that secret,' said
Fatty.

' Things like what ? ' asked Mr. Goon, pretending he didn't know what Fatty was talking about.

' Well—things like you-know-what,' said Fatty,
going all mysterious. ' I know you're going to set
to work on that little matter, Mr. Goon, and I wish
you luck. I hope, for poor Gladys's sake, you'll
soon get to the bottom of the matter.'

This was quite a shot in the dark, but it seemed
to surprise Mr. Goon very much. He blinked at
Fatty out of his bulging frog-eyes.

' Who told you about that there letter ? ' he
suddenly said.

' Oho,' thought Fatty, ' so it's something to do
with a letter ! ' He spoke aloud.

' Ah, I have ways and means of finding out these things, Mr. Goon. We'd like to help you if we can.'

Mr. Goon suddenly lost his temper, and his face went brick-red. ' I don't want none of your help ! ' he shouted. ' I've had enough of it ! Help ? Interference is what I calls it ! Can't I manage a case on my own without all you children butting in ? You keep out of it ! Mrs. Hilton, she promised me she wouldn't say nothing to any of you, no, nor show you that letter either. She didn't want you poking your noses in no more than I did. Anyway, this is a case for the police not for little busy-bodies like you ! Clear-orf now, and don't let me see you messing about any more.'

' I thought perhaps you would like your glove, Mr. Goon,' said Fatty politely, and he held out the policeman's big glove. ' You left it behind you yesterday.'

Mr. Goon snatched at it angrily. Buster growled. ' You and that dog of yours ! ' muttered Mr. Goon. ' Tired to death of both of you I am. Clear-orf ! '

Fatty cleared off. He was pleased with the result of his interview with Mr. Goon, but very puzzled. Mr. Goon had given a few things away—about that letter, for instance. But what letter ? What could have been in a letter to cause this mystery ? Was it something to do with Gladys ? Was it her letter ?

Puzzling out all these things Fatty cycled back to the others. He soon told them what he had learnt.

' I think possibly Mrs. Moon may know some-thing,' he said. ' Bets, couldn't you ask her ? If you just sort of prattled to her, she might tell you something.'

' I don't prattle,' said Bets indignantly. ' And I don't expect she'd tell me anything at all. I'm sure she's in this business of keeping everything secret from us. She wouldn't even tell us yesterday that Gladys had gone.'

' Well, anyway, see what you can do,' said Fatty. ' She's fond of knitting, isn't she ? Well, haven't you got a bit of tangled up knitting you could take down to her and ask her to undo for you—pick up the stitches or whatever you call it? Then you could sort of prat . . . er—talk to her about Gladys and Goon and so on.'

' I'll try,' said Bets. ' I'll go downstairs to her this afternoon when she's sitting down resting. She doesn't like me messing about in the morning.'

So that afternoon Bets went down to the kitchen with some very muddled knitting indeed. She had been planning earnestly what to say to Mrs. Moon, but she felt very nervous. Mrs. Moon could be very snappy if she wanted to.

There was no one in the kitchen. Bets sat down in the rocking-chair there. She always liked that old chair. She rocked herself to and fro.

From the back-yard came two voices. One was Mrs. Moon's and the other was Mrs. Cockles's. Bets hardly listened—but then she suddenly sat up.

' Well, what I say is, if a girl gets a nasty letter telling her things she wants to forget, and no name at the bottom of the letter, it's enough to give any one a horrid shock ! ' came Mrs. Moon's voice. ' And a nasty, yes right-down nasty thing it is to do ! Writing letters and putting no name at the bottom.'

' Yes, that's a coward's trick all right,' said Mrs. Cockles's cheerful voice. ' You mark my words, Mrs. Moon, there'll be more of those nonnimus letters, or whatever they calls them—those sort of letter-writers don't just stop at the one person. No, they've got too much spite to use up on one person, they'll write more and more. Why, *you* might get one next ! '

' Poor Gladys was right-down upset,' said Mrs. Moon. ' Cried and cried, she did. I made her show me the letter. All in capital letters it was, not proper writing. And I said to her, I said, " Now look here, my girl, you go straight off to your mistress and tell her about this. She'll do her best for you, she will." And I pushed her off to Mrs. Hilton.'

' Did she give her her notice ? ' asked Mrs. Cockles.

' No,' said Mrs. Moon. ' She showed Mr. Hilton the letter, and he rang up Mr. Goon. That silly, fussing fellow ! What do they want to bring *him* in for ! '

' Oh, he's not so bad,' said Mrs. Cockles's cheerful voice. ' Just hand me that broom, will you ? Thanks. He's all right if he's treated rough. I don't stand no nonsense from him, I don't. I've cleaned for him now for years, and he's never had a harsh word for me. But my, how he hates those children ! '

' Ah, that's another thing,' said Mrs. Moon. ' When Mr. Hilton told him about this here letter, he was that pleased to think those kids knew nothing about it—and he made Master and Mistress promise they'd not let those five interfere. And they promised. I was there, holding up poor Gladys, and I heard every word. " Mrs. Hilton," he said, " Mrs. Hilton, madam, this is not a case for children to hinterfere in and I must request you, in the name of the law, to keep this haffair to yourselves." '

' Lawks ! ' said Mrs. Cockles. ' He can talk grand when he likes, can't he ? I reckon, Mrs. Moon, maybe there's been more of these letters than we know. Well, well—so poor Gladys went home, all upset-like. And who's going to come in her place, I wonder ? Or will she be coming back ? '

' Well, it's my belief she'd better keep away from this village now,' said Mrs. Moon. ' Tongues will wag, you know. I've got a niece who can come next week, so it won't matter much if she keeps away.'

' What about a cup of tea ? ' said Mrs. Cockles. ' I'm that thirsty with all this cleaning. These rugs look a fair treat now, Mrs. Moon.'

Bets fled as soon as she heard footsteps coming in at the scullery door. Her knitting almost tripped her up as she went. She ran up the stairs and into the playroom, panting. Pip was there, reading and waiting for her.

' Pip ! I've found out everything, simply everything ! ' cried Bets. ' And there *is* a mystery to solve—a kind we haven't had before.'

Sounds of laughter floated up from the drive. It was the others coming. ' Wait a bit,' said Pip, excited. ' Wait till the others come up. Then you can tell the whole lot. Golly, you must have done well, Bets ! '

The others saw at once from Bets' face that she had news for them. ' Good old Bets ! ' said Fatty. ' Go on, Betsy. Spill the beans ! '

Bets told them everything. ' Somebody wrote a

nonnimus letter to Gladys,' she said. ' What *is* a
nonnimus letter, Fatty ? '

Fatty grinned. ' You mean an *anonymous* letter,
Bets,' he said. ' A letter sent without the name of
the sender at the bottom—usually a beastly cowardly
sort of letter, saying things that the writer wouldn't
dare to say to any one's face. So poor Gladys got
an anonymous letter, did she ? '

' Yes,' said Bets. ' I don't know what it said
though. It upset her. Mrs. Moon got out of her
what it was and made her go and see Mother and
Daddy about it. And they rang up Mr. Goon.'

' And he came popping along, his eyes bulging
with delight because he'd got a mystery to solve
that we didn't know about ! ' said Fatty. ' So
there's an anonymous letter-writer somewhere here,
is there ? A nasty, cowardly letter-writer—well,
here's our mystery, Find-Outers ! WHO is the
writer of the " nonnimus " letters ? '

' We shall never be able to find that out,' said
Daisy. ' How on earth could we ? '

' We must make plans,' said Fatty. ' We must
search for clues ! ' Bets' face lighted up at once.
She loved hunting for clues. ' We must make a
list of suspects—people who could do it and would.
We must . . .'

' We haven't got to work with Goon, have we ? '
said Pip. ' We don't need to let him know we
know, do we ? '

' Well—he already thinks we know most of this,'
said Fatty. ' I don't see why we shouldn't tell him
we know as much as he does, and not tell him how
we've found out, and make him think we know a
lot more than we do. That'll make him sit up
a bit ! '

So, the next time that the Five Find-Outers met the policeman, they stopped to speak to him.

' How are you getting on with this difficult case ? ' asked Fatty gravely.    It—er—it abounds with such strange clues, doesn't it ? '

Mr. Goon hadn't discovered a single clue, and he was astonished and annoyed to hear that there were apparently things the children knew and he didn't.   He stared at them.

' You tell me what clues you've found,' he said at last.   ' We'll swap clues.   It beats me how you know about this affair.   You wasn't to know a thing, not a thing.'

' We know much more than you think,' said Fatty solemnly.   'A very difficult and—er—enthralling case.'

' You tell me your clues,' said Mr. Goon again. ' We'd better swap clues, like I said.   Better help one another than hinder, I always say.'

' Now, where did I put those clues ? ' said Fatty, diving into his capacious pockets.   He brought out a live white rat and stared at it.   ' Was this a clue or not ? ' he asked the others.   ' I can't remember.'

It was impossible not to giggle.   Bets went off into a delighted explosion.   Mr. Goon glared.

' You clear-orf,' he said majestically.   ' Making a joke of everything !   Call yourself a detective ! Gah ! '

' What a lovely word ! ' said Bets, as they all walked off, giggling.   ' Gah !   Gah, Pip !   Gah, Fatty ! '

*Fatty brought out a live white rat*

EVERY one went to tea at Fatty's that day. Mrs. Trotteville was out, so the five children had tea in Fatty's crowded little den. It was more crowded than ever now that Fatty had got various disguises and wigs. The children exclaimed in delight over a blue-and-white striped butcher-boy's apron and a lift-boy's suit complete with peaked cap.

'But, Fatty, whenever could you disguise your-self as a lift-boy?' asked Larry.

'You never know,' said Fatty. 'You see, I can only get disguises that do for a boy. If I were a grown-up I could get dozens and dozens—a sailor's suit, a postman's, even a policeman's. But I'm a bit limited, being a boy.'

Fatty also had a bookcase crammed full of detective stories. He read every one he could find. 'I pick up quite a lot of hints that way,' he said. 'I think Sherlock Holmes was one of the best detectives. Golly, he had some fine mysteries to solve. I don't believe even I could have solved all of them!'

'You're a conceited creature,' said Larry, trying on the red wig. He looked very startling in it. 'How do you put those freckles on that you had with this?' he asked.

'Grease-paint,' said Fatty. 'There are my grease-paints over there—what actors use for make-up, you know. One day I'm going to make myself up as a black boy and give you all a fright.'

'Oh—do give old Clear-Orf a scare too!' begged Bets. 'Let me try on that wig, Larry; do let me.'

'We really ought to be making our plans to tackle this mystery,' said Fatty, taking a beautiful gold pencil out of his pocket. Pip stared.

'I say! Is that gold?'

'Yes,' said Fatty airily. 'I won it last term for the best essay. Didn't I tell you? It was a marvellous essay, all about . . .'

'All right, all right,' said Larry and Pip together. 'We'll take your word for it, Fatty!'

'I had a marvellous report again,' said Fatty. 'Did you, Pip?'

'You know I didn't,' said Pip. 'You heard my mother say so. Shut up, Fatty.'

'Let's talk about our new mystery,' said Daisy, seeing that a quarrel was about to flare up. 'Write down some notes, Fatty. Let's get going.'

'I was just about to,' said Fatty, rather pompously. He printed in beautiful small letters a heading to the page in the lovely leather notebook he held. The others looked to see what he had printed :

MYSTERY NO. 4.   BEGUN APRIL 5TH.

'Ooh—that looks fine,' said Bets.

'CLUES' was the next thing printed by Fatty, over the page.

'But we haven't got any,' said Pip.

'We soon shall have,' said Fatty. He turned over the page. 'SUSPECTS' was what he printed there.

'We don't know any of those yet either,' said
Daisy. 'And I'm sure I don't know how we're
going to find any.'

'Leave it to me,' said Fatty. 'We'll soon have
something to work on.'

'Yes, but what?' said Pip. 'I mean, it's no
use looking for footprints or cigarette-ends or
dropped hankies or anything like that. There's
just nothing at all we can find for clues.'

'There's one very important thing,' said Fatty.

'What's that?' said every one.

'That anonymous letter,' said Fatty. 'It's
most important we should get a glimpse of it.
Most important!'

'Who's got it?' asked Larry.

'My mother might have it,' said Pip.

'More likely Gladys has got it,' said Fatty.
'That's the first thing we must do. Go and see
Gladys, and ask her if she knows or guesses who
could have written her that letter. We must also
find out what's in it.'

'Let's go now,' said Pip, who always liked to
rush off as soon as anything had been decided.

'Right. You take us,' said Fatty. Pip looked
rather blank.

'But I don't know where Gladys lives,' he
said.

'Ha, I thought you didn't,' said Fatty. 'Well,
Pip, you must find out. That's the first thing we've
got to do—find out where Gladys lives.'

'I could ask Mother,' said Pip doubtfully.

'Now don't be such a prize idiot,' said Fatty
at once. 'Use your brains! You know jolly well
your parents don't want us mixed up in this mystery,
and we've got to keep it dark that we're finding out

things.   Don't on any account ask your mother anything—or Mrs. Moon either.'

'Well, but how am I to find out then ? ' said Pip, looking bewildered.

'I know a way, I know a way ! ' sang out Bets suddenly.   'Gladys lent me a book once and I didn't have time to give it her back before she left. I could go to Mrs. Moon and tell her, and ask her for Gladys's address so that I could send the book on to her.'

'Clever girl ! ' said Fatty.   'You're coming on well, you are, Bets !   Perhaps you'd better handle this, and not Pip.'

'I've got an idea too now,' said Pip, rather sulkily.

'What ? ' said Bets.

'Well—if I got a bit of paper and stuck it in an envelope, and wrote Gladys's name and our address on it and posted it—Mother would re-address it and I could hang about and see what it was, when she puts the letter on the hall-stand to be posted,' said Pip.

'Yes, that's a very fine idea too,' said Fatty. 'Couldn't have thought of a much better one myself.   Go to the top of the class, Pip.'

Pip grinned.   'Well—both Bets and I will carry out our ideas,' he said, ' and surely one of us will get Gladys's address ! '

'Here's a bit of paper and an envelope,' said Fatty.   'But disguise your writing, Pip.'

'Why ? ' said Pip, surprised.

'Well—seeing that your mother gets a letter from you every single week when you're away at boarding-school, it's likely she *might* recognize your writing and wonder why on earth you were writing

to Gladys when she was gone ! ' said Fatty, in a
very patient, but rather tired voice.

' Fatty thinks of everything ! ' said Daisy admiringly. Pip saw the point at once, but doubted
very much if he could disguise his writing
properly.

' Here—give it to me. I'll do it,' said Fatty,
who was apparently able to disguise his writing as
easily as he could disguise his appearance and his
voice. He took the envelope, and, to the children's
enormous admiration, wrote Gladys's name and
Pip's address in a small, extremely grown-up
handwriting, quite unlike his own.

' There you are,' he said. ' Elementary, my
dear Pip ! '

' Marvellous, Mr. Sherlock Holmes ! ' said Pip.
' Honestly, Fatty, you're a wonder. How many
different writings can you do ? '

' Any amount,' said Fatty. ' Want to see the
writing of a poor old charwoman ? Here it is ! '

He wrote a few words in a scrawling, untidy
writing. ' Oh, it's just like Mrs. Cockles's writing ! '
cried Bets in delight. ' Sometimes she puts out a
notice for the milkman — " TWO PINTS " or
something like that—and her writing is just like
that ! '

' Now write like old Clear-Orf,' said Larry.
' Go on ! What does *he* write like ? '

' Well, I've seen his writing, so I know what
it's like,' said Fatty, ' but if I hadn't seen it I'd
know too—he'd be bound to write like this. . . .'

He wrote a sentence or two in a large, flourishing
hand with loops and tails to the letters—an untidy,
would-be impressive hand—yes, just like Mr. Goon's
writing.

' Fatty, you're always doing something surprising,' said Bets, with a sigh. ' There's nothing
you can't do. I wish I was like you.'

' You be like yourself. You couldn't be nicer,'
said Fatty, giving the little girl a squeeze. Bets was
pleased. She liked and admired Fatty very much
indeed.

' You know, once last term I thought I'd try
out a new handwriting on my form-master,' said
Fatty. ' So I made up a marvellous handwriting,
very small and neat and pointed, with most of the
letters leaning backwards—and old Tubbs wouldn't
pass it—said I'd got some one to do that prep for
me, and made me do it all again.'

' Poor Fatty,' said Bets.

' Well, the next time I gave my prep in, it was
written in old Tubbs' own handwriting,' said
Fatty, with a grin. ' Golly, it gave him a start to
see a prep all done in his own writing ! '

' What *did* he say ? ' asked Pip.

' He said, " And who's done this prep for you
this time, Trotteville ? " And I said, " My goodness, sir, it looks as if *you* have ! " ' said Fatty. The
others roared with laughter. Whether Fatty's school
tales were true or not, they were always funny.

Pip slipped the blank piece of paper into the
envelope that Fatty had addressed and stuck it
down. He took the stamp that Fatty offered him
and put it on.

' There ! ' he said. ' I'll post it on my way
home to-night. It'll catch the half-past six post
and it will be there to-morrow morning. Then if I
don't manage to spot the re-addressed letter my
name isn't Pip.'

' Well, it isn't,' said Bets. ' It's Philip.'

' Very funny ! ' said Pip. ' I don't think ! '

' Now don't squabble, you two,' said Fatty. ' Well, we've done all we can for the moment. Let's have a game. I'll teach you Woo-hoo-colly-wobbles.'

' Gracious ! Whatever's that ? ' said Bets.

It was a game involving much woo-hoo-ing and groaning and rolling over and over. Soon all the children were reduced to tears of mirth. Mrs. Trotteville sent up to say that if anybody was ill they were to go down and tell her, but if they were just playing, would they please go out into the garden, down to the very bottom.

' Oooh. I didn't know your mother was back,' said Pip, who had really let himself go. ' We'd better stop. What an awful game this is, Fatty.'

' I say—it's almost half-past six ! ' said Larry. ' If you're going to post that letter, you'd better go, young Pip. Brush yourself down, for goodness sake. You look awful.'

' Gah ! ' said Pip, remembering Mr. Goon's last exclamation. He brushed himself down, and re-tied his tie. ' Come on, Bets,' he said. ' Well, so long, you others—we'll tell you Gladys's address to-morrow, and then we'll go and see her and examine our first clue—the " nonnimus " letter ! '

He ran down the path with Bets. Fatty leaned out of the window of his den and yelled, ' Oy ! You're a fine detective ! You've forgotten the letter ! '

' So I have ! ' said Pip and tore back for it. Fatty dropped it down. Pip caught it and ran off again. He and Bets tore to the pillar-box at the corner and were just in time to catch the postman emptying the letters from the inside.

'One more!' said Pip. 'Thanks, postman!
Come on, Bets. We'll try out your book-idea as
soon as we get home.'

## 7    DISAPPOINTMENT

### FOR PIP AND BETS

BETS flew to find the book that Gladys had lent
her, as soon as she got home. She found it at
once. It was an old school prize, called *The Little
Saint*. Bets had been rather bored with it. 'The
Little Saint' had been a girl much too good to be
true. Bets preferred to read about naughty, lively
children.

She wrapped the book up carefully, and then
went down to say good-night to her mother. Mrs.
Hilton was reading in the drawing-room.

'Come to say good-night, Bets?' she said, looking at the clock. 'Did you have a nice time at
Fatty's?'

'Yes! We played his new game, Woo-hoo-
colly-wobbles,' said Bets. 'It was fun.'

'I expect it was noisy and ridiculous if it was
anything to do with Frederick,' said her mother.
'What's that you've got, Bets?'

'Oh Mother, it's a book that Gladys lent me,'
said Bets. 'I was going to ask Mrs. Moon her
address so that I could send it to her. Could I
have a stamp, Mother?'

'You don't need to ask Mrs. Moon,' said her
mother. 'I'll see that Gladys gets it.'

'Oh,' said Bets. 'Well—I'll just put her address

on it. I've written her name. What's her address,
Mother ? '

' I'll write it,' said Mrs. Hilton. ' Now don't
stand there putting off time, Bets. Go up to bed.
Leave the parcel here.'

' Oh, do let me just write the address,' said poor
Bets, feeling that her wonderful idea was coming to
nothing, and that it wasn't fair. ' I feel like writing,
Mother.'

' Well, it must be for the first time in your life
then ! ' said Mrs. Hilton. ' You've always said how
much you hate writing before. Go up to bed,
Bets, now.'

Bets had to go. She left the book on the table
by her mother, feeling rather doleful. But perhaps
Pip would see the address later on in the evening,
if her mother wrote it on the parcel.

Pip said he'd keep an eye open. Anyway, what
did it matter ? His own letter would come in the
morning and they'd soon find out the right address.

He saw the book on the table when he went
down ready for dinner, cleaned and brushed. He
read the name on the wrapping-paper . . . but there
was no address there yet.

' Shall I write Gladys's address for you,
Mother ? ' he asked politely. ' Just to save you
time.'

' I can't imagine why you and Bets are so
anxious to do a little writing to-night ! ' said Mrs.
Hilton, looking up from her book. ' No, Pip. I
can't be bothered to look up the address now, and
I can't remember it off-hand. Leave it.'

So it had to be left. Pip was glad to think his
letter was coming in the morning. He was sure
that had been a better idea than Bets ' !

Pip was down early next morning, waiting for
the postman. He took all the letters out of the
box and put them by his mother's plate. His
own was there, addressed in Fatty's disguised
handwriting.

'There's a letter for Gladys, Mother,' said
Pip, at breakfast-time. ' We'll have to re-address it.'

'My dear boy, you don't need to tell me that!'
said Mrs. Hilton.

'Did you put the address on my parcel?'
asked Bets, attacking her boiled egg hungrily.

'No. I couldn't remember it last night,' said
Mrs. Hilton, reading her letters.

'Shall Pip and I take the letters and the parcel
to the post for you this morning?' asked Bets,
thinking this was really a very good idea.

'If you like,' said Mrs. Hilton. Bets winked
at Pip. Now things would be easy! They could
both see the address they wanted.

A telephone call came for Mrs. Hilton after
breakfast, whilst the children were hanging about
waiting to take the letters. Mrs. Moon answered it.
She went in to Mrs. Hilton.

'There's a call for you, Mam,' she said.

'Who is it?' asked Mrs. Hilton. Pip and Bets
were most astonished to see Mrs. Moon winking
and nodding mysteriously to their mother, but not
saying any name. However, Mrs. Hilton seemed
to understand all right. She got up and went
to the telephone, shutting the door behind her so
that the children could not follow without being
noticed.

'Well—who's on the phone that Mother doesn't
want us to know about?' said Pip, annoyed. 'Did
you see how mysterious Mrs. Moon was, Bets?'

'Yes,' said Bets. 'Can't we just open the door a bit and listen, Pip?'

'No,' said Pip. 'We really can't. Not if Mother doesn't want us to hear.'

Their mother came back after a minute or two. She didn't say who had telephoned to her and the children didn't dare to ask.

'Shall we go to the post-office now?' said Pip, at last. 'We're ready.'

'Yes. There are the letters over there,' said Mrs. Hilton.

'What about my parcel for Gladys?' said Bets.

'Oh, that doesn't need to go—nor the letter for her,' said Mrs. Hilton. 'Somebody's going to see her to-day and he will take them. That will save putting a stamp on the parcel.'

'Who's going to see Gladys?' asked Pip. 'Can we go too? I'd like to see Gladys again.'

'Well, you can't,' said Mrs. Hilton. 'And please don't start trying to find out things, Pip, because, as I've already told you, this is nothing whatever to do with you. You can take the other letters to the post for me. Go now and you will catch the ten o'clock post.'

Pip and Bets went off rather sulkily. Bets was near tears. 'It's too bad, Pip,' she said, when they got out-of-doors, 'we had such good ideas—and now they're no use at all!'

'We'll post the letters and then go up and see Fatty,' said Pip gloomily. 'I expect he'll think we ought to have done better. He always thinks he can do things so marvellously.'

'Well, so he can,' said Bets loyally. 'Let *me* post the letters, Pip. Here's the post office.'

' Here you are then. What a baby you are to like posting letters still ! ' said Pip. Bets slipped them into the letter-box and they turned to go up to Fatty's house. He was at home, reading a new detective book.

' Our ideas weren't any good,' said Pip. He told Fatty what had happened. Fatty was un-expectedly sympathetic.

' That was hard luck,' he said. ' You both had jolly fine ideas, and it was only a bit of bad luck that stopped them having their reward. Now—who is it that is going to see Gladys to-day ? '

' Mother said it was a " he," ' said Pip. ' She said, " Somebody's going to see Gladys to-day, and *he* will take them ! " '

' That's easy then,' said Fatty briskly. ' *He* can only mean one person—and that's old Clear-Orf ! Well, now we know what to do.'

' *I* don't know,' said Pip, still gloomy. ' You always seem to know everything, Fatty.'

' Brains, my dear fellow, brains ! ' said Fatty. ' Well, look here—if it's Goon that's going to see Gladys, we can wait about and follow him, can't we ? He'll go on his bike, I expect—well, we can go on ours ! Easy ! '

Pip and Bets cheered up. The idea of stalking old Clear-Orf was a pleasing one. They would have the fun of doing that, and would find out too where Gladys lived. Yes, to-day looked much more exciting now.

' You go and tell Larry and Daisy,' said Fatty. ' We shall have to keep a watch on old Goon's house so that we know when he leaves. I vote we ask our mothers for food again, so that we can go off at any time and come back when we like.'

'I'm going to buy Gladys some sweets,' said Bets. 'I like her.'

'It would be a good idea if we all took her some little present,' said Fatty thoughtfully. 'Sort of show we were sorry for her and were on her side, so that she'll be more willing to talk.'

'Well, I'll go and tell Larry and Daisy to get out their bikes and bring food along,' said Pip. 'I'd better hurry in case old Clear-Orf goes this morning. Bets, you'd better come back home with me too, and get your bike, because we'll both need them. Then we'll go to Larry's and then we'll buy some little things for Gladys.'

'I'll go and keep a watch on Goon's house in case he starts off before you're back,' said Fatty. 'I'll just get some sandwiches first. See you round the corner from Goon's!'

In about half an hour's time Larry, Daisy, Bets, and Pip were all with Fatty, round the corner near Clear-Orf's house, complete with sandwiches and little presents for Gladys. There had been no sign of Goon.

But in about ten minutes' time, Larry, who was on guard, gave a whistle. That was the signal to say that Goon was departing somewhere. He was on his bicycle, a portly, clumsy figure with short legs ending in enormous boots that rested on pedals looking absurdly small.

He set off down the road that led to the river. 'May be going across in the ferry!' panted Fatty, pedalling furiously. 'Come on! Don't all tear round the corners together in case he spots us. I'll always go first.'

But unfortunately all that Mr. Goon had gone to do down the river-lane was to leave a message with the farmer there. He saw the farmer in the field and called out the message to him, then quickly turned his bicycle round and cycled back up the lane again. He came round the corner very quickly and found himself wobbling in the middle of the Five Find-Outers !

He came off with a crash. The children jumped off and Fatty tried to help him up, whilst Buster, jumping delightedly out of Fatty's basket, yelped in delight.

'Hurt yourself, Mr. Goon ?' asked Fatty politely. 'Here, let me give you a heave up.'

'You let me alone !' said Mr. Goon angrily. 'Riding five abreast like that in a narrow lane ! What do you mean by it !'

'So sorry, Mr. Goon,' said Fatty. Pip gave a giggle. Old Clear-Orf looked so funny, trying to disentangle himself from his bicycle.

'Yes, you laugh at me, you cheeky little toad !' roared Mr. Goon. 'I'll tell of you, you see if I don't. I'll be seeing your Ma this morning and I'll put in a complaint. I'm going right along there now.'

Fatty brushed Mr. Goon down so smartly that the policeman jumped aside. 'You're all dusty, Mr. Goon,' said Fatty anxiously. 'You can't go to Mrs. Hilton's in this state. Just a few more whacks and you'll be all right !'

'Wait till you get the whacks *you* want !' said Mr. Goon, putting his helmet on firmly. 'Never knew such children in me life ! Nothing but trouble round every corner where you are ! Gah !'

He rode off, leaving the children standing in the lane with their bicycles. 'Well, that was a bit of a nuisance bumping into him like that,' said Fatty.

' I didn't particularly want him to see any of us
to-day. I don't want him to suspect we're on his
track. Now let me see—he's off to collect those
things for Gladys from your mother, Pip. There's
no doubt about that. So all we've got to do now is
to lie in wait for him somewhere and then follow
him very carefully.'

' Let's go to the church corner,' said Pip. ' He's
sure to pass there, wherever he goes. Come on ! '

So off they went, and hid behind some trees,
waiting for old Clear-Orf to show them the way to
where Gladys lived.


## 8    A TALK WITH POOR GLADYS

IN about half an hour Mr. Goon came cycling
along, and went right by the hidden children
without seeing them.

' Now listen ! ' said Fatty. ' It's no use us all
tearing after him in a bunch because we'd be so
easy to spot. I'll go first and keep a long way
ahead. You follow, see ? If I have to take a
turning you may not know I'll tear a sheet out of
my notebook and drop it the way I go.'

' It's windy to-day. Better hop off your bike
and chalk one of those arrows on the road that
gypsies always seem to make,' said Pip. ' Your
bit of paper might blow away. Got any chalk,
Fatty ? '

' Of course ! ' said Fatty and took a piece out
of his capacious pockets. ' Yes, that's a better

idea. Good for you, Pip! Well, I'll get along in front of you now. Look, there goes old Clear-Orf panting up the hill in the distance. Looks as if he's going to take the main road.'

Fatty rode off, whistling. The others waited a little while and then rode after him. It was easy to see him in the distance in the open country. But soon they came to where the road forked, and Fatty seemed nowhere in sight.

'Here you are! Here's his chalk arrow!' said Daisy, her sharp eyes spotting it at once, marked on the path at the side of one of the roads. 'This is the way!'

They rode on again. They rarely saw Fatty now, for he and Mr. Goon had left the main road and were cycling down narrow, winding lanes. But at every doubtful fork or corner they saw his chalk mark.

'This is fun,' said Bets, who liked looking for the little arrows. 'But oh dear—I hope it's not much farther!'

'Looks as if Gladys lives at Haycock Heath,' said Larry. 'This road leads there. My, here's a steep hill. Up we go! I bet old Fatty found it heavy going here, with Buster in his basket. Buster seems to weigh an awful lot when he's in a bicycle basket.'

At the top of the hill, just at a bend, Fatty was waiting for them. He looked excited.

'He's gone into the very last cottage of all!' he said. 'And isn't it good luck—it's got a notice with " Minerals " printed on it, in the window. That means lemonade or ginger-beer is sold there. We've got a fine excuse for going in, once Clear-Orf has gone.'

' Better get back into this other little lane here, hadn't we ? ' said Larry. ' I mean—if old Clear-Orf suddenly comes out, he'll find us ! '

So they all wheeled their bicycles into a crooked, narrow little lane, whose trees met overhead and made a green tunnel. ' Must give old Buster a run,' said Fatty and lifted him out of the basket. But most unfortunately a cat strolled down the lane, appearing suddenly from the hedge, and Buster immediately gave chase, barking joyfully. Cats and rabbits were his great delight.

The cat gave one look at Buster and decided to move quickly. She shot down the lane, and took a flying leap over the little wall surrounding the back-garden of the cottage into which Mr. Goon had disappeared. Buster tried to leap over too, and couldn't—but, using his brains as a Buster should, he decided that there must be another way in, and went to look for the front gate.

Then there was such a hurricane of barks and yowls, mixed with the terrified clucking of hens, that the children stood petrified. Out came Mr. Goon, with a sharp-nosed woman—and Gladys !

' You clear-orf ! ' yelled Mr. Goon to Buster. ' Bad dog, you ! Clear-orf ! '

With a bark of joy Buster flung himself at the policeman's ankles, and snapped happily at them. Mr. Goon kicked at him and let out a yell.

' It's that boy's dog ! Get away, you ! Now what's he doing here ? Has that boy Frederick Trotteville been messing about up here, now ? '

' Nobody's been here this morning but you,' said Gladys. ' Oh, Mr. Goon, don't kick at the dog like that. He wasn't doing much harm.'

It was quite plain that Buster meant to get a nip if he could. Fatty, feeling most annoyed at having to show himself, was forced to cycle out and yell to Buster.

'Hey, Buster! Come here, sir!'

Mr. Goon turned and gave Fatty a look that might have cowed a lion if Fatty had been a lion. But, being Fatty, he didn't turn a hair.

'Why, Mr. Goon!' he said, taking off his cap in a most aggravatingly polite manner, 'fancy seeing *you* here! Come for a little bike-ride too? Lovely day, isn't it?'

Mr. Goon almost exploded. 'Now what are *you* a-doing of here?' he demanded. 'You tell me that, see?'

'All I'm a-doing of at the moment is having a nice bike-ride,' answered Fatty cheerfully. 'What are *you* a-doing of, Mr. Goon? Having a ginger-beer? I see there's a card in the window. I think I'll have something to drink myself. It's a jolly hot day.'

And, to the other children's delight, and Mr. Goon's annoyance, Fatty strolled up the little front path and entered the door. Inside was a small table at which people could sit down to have their lemonade. Fatty sat down.

'You clear-orf out of here,' ordered Mr. Goon. 'I'm here on business, see? And I'm not having busy-bodies like you interfering. *I* know what you've come here for—snooping around—trying to find clues, and making nuisances of yourselves.'

'Oh, that reminds me,' said Fatty, beginning to feel in his pockets with a serious look, 'didn't we say we'd swap clues, Mr. Goon? Now where did I put that . . .'

'If you bring out that there white rat again I'll skin you alive!' boomed Mr. Goon, whose fingers were itching to box Fatty's ears.

'That white rat wasn't a clue after all,' said Fatty gravely. 'I made a mistake. That must have been a clue in another case I'm working on. Wait a bit—ah, this may be a clue!'

He fished a clothes-peg out of his pocket and looked at it solemnly. Mr. Goon, quite beside himself with rage, snatched at it, threw it down on the floor, and jumped on it! Then, looking as if he was going to burst, he took his bicycle by the handle-bars, and turned to Gladys and the other woman.

'Now don't you forget what I've said. And you let me hear as soon as anything else happens. Don't talk to nobody at all about this here case— them's my strict orders!'

He rode off, trying to look dignified, but unfortunately Buster flew after him, jumping up at his pedalling feet, so that poor Mr. Goon wobbled dreadfully. As soon as he had gone the children crowded up to Fatty, laughing.

'Oh, Fatty! How can you! One of these days old Clear-Orf will kill you!'

Gladys and her aunt had been listening and watching in surprise. Bets ran to Gladys and took her hand.

'Gladys! I *was* sorry you left! Do come back soon! Look, I've brought you something!'

The sharp-nosed aunt made an impatient noise. 'I'll never get to the shops this morning!' she said. 'I'm going right away now, Gladys. See and get the dinner on in good time—and mind you heed what the policeman said.'

Much to the children's relief, she put on an old hat and scarf, and disappeared down the lane, walking quickly. They were glad to see her go, for she looked rather bad-tempered. They crowded round Gladys, who smiled and seemed very pleased to see them.

'Gladys! We know something made you unhappy,' said little Bets, and pressed a bag of sweets in the girl's hand. 'We've come to say we're sorry and we've brought a few little things for you. And please, please come back!'

Gladys seemed rather overcome. She took them all into the little front-room and poured out some glasses of ginger-beer for them.

'It's right down kind of you,' she said, in a tearful voice. 'Things aren't too easy—and my aunt isn't too pleased to have me back. But I couldn't go on living in Peterswood when I knew that—that—that . . .'

'That what?' asked Fatty gently.

'I'm not supposed to talk about it,' said Gladys.

'Well—we're only children. It can't matter talking to *us*,' said Bets. 'We all like you, Gladys. You tell us. Why, you never know, we might be able to help you!'

'There's nobody can help me,' said Gladys, and a tear ran down her cheek. She began to undo the little things the children had brought her—sweets, chocolate, a little brooch with G on, and two small hankies. She seemed very touched.

'It's kind of you,' she said. 'Goodness knows I want a bit of kindness now.'

'Why?' asked Daisy. 'What's happened? You tell us, Gladys. It will do you good to tell some one.'

'Well—it's like this,' said Gladys. 'There's something wrong I once did that I'm ashamed of now, see? And I had to go into a Home to teach me right. It was a nice Home, and I liked it and I said I'd never do wrong again. Well, I left there and I got a job—with your mother, Master Pip, and wasn't I happy working away there, and everybody treating me nice, and me forgetting all about the bad days!'

'Yes?' said Fatty, as Gladys paused. 'Go on, Gladys. Don't stop.'

'Then—then . . .' began Gladys again, and burst into tears. 'Somebody sent me a letter, and said, "We know you're a wrong-un, and you didn't ought to be in a good place with decent people. Clear out or we'll tell on you!"'

'What a shame!' said Fatty. 'Who sent the letter?'

'I don't know that,' said Gladys. 'It was all in printed letters. Well, I was that upset I broke down in front of Mrs. Moon, and she took the letter from me and read it, and said I should ought to go to your mother, Master Pip, and tell her—but I didn't want to because I knew I'd lose my place. But she said, yes go, Mrs. Hilton would put things right for me. So I went, but I was that upset I couldn't speak a word.'

'Poor old Gladys!' said Daisy. 'But I'm sure Pip's mother was kind to you.'

'Oh yes—and shocked at the cruel letter,' said Gladys, wiping her eyes. 'And she said I could have two or three days off and go to my aunt to pull myself together, like—and she'd make inquiries and find out who wrote that letter—and stop them talking about me, so's I could have a chance. But my aunt wasn't too pleased to see me ! '

' Why didn't you go to your father and mother, Gladys ? ' asked little Bets, who thought that surely they would have been the best friends for any girl of theirs who was unhappy.

' I couldn't,' said Gladys, and looked so sad that the children felt quite scared.

' Why—are they—are they—dead ? ' asked Bets.

' No. They're—they're in prison ! ' said poor Gladys and wept again. ' You see—they've always been dishonest folk—stealing and that—and they taught me to steal too. And the police got them, and when they found I was going into shops with my mother and taking things I didn't ought, they took me away and put me into a Home. I didn't know it was so wrong, you see—but now I do ! '

The children were horrified that any one should have such bad parents. They stared at Gladys and tears ran down Bets' cheeks. She took Gladys's hand.

' You're good now, Gladys, aren't you ? ' said the little girl. ' You don't look bad. You're good now.'

' Yes—I've not done nothing wrong ever since,' said poor Gladys. ' Nor I never would now. They were so kind to me at the Home—you can't think ! And I promised the Matron there I'd always do my best wherever I was, and I was so glad when they sent me to your mother's, Miss Bets. But there—they say your sins will always find you out ! I guess I'll never be able to keep a good job for long. Somebody will always put it round that I was a thief once, and that my parents are still in prison.'

' Gladys—the person who wrote that letter and threatens to tell about you, is far, far wickeder than you've *ever* been ! ' said Fatty earnestly. ' It's a shame ! '

' There was another girl in the Home with me,' said Gladys. ' She's with old Miss Garnett at Lacky Cottage in Peterswood. Well, she's had one of them letters too—without any name at the bottom. But she doesn't mind as much as I do. She didn't give way like I did. But she met me and told me, that's how I know. She didn't tell nobody but me. And she don't know either who wrote the letters.'

' Did you tell Mr. Goon that ? ' asked Fatty.

' Oh yes,' said Gladys. ' And he went to see Molly straightaway. He says he'll soon get to the bottom of it, and find out the mischief-maker. But it seems to me that the mischief is done now. I'll never be able to face people in Peterswood again. I'll always be afraid they know about me.'

' Gladys, where is that letter ? ' said Fatty. ' Will you show it to me ? It might be a most important clue.'

Gladys rummaged in her bag. Then she looked up. ' No good me looking for it ! ' she said. ' I've given it to Mr. Goon, of course ! He came to fetch it this morning. He's got Molly's letter too. He reckons he'll be able to tell quite a lot from the writing and all ! '

' Blow ! ' said Fatty, in deep disappointment. ' There's our one and only clue gone ! '

THE children sat and talked to Gladys for a little while longer. They were so disappointed about the letter being given to Mr. Goon that she felt quite sorry for them.

' I'll get it back from him, and Molly's letter too,' she promised. ' And I'll show you them both. I'll be going down to see Molly this evening, when it's dark and no one will see me—and I'll pop into Mr. Goon's, say I want to borrow the letters, and I'll lend them to you for a little while.'

' Oh thanks ! ' said Fatty, cheering up. ' That'll be splendid. Well, now we'd better be going. We've got our lunch with us and it's getting a bit late-ish. You haven't put that dinner on yet, Gladys, either ! '

' Oh lawks, nor I have ! ' said Gladys, and began to look very flustered. ' I've been that upset I can't think of a thing ! '

' You'll be passing my door on your way to Molly's to-night,' said Fatty. ' Could you pop the letters in at my letter-box, and call for them on your way back ? '

' Yes, I'll do that,' said Gladys. ' Thank you for all your kindness. You've made me feel better already.'

The children went off. ' A nice girl, but not very bright,' said Fatty, as they cycled away. ' What a mean trick to play on her—trying to make her lose her job and get all upset like that ! I

wonder who in the world it is ? I bet it's some
one who knows the Home Gladys went to, and
has heard about her there. My goodness, I'm
hungry ! '

'We've had quite an exciting morning,' said
Larry. 'It's a pity we couldn't see that letter
though.'

'Never mind—we'll see it this evening—if old
Clear-Orf will let Gladys have it ! ' said Fatty.
'Which I very much doubt. He'll suspect she's
going to show it to us ! '

'We'll all come round to you after tea,' said
Larry. 'And we'll wait for the letters to come. I
think you'd better wait about by the front gate,
Fatty—just in case somebody else takes them out of
the letter-box instead of you.'

So, when it was dark, Fatty skulked about by
the front gate, scaring his mother considerably
when she came home from an outing.

'Good gracious, Fatty ! Must you hide in the
shadows there ? ' she said. 'You gave me an
awful fright. Go in at once.'

'Sorry, Mother,' said Fatty, and went meekly
in at the front door with his mother—and straight
out of the garden door, back to the front gate at
once ! Just in time too, for a shadowy figure
leaned over the gate and said breathlessly : ' Is that
Master Frederick ? Here's the letters. Mr. Goon
was out, so I went in and waited. He didn't come,
so I took them, and here they are.'

Gladys pushed a packet into Fatty's hands and
hurried off. Fatty gave a low whistle. Gladys
hadn't waited for permission to take the letters !
She had reckoned they were hers and Molly's and
had just taken them. What would Mr. Goon say

*Gladys pushed the letter into Fatty's hand*

to that ?   He wouldn't be at all pleased with Gladys
—especially when he knew she had handed them to
him, Fatty !   Fatty knew perfectly well that Mr.
Goon would get it all out of poor Gladys.

He slipped indoors and told the others what
had happened.  ' I think I'd better try and put the
letters back without old Clear-Orf knowing they've
gone,' he said.  ' If I don't, Gladys will get into
trouble.  But first of all, we'll examine them ! '

' I   suppose   it's   all   right   to ? '   said   Larry
doubtfully.

' Well—I don't see that it matters, seeing that
Gladys has given us her permission,' said Fatty.
He looked at the little package.

' Golly ! ' he said.   ' There are more than two
letters here !   Look—here's a post-card—an anonymous one to Mr. Lucas, Gardener, Acacia Lodge,
Peterswood—and do you know what it says ? '

' What ? ' cried every one.

' Why,  it  says :  '' WHO LOST HIS JOB
THROUGH    SELLING    HIS    MASTER'S
FRUIT ? '  said  Fatty,  in  disgust.   ' Gracious !
Fancy sending a *card* with that on—to poor old
Lucas too, who must be over seventy ! '

' So other people have had these beastly things
as well as Gladys and Molly ! ' said Larry.   ' Let's
squint at the writing, Fatty.'

' It's all the same,' said Fatty.   ' All done in
capital letters, look—and all to people in Peterswood.   There are five of them—four letters and a
card.   How disgusting ! '

Larry  was  examining  the  envelopes.   They
were all the same, square and white, and the paper
used was cheap.  ' Look,' said Larry, ' they've all
been sent from Sheepsale—that little market-town

we've sometimes been to. Does that mean it's somebody who lives there ? '

' Not necessarily,' said Fatty. ' No, I reckon it's somebody who lives in Peterswood all right, because only a Peterswood person would know the people written to. What exactly does the post-mark say ? '

' It says, " Sheepsale, 11.45 a.m. April 3rd," said Daisy.

' That was Monday,' said Fatty. ' What do the other post-marks say ? '

' They're all different dates,' said Daisy. ' All of them except Gladys's one are posted in March—but all from Sheepsale.'

Fatty made a note of the dates and then took a small pocket calendar out. He looked up the dates and whistled.

' Here's a funny thing,' he said. ' They're all a Monday ! See—that one's a Monday—and so is that—and that—and that. Whoever posted them must have written them on the Sunday, and posted them on Monday. Now—if the person lives in Peterswood, how can he get to Sheepsale to post them in time for the morning post on a Monday ? There's no railway to Sheepsale. Only a bus that doesn't go very often.'

' It's market-day on Mondays at Sheepsale,' said Pip, remembering. ' There's an early bus that goes then, to catch the market. Wait a bit—we can look it up. Where's a bus time-table ? '

As usual, Fatty had one in his pocket. He looked up the Sheepsale bus.

' Yes—here we are,' he said. ' There's a bus that goes to Sheepsale from Peterswood each Monday—at a quarter-past ten—reaching there at one minute past eleven. There you are—I bet our letter-writing friend leaves Peterswood with a nasty letter in his pocket, catches the bus, gets out at Sheepsale, posts the letter—and then gets on with whatever business he has to do there ! '

It all sounded extremely likely, but somehow Larry thought it was *too* likely. ' Couldn't the person go on a bike ? ' he said.

' Well—he *could*—but think of that awful hill up to Sheepsale,' said Fatty. ' Nobody in their senses would bike there when a bus goes.'

' No—I suppose not,' said Larry. ' Well—I don't see that all this gets us much farther, Fatty. All we've found out is that more people than Gladys and Molly have had these letters—and that they all come from Sheepsale and are posted at or before 11.45—and that possibly the letter-writer may catch the 10.15 bus from Peterswood.'

' *All* we've found out ! ' said Fatty. ' Gosh, I think we've discovered an enormous lot. Don't you realize that we're really on the track now—the track of this beastly letter-writer. Why, if we want to, we can go and see him—or her—on Monday morning ! '

The others stared at Fatty, puzzled.

' We've only got to catch that 10.15 bus ! ' said Fatty. ' See ? The letter-writer is sure to be on it. Can't we discover who it is just by looking at their faces ? I bet *I* can ! '

' Oh, Fatty ! ' said Bets, full of admiration. ' Of course—we'll catch that bus. But, oh dear, *I* should never be able to tell the right person, never. Will you really be able to spot who it is ? '

' Well, I'll have a jolly good try,' said Fatty. ' And now I'd better take these letters back, I think.

But first of all I want to make a tracing of some of
these sentences—especially words like " PETERS-
WOOD " that occur in each address—in case I
come across somebody who prints their words in
just that way.'

' People don't print words, though—they write
them,' said Daisy. But Fatty took no notice. He
carefully traced a few of the words, one of them
being ' PETERSWOOD.' He put the slip into his
wallet. Then he snapped the bit of elastic round
the package and stood up.

' How are you going to get the letters back
without being seen ? ' asked Larry.

' Don't know yet,' said Fatty, with a grin.
' Just chance my luck, I think. Wait about for
Gladys, will you, and tell her I didn't approve of
her taking the letters like that in case Mr. Goon
was angry with her—and tell her I'm returning him
the letters, and hope he won't know she took them
at all.'

' Right,' said Larry. Fatty was about to go
when he turned and came back. ' I've an idea I'd
better pop on my telegraph-boy's uniform,' he said.
' Just in case old Goon spots me. I don't want him
to know I'm returning his letters ! '

It wasn't long before Fatty was wearing his
disguise, complete with freckles, red eyebrows and
hair. He set his telegraph-boy's cap on his head.

' So long ! ' he said, and disappeared. He
padded off to Mr. Goon's, and soon saw, by the
darkness of his parlour, that he was not yet back.
So he waited about, until he remembered that there
was a darts match at the local inn, and guessed Mr.
Goon would be there, throwing a dart or two.

His guess was right. Mr. Goon walked out of

the inn in about ten minutes' time, feeling delighted with himself because he had come out second in the match. Fatty padded behind him for a little way, then ran across the road, got in front of Mr. Goon, came across again at a corner, walked towards the policeman and bumped violently into him.

'Hey!' said the policeman, all his breath knocked out of him. 'Hey! Look where you're going now.' He flashed his torch and saw the red-headed telegraph-boy.

'Sorry, sir, I do beg your pardon,' said Fatty earnestly. 'Have I hurt you? Always seem to be damaging you, don't I, sir? Sorry, sir.'

Mr. Goon set his helmet straight. Fatty's apologies soothed him. 'All right, my boy, all right,' he said.

'Good-night, sir, thank you, sir,' said Fatty and disappeared. But he hadn't gone more than three steps before he came running back again, holding out a package.

'Oh, Mr. Goon, sir, did you drop these, sir? Or has somebody else dropped them?'

Mr. Goon stared at the package and his eyes bulged. 'Them letters!' he said. 'I didn't take them out with me, that I do know!'

'I expect they belong to somebody else then,' said Fatty. 'I'll inquire.'

'Hey, no you don't!' said Mr. Goon, making a grab at the package. 'They're my property. I must have brought them out unbeknowing-like. Dropped them when you bumped into me, shouldn't wonder. Good thing you found them, young man. They're valuable evidence, they are. Property of the Law.'

' I hope you won't drop them again, then, sir,' said Fatty earnestly. 'Good-night, sir.'

He vanished. Mr. Goon went home in a thoughtful frame of mind, pondering how he could possibly have taken out the package of letters and dropped them. He felt sure he *hadn't* taken them out—but if not, how could he have dropped them ?

' Me memory's going,' he said mournfully. ' It's a mercy one of them kids didn't pick them letters up. I won't let that there Frederick Trotteville set eyes on them. Not if I know it ! '

## 10    ON THE BUS TO SHEEPSALE

THERE was nothing more to be done until Monday morning. The children felt impatient, but they couldn't hurry the coming of Monday, or of the bus either.

Fatty had entered a few notes under his heading of Clues. He had put down all about the anonymous letters, and the post-marks, and had also pinned to the page the tracings he had made of the printed capital letters.

' I will now write up the case as far as we've gone with it,' he said. ' That's what the police do—and all good detectives too, as far as I can see. Sort of clears your mind, you see. Sometimes you get awfully good ideas when you read what you've written.'

Every one read what Fatty wrote, and they thought it was excellent. But unfortunately nobody had any good ideas after reading it. Still, the bus passengers to Sheepsale might provide further clues.

The five children couldn't help feeling rather excited on Monday morning. Larry and Daisy got rather a shock when their mother said she wanted them to go shopping for her—but when she heard that they were going to Sheepsale market she said they could buy the things for her there. So that was all right.

They met at the bus stopping-place ten minutes before the bus went, in case Fatty had any last-minute instructions for them. He had !

' Look and see where the passengers are sitting when the bus comes up,' he said. ' And each of you sit beside one if you can, and begin to talk to him or her. You can find out a lot that way.'

Bets looked alarmed. ' But I shan't know what to say ! ' she said.

' Don't be silly,' said Pip. ' You can always open the conversation by saying, " Isn't that a remarkably clever-looking boy over there ? " and point to Fatty. That's enough to get any one talking.'

They all laughed. ' It's all right, Bets,' said Fatty. ' You can always say something simple, like " Can you tell me the time, please ? " Or, " What is this village we're passing now ? " It's easy to make people talk if you ask them to *tell* you something.'

' Any other instructions, Sherlock Holmes ? ' said Pip.

' Yes—and this is most important,' said Fatty. ' We must watch carefully whether anybody posts a letter in Sheepsale—because if only one of the passengers does, that's a pretty good pointer, isn't it ? The post-office is by the bus-stop there, so we can easily spot if any one catches the 11.45 post. We can hang around and see if any of the bus passengers posts a letter before that time, supposing they don't go to the letter-box immediately. That's a most important point.'

'Here comes the bus,' said Bets in excitement. 'And look—there are quite a lot of people in it!'

'Five!' said Larry. 'One for each of us. Oh gosh! One of them is old Clear-Orf!'

'Blow!' said Fatty. 'So it is. Now whatever is he doing on the bus this morning ? Has he got the same idea as we have, I wonder ? If so, he's brainier than I thought. Daisy, you sit by him. He'll have a blue fit if I do and I know Buster will try to nibble his ankles all the time.'

Daisy was not at all anxious to sit by Mr. Goon, but there was no time to argue. The bus stopped. The five children and Buster got in. Buster gave a yelp of joy when he smelt the policeman. Mr. Goon looked round in astonishment and annoyance.

'Gah!' he said, in tones of deep disgust. 'You again! Now, what you doing on this bus to-day! Everywhere I go there's you children traipsing along!'

'We're going to Sheepsale market, Mr. Goon,' said Daisy politely, sitting beside him. 'I hope you don't mind. Are you going there too ?'

'That's *my* business,' said Mr. Goon, keeping a watchful eye on Buster, who was trying to reach his ankles, straining at his lead. 'What the Law does is no concern of yours.'

Daisy wondered for a wild moment if Mr. Goon could possibly be the anonymous letter-writer. After all, he knew the histories of every one in the

village.  It was his business to.  Then she knew it
was a mad idea.  But what a nuisance if Mr. Goon
was on the same track as they were—sizing up the
people in the bus, and going to watch for the one
who posted the letter to catch the 11.45 post.

Daisy glanced round at the other people in the
bus.  A Find-Outer was by each.  Daisy knew two
of the people there.  One was Miss Trimble who
was companion to Lady Candling, Pip's next-door
neighbour.  Larry was sitting by her.  Daisy felt
certain Miss Trimble—or Tremble as the children
called her, could have nothing to do with the case.
She was far too timid and nervous.

Then there was fat little Mrs. Jolly from the
sweet-shop, kindness itself.  No, it couldn't possibly
be her !  Why, every one loved her, and she was
exactly like her name.  She was kind and generous
to every one, and she nodded and smiled at Daisy as
she caught her eye.  Daisy was certain that before
the trip was ended she would be handing sweets out
to all the children !

Well, that was three out of the five passengers !
That only left two possible ones.  One was a thin,
dark, sour-faced man, huddled up over a newspaper,
with a pasty complexion, and a curious habit of
twitching his nose like a rabbit every now and again.
This fascinated Bets, who kept watching him.

The other possible person was a young girl about
eighteen, carrying sketching things.  She had a
sweet, open face, and very pretty curly hair.  Daisy
felt absolutely certain that she knew nothing whatever about the letters.

' It must be that sour-faced man with the
twitching nose,' said Daisy to herself.  She had
nothing much to do because it was no use tackling

Mr. Goon and talking to him. It was plain that he
could not be the writer of the letters. So she watched
the others getting to work, and listened with much
interest, though the rattling of the bus made her
miss a little of the conversation.

'Good morning, Miss Trimble,' Daisy heard
Larry say politely. 'I haven't seen you for some
time. Are you going to the market too? We
thought we'd like to go to-day.'

'Oh, it's a pretty sight,' said Miss Trimble,
setting her glasses firmly on her nose. They were
always falling off, for they were pince-nez, with no
side-pieces to hold them behind her ears. Bets
loved to count how many times they fell off. What
with watching the man with the twitching nose and
Miss Trimble's glasses, Bets quite forgot to talk to
Mrs. Jolly, who was taking up most of the seat she
and Bets was sitting on.

'Have you often been to Sheepsale market?'
asked Larry.

'No, not very often,' said Miss Trimble. 'How
is your dear mother, Laurence?'

'She's quite well,' said Larry. 'Er—how is
*your* mother, Miss Tremble? I remember seeing
her once next door.'

'Ah, my dear mother isn't too well,' said Miss
Trimble. 'And if you don't mind, Laurence dear,
my name is *Trim*ble, not Tremble. I think I have
told you that before.'

'Sorry. I keep forgetting,' said Larry. 'Er—
does your mother live at Sheepsale, Miss Trem—er
Trimble? Do you often go and see her?'

'She lives just outside Sheepsale,' said Miss
Trimble, pleased at Larry's interest in her mother.
'Dear Lady Candling lets me go every Monday to

see her, you know—such a help. I do all the old
lady's shopping for the week then.'

' Do you always catch this bus ? ' asked Larry,
wondering if by any conceivable chance Miss Trimble
could be the wicked letter-writer.

' If I can,' said Miss Trimble. ' The next one is
not till after lunch you know.'

Larry turned and winked at Fatty. He didn't
think that Miss Trimble was the guilty person, but
at any rate she must be put down as a suspect.
But her next words made him change his mind
completely.

' It was such a nuisance,' said Miss Trimble.
' I lost the bus last week, and wasted half my
day ! '

Well ! That put Miss Trimble right out of the
question, because certainly the letter-writer had
posted the letter to poor Gladys the Monday before
—and if Miss Trimble had missed the bus, she
couldn't have been in Sheepsale at the right time
for posting !

Larry decided that he couldn't get any more out
of Miss Trimble that would be any use and looked
out of the window. Bets seemed to be getting on
well with Mrs. Jolly now. He couldn't hear what
she was saying, but he could see that she was busy
chattering.

Bets was getting on like a house on fire ! Mrs.
Jolly greeted her warmly and asked after her mother
and father, and how the garden was, and had they
still got that kitchen cat that was such a good hunter.
And Bets answered all her questions, keeping an
interested eye on Miss Trimble's glasses, which
had already fallen off twice, and on the sour-faced
man's twitching nose.

It was not until she saw how earnestly Fatty was trying to make the sour-faced man talk to him that she suddenly realized that she too ought to find out a few things from Mrs. Jolly. Whether, for instance, she always caught this bus !

' Are you going to the market, Mrs. Jolly ? ' she asked.

' Yes, that I am ! ' said Mrs. Jolly. ' I always buy my butter and eggs from my sister there. You should go to her stall too, Miss Bets, and tell her you know me. She'll give you over-weight in butter then and maybe a brown egg for yourself ! '

' She sounds awfully kind—just like you ' said Bets.

Mrs. Jolly was pleased and laughed her hearty laugh. ' Oh, you've got a soft tongue, haven't you ? ' she said. Bets was surprised. She thought all tongues must surely be soft.

She looked at Mrs. Jolly, and decided not to ask her any more questions about going to Sheepsale every Monday because nobody, nobody with such kind eyes, such a lovely smile, such a nice apple-cheeked face could possibly write an unkind letter ! Bets felt absolutely certain of it. Mrs. Jolly began to fumble in her bag.

' Now where did I put those humbugs ? ' she said. ' Ah, here they are ? Do you like humbugs, Miss Bets ? Well, you help yourself, and we'll pass them over to the others as well.'

Pip was sitting by the young girl. He found it easy to talk to her.

' What are you going to paint ? ' he asked.

' I'm painting Sheepsale market,' she answered. ' I go every Monday. It's such a jolly market— small and friendly and very picturesque, set on the

top of the hill, with that lovely country all round.
I love it.'

'Do you always catch the same bus?' asked
Pip.

'I have to,' she said. 'The market's in the
morning, you know. I know it by heart now—where
the hens and ducks are, and the sheep, and the
butter-stalls and the eggs and everything!'

'I bet you don't know where the post-office is!'
said Pip quickly.

The girl laughed and thought. 'Well, no, I
don't!' she said. 'I've never had to go there and
so I've never noticed. But if you want it, any one
would tell you. There can't be much of a post-
office at Sheepsale, though. It's only a small place.
Just a market really.'

Pip felt pleased. If this girl didn't know where
the post-office was, she could never have posted a
letter there. Good. That ruled her out. Pip felt
very clever. Anyway, he was certain that such a nice
girl wouldn't write horrid letters.

He looked round at the others, feeling that his
task was done. He felt sorry for Daisy, sitting next
to the surly Mr. Goon. He wondered how Fatty
was getting on.

He wasn't getting on at all well! Poor Fatty—
he had chosen a very difficult passenger to talk to.

THE sour-faced man appeared to be very deep indeed in his paper, which seemed to Fatty to be all about horses and dogs.

Buster sniffed at the man's ankles and didn't seem to like the smell of them at all. He gave a disgusted snort and strained away towards where Mr. Goon sat, a few seats in front.

'Er—I hope my dog doesn't worry you, sir,' said Fatty.

The man took no notice. 'Must be deaf,' thought Fatty and raised his voice considerably.

'I hope my DOG doesn't WORRY you, sir,' he said. The man looked up and scowled.

'Don't shout at me. I'm not deaf,' he said.

Fatty didn't like to ask again if Buster worried him. He cast about for something interesting to say.

'Er—horses and dogs are very interesting aren't they?' he said. The man took no notice. Fatty debated whether to raise his voice or not. He decided not.

'I said, horses and dogs are very interesting, aren't they?' he repeated.

'Depends,' said the man, and went on reading.

That wasn't much help in a conversation, Fatty thought gloomily. The others were jolly lucky to have got such easy people to tackle. But still—of all the passengers in the bus, this man looked by far the most likely to be the letter-writer—sour-faced, scowling, cruel-mouthed! Fatty racked his brains and tried again.

'Er—could you tell me the time?' he said, rather feebly. There was no reply. This was getting boring! Fatty couldn't help feeling annoyed too. There was no need to be so rude, he thought!

'Could you tell me the time?' he repeated.

'I could, but I'm not going to, seeing that you've got a wrist-watch yourself,' said the man. Fatty could have kicked himself.

'You're not being much of a detective this morning!' he told himself. 'Buck up, Frederick Algernon Trotteville, and look sharp about it!'

'Oh—look at that aeroplane!' said Fatty, seeing a plane swoop down rather low. 'Do you know what it is, sir?'

'Flying Fortress,' said the man, without even looking up. As the aeroplane had only two engines and not four, this was quite wrong and Fatty knew it. He looked at his fellow passenger in despair. How could he ever get anything out of him?

'I'm going to Sheepsale market,' he said. 'Are you, sir?'

There was no answer. Fatty wished Buster would bite the man's ankles. 'Do you know if this is Buckle Village we're passing?' asked Fatty, as they passed through a pretty little village. The man put down his paper and glared at Fatty angrily.

'I'm a stranger here,' he said. 'I know nothing about Buckle or Sheepsale or its market! I'm just going there to be picked up by my brother, to go on somewhere else—and all I can say is that the further I get away from chatterboxes like you, the better I shall like it!'

As this was all said very loudly, most of the people in the bus heard it. Mr. Goon chuckled heartily.

' Ah, I've had some of him too ! ' he called. ' Proper pest, I reckon he is.'

' Go and sit somewhere else and take your smelly dog with you,' said the sour-faced man, pleased to find that somebody else agreed with his opinion of poor Fatty.

So Fatty, red in the face, and certain that he would not be able to get anything more out of the annoyed man, got up and went right to the front of the bus, where nobody was sitting. Bets was sorry for him and she left Mrs. Jolly and joined him.

Larry, Pip and Daisy came across too, and they talked together in low voices.

' I can't see that it can be any one here,' said Fatty, when he had heard all that the others had to say. ' It's obviously not old Clear-Orf—and we can rule out Miss Tremble and Mrs. Jolly surely. And I agree with Pip that the artist girl isn't very likely either, especially as she doesn't even know where the post-office is. And my man said he was a stranger here, so it doesn't look as if he could be the one. A stranger wouldn't know any of the Peterswood people.'

' Does he come on this bus every Monday ? ' asked Pip, in a low voice.

' I didn't get as far as asking him that,' said Fatty gloomily. ' Either he wouldn't answer, or he just snapped. He was hopeless. It doesn't look really as if any of the people here could have posted those letters.'

' Look—there's somebody waiting at the next bus-stop ! ' said Bets suddenly. ' At least—it isn't a bus-stop—it's just somebody waving to the bus to stop it for himself. That must be the person we want, if there's nobody else.'

' Perhaps it is,' said Fatty hopefully, and they all waited to see who came in.

But it was the vicar of Buckle ! The children knew him quite well because he sometimes came to talk to them in their own church at Peterswood. He was a jolly, burly man and they liked him.

' Can't be him ! ' said Fatty, disappointed. ' Can't possibly. Blow ! We're not a bit further on.'

' Never mind—perhaps one of them will post a letter when they get out of the bus,' said Pip. ' We'll hope for that. Maybe your sour-faced man will, Fatty. He looks the most likely of the lot. He may be telling lies when he says he is a stranger.'

The vicar talked to every one in the bus in his cheerful booming voice. The thin huddled man took no notice, and as the Vicar did not greet him, the children felt sure that he did not know him. So perhaps he *was* a stranger after all ?

' Soon be at Sheepsale now,' said Fatty. ' Golly, isn't this a steep pull-up ? They say it wanted eight horses to pull the coach up in the old days before motor-buses.'

The bus stopped under some big trees in Sheep-sale. A babel of baaing, mooing, clucking and quacking came to every one's ears. The market was in full swing !

' Quick—hop out first ! ' said Fatty to the others. ' Stand by the post-office—and keep a close watch.'

The children hurried off. Miss Trimble nodded to them and walked away down a little lane. The

Find-Outers spotted the post-office at once and went over to it. Fatty produced a letter, and began to stamp it carefully.

'Don't want Goon to wonder why we're all standing about here,' he murmured to the others. 'May as well post this letter.'

Mrs. Jolly went off to the market to find her sister. The children watched her go.

'Well, neither Miss Trimble nor Mrs. Jolly have posted letters,' said Fatty. 'That lets those two out. Ah—here comes the artist girl.'

The girl smiled at them and went on. Then she suddenly turned back. 'I see you've found the post-office!' she called. 'I'm so glad! How silly of me never to have noticed it when I pass it every single Monday. But that's just like me!'

'She's not the one, either,' said Pip, as she disappeared in the direction of the market. 'I didn't think she was. She was too nice.'

The vicar disappeared too, without coming in their direction at all. Now only Mr. Goon and the sour-faced man were left. Mr. Goon stared at Fatty, and Fatty raised his eyebrows and smiled sweetly.

'Anything I can do for you, Mr. Goon?'

'What you hanging about here for?' said the policeman. 'Funny thing I can't seem to get rid of you children. Always hanging on my tail, you are.'

'We were thinking the same thing about you too,' said Fatty. He watched the sour-faced man, who was standing nearby at the kerb, still reading his paper about dogs and horses. Fatty wondered if he wanted to post a letter, but was waiting till the children and Mr. Goon had gone. Or was he *really* waiting for his brother, as he had said?

' There's the sweet-shop over the road,' said Fatty, in a low voice, popping his letter into the post-box. ' Let's go over there and buy something. We can keep a watch on the post-box all the time. Then if dear old Clear-Orf or the sour-faced fellow are bursting to post letters, they can do it without feeling that we are watching ! '

So they all crossed to the sweet-shop and went in. Larry and Daisy started an argument about whether to buy peppermints or toffees, and Fatty watched the post-office carefully through the glass door. He could see, but could not be seen, for it was dark in the little shop.

The sour-faced man folded up his paper and looked up and down the village street. Mr. Goon disappeared into a tobacco shop. Fatty watched breathlessly. There was no one about in the street now—would that man quickly slip a letter into the post-box ?

A car drove up. The driver called out a greeting, and the sour-faced man replied. He opened the door and got in beside the driver. Then they drove off quickly. Fatty gave such a heavy sigh that the others looked round.

' He didn't post a letter,' said Fatty. ' He was telling the truth. Somebody picked him up in a car. Blow ! Bother ! Dash ! '

' Well, even if he *had* posted a letter, I don't see that we could have collared him,' said Pip. ' We didn't know his name or anything about him. But I say—it's pretty peculiar, isn't it—not a single one of the passengers posted a letter—and yet one is always posted every single Monday ! '

' Well—we'll just wait till 11.45 when the post-man comes to collect the letters,' said Fatty. ' In

case one of the passengers comes back.   Ah, there
goes Goon, off to the market.   I suppose he's buying
butter and cream to make himself a bit fatter ! '

The children waited patiently by the post-
office till the postman came and took out the letters.
Nobody came to post any.   It was most disappointing.

' We're just where we were ! '   said Fatty
gloomily.   ' Sickening, isn't it ?   I don't think we're
such good detectives as we hoped we were !   You
go off to the market.   I want to have a good think.
I may get a much better idea soon ! '

So off to Sheepsale market went the others,
leaving poor Fatty behind, looking extremely gloomy.

## 12    A LOVELY DAY

THE children had a really lovely time at the market.
They loved every minute of it.   It was such a noisy,
lively, friendly place, the birds and animals were so
excited, the market-folk so good-humoured and
talkative.

They found Mrs. Jolly's sister, and she insisted
on giving each of them a large brown egg, and a
small pat of her golden home-made butter for their
breakfast.   Bets was simply delighted.   She always
loved an unexpected present more than any other.

' Oh *thank* you ! ' she said.   ' You *are* kind—
just exactly like Mrs. Jolly.   She gives us sweets.
Is your name Jolly, too ? '

' No.   I'm Mrs. Bunn,' said Mrs. Jolly's sister
and Bets very nearly said, ' Oh, that's *just* the right

name for you!' but stopped herself in time. For Mrs. Bunn was exactly like her name—big and round, and soft and warm, with eyes like black-currants.

'Let's go and find Fatty and tell him to come and see the market,' said Bets. 'I don't like to think of him glooming by himself. We're stuck over this case, and I don't believe even Fatty can unstick us.'

'There's the artist girl, look!' said Pip. And there she was, in the middle of the market, painting hard, gazing at all the animals and birds around her in delight. The children went and looked at her picture and thought it was very good indeed.

Bets went to find Fatty. He was sitting on a bench in the village street, lost in thought. Bets looked at him in admiration. She could quite well imagine him grown-up, solving deep mysteries that nobody else could. She went up to him and made him jump.

'Oh, Fatty, sorry! Did I make you jump? Do come and see the market. It's marvellous.'

'I haven't quite finished my pondering yet,' said Fatty. 'Perhaps if I talk to you, Bets, I might see things a little more clearly.'

Bets was thrilled and proud. 'Oh yes, *do* talk to me, Fatty. I'll listen and not say a word.'

'Oh, you can talk too,' said Fatty. 'You're a very sensible little person, I think. I haven't forgotten how you guessed that telegraph-boy was me, just because you happened to see Buster staring up at me adoringly.'

Buster looked up at the mention of his name. He was looking gloomy, because he was still on the lead. He badly wanted to go off to the market, because the smells that came from it were too exciting for words. He wagged his tail feebly.

'Buster looks as if he's pondering too,' said Bets. Fatty took no notice. He was looking off into the distance, deep in thought. Bets decided not to disturb him. He could talk to her when he wanted to. She began to practise twitching her nose just as she had seen the sour-faced man do. Buster watched her.

Fatty suddenly noticed it too and stared. 'Whatever's the matter with your nose ? ' he said.

'I'm only just twitching it like that man did,' said Bets. 'Talk to me, Fatty.'

'Well, I'm trying to work out what's best to do next,' said Fatty. 'Now—every Monday for some weeks past somebody has posted a letter to catch the 11.45 post here in Sheepsale—and each of those letters has gone to people in Peterswood. Well, if you remember, I said that that looked as if somebody living in Peterswood, who knew those people and possibly their histories, must have posted them.'

'Yes, that's right,' said Bets.

'And we worked out that the letter-writer probably caught that bus on a Monday and posted the letter on getting out,' said Fatty. 'So we caught the same bus, but we haven't found any one we could *really* suspect—though mind you every one of those bus passengers must go down on our list of Suspects—and we didn't catch any one posting a letter either.'

'You're not going to put Clear-Orf or the vicar down on the list, are you ? ' said Bets, astonished.

'Every single person is being put there,' said Fatty firmly. 'We can easily cross them out if we think we should—but they've all got to go down.'

'I dare say Clear-Orf has put *us* all down on *his* list of Suspects too then,' said Bets unexpectedly. 'I expect he was on that bus for the same reason as we were—to have a look at the passengers and watch who posted a letter.'

Fatty stared at Bets. Then he burst out into such a hearty laugh that Bets was startled. 'Have I said something funny ? ' she asked.

'No, Bets. But don't you realize which of the passengers posted a letter ? ' said Fatty, grinning.

'Nobody did,' said Bets. 'Well—except you, of course ! '

'Yes—me ! ' said Fatty. 'And it's going to make old Goon scratch his head hard when he thinks that of all his precious Suspects only one posted a letter—and that was his pet aversion, Frederick Trotteville ! '

Bets laughed too. 'That's funny ! ' she said. 'But, Fatty, nobody could possibly think *you* would write horrid letters like that ! '

'Old Clear-Orf would believe I'd stolen the Crown Jewels, if there was any suspicion of it,' said Fatty. 'He's got such a bad opinion of me ! He'd think me capable of anything. Golly—he must be in a state, wondering who's going to get that letter to-morrow morning ! '

'And nobody *will* get a letter ! ' said Bets. 'Because one hasn't been posted. It will be the first Monday that is missed for six weeks. I wonder why ? '

'So do I,' said Fatty. 'Of course—if one *does* arrive—it will mean that the writer lives in Sheep-sale after all, and has just posted the letter any

time this morning, before the bus came up. Then
we shall be properly stuck. We can't watch all
the inhabitants of Sheepsale posting letters ! '

' Perhaps whoever comes up on the bus to post
the letters each Monday didn't come to-day for
some reason,' said Bets.

' That's an idea,' said Fatty. ' When we go
back on the bus we'll ask the conductor if he
always has his regular passengers each Monday,
and see if any didn't go this morning. We could
make inquiries about them too—see if they've got
any spite against Gladys or Molly or the others,
and so on.'

' When's the next bus back ? ' asked Bets. ' I
wish we could stay here for the day, Fatty. You'd
love the market. But we haven't got our lunch
with us.'

' We could have it in that little shop over there,'
said Fatty, pointing. ' Look—it says, ' Light
Lunches.' That probably means eggs and bread,
and butter and cake. How would you like that ? '

' Oh, it would be *lovely*,' said Bets. ' You do
have good ideas, Fatty. But Mother would be
anxious if we didn't come back.'

' I'll do a spot of phoning,' said Fatty, who never
minded doing things of that sort. Bets thought how
like a grown-up he was, always deciding things, and,
what was more, always seeming to have plenty of
money to pay for everything !

Fatty disappeared into the post-office and went
into the telephone box. He made three calls very
quickly and came out.

' It's all right,' he said. ' I phoned up your
mother and Larry's mother and mine—and they all
said, ' Good riddance to you for the day ! '

' They didn't, Fatty ! ' said Bets, who simply couldn't imagine her mother saying any such thing.

' Well—not exactly those words,' grinned Fatty. ' But I could tell they weren't sorry to be rid of us for the day. I don't think my mother, for instance, liked that new game of ours very much.'

' I shouldn't think she did, really,' said Bets, remembering the yowling and groaning and rolling over and over that went with Fatty's new game. ' Let's go and tell the others we can stay here for lunch. Won't they be thrilled ! '

They were. ' Good old Fatty ! ' said Larry. ' It's a treat to be up here on a day like this, among all the farming folk and their creatures. What's the time ? I'm getting jolly hungry.'

' It's a quarter to one,' said Fatty. ' I vote we go and have some lunch now. Come on. It looks a nice little place like a dairy and cake shop mixed.'

It *was* a nice little place—shining and spotless, with a plump woman in a vast white apron to serve them and beam at them.

Yes, she could do two boiled eggs apiece and some plates of bread and butter, and some of her own bottled gooseberries if they liked, with a jug of cream. And she'd made some new buns, would they like some ?

' This is just the kind of meal I like,' said Bets, as the eggs arrived, all brown and smooth and warm. ' I like it much better than meat. Oh—is that strawberry jam, how lovely ! '

' I thought you might like some with the bread and butter, after you've had your eggs,' said the plump woman, smiling at them all. ' They're my own growing, the strawberries.'

' I think,' said Daisy, battering with her spoon
at her egg, ' I think that there can't be any thing
nicer than to keep your own hens and ducks, and
grow your own fruit and vegetables, and do your
own bottling, and pickling, and jamming. When I'm
grown-up I'm not going to get a job in an office and
write dreary letters, or things like that—I'm going
to keep a little house and have my own birds and
animals and make all kinds of delicious food like
this ! '

' In that case,' said Larry, ' I shall come and live
with you, Daisy—especially if you make jam like
this ! '

' I'll come too,' said both Fatty and Pip at
once.

' Oh—wouldn't it be lovely if we could *all* live
together, and have lovely meals like this, and solve
mysteries for the rest of our lives ! ' said Bets
fervently.

Everybody laughed. Bets always took things they
said so seriously.

' Well, I can't say we've made much headway at
solving *this* one ! ' said Fatty, beginning his second
egg. ' All right, Buster, old fellow, we'll get you a
meal too when we've finished. Be patient ! '

Fatty paid the smiling woman for the meal when
they had finished. The others wanted to pay their
share, but hadn't enough money. ' We'll take it out
of our money-boxes when we get home,' said Larry.
' And give it to you, Fatty.'

' That's all right,' said Fatty. ' Now let's go and
watch them clearing up the market. Then we'd
better inquire about our bus.'

They spent a lovely time watching the market
folk packing up their unsold goods, taking away the

birds and animals bought and sold, talking, laughing, and clapping one another on the back. Mrs. Jolly was there, talking to her sister, and she called to them.

' Don't you miss that bus back now ! There's only two more to-day, and the last one goes too late for you ! '

' Golly ! We forgot to look up the bus-time,' said Fatty, and ran to a bus time-table to look. ' We've only got three minutes ! ' he said. ' Come on, we must run for it ! '

They caught the bus with about half a minute to spare. But to Fatty's deep disappointment the driver and conductor were different. Apparently the morning and afternoon buses were manned by different men.

' Blow ! ' said Fatty, sitting down at the front. ' I call this a real waste of a day ! '

' Oh *Fatty*—how can you say that ? ' said Daisy, who had enjoyed every single minute of it. ' Why, it's been the nicest day we've had these hols ! '

' I daresay,' said Fatty. ' But if you remember, we came up here to try and get a bit further forward in our Mystery—and all we've done is to have a jolly good time, and not find out anything at all. A good day for five children—but a poor day for the Find-Outers—and Dog ! '

NEXT day the children felt rather dull after their exciting time at the market. They met in Pip's playroom, and Fatty seemed rather gloomy.

' I wish we could find out if any one has had an anonymous letter *this* Tuesday,' he said. ' But I don't see how we can. Old Clear-Orf is in a much better position than we are—such a thing would probably be réported to him at once ! '

' Well—never mind about the letters to-day,' said Pip. ' My mother's out—so if you want to play that woo-hoo-colly-wobbles game, we can.'

' Won't Mrs. Moon object ? ' asked Fatty.

' I shouldn't think she'd hear, away down in the kitchen,' said Pip. ' Anyway, we don't need to bother about her ! '

They were just beginning their extremely hilarious game, when a knock came at the playroom door and Mrs. Moon stuck her head in. The children looked at her, expecting a complaint.

But she hadn't come to complain. ' Master Philip, I've got to run down to the shops,' she said. ' The butcher hasn't sent me my kidneys this morning. Will you answer the telephone whilst I'm gone, and listen for the milkman ? '

' But isn't Mrs. Cockles here ? ' asked Pip. She always comes on Tuesdays, doesn't she ? '

' She does, usually,' said Mrs. Moon. ' But she hasn't turned up yet, so I'm all on me own.

I won't be above ten minutes gone—but I must get my kidneys.'

She disappeared. The children giggled. ' I hope the butcher hands her her kidneys all right,' said Larry. ' I shouldn't like to be without mine ! '

' Idiot ! ' said Daisy. ' Come on now—we can really let ourselves go, now the house is empty ! '

In the middle of all the hullabaloo, Pip heard a noise. He sat up, trying to push Fatty off him. ' Listen—is that the telephone ? ' he asked.

It was. Goodness knows how long the bell had been ringing ! ' I'll go, if you like,' said Fatty, who knew that Pip hated answering the telephone. ' It's probably from the butcher to say he's sending Mrs. Moon's kidneys ! '

He ran downstairs. He lifted the telephone receiver and spoke into it. ' Hallo ! '

' 'Allo ! ' said a voice. ' Can I speak to Mrs. Hilton, please ? '

' She's out,' said Fatty.

' Oh. Well, is Mrs. Moon there ? ' said the voice. ' It's Mrs. Cockles speaking.'

' Oh, Mrs. Cockles, this is Frederick Trotteville here, answering the phone for Philip Hilton,' said Fatty. ' Mrs. Moon has just gone down to— er—fetch her kidneys. Can I give her a message when she comes back ? '

' Oh yes, Master Frederick, please,' said Mrs. Cockles. ' Tell her, I'm that sorry I can't come to-day—but my sister's upset and I've had to go round to her. Tell Mrs. Moon she's had one of them there letters. She'll know what I mean.'

Fatty at once pricked up his ears. ' One of them there letters ! ' That could only mean one thing surely—that the wicked letter-writer had been busy again as usual, and had sent a letter to somebody else—Mrs. Cockles's sister this time. His brain worked quickly.

' Mrs. Cockles, I'm so sorry to hear that,' he said in a rather pompous, grown-up tone. ' Very sorry indeed. So upsetting, those anonymous letters, aren't they ? '

' Oh—you've heard about them then,' said Mrs. Cockles. ' Yes, right down wicked they are. Upset folks properly they do. And to think as my pore innocent sister should have had one of them. Mrs. Moon will be sorry to hear that—not that she ever had much time for my pore sister, they never did get on, but Mrs. Moon she knows how it upsets people to get one of these here nonnimus letters, and she'll understand why I've got to be with my pore sister this day instead of coming to help as I usually do. . . .'

This was all said without Mrs. Cockles taking a single breath, and Fatty felt slightly dazed. He felt that if he didn't interrupt, Mrs. Cockles might quite well go on for another ten minutes.

' Mrs. Cockles, do you think your sister would let me see the letter ? ' he asked. ' I'm—er—very interested in these things—and, as you perhaps know, I am quite good at solving mysteries, and . . .'

' Yes, I've heard how you found Lady Candling's cat for her, and found the real guilty person too,' said Mrs. Cockles. ' You come round to my sister's if you like, and she'll show you the letter. She lives at 9, Willow Lane. I'll be there. And give my regrets to Mrs. Moon and say I'll be along on Thursday for sure.'

Fatty replaced the receiver and rushed upstairs in the greatest excitement. He burst into the play-room and stood dramatically in the doorway.

'What do you *think*!' he said. 'There's been another of those beastly letters—sent to Mrs. Cockles's sister! She got it this morning and is all upset and that's why Mrs. Cockles didn't turn up to help Mrs. Moon! And Mrs. Cockles said if I go round to her sister's, she'll show me the letter. I simply *must* find out where it was posted and when.'

'Golly!' said every one.

'Let me come too,' said Pip.

'No. Best for only one of us to go,' said Fatty. 'Give Mrs. Moon this message when she comes back, Pip—say that Mrs. Cockles rang up and said she had to go to her sister, who was upset because she'd had a nasty letter. Don't let on that you know any more than that.'

'Right,' said Pip. 'Well, you hop off now, Fatty, before old Goon gets going on the job. He'll be round at Mrs. Cockles's sister in no time, as soon as he hears about the letter.'

Fatty shot off. He knew where Willow Lane was. He found number 9 and went to the little front door. It was a dirty, untidy little place. He rapped on the wooden door.

'Come in!' called Mrs. Cockles's voice. 'Oh, it's you, Master Frederick. Well, my sister says she won't show you the letter. She says what's in it isn't for any one to read but me and the police. And I won't say but what she's right, now I've read the letter properly.'

Fatty was most bitterly disappointed. 'Oh, I say!' he said. 'You might just let me have a

squint. I've seen all the others. Go on, be a sport
and let me see it.'

Mrs. Cockles's sister was a fat, untidy woman,
who breathed very loudly through her mouth and
talked through her nose.

' 'Taint fit for a child to read,' she said. ' It's
a right down spiteful letter, and not a word of truth
in it, neither ! '

' I'm not a child ! ' said Fatty, making himself
as tall as he could. ' You can trust me to read the
letter and not say a word to anyone. I'm—er—I'm
investigating the case, you see.'

Mrs. Cockles was very much impressed. But she
still agreed with her sister that the letter was not one
for him to read. Fatty, of course, was not in the least
curious about its contents—but he did badly want
to see the printing and, of course, the envelope.

' Well—could I just see the envelope ? ' he asked.
' That would do quite well.'

Neither Mrs. Cockles nor Mrs. Lamb, her sister,
could see any reason why he should not see the
envelope. They handed it to him. Fatty looked at
it eagerly, to make out the post-mark.

But there was none ! There was no stamp, no
post-mark ! Fatty stared in surprise.

' But—it didn't come by post ! ' he said.

' I never said it did,' said Mrs. Lamb. ' It
come this morning, very early—about half-past six,
I reckon. I heard something being pushed under
the door, but I was too sleepy to get up. So I
didn't get it till about half-past eight—and then I
was that upset, I sent for Mrs. Cockles here. And
you come at once, didn't you, Kate ? '

' Course I did,' said Mrs. Cockles. ' Only
stopped to have a word with Mr. Goon about it.

He'll be along soon to have a look at the letter too.'

Fatty felt slightly alarmed. He didn't want to bump into Clear-Orf at the moment. He stared hard at the envelope once more. The name and address were printed in capital letters again, and the square envelope was the same as the others that had been used. Fatty took his note-book out of his pocket and looked at the page headed CLUES.

He compared the tracing of the word PETERS-WOOD with the same word on the envelope. Yes, there was no doubt at all, but that the same hand wrote both words. They were exactly alike.

Fatty handed the envelope back to Mrs. Lamb. He had got from it all he wanted. He didn't want to see the letter inside. He could imagine it—a few sentences of spite and hurtfulness, with perhaps a little truth in them. He had enough to puzzle himself with—here was the usual letter, received on a Tuesday morning—but this time not through the post, and not from Sheepsale. Funny !

' Well, I'll be going,' said Fatty. ' Thanks for showing me the envelope, Mrs. Lamb. I'm so sorry you had one of these beastly letters. I shan't rest till I find out who is the writer of them.'

' Mr. Goon, he's on to them too,' said Mrs. Cockles. ' Says he's got a very good idea who it is, too.'

Fatty doubted that. He was sure that Mr. Goon was as puzzled as he was. He said good-bye and went out of the dirty little room.

But coming in at the front gate was the burly figure of Mr. Goon ! Fatty was annoyed. He tried to get out of the gate before Mr. Goon came in, but the policeman, surprised and exasperated at

seeing Fatty there, caught hold of his arm. He
pulled the boy inside the cottage.

' Has this boy been interfering with the Workings
of the Law ? ' he demanded, in an angry voice.
' What's he doing here, that's what I want to know ? '

Mrs. Lamb was afraid of Mr. Goon, but Mrs.
Cockles was not.

' He's not been interfering,' she said. ' Only
taking a friendly interest like.'

' How did he know that Mrs. Lamb had received
one of these here letters ? ' inquired Mr. Goon, still
in a furious voice.

' Well, I had to ring up Mrs. Moon to tell her
as how I wouldn't be along this morning, because
my sister had had a letter,' said Mrs. Cockles. ' And
Master Frederick, he happened to be there, and he
took the message. And he said he knew all about
the letters and would like to see this one, and I knew
he wasn't half-bad at snooping out things, so . . .'

' Mrs. Lamb, you didn't show this interfering
boy that letter before you showed it to me, did
you ? ' thundered Mr. Goon.

' Well—well, sir—he did say as he's seen them
all,' stammered poor Mrs. Lamb, frightened out of
her life. ' So I thought there wouldn't be much
harm. I only showed him the envelope though, Mr.
Goon, sir.'

Mr. Goon turned his frog-like gaze on to
Fatty. ' What's that mean—that you've seen all the
letters ? ' he demanded. ' They've been in my
possession—never out of it for a minute. What
you mean—you've seen them all ? '

' I must have been dreaming,' answered Fatty,
in an amiable voice. This was the voice that drove
poor Mr. Goon to fury. He snorted.

*Mr. Goon caught hold of Fatty's arm*

' You're telling untruths,' he said. ' Yes, you know you are. Them letters haven't been out of my possession, not for one minute ! '

' Haven't they really ? ' said Fatty. ' Well, I couldn't have seen them then.'

' Unless you know more about them than you make out ! ' said Mr. Goon, darkly and mysteriously, suddenly remembering how he had seen Fatty post a letter at Sheepsale the morning before. ' Ho, you're a deep one, you are—never know what your game is, I don't ! I wouldn't put anything past you, Master Frederick Trotteville ! '

' Thank you, Mr. Theophilus Goon,' said Fatty, and grinned. Mr. Goon longed to box his ears. Then he suddenly remembered that those letters *had* been out of his possession once—that time when he had apparently dropped them in the road, after colliding with the red-haired telegraph-boy. He stared suspiciously at Fatty.

' That telegraph-boy your friend ? ' he asked suddenly. Fatty looked mildly surprised.

' What telegraph-boy ? ' he asked.

' That red-haired fellow with the freckles,' said Mr. Goon.

' I'm afraid I've no red-haired, freckled tele-graph-boy for a friend, much as I would like one,' said Fatty. ' But why all these questions about a telegraph-boy ? '

Mr. Goon wasn't going to tell him. But he made a mental note to get hold of that telegraph-boy and ask him a few questions. Perhaps he and Fatty were in league together !

' Well, I'll go now,' said Fatty politely, ' unless you've got any more questions to ask me about telegraph-boys, Mr. Goon ? Oh—and would you

like another clue ?   Wait a bit, I'll see if I've got
one about me ! '

To Mr. Goon's rage he felt in his pockets and
produced a doll's straw hat. ' Now was that a
clue ? ' murmured Fatty, but, seeing Mr. Goon
gradually turning a familiar purple, he moved
swiftly through the door.

' If you don't clear-orf,' said Mr. Goon, between
his teeth, ' if you don't clear-orf . . . I'll . . .
I'll . . .'

But Fatty had cleared-orf.  He sprinted back to
Pip's.  The mystery of the letters was warming up
again !


## 14    THREE MORE SUSPECTS

HE was soon back in the playroom, relating everything to the others.  How they roared when they
heard about Mr. Goon coming in and hearing that
Fatty had seen all the letters !

' That must have given him a shock ! ' said Pip.
' He'll wonder for hours how you've seen them.
I bet he'll go about looking for that telegraph-boy
now—he knows he's the one who handed him the
letters he was supposed to have dropped.'

' Well, he'll be lucky if he finds the telegraph-
boy, even if he goes up to the post-office to look
for him ! ' said Fatty.  ' But I say—*now* we know
why none of the bus passengers posted the letter !
It was delivered by hand instead !  No wonder
we didn't see any one popping the letter into
Sheepsale post-box ! '

'It must be some one who didn't catch the bus yesterday for some reason,' said Daisy thoughtfully. 'We really must find out if any one who regularly catches that bus, didn't take it yesterday. If we can find out the person who didn't go as usual, we *may* have discovered who the letter-writer *is*!'

'Yes—you're right, Daisy,' said Larry. 'Shall one of us catch the 10.15 bus to-morrow, Fatty, and ask the conductor a few questions?'

'Perhaps we'd better not,' said Fatty. 'He might think it a bit funny, or think us cheeky, or something. I've got a better idea than that.'

'What?' asked the others.

'Well, what about going in to see Miss Tremble this morning?' said Fatty. 'We know she usually takes the Monday morning bus. We could get from her the names of all the people who always catch it at Peterswood. After all, it starts off by the church, and that's where she gets in. She must know every one who takes it on Mondays.'

'Yes. Let's go and see her now,' said Bets. 'Mrs. Moon is back with her kidneys, Fatty. She wasn't long. Pip gave her the message, and she said, 'Well, well, she wasn't surprised to hear that Mrs. Lamb had got one of those letters, she was the dirtiest, laziest woman in the village!'

'Well, I must say her cottage was jolly smelly,' said Fatty. 'Come on—let's go in next door. We'll ask Miss Trimble if she's seen your cat, Pip.'

'But Whiskers is here,' said Pip in surprise, pointing to the big black cat.

'Yes, idiot. But Miss Trimble's not to know that,' said Fatty. 'We've got to have *some* excuse for going in. She'll probably be picking flowers in the garden, or taking the dog for an airing. Let's look over the wall first.'

Their luck was in. Miss Trimble was in the garden, talking to Miss Harmer, who looked after Lady Candling's valuable Siamese cats for her.

'Come on. We'll go up the front drive and round to where she's talking,' said Fatty. 'I'll lead the conversation round to the bus.'

They set off, and soon found Miss Trimble. Miss Harmer was pleased to see them too. She showed them all the blue-eyed cats.

'And you really must come and see the daffodils in the orchard,' said Miss Trimble, setting her glasses firmly on her nose. Bets gazed at them, hoping they would fall off.

They all trooped after her. Fatty walked politely beside her, holding back any tree-branches that might catch at her hair. She thought what a very well-mannered boy he was.

'I hope you found your mother well on Monday,' said Fatty.

'Not so very well,' said Miss Trimble. 'She's got a bad heart, you know, poor old lady. She's always so glad to see me on Mondays.'

'And you must quite enjoy Mondays too,' said Fatty. 'Such a nice trip up to Sheepsale, isn't it, and such a fine little market!'

Miss Trimble's glasses fell off, and dangled on the end of their little gold chain. She put them on again, and smiled at Fatty.

'Oh yes, I always enjoy my Mondays,' she said.

'I expect you know all the people who go in the bus!' said Daisy, feeling that it was her turn to say something now.

'Well, I do, unless there are strangers, and we don't get many of those,' said Miss Trimble. 'Mrs. Jolly always goes, of course—such a nice person. And that artist-girl goes too—I don't know her name—but she's always so sweet and polite.'

'Yes, we liked her too,' said Fatty. 'Did you see the man I sat by, Miss Trimble? Such a surly fellow.'

'Yes. I've never seen him before,' said Miss Trimble. 'The vicar often gets on the bus at Buckle, and I usually have such a nice talk with him. Mr. Goon sometimes goes up on that bus too, to have a word with the policeman in charge of Sheepsale. But I'm always glad when he's not there, somehow.'

'I suppose one or two of the regular Monday bus-people weren't there yesterday, were they?' said Fatty innocently. 'I thought the bus would be much more crowded than it was.'

'Well, let me see now—yes, there *are* usually more people,' said Miss Trimble, her glasses falling off again. The children held their breath. Now they would perhaps hear the name of the wicked letter-writer!

'Anyone *we* know?' asked Fatty.

'Well, I don't know if you know Miss Tittle, do you?' said Miss Trimble. 'She *always* goes up on a Monday, but she didn't yesterday. She's a dressmaker, you know, and goes up to Sheepsale House to sew all day Mondays.'

'Really?' said Fatty. 'Is she a special friend of yours, Miss Trimble?'

'Well, no,' said Miss Trimble. 'I can't say she is. She's like a lot of dressmakers, you know—full of gossip and scandal—a bit spiteful, and I don't like that. It's not Christian, I say. She pulls people to pieces too much for my liking. Knows a bit too much about everybody ! '

The children immediately felt absolutely certain that Miss Tittle was the writer of those spiteful letters. She sounded exactly like them !

' Aren't the daffodils simply lovely ? ' said Miss Trimble, as they came to the orchard.

' Glorious ! ' said Daisy. ' Let's sit down and enjoy them.'

They all sat down. Miss Trimble looked anxiously at the children and went rather red.

' I don't think I should have said that about Miss Tittle,' she said. ' I wasn't thinking. She some-times comes here to sew for Lady Candling, you know, and I do find it very difficult not to be drawn into gossip with her—she asks me such questions ! She's coming here this week, I believe, to make up the new summer curtains—and I'm not looking forward to it. I can't bear all this nasty spitefulness.'

' No, I should think not,' said Bets, taking her turn at making a remark. ' You're not a bit like that.'

Miss Trimble was so pleased with this remark of Bets that she smiled, wrinkled her nose, and her glasses fell off.

' That's three times,' said Bets. Miss Trimble put back her glasses and did not look quite so pleased. She couldn't bear Bets to count like that.

' We'd better be going,' said Fatty. Then a thought struck him. ' I suppose there aren't any other Monday regulars on that bus, Miss Tremble— Trimble, I mean ? '

' You seem very interested in that bus ! ' said Miss Trimble. ' Well, let me think. There's always old Nosey, of course. I don't know why he didn't go yesterday. He always goes up to the market.'

' Old Nosey ? Whoever is he ? ' asked Fatty.

' Oh, he's the old fellow who lives with his wife in the caravan at the end of Rectory Field,' said Miss Trimble. ' Maybe you've never seen him.'

' Oh yes, I have ! Now I remember ! ' said Fatty. ' He's a little stooping fellow, with a hooked nose and a droopy little moustache, who goes about muttering to himself.

' He's called Nosey because he's so curious about everyone,' said Miss Trimble. ' The things he wants to know ! How old my mother is—and how old I am too—and what Lady Candling does with her old clothes—and how much the gardener gets in wages. I don't wonder people call him Old Nosey.'

Fatty looked round at the others. It sounded as if old Nosey, too, might be the letter-writer. He might be a bit daft and write the letters in a sort of spiteful fun. Fatty remembered a boy at his school who had loved to find out the weak spots in the others, and tease them about them. It was quite likely that Old Nosey was the letter-writer !

' And then, of course, there's always Mrs. Moon, your cook, Pip,' said Miss Trimble, rather surprisingly. ' She always has Mondays off to go and see to her old mother, just like me—and I usually see her every single Monday. But I didn't see her yesterday.'

' Well, you see, our housemaid, Gladys, has gone away for a few days,' explained Pip. ' And so I suppose Mother couldn't let Mrs. Moon off for the day. Yes—now I think of it—Mrs. Moon does go off on Mondays.'

' Any one else a regular passenger on the bus ? ' asked Larry.

' No, nobody,' said Miss Trimble. ' You *do* seem interested in that bus. But I'm sure you didn't come in here to ask me about that Monday morning bus, now did you ! What did you come to ask ? '

The children had forgotten what reason they were going to give ! Bets remembered just in time.

' Oh—we were going to ask if you'd seen our cat ! ' she said.

' So that's what you came in for ! ' said Miss Trimble. ' No—I'm afraid I haven't seen your cat. It's that big black one, isn't it ? I shouldn't think you need to worry about *him* ! He can look after himself all right.'

' I've no doubt he's indoors sitting by the fire this very minute,' said Pip, quite truthfully. ' Well, we must go, Miss Tremble.'

' Trimble, dear boy, not Tremble,' said Miss Trimble, her glasses falling off again. ' I simply cannot imagine why you keep making that mistake. Any one would think I was like an aspen leaf, all of a tremble ! '

The children laughed politely at this small joke, said good-bye and went. They said nothing at all till they were safely in Pip's playroom with the door shut. Then they looked at one another in excitement.

' Well ! Three more really fine Suspects ! ' said Fatty, opening his notebook. ' Would you believe it ? I think there's no doubt that one of them is the letter-writer.'

' Not Mrs. Moon,' said Bets. ' She was so kind to Gladys. Gladys said so. She couldn't be mean to her and kind to her as well.'

' I suppose not,' said Fatty. ' But all the same she's going down on our list. Now then—Miss Tittle-Tattle.'

The others laughed. ' Miss Tittle, not Tittle-Tattle ! ' said Pip.

' I know, idiot,' said Fatty. ' But I think Tittle-Tattle suits her jolly well. Miss Tittle—old Nosey —and Mrs. Moon. We're getting on. Now we'll have plenty more inquiries to make.'

' What inquiries ? ' asked Pip.

' Well—we must try and find out if Old Nosey, Miss Tittle, and Mrs. Moon were out early this morning,' said Fatty. ' That letter was pushed under Mrs. Lamb's door at about half-past six. It was only just getting light then. If we can find out that any of those three were out early, we've got the right one ! '

' However are you going to find that out ? ' said Larry. ' I shouldn't have thought even you were clever enough for that, Fatty ! '

' Well, I am ! ' said Fatty. ' And what's more I'll go and do it now—and come back and tell you all about it in an hour's time ! '

FATTY went off, whistling. The others watched him from the window. ' I suppose he's going to interview Old Nosey, Miss Tittle, and Mrs. Moon ! ' said Pip. ' He's a wonder ! Never turns a hair, no matter what he's got to do.'

' All the same, he won't find Mrs. Moon an easy one to interview,' said Larry. ' She doesn't seem to me to be in a very good temper to-day— because Mrs. Cockles hasn't turned up, I suppose.'

An hour went by. It was a quarter to one. The children went to the window and watched for Fatty. He came cycling up the drive—but dear me, how different he looked ! He had put on his red wig again, but with black eyebrows this time, and had reddened his face till it looked weather-beaten. He wore a dirty old suit and a butcher-boy apron round his waist !

But the children knew it was Fatty all right, by his whistle ! He stopped under their window. ' Any one about ? ' he said. ' Shall I come up ? '

' It's safe,' said Pip, leaning out of the window. ' Mrs. Moon's in the back-yard.'

Fatty came up, looking a real, proper butcher-boy. It was amazing how he could alter even his expression when he was supposed to be somebody else. He took off his apron and wig, and looked a bit better.

' Well—what have you found out ? ' said Larry eagerly. ' And why ever are you dressed like that ? '

' I've found out a lot,' said Fatty. ' But I
don't know that I'm any further forward really !
I'll tell you everything. I'm dressed like this
because it's natural for a butcher-boy to hang
about and gossip.'

He opened his notebook, and turned to the
pages headed ' SUSPECTS.'

' Old Nosey,' he began. ' Old Nosey was up
and about before half-past six this morning, with
his dog, Lurcher. He left his caravan and went
down Willow Lane, and into the village. He was
back at eight o'clock.'

He turned over another page.

' Miss Tittle,' he said. ' Miss Tittle was about
with her dog at half-past six, as she is every single
morning. She lives in a turning off Willow Street.
She always wears an old red shawl in the mornings.'

' Mrs. Moon,' went on Fatty, turning over a
page again. ' Mrs. Moon was out this morning
early, and was seen talking to Old Nosey. Well,
there you are, Find-Outers. What do you make
of that ? Every one of our three Suspects could
have popped that letter under the door ! '

' But, Fatty—however did you find out all
this ? ' said Bets, in great admiration. ' You really
are a most marvellous Find-Outer.'

' Elementary, my dear Bets ! ' said Fatty, putting
his notebook down. ' You know the field opposite
Willow Lane ? Well, old Dick the shepherd lives
there in a little hut. I noticed him this morning.
So all I had to do was to go and engage him in
conversation, and ask him a few innocent questions
—and out it all came ! Old Dick was wide awake
at five o'clock—always is—and he takes a great
interest in the people that pass up and down by

his field. They're about all he has to see, except his sheep. He says Nosey's always up and about at unearthly hours—a poacher most likely. He's a gypsy anyway. And apparently Miss Tittle always takes her dog for a trot early in the morning. So there's nothing unusual about that. He says he saw Mrs. Moon quite distinctly, and heard her voice too, talking to Old Nosey.'

' I'm sure it's Mrs. Moon ! ' said Larry. ' She *never* goes out so early, surely. I've heard your mother say she gets up too late, Pip.'

' Sh ! Here she comes, to say our lunch is ready,' said Pip warningly. Sure enough, it was Mrs. Moon.

She put her head in at the door. ' Will you come now, Master Philip ? ' she said, ' I've put your lunch and Miss Bets' in the dining-room.'

' Thank you, Mrs. Moon,' said Pip. Then, on a sudden impulse, he called out.

' I say, Mrs. Moon—isn't it queer, the old shepherd told Fatty that he saw you out at half-past six this morning ! He must be dreaming, mustn't he ! '

There was a sudden pause. Mrs. Moon looked startled and surprised.

' Well there now,' she said at last. ' Who would have thought any one'd be peeping out at that time of day. Yes, it's quite right. I *was* out early this morning. You see, I usually go up to see my old mother at Sheepsale on a Monday, and I couldn't let her know in time that I wasn't coming yesterday. I knew she'd be worrying, and I remembered that Old Nosey, the gypsy fellow, might be going up to-day, so I got out early and gave him a note for my mother, and a packet of food in case she hasn't been able to get some one to buy any for her. He'd be taking the 10.15 bus.'

' Oh,' said the children, really quite relieved at this explanation.

' So that's it ! ' said Pip, without thinking.

' That's what ? ' asked Mrs. Moon sharply.

' Nothing,' said Pip hastily, feeling a nudge from Fatty. ' Nothing at all ! '

Mrs. Moon looked at the children curiously. Fatty got up. He didn't want to make Mrs. Moon suspicious about anything.

' Time I went,' he said. ' Your lunch will get cold, Pip and Bets, if you don't go and have it. See you later.'

'Here's your notebook, Fatty ! ' Bets called after him, as he went downstairs. ' Your precious notebook with all its Clues and Suspects ! Fatty, are you going to write up the case again ? You've got some more to put down now, haven't you ? '

' Chuck the book down to me,' said Fatty. ' Yes, I'll write up the case as far as it's gone. I bet old Goon would like to see my notes ! '

He went out of the garden-door with Larry and Daisy. Fatty did not put on his wig or apron again. He stuffed them into his bicycle basket. ' Good thing I'd taken them off before Mrs. Moon came in,' he said. ' She'd have wondered why you were hobnobbing with the butcher-boy ! '

' Fatty, who do you think is the letter-writer ? ' said Daisy, who was burning with curiosity. ' I think it's Mrs. Moon. I do really.'

' I do too,' said Larry. ' But I don't see how we are to get any proof.'

' Yes, it certainly *might* be Mrs. Moon,' said Fatty thoughtfully. ' You remember that Pip told

us she wanted her niece to come here ?  She might
have got Gladys out of the way for that.  And yet
—there are all the other letters too.  Whoever
wrote them must be a bit mad, I think.'

' What do we do next ? ' asked Larry.

' I think we'll try and find out a bit more about
Mrs. Moon,' said Fatty.  ' We'll meet at Pip's at
half-past two.'

When they arrived back at Pip's, they found
him and Bets in a great state of excitement.

' What do you think !  Old Clear-Orf is here
and he's been going for Mrs. Moon like anything ! '
cried Pip.  ' We heard a lot of it, because the
kitchen window's open and it's just under our
playroom ! '

' What's he been going at her for ? ' asked
Fatty.

' Well, apparently she used to live near the
Home where Gladys was,' said Pip.  ' And once
she was working there as cook, and she got the
sack because the girls complained of her bad temper.
Maybe Gladys was one of those that complained !
Old Clear-Orf has been making inquiries himself,
I suppose, and when he found out that Mrs. Moon
actually knew the Home Gladys had been in, I
suppose he came over all suspicious.  He shouted
at her like anything—and she shouted back ! '

A noise of voices arose again.  The children
leaned out of the window.

' And what right have you got to come here
and talk to an innocent woman like you have ! '
shouted Mrs. Moon.  ' I'll have the law on you ! '

' I *am* the Law,' came Mr. Goon's ponderous
voice.  ' I'm not accusing you of anything, Mrs.
Moon, please understand that.  I'm just asking you

a few questions in the ordinary way of business, that's all. Routine questions is what we call them. Checking up on people, and finding out about them. Clearing them if they're innocent—as I've no doubt you are. You didn't ought to go on like this just because the Law asks you a few civil questions ! '

' There's others you could well ask questions of,' said Mrs. Moon darkly. ' Yes, others I could tell you of.'

' I've got a list of people I'm asking questions of,' said Mr. Goon. ' And all I hope is they'll be more civil than you've been. You don't make a good impression, Mrs. Moon, you don't, and that's flat.'

Whereupon Mr. Goon took his departure, and cycled slowly and heavily up the drive, the back of his neck looking bright red with rage.

' Old Goon's a bit brighter than we think,' said Fatty. ' He seems to have got his list of Suspects just as we have—and Mrs. Moon is down on his too ! '

' I thought when he saw you posting that letter yesterday at Sheepsale he'd suspect *you* ! ' said Larry.

' Oh, I think he's sure I'm " messing about " somehow, as he puts it,' said Fatty. ' He's probably expecting some one to get a stupid letter from *me*, as well as from the real letter-writer. Well—I've a jolly good mind to let him have one ! '

' Oh no, Fatty ! ' said Daisy.

Fatty grinned. ' No, I didn't mean it. Well, let's go out into the garden, shall we ? We'll go up to that old summer-house. I'll write up my notes there, whilst you all read or do something. It's too hot to stay indoors.'

They all went up to the summer-house. It backed on to the next-door garden, and was a nice, secluded little place, well away from the house. The children pulled some early radishes from the garden and washed them, meaning to nibble them all the afternoon.

They all talked hard about their mystery. They discussed everything and everybody. They read out loud what Fatty had written. It sounded very good indeed. He had even written up the interview between Mr. Goon and Mrs. Moon that afternoon. It began :

' Said Mr. Goon
To Mrs. Moon '

and went on in such a funny strain that the children roared.

Then, quite suddenly, they heard voices very near them. They stopped their talk, startled. Who could be so near ?

They peeped out of the summer-house. They saw Mrs. Moon, with some lettuces in her hand, talking to a stranger over the wall, almost within touch of their summer-house.

' Well, that's what I always say, Miss Tittle,' they heard Mrs. Moon say. ' If a thing's too tight, it's not worth wearing ! '

' You're quite right,' said the little, neat woman looking over the wall. ' But people will have their things made so tight. Well, do come in and see me about that dress of yours, Mrs. Moon, sometime. I'd enjoy a good talk with you.'

' I bet she would,' whispered Daisy. ' The two of them together would just about pull every one in Peterswood to pieces ! '

' Miss Tittle didn't look a very nice person,' said Bets, watching Mrs. Moon go down the path with her lettuces. She had obviously just been up the kitchen garden nearby to pull them.

' I suppose you realize that we've been talking very loudly, and that both Miss Tittle and Mrs. Moon could have heard every word, if they'd been listening ? ' said Fatty, with a groan. ' I never thought of any one coming up here. Miss Tittle must have been just the other side of the wall, and Mrs. Moon must have come up to get the lettuces. They grow quite near the summer-house. Now both will be on their guard, if they've heard what we've been saying ! '

' They won't have heard ! ' said Pip.

' They may quite well have done,' said Fatty. ' What idiots we are. Really ! Giving all our clues and facts away at the tops of our voices. And Bets reading out loud from my notes ! '

' Why didn't Buster bark ? ' said Bets.

' Well, he knows Mrs. Moon all right and wouldn't bark if she came by,' said Fatty. ' And I don't expect he bothers about any one in the next garden. Do you, Buster, old fellow ? '

' Woof,' said Buster lazily. He was lying in a patch of sun and it was pleasantly warm on him. He cocked his ears up, hoping to hear the magic word ' Walk.'

He soon heard it. ' I vote we go for a walk,' said Larry. ' It's getting stuffy here. Let's go down to the river and watch the swans. We'll take some bread.'

Pip asked Mrs. Moon for some bread. She seemed sulky and upset. ' No wonder,' thought Pip, ' after having Mr. Goon bellowing at her ! '

They had a lovely time by the river. They sauntered back to tea, but parted at Pip's, because each had to get back home for tea that afternoon.

' See you to-morrow,' said Fatty. ' We seem to be rather stuck again, don't we ? This mystery wants oiling a bit ! Well—maybe something will happen to-morrow ! '

Fatty was quite right. Plenty happened—and it was very exciting too !

## 16     MR. GOON IS PUZZLED

FATTY thought he would wear his butcher-boy disguise the next morning, in case he had to go and do a bit more snooping or interviewing. It was a simple disguise, and very effective. He put on his red wig, with no cap. He adjusted the black eyebrows and made his face red. Then, with his striped apron tied round his middle, he set off to Pip's.

Mrs. Hilton saw him as he flashed by the window. ' Ah, the butcher-boy,' she thought. ' Now Mrs. Moon won't have to go and fetch the meat again.'

The others greeted Fatty with delight. They were always thrilled when he disguised himself. He pulled off his wig, eyebrows, and apron when he got up into the playroom in case Mrs. Hilton should come in and see him.

He had no sooner done this than a great commotion began downstairs. The children listened, quite startled. They heard wails and groans, and somebody speaking sharply, then more wails.

They went to the head of the stairs and listened. ' It's Mrs. Moon—and Mother,' said Pip. ' Whatever is happening ? Mrs. Moon is crying and howling like anything and Mother is trying to make her stop. Gracious, what can be the matter ? '

' Perhaps Mother's discovered that Mrs. Moon is the bad letter-writer ! ' suggested Bets, looking rather scared.

' I'll go down and see what's up,' said Fatty, rising to the occasion as usual. He went downstairs quietly. He heard Mrs. Hilton's stern voice.

' Now Mrs. Moon, you are not to go on like this. I won't have it ! Pull yourself together at once ! '

' Oh Mam, to think I'd get one of those nasty letters ! ' wailed Mrs. Moon's voice. ' And such a spiteful one too ! Look here what it says.'

' I don't want to see, Mrs. Moon. Pay no attention to it,' said Mrs. Hilton. ' You know quite well it is only something written out of somebody's spiteful imagination. Let Mr. Goon see it, and then forget all about it.'

' That Mr. Goon ! ' wailed Mrs. Moon. ' Didn't he come here yesterday and tell me I might be one of them he suspects could have written the letters— me, a law-abiding, peaceful woman that never did no one no harm. Oooooo-o-oh ! '

' Pull yourself together at once,' said Mrs. Hilton sharply ! ' You're getting hysterical and I won't have it ! When did the letter come ? '

' Just this minute as ever was ! ' wailed Mrs. Moon. ' Somebody pushed it in at the kitchen door, and I picked it up and opened it—and there was that nasty spiteful message—oh, to think somebody could write to me like that, me that hasn't an enemy in the world.'

' Somebody pushed it in just *now* ? ' said Mrs. Hilton thoughtfully. ' Well now—I saw the butcher-boy coming by my window a minute ago.'

' He never came to my back door ! ' declared Mrs. Moon. ' Never left any meat or nothing.'

' Strange,' said Mrs. Moon. ' Could it possibly have been that boy who delivered the note—for somebody else ? Well, we can easily make inquiries at the butcher's.'

Fatty wished heartily that he hadn't put on his butcher-boy disguise. He must hide it well away when he went upstairs.

' I'll go and telephone to Mr. Goon now,' said Mrs. Hilton. ' Make yourself a cup of tea, Mrs. Moon, and try and be sensible.'

Fatty shot upstairs as Mrs. Hilton came out into the hall to telephone. The others clutched him.

' What's the row about ? ' they asked. ' Quick, tell us ! '

' What do you think ! ' said Fatty. ' Mrs. Moon's had one of those letters—delivered by hand a few minutes ago. We might any of us have seen who it was that left it here—but we didn't. But your mother spotted me in my butcher-boy disguise, Pip, and that's a pity, because she thinks *I'm* the one that delivered the letter ! '

' Mrs. *Moon's* had a letter ! ' said Larry, and gave a low whistle. ' Well, that rules *her* out then. That leaves only Nosey and Miss Tittle.'

' Let's watch for Mr. Goon,' said Bets. So they watched. He came cycling up the drive and dismounted by the front door. Mrs. Hilton let him in. The children stood at the top of the stairs, but Mrs. Hilton, worried and puzzled, did not even see them.

' I sent for you to say that Mrs. Moon has now had one of those unpleasant letters,' said Mrs. Hilton. ' She is naturally very upset.'

' Well, Madam, I may tell you that *I've* had one too, this morning ! ' said Mr. Goon. ' It's getting beyond a joke, this is. I found mine in the letter-box this morning. Course, it may have been delivered in the dark of night, probably was. Making fun of the Law like that. Things have come to a pretty pass if the Law can be treated like that ! '

' It's very worrying,' said Mrs. Hilton. ' I can't imagine any one wanting to send *you* that kind of letter, Mr. Goon.'

' Ah, no doubt the wrong-doer knows I'm on their track,' said Mr. Goon. ' Thinks to put me off, no doubt ! Tells me I'm a meddler and a muddler ! Ah, wait till I get me hands on them ! '

' Well—come and see Mrs. Moon,' said Mrs. Hilton. ' Please handle her carefully, Mr. Goon. She's almost hysterical.'

Obviously Mr. Goon couldn't handle a hysterical person, judging by the angry voices soon to be heard from the kitchen. The door opened again at last and Mr. Goon came out into the hall, looking extremely flustered, to find Mrs. Hilton, who had retired to the drawing-room.

' And that'll teach you to come pestering and accusing a poor, innocent woman ! ' Mrs. Moon's voice came from the kitchen. ' Pestering me yesterday like you did—and me struck all of a heap to-day ! '

Mr. Goon heard next about the red-headed butcher-boy, who had so mysteriously ridden up and left no meat, and had apparently departed without being seen.

Mr. Goon immediately thought of the red-headed telegraph-boy. ' Funny goings-on ! ' he said to himself. ' Them dropped letters now—and that telegraph-boy picking them up—and now this red-headed butcher-boy, without his meat—and maybe delivering that letter to Mrs. Moon. This wants looking into.'

' The five children are upstairs,' said Mrs. Hilton. ' I don't know if you want to ask them if they saw the butcher-boy. They may give you a few more details.'

' I'll see them,' said Mr. Goon, and went upstairs to the playroom. When he got there the children were apparently playing a game of snap. They looked up as Mr. Goon walked heavily into the room.

' Good morning,' he said. ' Did any of you see a red-headed butcher-boy coming along here this morning ? '

' Yes, I saw him,' said Pip with a grin.

' Ho, you did ! What did he do ? ' asked Mr. Goon.

' Just rode up the drive,' said Pip.

' And rode down again at once, I suppose,' said Mr. Goon.

' No. I didn't see him ride down,' said Pip. Nobody had apparently. Mr. Goon began to feel that this mysterious red-headed boy must be somewhere about the premises.

' He a friend of yours ? ' he said.

Pip hesitated. Fatty *was* his friend—and yet
to say that the butcher-boy was his friend would
lead him into difficulties. Fatty saw him hesitate
and came to the rescue.

' We've got no butcher-boy friends,' he said.
' And no telegraph-boy friends either. You remember you asked me that one too ? '

' I'm not speaking to you,' said Mr. Goon, with
a scowl. ' I'm speaking to Master Philip here.
I'd like to get hold of them two red-headed lads !
And I will too, if I have to go to the post-office
and speak to the postmaster, and ask at every
butcher's in the town ! '

' There are only two butchers,' said Pip.

' Mr. Goon, I'm so sorry to hear you've had
one of those horrid letters too,' said Fatty earnestly.
' I can't think how any one could have the nerve
—er, I mean—the heart to write to you like
that.'

' Like what ? ' said Mr. Goon sharply. ' What
do *you* know about any letters I've had ? I suppose
you'll tell me next you've seen the letter and know
what's in it, hey ? '

' Well, I can more or less guess,' said Fatty
modestly.

' You tell me what was in that letter then,' said
Mr. Goon, growing angry.

' Oh I couldn't,' said Fatty. ' Not with all the
others here.' He didn't know, of course, what was
in the letter at all, beyond that Goon was a meddler
and a muddler, but it was amusing to make the
policeman think he did.

' Well, it wouldn't surprise me at all if *you*
didn't write that there letter to me ! ' said Mr. Goon.

' It might not be the letter-writer at all—it might just be *you* ! '

' Oh, you *couldn't* think that of me ! ' said Fatty, looking pained. Larry and Daisy, rather alarmed, looked at him. They remembered how he had said he would love to write a letter to Mr. Goon. Surely he *hadn't* ?

Mr. Goon departed, determined to run the red-headed butcher-boy, and the equally red-headed telegraph-boy to earth. Larry turned to Fatty.

' I say ! You didn't really write to him, did you, Fatty ? '

' Of course not, silly ! As if I'd send an anonymous letter to any one, even for fun ! ' said Fatty. ' But my word, fancy somebody delivering a letter right into the lion's mouth ! To Goon himself. I can't see Miss Tittle doing that—or even Old Nosey the gypsy.'

' And now Mrs. Moon's ruled out,' said Larry. ' Gracious—it seems more of a muddle than ever, really it does. Got any ideas as to what to do next, Fatty ? '

' One or two,' said Fatty. ' I think it would be rather helpful to get specimens of Miss Tittle's writing and Old Nosey's. Just to compare them with my tracing. That might tell us something.'

' But how in the world can you do that ? said Daisy. ' I wouldn't be able to get Old Nosey's writing if I thought for a month ! '

' Easy ! ' said Fatty. ' You wait and see ! '

THE next day both Mr. Goon and Fatty were very busy. Fatty was trying to get specimens of Nosey's writing and Miss Tittle's, and Mr. Goon was trying to trace the two red-headed boys.

Fatty pondered whether to disguise himself or not, and then decided that he would put on the red wig, red eyebrows, and freckles, and a round messenger-boy's hat. It was essential that people should think he was a delivery boy of some sort, in order for him to get specimens of their writing—or so Fatty worked it out.

He set off on his bicycle to the Rectory Field, where Old Nosey, the gypsy, lived in a dirty caravan with his wife. In his basket he carried a parcel, in which he had packed two of his father's old pipes, and a tin of tobacco he had bought. Larry met him as he cycled furiously down the village street, keeping a sharp look-out for Goon.

'Fatty!' said Larry, and then clapped his hand over his mouth, hoping that no passer-by had heard.

'Fathead!' said Fatty, stopping by Larry. 'Don't yell my name out when I'm in disguise! Yell out Bert, or Alf, or Sid—anything you like, but not Fatty.'

'Sorry! I did it without thinking,' said Larry. 'I don't think any one heard. What *are* you going to do, Fatty—er, I mean Sid?'

'I'm going to deliver a parcel to Old Nosey,' said Fatty. 'From an Unknown Friend! And he's got to sign a receipt for it. See?'

'Golly, you're clever,' said Larry, filled with admiration. 'Of course—you can easily get him to sign his name—and address too, I suppose— by delivering a parcel to him and asking for a receipt! I'd never have thought of that. Never.'

'I've put a couple of old pipes and some tobacco in,' said Fatty, with a grin. 'Nice surprise for Old Nosey! I'm delivering a parcel to Miss Tittle too—and one to Mrs. Moon later. I've a feeling that if we've got specimens of all three in the way of hand-writing, we shall soon be able to spot the real letter-writer! I'm going to ask them to give me a receipt in capital letters, of course.

'Good for you,' said Larry. 'I'll tell Pip and Bets to look out for you later—delivering something to Mrs. Moon!'

Fatty rode off, whistling. He soon came to Rectory Field. He saw the caravan standing at the end, its little tin chimney smoking. Mrs. Nosey was outside, cooking something over a fire, and Nosey was sitting beside it, sucking at an empty pipe. Fatty rode over the field-path and jumped off his bicycle when he came to Nosey.

'Good morning,' he said. 'Parcel for you! Special delivery!'

He handed the parcel to the surprised Old Nosey. The gypsy took it and turned it round and round, trying to feel what was inside. 'Anythink to pay?' asked Mrs. Nosey.

'No. But I must have a receipt, please,' said

'*Good morning. Parcel for you*'

Fatty, briskly, and whipped out a notebook, in
which was printed in capital letters :

RECEIVED, ONE PARCEL,

       by . . . . . . . . . . . .

'Will you sign your name and address there,
please, in capital letters ? ' he asked, showing Nosey
where he meant.

'I'm not signing nothing,' said Nosey, not
looking at Fatty.

'Well, if you want the parcel, you'll have to sign
for it,' said Fatty. 'Always get a receipt, you know.
It's the only thing I've got, to show I've delivered
the parcel. See ? '

'*I'll* sign it,' said Mrs. Nosey, and held out her
hand for the pencil.

'No,' said Fatty. 'The parcel is for your
husband. I'm afraid he must sign it, Madam.'

'You let me,' said Mrs. Nosey. 'Go on—you give
it to me to sign. It don't matter which of us does it.'

Fatty was almost in despair. Also he thought
it a very suspicious sign that Nosey didn't seem to
want to sign his name and address in capital letters.
It rather looked as if he was afraid of doing so.

'I shall have to take the parcel back if your
husband doesn't give me a proper receipt for it,' he
said, in as stern a voice as he could manage. 'Got
to be business-like over these things, you know.
Pity—it smells like tobacco.'

'Yes, it do,' said Old Nosey, and sniffed the
parcel eagerly. 'Go on, wife, you sign for it.'

'I tell you,' began Fatty. But Nosey's wife
pulled at his elbow. She spoke to him in a hoarse
whisper.

'Don't you go bothering 'im. 'E can't write nor read!'

'Oh,' said Fatty blankly, and let Mrs. Nosey sign a receipt without further objection. He could hardly read what she wrote, for she put half the letters backwards, and could not even spell Peterswood.

Fatty cycled off, thinking. So Old Nosey couldn't write. Well, *he* was ruled out too, then. That really only left Miss Tittle—because Mrs. Moon had had one of the letters and could be crossed off the List of Suspects.

He went home and fetched a cardboard box into which he had packed a piece of stuff he had bought from the draper's that morning. He was just in time to catch Miss Tittle setting out to go for the day to Lady Candling's again.

'Parcel for you,' said Fatty briskly. 'Special delivery. Will you please sign for it—here—in capital letters for clearness—name *and* address, please.'

Miss Tittle was rather surprised to receive a parcel by special delivery, when she was not expecting one, but she supposed it was something urgent sent to be altered by one of her customers. So she signed for it in extremely neat capital letters, small and beautiful like her stitches.

'There you are,' she said. 'You only just caught me! Good morning.'

'That was easy!' thought Fatty, as he rode away. 'Now—I wonder if it's really necessary to get Mrs. Moon's writing? Better, I suppose, as she's been one of the Suspects. Well, here goes!'

He rode up the drive of Pip's house. Pip and

the others were lying in wait for him, and they called out in low voices as he went past.

'Ho there, Sid!'

'Hallo, Bert!'

'Wotcher, Alf!'

Fatty grinned and went to the back door. He had a small and neat parcel this time, beautifully wrapped up and tied with string and sealed. It really looked a very exciting parcel.

Mrs. Moon came to the kitchen door. 'Parcel for you,' said Fatty, presenting it to her. 'Special delivery. Sign for it here, please, in capital letters for clearness, name *and* address.'

'Me hands are all over flour,' said Mrs. Moon. 'You just sign it for me, young man. Now who can that parcel be from, I wonder!'

'' 'Fraid you'll have to sign it yourself,' said Fatty. Mrs. Moon made an exasperated noise and snatched the pencil from Fatty's hand. She went and sat down at the table and most laboriously pencilled her name and address. But she mixed up small letters and capital letters in a curious way. The receipt said:

RECEIVED, ONE PARCEL,

by..............................

WInnIe MOOn,

ReDhoUSe

peTeRSWOOD

'Thank you,' said Fatty, looking at it closely. 'But you've mixed up small letters and capital ones, Mrs. Moon! Why did you do that?'

'I'm no writer!' said Mrs. Moon, annoyed. 'You take that receipt and be off. Schooling in my days wasn't what it is now, when even a five-year-old knows his letters.'

Fatty went off. If Mrs. Moon didn't very well know the difference between small and capital letters, he didn't see how she could have printed all those spiteful anonymous letters. Anyway, he didn't really suspect her. He thought about things as he rode down the drive and back through the village. Nosey couldn't write. Rule him out. Mrs. Moon couldn't have done it either. Rule her out. That only left Miss Tittle—and the difference between her small and beautiful printing and the untidy, laboured scrawl of the nasty letters was amazing.

'I can't think it can be *her* writing, in those letters,' thought Fatty. 'Well, really, this case is getting more and more puzzling. We keep getting very good ideas and clues—and then one by one they all fizzle out. Not one of our Suspects really seems possible now—though I suppose Miss Tittle is the likeliest.'

He was so deep in thought that he didn't look where he was going, and he almost ran over a dog. It yelped so loudly with fright that Fatty, much concerned, got off his bicycle to comfort it.

'What you doing to make that dog yelp like that?' said a harsh voice suddenly, and Fatty looked up, startled, to see Mr. Goon standing over him.

'Nothing, sir,' stammered Fatty, pretending to be scared of the policeman. A curious look came into Mr. Goon's eyes—so curious that Fatty began to feel *really* scared.

Mr. Goon was gazing at Fatty's red wig. He looked at Fatty's messenger-boy hat. He looked very hard indeed. Another red-headed boy! Why, the village seemed full of them!

' You come-alonga me ! ' he said suddenly, and clutched hold of Fatty's arm. ' I want to ask you a few questions, see ? You just come-alonga me ! '

' I've done nothing,' said Fatty, pretending to be a frightened messenger-boy. ' You let me go, sir. I ain't done nothing.'

' Then you don't need to be scared,' said Mr. Goon. He took firm hold of Fatty's arm and led him down the street to his own small house. He pushed him inside, and took him upstairs to a small box-room, littered with rubbish of all kinds.

' I've been looking for red-headed boys all morning ! ' said Mr. Goon grimly. ' And I haven't found the ones I want. But maybe *you'll* do instead ! Now you just sit here, and wait for me to come up and question you. I'm tired of red-headed boys, I am—butting in and out—picking up letters and delivering letters and parcels—and disappearing into thin air. Ho yes, I'm getting a bit tired of these here red-headed boys ! '

He went out, shut the door and locked it. He clumped downstairs, and Fatty heard him using the telephone though he couldn't hear what he said.

Fatty looked round quickly. It was no use trying to get out of the window, for it looked on to the High Street and heaps of people would see him trying to escape that way and give the alarm.

No—he must escape out of the locked door, as he had done once before when an enemy had locked him in. Ah, Fatty knew how to get out of a locked room ! He felt in his pocket and found a folded newspaper there. It was really amazing what Fatty kept in his pockets ! He opened the news-paper, smoothed it out quite flat, and pushed it quietly under the crack at the bottom of the door.

Then he took a small roll of wire from his pocket, and straightened one end of it. He inserted the end carefully into the lock. On the other side, of course, was the key that Mr. Goon had turned to lock the door.

Fatty jiggled about with the piece of wire, pushing and moving the key a little. Suddenly, with a soft thud, it fell to the floor outside the door, on to the sheet of newspaper that Fatty had pushed underneath to the other side. He grinned.

He had left a corner of the newspaper on his side, and this he now pulled at very gently. The whole of the newspaper sheet came under the door —bringing the key with it ! Such a clever trick— and *so* simple, thought Fatty.

It took him just a moment to put the key into the lock his side, turn it and open the door. He took the key, stepped out softly, locked the door behind him and left the key in.

Then he stood at the top of the little stairway and listened. Mr. Goon was evidently in the middle of a long routine telephone call, which he made every morning about this time.

There was a small bathroom nearby. Fatty went into it and carefully washed all the freckles off his face. He removed his eyebrows and wig and stuffed them into his pocket. He took off his rather loud tie and put another one on, also out of his pocket.

Now he looked completely different. He grinned at himself in the glass. ' Disappearance of another red-headed boy,' he said, and crept downstairs as quietly as he could. Mr. Goon was still in his parlour, telephoning. Fatty slipped into the small empty kitchen. Mrs. Cockles was not there to-day.

He went out of the back door, down the garden and into the lane at the end. He had to leave his bike behind—but never mind, he'd think of some way of getting it back! Off he went, whistling, thinking of the delight of the Find-Outers when he told them of his adventurous morning!

## 18    THE MYSTERY OF THE

### RED-HEADED BOYS

MR. GOON finished his telephoning and went clumping upstairs to give that boy What-For, and to Properly-Put-Him-Through-It. Mr. Goon was sick and tired of chasing after red-headed boys that nobody seemed to have heard of. Now that he had got one really under his thumb, he meant to keep him there and find out a great many things he was bursting to know.

He stood and listened outside the door. There wasn't a sound to be heard. That boy was properly scared. That's how boys should feel, Mr. Goon thought. He'd no time for boys—cheeky, don't-care, whistling creatures! He cleared his throat and pulled himself up majestically to his full height. He was the Law, he was!

The key was in the lock. The door was locked all right. He turned the key and flung open the door. He trod heavily into the room, a pompous look on his red face.

There was nobody there. Mr. Goon stared all round the room, breathing heavily. But there simply wasn't anybody there. There was nowhere to hide at all—no cupboard, no chest. The window was still shut and fastened. No boy had got out that way.

Mr. Goon couldn't believe his eyes. He swallowed hard. He'd been after two red-headed boys that morning, and nobody seemed to have heard of either of them—and now here was the third one gone. Disappeared. Vanished. Vamoosed. But WHERE? And HOW?

Nobody could walk through a locked door. And the door *had* been locked, and the key his side too. But that boy had walked clean through that locked door. Mr. Goon began to feel he was dealing with some kind of Magic.

He walked round the room just to make sure that the boy hadn't squeezed into a tin or a box. But he had been such a plump boy! Mr. Goon felt most bewildered. He wondered if he had got a touch of the sun. He had just reported over the telephone his capture of a red-headed boy, for questioning—and how was he to explain his complete disappearance? He didn't feel that his superior officer would believe a boy could walk out of a locked door.

Poor Mr. Goon! He had indeed had a trying morning—a real wild-goose chase, as he put it to himself.

He had first of all gone to the post-office to ask the post-master to let him talk to the red-headed telegraph-boy.

But when the telegraph-boy had come, he wasn't red-headed! He was mousey-brown, and was a thin, under-sized little thing, plainly very frightened indeed to hear that Mr. Goon wanted to speak to him.

' This isn't the lad,' said Mr. Goon to the post-master. ' Where's your other boy ?   The red-headed one ? '

' We've only got the one boy,' said the post-master, puzzled. ' This is the one.  We've never had a red-headed fellow, as far as I can remember. We've had James here for about fourteen months now.'

Mr. Goon was dumbfounded.  No red-headed telegraph-boy ?  Never had one !  Well then, where did that fellow come from ?  Telegraph-boys were only attached to post-offices, surely.

' Sorry I can't help you,' said the post-master. ' But I do assure you we've got no red-headed boys at all here.  But we've got a red-headed girl here— now would you like to see *her* ? '

' No,' said Mr. Goon.  ' This was a boy all right, and one of the civilest I ever spoke to—too civil by a long way.  I see now !  Pah !  I'm fed up with this.'

He went out of the post-office, feeling very angry, knowing that the post-master was thinking him slightly mad.  He made his way to one of the butcher's, frowning.  Just let him get hold of that there red-headed butcher-boy, delivering letters for the anonymous letter-writer.  Ho, just let him ! He'd soon worm everything out of him !

Mr. Veale, the butcher, was surprised to see Mr. Goon.  ' Bit of nice tender meat, sir, for you to-day ? ' he asked, sharpening his knife.

' No thanks,' said Mr. Goon.  ' I want to know if you've got a red-headed boy here, delivering your meat.'

' I've got no boy,' said Mr. Veale.  ' Only old Sam, the fellow I've had for fifteen years.  Thought you knew that.'

'Oh, I know old Sam,' said Mr. Goon. ' But
I thought maybe you had a new boy as well. I
expect it's the other butcher's delivery-boy I want.'

He went off to the other shop. This was a
bigger establishment altogether. Mr. Cook, the
owner, was there, cutting up meat with his two
assistants.

'You got a boy here, delivering your meat for
you ? ' asked Mr. Goon.

'Yes, two,' said Mr. Cook. ' Dear me, I hope
they haven't either of them got into trouble, Mr.
Goon. They're good boys, both of them.'

'One of them isn't,' said Mr. Goon grimly.
'Where are they ? You let me see them.'

'They're out in the yard at the back, packing
their baskets with meat-deliveries,' said Mr. Cook.
'I'll come with you. Dear me, I do hope it's nothing
serious.'

He took Mr. Goon out to the back. The
policeman saw two boys. One was fair-haired with
blue eyes and the other was black-haired, dark as
a gypsy.

'Well, there they are, Mr. Goon,' said Mr.
Cook. ' Which of them is the rascal ? '

The boys looked up, surprised. Mr. Goon took
one look and scowled. ' They're neither of them
the boy I want,' he said. ' I want a red-headed
fellow.'

'There aren't any red-headed delivery-boys here,
sir,' said the fair-haired lad. ' I know them all.'

Mr. Goon snorted and went back into the shop.

'Well, I'm glad it wasn't one of my boys,' said
Mr. Cook. ' The fair-haired one is really a very
clever fellow—he . . .'

But Mr. Goon didn't want to hear about any

clever fair-haired boys. He wanted to see a red-headed one—and the more he tried to, the less likely it seemed he would ever find one.

He clumped out of the shop, disgusted. Who was the telegraph-boy ? Hadn't he seen him delivering a telegram to those children some time back—and again at night when he had bumped into him ? And what about that red-headed butcher-boy that Mrs. Hilton and Philip Hilton both said they had seen ? Who were these red-headed fellows flying around Peterswood, and not, apparently, living anywhere, or being known by any one ?

Mr. Goon began to feel that he had red-headed boys on the brain, so, when he suddenly heard the loud yelping of a frightened dog, and looked up to see, actually to *see* a red-headed messenger-boy within reach of him, it was no wonder that he reached out and clutched that boy hard !

That was when Fatty had been trying to comfort the dog he had nearly run into. Mr. Goon had felt that it was a miracle to find a red-headed boy, even if he wasn't a telegraph-boy or a butcher-boy. He was red-headed, and that was enough !

And now he had lost that boy too. He had just walked out of a locked room and disappeared into thin air. Hey presto, he was there, and hey presto, he wasn't.

Mr. Goon forgot all about the boy's bicycle in his worry. It had been left out in the little front garden when he had pushed the boy into his house. The policeman didn't even notice it there when he went out to get his mid-day paper. Nor did he notice Larry waiting about at the corner.

But Larry had been posted there by Fatty to watch what Mr. Goon did with his bike. Fatty was afraid that Mr. Goon might make inquiries and find out who the right owner was, and he didn't want the policeman to know that.

Larry saw Mr. Goon come out. He imagined that having found that Fatty was gone, he would at least lock up his bicycle, and take a delight in doing it. He didn't realize poor Mr. Goon's stupefied state of mind. The puzzled man had sat down in his chair to think things out, but had got into such a muddle that he had decided to go out, get his paper and have a drink. Maybe he would feel better then.

Mr. Goon went out of his little front garden as if he was walking in a dream. He saw neither Larry nor the bicycle. He drifted on towards the paper-shop.

Larry gaped. Wasn't old Goon going to lock up the bicycle ? Surely he ought to do that ? Could he possibly have overlooked it ? It really did seem as if he had.

Mr. Goon went into the paper-shop. Larry acted like lightning ! He shot across the road, went into the little garden, took Fatty's bike out, mounted it and rode off at top speed. Nobody even saw him !

Mr. Goon got his paper, and had a little talk with the owner of the shop. As he went out again, he suddenly remembered the bicycle.

"Lawks ! I ought to have locked it up at once ! ' thought Mr. Goon, and began to hurry back to his house. ' How did I come to forget it ? I was that mazed.'

He hurried into his front garden—and then stopped short in dismay. The bicycle was gone ! It was now of course, half-way to Pip's house, ridden furiously by Larry, who was absolutely

longing to know the whole of Fatty's story. But
Mr. Goon didn't know that.

He gulped. This was getting too much for
him. Three red-headed boys all vanishing into thin
air—and now a completely solid bicycle doing the
same thing. He supposed that red-headed fellow
must have taken it somehow without his seeing—
but how ?

' Gah ! ' said Mr. Goon, wiping his hot forehead.
' What with these here letters—and hysterical women
—and red-headed disappearing fellows—and that
cheeky toad, Frederick Trotteville—my life in
Peterswood ain't worth living ! First one thing
and then another. I'd like to talk to that Frederick
Trotteville. I wouldn't put it past him to write
me that cheeky anonymous letter. It's him that
done that—I'd lay a million dollars it was. Gah ! '


## 19    CLUES, REAL CLUES AT LAST!

THE Five-Find-Outers and Buster met in the
little summer-house at the top of Pip's garden that
afternoon. It was warm and sunny there, and they
wanted to be quite alone and hear again and again
of all that Fatty had done that morning—especially
of his neat escape from Mr. Goon's boxroom.

' I simply can't *imagine* what he said when he
unlocked the door and found you gone, Fatty ' said
Bets. ' I'd have loved to be there ! '

Fatty showed them the two specimens of handwriting he had taken from Miss Tittle and Mrs.

Moon. He told them that Nosey couldn't write, so that ruled him out completely. 'And if you look at this receipt, which Mrs. Nosey signed, you'll see she could never have written those letters either, even if Nosey had told her what to put into them,' said Fatty.

'It's a funny thing,' said Daisy, 'we've had plenty of Suspects—but one by one we've had to rule them out. There honestly doesn't seem to be a single real Suspect left, Fatty.'

'And except for seeing the letters, we've got no real Clues either,' said Larry. 'I call this a most disappointing Mystery. The letter-writer went a bit mad this week, didn't he—or she—sending letters to Mrs. Lamb—and Mrs. Moon *and* Mr. Goon. Before that, as far as we know, only one a week was sent.'

'Isn't old Clear-Orf funny when I keep pretending I've got a new Clue?' said Fatty, grinning. 'Do you remember his face when I pulled old Waffles, the white rat, out of my pocket? I just happened to have him there that day.'

'Poor old Clear-Orf doesn't believe anything we say any more,' said Pip. 'I do wonder if he really suspects somebody of writing those letters —some one we don't know about?'

'He may have some clues or ideas we haven't been able to get,' said Fatty. 'I shouldn't be surprised if he solves this Mystery after all—and not us.'

'Oh, *Fatty*!' cried every one in dismay.

'How *can* you say that?' said Bets. 'Wouldn't it be dreadful if he did—so that Inspector Jenks was pleased with him, and not with us.'

Inspector Jenks was their very good friend, and

had always been very pleased with them because they had managed to solve some curious mysteries in Peterswood before. They had not seen him since the Christmas holidays.

' Let's get out of this summer-house,' said Larry. ' It's absolutely melting in here ! Fatty, don't forget to take your red-haired wig and things back with you to-night. This summer-house isn't an awfully safe hiding-place for them. Pip's mother might easily walk in and see them stuffed under the seat.'

' I'll remember,' said Fatty, yawning. ' Golly, it was funny going into Goon's house this morning as a red-headed messenger-boy—and coming out just myself, and nobody spotting me ! Come on—let's go for a walk by the river. It'll be cool there. I shall fall asleep in this heat ! '

As they went down the drive they met Mr. Goon cycling up. They wondered which of the household he was going to see. He stopped and got off his bike.

' You know that there telegraph-boy, that brought you that telegram some time back ? ' he said. ' Well, I happen to know he's a fake, see ? There's no telegraph-boy like that. And I'm making strict inquiries into the matter, I am—yes and into fake telegrams too, see ? And I warn you all, if you hob-nob with red-heads, you'll get into Serious Trouble. Very Serious Trouble.'

' You do frighten me,' said Fatty, making his eyes go big.

' And I'll have None of your Sauce ! ' said Mr. Goon majestically. ' I know more than what you think, and I advise you all to be careful. Call that dog orf ! '

'Come here, Buster,' said Fatty, in such a mild voice that Buster took no notice at all. He went on prancing round Mr. Goon's ankles.

'I said, call him *orf*!' repeated Mr. Goon, doing little prances too, to avoid sudden rushes by Buster.

'Come here, Buster,' said Fatty again, in an extremely polite voice. Buster ignored him completely.

'That's not calling him orf!' shouted Mr. Goon, beginning to lose his temper. 'Yell at him, go on! Nuisance of a dog!'

Fatty winked at the others, and with one accord they all opened their mouths and yelled at the top of their voices. 'COME HERE, BUSTER!'

Mr. Goon jumped violently at the noise. He glared. Buster also jumped. He went to Fatty.

'Not pleased even now, Mr. Goon?' said Fatty sweetly. 'Oh dear—there's no pleasing you at all, I'm afraid. Wait a minute—I believe I've got a really good clue to hand you—ah, here it is!'

He took out a match-box and gave it to the policeman. Mr. Goon opened it suspiciously. It was a trick match-box, and, as Mr. Goon opened it, he released a powerful spring inside which sprang up and shot the match-box high in the air. Mr. Goon got quite a shock.

He went purple, and his eyes bulged.

'So sorry, so sorry,' said Fatty hastily. 'It must have been the wrong match-box. Wait a bit—I've got another. . . .'

If Buster had not been there with his ready teeth Mr. Goon might quite well have boxed Fatty's ears. He looked ready to burst. Fearing that he might say something he ought not to, poor Mr. Goon hurriedly mounted his bicycle and rode up the drive, breathing so heavily that he could be heard all the way to the kitchen-door.

' He's gone to talk to Mrs. Moon again,' said Pip. ' I expect they'll come to blows ! Let's get on. Oh, Fatty, I thought I should burst when that trick match-box went up in the air. Goon's face !

They strolled down the lane to the river. It was pleasant there, for a breeze blew across the water. The children found a sunny place beside a big bush and lay down lazily. A swan came swimming by, and two moor-hens chugged across the water, their heads bobbing like clock-work.

' Let's forget all about the Mystery for a bit,' said Daisy. ' It's so nice here. I keep on thinking and thinking about those letters, and who could be writing them—but the more I think the less I know.'

' Same here,' said Pip. ' So many Suspects— and not one of them could apparently have Done the Deed. A most mysterious mystery.'

' One that even the great detective, Mr. Frederick Sherlock Holmes Trotteville can't solve either ! ' said Larry.

' Correct ! ' said Fatty, with a sigh. ' I almost— but not quite—give it up ! '

Larry's hat blew away and he got up to go and get it. ' Blow ! ' he said. ' There's old Clear-Orf again—cycling over the field-path. He's seen me too. Hope he doesn't come and make a row again. He'd like to eat you alive, Fatty, you're so aggravating.'

'Sit down quickly, in case he hasn't seen you,' said Daisy. 'We don't want him here.'

Larry sat down. They all watched the blue water flowing smoothly by. The moor-hens came back again, and a fish jumped at a fly. A very early swallow dipped down to the water. It was all very peaceful indeed.

'I should think old Clear-Orf didn't see me after all,' said Larry. 'Thank goodness. I think I'm going to sleep. There's something very soothing about the gurgling of the water—a lovely, peaceful afternoon.'

Heavy breathing disturbed the peace, and clumsy footsteps came over the grass towards their bush. Mr. Goon appeared, his face a familiar purple. He carried a small sack in his hand, and looked extremely angry. He flung the little sack down fiercely.

'More Clues, I suppose!' he sneered. 'More of your silly, childish jokes! White rats and match-boxes! Huh! Gah! What a set of children! And now *these* Clues—hidden nicely under a bush for me to find, I suppose? What do you think I am? A nitwit?'

The children were astonished at this outburst, and Bets was really alarmed. Fatty put out a quick hand on Buster's collar, for the little Scottie had got his hackles up and was growling fiercely, showing all his teeth.

'What's up, Goon?' said Fatty, in a sharp, rather grown-up voice.

'You know as well as I do!' said the policeman. 'More Clues! I suppose you'll tell me next that you don't know anything about that sack of Clues! Gah!'

'What sack? What clues?' said Fatty, really

puzzled. ' No—I really don't know what you're talking about, Mr. Goon.'

' You don't know—ho no, you don't know ! ' said Mr. Goon, and he laughed a nasty laugh. ' You don't know anything about red wigs, either, I suppose ? Or writing rude letters to the Law ? Well, I know a lot ! Oho, don't I ? I'll teach you to lay clues about for me to find. Think I'm a real hignoramus, don't you ? '

' Shut up, Buster,' said Fatty, for Buster was now snarling very loudly indeed. ' Mr. Goon, please go. You're frightening little Bets, and I don't think I can hold Buster in much longer. I don't know *what* you're talking about—and certainly I've never seen the sack before.'

Buster gave such a fearfully loud snarl that Mr. Goon thought it would be best to do as Fatty said and go. He went, leaving the little sack on the ground, and stepped heavily away, looking as majestic as he could.

' Well, what an unpleasant fellow,' said Fatty, slipping his arm round Bets, who was in tears. ' Don't bother about him, Bets. We know the blustering, roaring old fellow by now. You need never be scared of *him* ! '

' I don't like p-p-people to shout like that,' sobbed Bets. ' And oh Fatty, he said about your red wig ! Has he found it ? '

' I wondered about that too,' said Fatty. ' We'll look when we go back. I left it in the summer-house, didn't I ? Wish I hadn't now.'

' What's this sack of clues that old Clear-Orf kept yammering about ? ' said Larry. He pulled it towards him. ' Some old collection of rubbish some tramp had left behind him under a bush, I suppose—and Mr. Goon found it and thought it was some more of your false clues, Fatty, planted for him to find.'

Larry undid the neck of the little sack. It was not much bigger than a three-pound flour bag. Inside, half-wrapped in brown paper, were some curious things.

There was a small school dictionary—and when he saw it Pip sat up in surprise. ' Golly ! That's my dicky, I do declare ! ' he said. ' The one I lost last hols. Isn't it, Bets ? Gracious, how *did* it get into this sack ? '

This made every one sit up and take notice at once. Fatty reached out his arm and took the sack. He ran his fingers quickly through the dictionary, and noted that several words were underlined. One of them was ' thief.' Another was ' fruit.' Fatty found others, all underlined.

Pip's name was in the front of the dictionary. There was no doubt at all but that it was his lost book. Fatty put his hand into the sack to see what else there was there.

He drew out—an alphabet book. ' A is for Apple, so rosy and red ! ' he chanted, ' B is for Baby who's just off to Bed.' My goodness, no wonder old Clear-Orf thought we'd planted these things for him—a dictionary—and an alphabet book. Most peculiar ! '

The next thing was a child's copy-book with some of the pages filled in, not very neatly. Larry laughed.

' This is some village kid's little treasure-store, I should think,' he said. ' Though goodness knows how the kid got hold of Pip's dictionary.'

Fatty dipped his hand in again. His eyes were

*Fatty dipped his hand in again*

suddenly very bright indeed. He pulled out an old bus time-table. He looked at it and then flipped it. It fell open at one much-thumbed page—and on that page there was a mark.

'Do you know what is marked?' said Fatty. 'The 10.15 bus to Sheepsale! What do you think of that?'

The others stared at him. They were all very puzzled now. Fatty spoke excitedly.

'These are *real* Clues! Don't you understand, you donkeys? Goon thought they were silly, false ones put there by us to deceive him—but they're *real* ones, ones that may help us to put our hand on the letter-writer this very day.'

Now it was the turn of the others to get excited. 'Oooh,' said Bets. 'How silly of Mr. Goon to give them all to *us*.'

Fatty put his hand in once again and drew out a little, torn scrap of paper with some untidy writing on it. There were only two or three words to be made out. One was 'spoonful,' another was 'stir,' and another was 'oven.' Fatty read them and nodded. He was evidently very pleased indeed with this find.

'Poor old Goon!' he said. 'He makes the one glorious find in this Mystery—and throws it down at our feet. Won't he kick himself when he knows? What a bit of luck, oh what a bit of luck!'

THE other four tried in vain to make Fatty tell them more. But he wouldn't. ' You can look at all these clues as much as you like,' he said, ' and if you use your brains they will tell you exactly what they tell me. Exactly. I could tell you everything in two minutes—but I do really think you should try to find out what I have found out.'

' But that silly alphabet book ! ' said Daisy. ' It doesn't tell me a thing ! '

' And all that time-table tells me is that there's a bus to Sheepsale at 10.15, and it's the bus the letter-writer probably took—but it doesn't tell me anything else,' said Pip. ' As to my dictionary— well, that beats me ! '

' Come on—let's get back home,' said Fatty. ' I've got to think this all out. It's not a scrap of good going to Goon about it. He won't believe a word. In fact I think he's got it firmly in his head that I'm mixed up in all this letter-writing. I'm sure he thinks *I* wrote the letter to him ! '

' Well—who are we going to, then ? ' asked Bets. ' Inspector Jenks ? I'd like that ! '

' I thought perhaps we'd better tell your mother first,' said Fatty. ' I don't somehow feel as if I want to bring Inspector Jenks down here for an affair like this—and go right over Goon's head with the clues that Goon himself presented us with. Doesn't seem quite fair somehow.'

' It seems quite fair to *me* ! ' said Bets, who

disliked Mr. Goon more than any of the others did.
' Oh, Fatty—tell us all you know from these clues,
do, do, do ! '

' Now, Bets, if you like to think hard and study
these clues, *you* would know as much as I do,' said
Fatty. ' Come on—let's go home—and on the way
you can all think hard and if nobody can find out
what these clues mean, or who they're pointing to,
then I'll tell you myself. But give your brains a
chance, do ! '

In silence except for Buster's occasional yaps
at a stray cat, they went home to Pip's. When they
got into the drive they saw a big black car there.

' Whose is that ? ' said Bets, in wonder.

' And there's Mr. Goon's bike,' said Daisy,
pointing to where it stood by the front door. ' He's
here too.'

Mrs. Hilton suddenly opened the front door and
stood there, waiting for them, looking pale and
worried.

' Come in this way,' she said. ' I'm glad you've
come. Mr. Goon is here—saying most peculiar
things—and he's got Inspector Jenks over too ! '

' Oh ! Is *he* here ? ' cried Bets in delight, and
rushed into the drawing-room. The big Inspector
sat there, his eyes twinkling as he saw Bets. He
was very fond of her.

She flung herself on him. ' I haven't seen you
since the Christmas holidays ! You're bigger than
ever ! Oh—there's Mr. Goon ! '

So there was, sitting upright in a corner,
looking curiously pleased with himself.

The other four came in more quietly, and shook
hands with the big Inspector. They knew him well,
for he had come to their help very often, when they

were solving other problems. Buster capered round
his ankles in delight, awaiting for the pat he knew
would come.

Mrs. Hilton waited till the greetings were over,
and then spoke in a worried voice.

' Children ! Mr. Goon brought Inspector Jenks
over here to-day, when he was visiting Peterswood,
because he had a serious complaint to make of your
behaviour, especially one of you, and he thought that
it would be a good thing if the Inspector reprimanded
you himself. But I cannot imagine what you have
been doing—unless you have been interfering in this
anonymous letter business—and I said you were
not to.'

Nobody said anything. Fatty looked politely
and inquiringly at the Inspector.

' Suppose you hold forth, Goon,' said the
Inspector, in his pleasant, courteous voice. ' You
have quite a lot to say, I believe.'

' Well, sir,' began Mr. Goon, in a righteous
sort of voice, ' I know your opinion of these here
children has always been high—but I've always
known more of them than you have, if you'll pardon
me saying so, sir—and they've bin getting above
themselves, sir—meddling in things that don't
concern them, and hindering me in my business,
sir—and one of them—this here boy by name of
Frederick Trotteville, sir, I regret to inform you
that he has meddled in this anonymous writing, and
sent me a most rude and incivil letter, sir—and
what's more he goes about pretending to be what
he's not, sir—and deceiving me proper-like. . . .'

' Exactly what do you mean by that, Goon ? '
asked the Inspector mildly. ' Going about pretending to be what he's not ? '

' Well, sir, he's a whole lot of red-headed boys,
sir,' said Mr. Goon, to the great mystification of the
Inspector and Mrs. Hilton. ' Took me in proper,
he did. First he was a red-headed telegraph-boy,
sir—then he was a butcher-boy—and a messenger-
boy, sir—tearing round on his bike, a public danger,
sir, and a nuisance. But as soon as I found the red
wig, sir . . .'

' Who told you where it was ? ' asked Fatty.

' Mrs. Moon showed me,' said Mr. Goon.
' Yes, and she told me, too, all the things you've
been saying about me, Master Frederick—you
and the others—and how she overheard you
planning to write that there cheeky letter to
me ! '

' Really ? ' said Fatty, his eyes gleaming curiously.
' Perhaps she told you also, who is the writer of
those other anonymous letters ? '

' Well, no, she didn't,' admitted Mr. Goon.
' Unless it was some one she's Got Her Eye On.
But she wasn't mentioning any names just yet.'

Frederick, this is all very disturbing,' said Mrs.
Hilton. ' I cannot imagine what you have been
doing ! And surely, surely you did not write that
letter to Mr. Goon ! '

' No, Mrs. Hilton, of course I didn't,' said Fatty.
' As for the disguises—well, I mean to be a famous
detective when I grow up—and I'm just practising,
that's all. I *have* been looking into the mystery of
the anonymous letter-writing—and by great good
luck I've had a whole lot of clues thrust upon me.
As a matter of fact we were going to tell you the
whole thing as soon as we got back.'

' Ho yes ! ' said Mr. Goon disbelievingly.

' That will do, Goon,' said the Inspector. ' What

are these clues, Frederick, that you've had thrust upon you ? '

Fatty went into the hall and came back with the little sack. He placed it on the table. Mr. Goon stared at it and his eyes bulged.

' Those clues ! ' he said, scornfully. ' Those clues you planted for me to find ! Ho ! Copybooks and alphabet books ! White rats and match-boxes that jump ! Clothing pegs and dolls' hats ! '

The Inspector looked most astonished at this long list of things. Fatty looked a little uncomfortable.

' Just my little joke,' he murmured.

' Well, your little jokes have landed you into Serious Trouble,' said Mr. Goon. ' Just like I said they would. It was lucky the Inspector was in Peterswood to-day. Soon as I told him about everything, along he came.'

' Very kind of him,' said Fatty. ' In fact, as far as we are concerned, he has come at exactly the right moment. We were just discussing whether or not we should telephone him and ask him to come over. Now he's here ! '

' And what did you want to see me about ? ' asked the Inspector.

' About this anonymous letter-writing business, sir,' said Fatty. ' You see, we couldn't let a mystery like that happen under our very noses, so to speak, without going into it a bit. And we were all sorry for Gladys.'

' Quite so,' said the Inspector. ' Another case for the Five Find-Outers—and Dog ! '

' Yes, sir,' said Fatty. ' A very difficult affair too, sir. We got on a lot of wrong trails.'

' We found out that the letter-writer caught the 10.15 bus to Sheepsale,' said Bets. ' And we went on it on Monday, to see who the passengers were. But nobody posted a letter there ! '

' Except Master Frederick ! ' shot out Mr. Goon.

' There—I told you Mr. Goon would put you down on his List of Suspects if he saw you posting that letter ! ' said Bets.

' I rather hoped he would ! ' said Fatty, with a grin. Mr. Goon scowled. This interview wasn't coming off quite as he had hoped it would. That wretched boy, Fatty ! He always seemed to get away with anything. And the Inspector didn't seem to be taking the matter very seriously, either. It was too bad.

' I expect Mr. Goon has told you about the bus to Sheepsale, though, sir, and how the letters were always posted there by the 11.45 post,' said Fatty. ' And how nobody posted any that day—except me ! —and I expect, like us, he made inquiries to see if any of the regular bus-passengers failed to go on the bus that day for some reason or other—and got his Suspects narrowed down to Old Nosey, Miss Tittle, and Mrs. Moon.'

' Yes. He did tell me,' said the Inspector. ' And I think, if I may say so, that it was pretty smart work on the part of you children to work all that out ! '

This was too much for Mr. Goon. ' Smart work ! Interfering with the Law, that's what I call it ! ' he said. ' I suppose he'll tell you next that he knows who that letter-writer is ! '

' Yes. I was going to come to that,' said Fatty quietly. ' I *do* know who the letter-writer is ! '

Every one gaped at Fatty. Even the Inspector sat up straight at once. As for Goon, his mouth fell open and he goggled at Fatty in disbelief.

' Who is it ? ' he said.

' Mrs. Hilton—may I ring the bell ? ' said Fatty.
She nodded.   He went over to the wall and rang
the bell hard.   Every one waited.


## 21    WELL DONE, FATTY!

THE bell sounded loudly.   The door opened in the
kitchen and footsteps came up the hall.   Mrs. Moon
appeared in the drawing-room.   She looked surprised and rather scared when she saw so many
people sitting quietly there.

' Did you ring, Madam ? ' she asked, and her
voice shook a little.

' I rang,' said Fatty.   He turned to the Inspector.   ' This is the anonymous letter-writer,' he
said.   ' Mrs. Moon ! '

Mrs. Hilton gasped.   Mr. Goon snorted loudly.
All the children drew in their breath sharply.   Only
the Inspector seemed unperturbed.

Mrs. Moon went pale.   She stared at Fatty.
' What do you mean ? ' she said fiercely.   ' How
dare you say things like that to a respectable law-
abiding woman ? '

' Hardly law-abiding, Mrs. Moon,' said the Inspector's stern voice.   ' It is against the law to send
spiteful and untrue letters through the post anony-
mously.   But Frederick—please explain.   I have
enough faith in your intelligence to know that you
are making no mistake, if I may say so—but I want
to know all about it.'

Mrs. Moon began to cry. ' Sit down and keep quiet,' commanded Inspector Jenks.

' I won't be treated like this, I won't ! ' wailed Mrs. Moon. ' An innocent woman like me ! Why, I've even had one of them awful letters meself ! '

' Yes—you nearly took me in over that,' said Fatty. ' I thought that ruled you out—but it was just a bit of artfulness on your part. I see that now.'

' You bad, wicked boy ! ' moaned Mrs. Moon.

' Silence ! ' said the Inspector, in such a fierce voice that Bets jumped. ' Speak when you're spoken to, Mrs. Moon, and not unless. If you are innocent you will be given plenty of chance to prove it. We will hear what you have to say when Master Frederick has told his story. Frederick, begin.'

Fatty began, and the other children leaned forward, knowing most of the story well, but longing to hear what the end of it was. Only Fatty knew that.

' Well, sir, you know already that we worked out that as the letters were posted in Sheepsale each Monday to catch the 11.45 post there, that it was probable the guilty person was some one who took the 10.15 bus from Peterswood to Sheepsale,' said Fatty.

' Quite so,' said the Inspector.

' Well, we found that none of the bus-passengers last Monday could be the letter-writer,' said Fatty, ' and certainly none of them posted a letter. So then we decided to find out if any regular Monday passenger was *not* on the bus that Monday, and make inquiries about them. And as you know, we found that three regular passengers didn't travel that day—Miss Tittle, Old Nosey, and Mrs. Moon.'

' Mr. Goon also worked on the same lines,' said the Inspector. A sound from Goon made every one look up.

' How did you get to see them letters, and see the post-mark ? ' demanded Mr. Goon. ' That's what I want to know.'

' Oh, that's not an important detail,' said Fatty, anxious not to give away Gladys's part in that affair. ' Well, to continue, sir—we found out next that another letter had been sent that Monday— but not from Sheepsale—it had been delivered by hand. So that definitely pointed to somebody in Peterswood, and possibly one of our three Suspects —Old Nosey, Miss Tittle, or Mrs. Moon.'

' Quite,' said the Inspector, deeply interested. ' I must say that your powers of deduction are good, Frederick.'

' Well, the letter was delivered very early in the morning,' said Fatty, ' so I had to find out which of the three Suspects was up early that Tuesday. And I found that all of them were ! '

' Very puzzling,' said the Inspector. ' I don't think Mr. Goon got quite as far as that, did you, Mr. Goon ?  Go on, Frederick.'

' That rather shook me,' said Fatty, ' and the only thing I could think of next was getting speci- mens of the handwriting of each of the three—to compare with the printed letters, you see.'

' A good idea,' said Inspector Jenks, ' but surely a little difficult ? '

' Not very,' said Fatty modestly. ' You see, I put on a disguise—a red-headed delivery-boy I was.'  There was a snort from Mr. Goon at this.

' And,' went on Fatty, ' I just delivered parcels to all three, and got them to sign receipts in capital letters—so that I could compare them with the capital letters in the anonymous notes ! '

' Most ingenious, if I may say so,' said the Inspector. He turned to Mr. Goon, whose eyes were bulging at hearing about all this detective work on Fatty's part. ' I am sure you agree with me ? ' said the Inspector. Mr. Goon did not agree with him at all, but couldn't very well say so.

' Well, I found that Nosey couldn't write at all,' said Fatty. ' So that ruled him out. Then I saw that Miss Tittle's printing, very small and neat and beautiful, wasn't anything at all like the printing of the letters in the anonymous notes—and that rather ruled *her* out too—and to my surprise Mrs. Moon's printing was such a mixture of big and small letters that I couldn't think she could be the culprit either.'

' And I'm not ! ' said Mrs. Moon, rocking herself to and fro. ' No, I'm not.'

' Here's a specimen of her writing—or rather, printing, sir,' said Fatty, opening his notebook and showing the Inspector Mrs. Moon's curious printing, big and small letters mixed. ' When I asked her about it, she gave me to understand that she couldn't help it—it appeared to me, sir, that she was muddled in her mind as to which were big and which were small letters.'

' Quite,' said Inspector Jenks. ' So you ruled her out too, as the messages and the addresses on the anonymous letters were apparently printed quite correctly in capitals, with no small letters at all ? '

' Yes, sir,' said Fatty. ' And I almost gave up the case. Couldn't see any light anywhere—and hadn't got any real clues, either. I didn't think at the time, either, that Mrs. Moon would write an anonymous letter to herself—though I *should* have thought of that, of course. . . .'

'And what about that letter to *me*?' said Mr. Goon, suddenly. 'That was you, wasn't it, Master Frederick? Come on, you own up now—that was you, calling me a meddler and a muddler and cheeking me like you always do!'

'No—I certainly didn't write you that letter,' said Fatty. 'And I think if you compare it with the others, Mr. Goon, you'll see it's just like them.'

'Well, Frederick—how did you come to know in the end that it *was* Mrs. Moon and nobody else?' inquired the Inspector.

'I tell you it wasn't, it wasn't,' moaned Mrs. Moon.

'That was a sheer bit of luck, sir,' said Fatty, modestly. 'Can't give myself any marks for that! It was Mr. Goon who put me right on the track!'

'Gah!' said Mr. Goon disbelievingly.

'Yes—he suddenly gave us a whole sack of clues—that sack of things on the table!' said Fatty. 'And, as soon as I saw them I was able to piece things together and know who had written those disgusting, spiteful letters!'

The Inspector picked up the things one by one and looked at them with interest. 'Exactly what did these things tell you?' he said curiously.

'There's a dictionary, sir—with Pip's name in,' said Fatty. 'That told me that it probably came from this house and was used by somebody living here. Then I noticed that various words had been

looked up for the spelling, and had been underlined
—and every one of those words, sir, has been used
in the anonymous letters ! '

Mr. Goon's face went redder than ever. To
think that boy had got all that out of the things in
that sack !

' The next thing, sir, was the alphabet book,'
said Fatty. ' And, as I daresay you've noticed, the
alphabet letters in such a book are always in capitals.
A is for Apple, and so on. So I guessed that book
had been bought as a kind of reference book for
capital letters, by somebody who wasn't quite sure
of the difference in shape of big and small letters.
The capital letter G, for instance, is quite different
from the small letter g. Naturally the anonymous
letter-writer didn't want to give away the fact that
she hadn't had enough education to know the
difference.'

' Well worked out, Frederick, well worked out,'
said the Inspector, most interested. ' What about
this ? ' He held up the copybook.

' That's easy, sir,' said Fatty. ' Even Bets
could read *that* clue now ! '

' Yes, I can ! ' called Bets. ' That's a copybook
Mrs. Moon must have bought to practise writing
capital letters in. There's lots of capitals printed
there in pencil.'

' I expect if you ask at the stationer's, Inspector,
you'll find that Mrs. Moon did buy a copybook there
some weeks ago ! '

' Make inquiries, Goon,' said the Inspector.
Goon hurriedly made a note in his notebook.

' The bus time-table was an easy clue,' said
Fatty. ' I guessed I'd find that 10.15 bus marked.
And this bit of torn paper, sir—used as a bookmark

in the dictionary, I should think—must have been torn from a recipe of some sort. I knew that as soon as I read the words—' spoonful '—' stir '—' oven.' I expect you will find that they are in Mrs. Moon's ordinary handwriting, and torn from her kitchen recipe-book.'

' A most ingenious reading of rather peculiar clues ! ' said the Inspector, looking really pleased. ' What a pity, Mr. Goon, you didn't take the trouble to look carefully through the clues yourself, and deduct from them all that Frederick has done.'

' Thought they was all false clues,' muttered Mr. Goon. ' Made me angry, they did.'

' It's a mistake to let anger cloud your thinking, Goon,' said the Inspector. ' If you had only examined these clues carefully, you might have arrived at the same conclusions as Frederick here—but again, you might not ! '

It was apparent that the Inspector believed that Goon would certainly not have made such good use of the clues as Fatty had !

Mrs. Moon suddenly threw her apron over her head and wailed loudly. She rocked to and fro again, and Bets watched her in dismay. She didn't like people who shouted and howled.

' You're all against me, you are ! ' wailed Mrs. Moon. ' Not a friend have I got in the world ! You're all against me ! '

' You have only yourself to blame, my good woman,' said Inspector Jenks sharply. ' You yourself are apparently filled with spite against a great many people—and you cannot be surprised if you have no friends. I'm afraid you must come with me for further questioning. Mrs. Hilton, I fear that Mrs. Moon will not be returning to you.'

' I don't want her,' said Mrs. Hilton, with a
shudder. ' A cruel, underhand, spiteful woman like
that in my house ! No, never. Poor Gladys. I'll
fetch her back at once. I'm horrified and disgusted,
Mrs. Moon. You have caused a great deal of pain
and grief to many people, and I hope you will be
well punished.'

' You don't mind us having investigated the
case now, Mother, do you ? ' said Pip, thinking
this was a good opportunity to get his mother
to agree.

' Well—I didn't want you mixed up in such an
unpleasant business,' said Mrs. Hilton. ' And I
must say that I thought Mr. Goon could manage it
himself. But I do think you worked out things very
cleverly—especially Fatty, of course.'

' Oh, all the Find-Outers did their bit,' said
Fatty loyally. ' I couldn't have done without them.
And,' he said, with a glance at Mr. Goon, ' we did
have a lot of fun at times—didn't we, Pip ? '

' We did ! ' said all the others, and grinned at
poor Mr. Goon, who did one of his snorts, and
scowled heavily at them.

The Inspector got up. ' Get your outdoor
things, Mrs. Moon,' he said. ' You must come with
me. Goon, I want you too. But perhaps, when I
have finished my work here, at about four o'clock
this afternoon, Mrs. Hilton, the children could come
over to Nutting, where I'm going then, and have
tea with me in the big hotel there ? I feel I would
like to have a little chat with the Five Find-Outers—
and Dog—again ! '

' Oooh ! ' said Bets, delighted.

' Woof,' said Buster, pleased.

' Oh *thanks* ! ' said the others.

Mrs. Moon went out, weeping. The Inspector shook hands with Mrs. Hilton and went out to his car. ' See you this afternoon ! ' he said, to the delighted children.

Mrs. Hilton went out to see that Mrs. Moon did what she was told. The children followed the Inspector to his big black car. Mr. Goon was left behind in the drawing-room, looking gloomily at the carpet. He was alone with his thoughts.

No—he wasn't alone ! Buster was there too, regarding his old enemy with a bright eye. No one was there to say, ' Come here, Buster ! ' What a chance !

With a joyful yelp he flung himself at Mr. Goon's ankles, and pulled at his blue trousers. Mr. Goon rose up in alarm.

' Clear-orf ! ' he yelled. ' Clear-orf, you ! Leave my trousers alone ! You want reporting, you do. Clear-orf ! '

The children heard the shouting and laughed at the familiar words. ' Poor old Clear-Orf,' said Bets. ' Always in trouble. Fatty, go and rescue him.'

Fatty went. Mr. Goon came out, frowning, trying to see if his trouser-ankles had been torn. Buster struggled in Fatty's arms.

' Get in, Goon, whilst you're safe,' said the Inspector, opening the door of the car. ' Ah, here is Mrs. Moon. The other side, please, Mrs. Moon. Goodbye, children—and thanks for your help once more. I must say I'm pleased with the Five Find-Outers and Dog ! '

' Oh well—I suppose we ought to thank Mr. Goon for all those clues ! ' said Fatty. He winked at the others, and they all opened their mouths together at once and chanted :

'THANKS,  MR.  GOON ! '

And what did Mr. Goon reply ?   Exactly what you would expect.

'GAH ! '

BOOK TWO

# The
# Mystery
## of the
# Missing
# Necklace

# I     OH, FOR A MYSTERY!

PIP and Bets sat in their garden, in the very coolest place they could find. They had on sun-suits and nothing else, for the August sun was blazing hot.

' A whole month of the summer hols gone already ! ' said Pip. ' And except that we've been away to the seaside for two weeks, absolutely nothing else has happened. Most boring.'

' The boringest hols we've ever had,' said Bets. ' Not even the smell of a mystery to solve ! And not even Larry, Daisy, Fatty, or Buster to play with —they've been away at the sea for ages ! '

Larry and Daisy were friends of Pip and Bets, and so was Frederick—or Fatty as everyone called him. Buster was his Scottie dog, loved by all the children.

The five children called themselves the Five Find-Outers and Dog, because for the last four holidays they had tackled curious mysteries and solved them all—much to the annoyance of the village policeman, Mr. Goon.

' But now it seems as if you and I, Pip, are the only Find-Outers left,' said Bets. ' I don't feel as if the others will ever come back ! Soon the hols will be over, you'll all be back at boarding-school again, except me, and we shan't solve any mystery at all these hols.'

' There are still four weeks left, so cheer up, baby ! ' said Pip. ' And the others come back this week—and I bet old Fatty will have heaps of new disguises to try out on us ! We'll be on the look-out for him this time, though—and we jolly well won't be taken in ! '

Bets laughed. She remembered how Fatty had disguised himself as a French boy, and deceived them all beautifully. And in the last holidays he had produced all kinds of disguises, which he wore with a red wig and eyebrows. There was no knowing what old Fatty would be up to next !

' But *this* time he won't deceive us,' said Pip again. ' I shall be very suspicious of any peculiar-looking stranger who tries to talk to me, or comes to call on us. I shall say to myself, " It's you all right, Fatty," and I shan't listen to a word ! '

' Do you think there will be a mystery for us to solve these hols ? ' asked Bets. ' I do so like looking for clues, and making out lists of Suspects, and crossing people off the list when we've made enquiries—and finding the real Suspect at the end ! '

' We've been jolly lucky so far,' said Pip, sitting up and looking round for the bottle of lemonade he had brought out. ' We've been able to solve every single mystery. We can't always be successful, though. I don't expect even real detectives are always successful. Bets, you pig, you've finished the lemonade. Go and ask Gladys for some iced water.'

Bets was too lazy to move. She rolled over out of Pip's reach, and yawned loudly. ' I'm bored ! I want the others to come back so that we can have games with them. I want a mystery—a really good one. And I want to solve it before Old Clear-Orf does ! '

Old Clear-Orf was Mr. Goon the policeman. He told children and dogs to ' clear-orf ' whenever he saw them. He disliked all the Find-Outers intensely, and never had a good word to say for them.

Pip and Bets hadn't seen much of him in the summer holidays, and were very glad, for he had often been to their parents to complain of the behaviour of the Five Find-Outers. Bets was afraid of him, because when he lost his temper he shouted, and was very unpleasant indeed.

'Bets, didn't you hear me tell you to go in and fetch some iced water?' said Pip crossly. 'Go on!'

'I'm not going to be ordered about by you,' said Bets, rolling a bit farther away. 'I suppose you order all the little boys about in your school, and then when you come home you think you can order me about too. Well, I shall soon be ten, and you're not to!'

'Don't you cheek me, young Bets!' said Pip, sitting up. 'You're much younger than I am, and you've got to do as you're told! Go and get that iced water—or I'll catch you and give you a jolly good smacking.'

'I think you're a horrid brother to have,' said Bets. 'I'd much rather have Fatty. He's always kind to me!'

'He wouldn't be, if you were his sister,' said Pip. 'He hasn't got any sisters—if he had, he'd know what a nuisance they are. Now—are you going to go and . . .'

'Yes, I'll get it!' said Bets, getting up, 'but only because *I'm* thirsty, and *I* want some to drink, see? I don't mind bringing you out a little too, as I'm going to get some for myself, but I'm really going for myself, and . . .'

Pip pretended to be getting up, and Bets fled. If only the others would come back! She and Pip were getting tired of one another.

Bets hadn't long to wait before the others came back. In two days' time Larry, Daisy, Fatty, and

Buster all turned up together, looking so brown that
Pip and Bets had to gaze earnestly at them to make
sure they really were their friends.   Buster wasn't
brown, of course—he was still jet-black, and he
flung himself on Pip and Bets in joy and delight,
barking and licking and whining as if he had gone
mad.

'Buster, darling!   You're fatter!   Oh, Larry,
I'm glad you're back!   Daisy, you're terribly brown.
And oh, Fatty—you've *grown*!'

Fatty certainly had grown in the last four months.
He was still plump, but he was taller, taller even
than Larry now, and much taller than Pip, who
didn't seem to have grown at all in the last year.

'Hallo, every one!' he said, and Bets gave a cry
of surprise.

'Fatty!   You've got a different voice!   It's a
grown-up voice!   Are you putting it on—disguising
it, I mean?'

'No,' said Fatty, pulling Bets' hair teasingly.
'It's just broken, that's all.'

'Who broke it?' said Bets, in alarm, and the
others roared at her till their sides ached.

'She'll never be anything but a baby!' said
Pip.   'Never.'

Bets looked so upset and puzzled that Fatty put
his arm round her and gave her a squeeze.   'Bets,
don't be silly.   You know that when they grow up,
boys get deep voices like men's, don't you?   Well,
when boys' voices change like that we say that
their voices *break*—that's all.   We don't mean
broken in half, or smashed to pieces!'

'Oh, Fatty—I don't know you with such a deep
voice,' said Bets, half-alarmed.   'You don't sound
the same.   You *look* like Fatty—but you don't
sound like him!   I wish you had your old voice.'

' Bets, you've no idea what a difference it makes to me, now I've got a proper grown-up voice,' said Fatty earnestly. ' It means that I can disguise myself as a grown-up instead of always like some kind of boy ! It gives me much more scope—and I've got some fine grown-up disguises ! '

Bets immediately changed her mind about not liking Fatty's new voice. More disguises ! Now life would be exciting and thrilling and unexpected things would happen. Fatty would disguise himself as all kinds of grown-up people—the Find-Outers would have a simply gorgeous time. She stared at Fatty happily.

' Oh, Fatty ! You've only been able to dress up as telegraph boys or butcher boys or messenger boys before ! Now you can be all kinds of things —old men with beards—a postman—a dustman— a window-cleaner with a ladder—even a sweep ! Oh, Fatty, do be all those things and let's see you ! '

Every one laughed. ' Give me a chance ! ' said Fatty. ' I'm going to practise a bit these hols. I didn't have much chance whilst I was away, because Mother wouldn't let me take much luggage—but I don't mind telling you I'm going to collect a few things now ! I've got taller too, so I can almost wear grown-ups' things. By the time our next mystery comes along I shall be able to tackle it in whatever disguise is necessary.'

' You do sound grown-up,' said Bets. ' Doesn't he, everybody ? '

' Well, as a matter of fact,' said Fatty, swelling up a little with pride, ' I'm the tallest boy in my form now, and you should just see the muscles in my arms. I'll show you ! '

' Same old Fatty ! ' said Larry. Best in everything, aren't you ? Nobody to beat you ! '

Fatty grinned and peeled off his shirt.  He bent his arm and shewed them how his muscles came up in a big lump.  Bets looked on in awe, but Larry and Pip did not seem to be much impressed.

'Fair !' said Larry.  'I've seen better ones on a boy of twelve !'

'Huh !  You're jealous !' said Fatty, good-humouredly.  'Now then—let's hear any Peterswood news, Pip and Bets.  The village seemed pretty crowded when I came through it just now.'

'Too jolly crowded for anything !' said Pip. 'This hot weather is drawing the people to the river in their hundreds !  We get motor-coaches all day long—and down by the river there are all sorts of shows to amuse the people when they get tired of the river, or it's raining.'

'What sort of shows ?' asked Fatty, lying down on the grass, and tickling Buster on his tummy. 'Any good ?'

'Not much,' said Pip.  'There's a Waxwork Show—pretty dull really—you know, figures made of wax, all dressed up—and there are those Bumping Motor-Cars—they're quite fun for the first two or three times you go in them. . . .'

'And a Hoopla game,' said Bets.  'You buy three wooden rings for twopence, and you try to throw them over any of the things arranged on a big round table—and if the ring goes right over anything, you can have whatever you've ringed.  I like that game.'

'You would !' said Pip.  'She spends a whole shilling on hiring the wooden rings—and then wins a mouldy little brooch worth a penny, that Mother can't bear and won't let her wear !'

'Well, Pip, you spent tenpence once, and you

didn't win a thing ! ' began Bets hotly. But Fatty interrupted.

' Sounds as if Peterswood is going quite gay ! ' he said. ' We'll have to make up a party and go down to all these shows one wet afternoon. If it ever *is* wet again ! '

' Fatty, will you go in one of your new grown-up disguises ? ' asked Bets excitedly. ' Oh, do! It would be lovely to see you acting like a grown-up, and taking everybody in ! '

' I'll see,' said Fatty. ' I'd like to take in Old Clear-Orf, I must say ! He's up to all my boy-disguises now—he'd see through them at once—but I bet he wouldn't see through a grown-up disguise ! '

' What will you go as ? ' asked Daisy.

' Don't know,' said Fatty. ' And listen, all of you—if you can get any old things of your fathers' —you know, old hats they don't want, or boots, or even old coats—they'd come in mighty useful for me. I'm afraid if I take too many of my father's things, he'll be annoyed. Mother doesn't let him keep any of his old things, she gives them away—so he's only got rather newish clothes.'

' We'll do what we can,' promised Larry, and Pip nodded too. Anything to help old Fatty to disguise himself ! Bets sighed with joy to think that Fatty was back again. Now life would really be exciting once more. And oh, if *only* a mystery turned up, how heavenly the rest of the hols would be !

IT was lovely to be all together again, day after day. The Five bathed in the river, went for long bicycle rides, lazed in the garden, squabbled, drank pints of iced drinks, and ate hundreds of ices. Buster liked both lemonade and ices and had his full share. He got rather fat and Pip teased him.

'You're too fat to go after rabbits, Buster!' he said. 'Why, even a mouse would escape you now. You don't walk any more, you waddle. You don't breathe, you wheeze! You . . .'

'Oh, don't tease him so,' said Bets, who was always quite certain that Buster could understand every single word said to him. 'He *doesn't* waddle. I bet if he saw Old Clear-Orf this very minute he'd be after him like a shot!'

'By the way, what's happened to Goon?' asked Fatty. 'I saw him yesterday, in a great hurry and looking frightfully important.'

'Probably solving some Mystery we don't know anything about,' said Larry gloomily. 'There have been a lot of burglaries lately, and perhaps Goon is getting at the bottom of them.'

'Yes—but the burglaries haven't been in his district,' said Fatty. 'They've mostly been miles away. I've read about them in the paper. Lady Rexham's jewels were stolen only last week—and somebody else's famous diamonds the week before. It's a clever gang of thieves—but they're not working this district, as far as I know.'

'I wish they were!' said Bets. 'Then we could

catch them. You could put on one of your new disguises, Fatty, and track them down.'

' It's not as easy as all that, little Bets, and you know it ! ' said Fatty, with a laugh. ' You just think of all the difficulties we had in our other mysteries.'

' We haven't seen you in any grown-up disguise yet, Fatty,' said Daisy. ' Do put one on, so that we can spot you in it, if we can.'

' I've been practising in my bedroom,' said Fatty. ' I don't want to try anything out on you till I'm perfect. I'll try it on you when I'm ready, I promise. And I'll give my second-best propelling-pencil to any one of you that spots me first, see ? '

' Oooh, Fatty—the pencil that can write in lead, or in red, or in blue ? ' said Bets. ' Can you really spare it ? '

' I'll certainly give it to any of the Find-Outers if they're bright enough to spot me in my first grown-up disguise,' said Fatty. ' It's a bargain ! '

' I bet I'll spot you first,' said Larry. ' The girls won't, I'm sure. Pip might—but I'll be first ! '

' We'll have to leave Buster behind when we try to do the spotting,' said Pip. ' Or he'll simply rush up to you and bark madly to tell every one it's you ! '

' Yes. Buster's out of this,' said Fatty, and Buster cocked up his ears at his name. ' Sorry, Buster, old boy—but to-morrow you must stay at home with the cat.'

' Oh, Fatty—are you going to dress up to-morrow ? ' asked Bets, in delight. ' Really to-morrow ? Well, you won't deceive me ! I shall look at every one with an eagle eye ! '

' Right,' said Fatty. ' But all the same—I have a feeling that my propelling-pencil will still be safely in my pocket to-morrow night ! You may be quite good Find-Outers—but I'm a bit cleverer than any of you !'

'You're certainly best at boasting !' said Larry 'That trumpet of yours must be quite worn out by now.'

'What trumpet ?' said Bets, in curiosity. 'I've never seen Fatty with a trumpet.'

'No, but surely you've heard him blowing his own trumpet ?' said Larry. 'It's deafening at times ! It's . . .'

And then Fatty sat up and flung himself on Larry and there was a great deal of shouting and yelling and squealing, with Buster plunging into the middle of the brawl and getting wildly excited too.

Mrs. Hilton, Pip's mother, appeared. 'Children ! You do know I've visitors in the garden, surely ? If you want to yell and squeal and fight, will you go somewhere else ? What about a nice walk ?'

'Oh, *Mother*—it's too hot for a walk !' groaned Pip.

'Well, I should have thought it was much too hot to fight,' said Mrs. Hilton disapprovingly. '.Really, Larry and Frederick, you look very dirty and untidy !'

'Sorry, Mrs. Hilton,' said Fatty meekly, and Larry tried to smooth his hair down. 'We'll go for a walk. I forgot you had people to tea in the garden. I really do apologise.'

Fatty had marvellous manners with grown-up people, and Mrs. Hilton began to smile again. 'Go down to the dairy and get yourselves an ice-cream each,' she said. 'That will get rid of you for a bit. Here's the money, Pip.'

'Oh thanks, Mother,' said Pip, and they all got up, pleased. It was the fourth ice-cream that day, but it didn't seem worth while mentioning that to

Mrs. Hilton. Fatty's mother had already provided ice-creams and so had Larry's, and Fatty had generously given them one each as well. Now this was the fourth lot. Goody !

They walked sedately down the garden and round the drive to the gates. They went to the dairy, which made real cream-ices that were most delicious, and sat down at the little table in the window to eat them.

Mr. Goon passed by on his bicycle as they sat there. He pedalled furiously, his face hot and red.

' Spot of hard work for Goon,' said Fatty, letting a cold spoonful of ice-cream slide as slowly down his throat as possible. ' Looks busy, doesn't he ? '

Before they had finished their ices, Goon came pedalling back again, as furiously as before. The police-station was just opposite the dairy, and the children watched the policeman go smartly up the steps. Then they saw his head behind the frosted window-pane of one of the rooms in the police-station, talking to somebody else. Goon was talking the most and was nodding vigorously.

' Never seen Goon so busy before ! ' said Fatty, in astonishment. ' Do you think he's really got a case to work on—a mystery to solve that we don't know anything about ? '

' Golly, here he comes again ! ' said Pip, as Goon scuttled out of the police-station, buttoning a big sheaf of papers into his breast-pocket. ' He's simply bursting with importance.'

' He's feeling jolly pleased about something,' said Fatty. ' I *should* be mad if something had cropped up in Peterswood whilst I've been away, and we don't know anything about it ! '

Goon jumped on to his bicycle and pedalled

away again.   It was maddening to sit there and watch him so busy and important and not know why. Fatty felt as if he was bursting with curiosity.

'He's on to something !' he said.  'He really is.  I know that look on his face.  We *must* find out what it is !'

'Well, you find out then,' said Larry.  'And if he tells you, you'll be lucky !  It's what Goon has dreamed of for months—a mystery all to himself, that the Five Find-Outers don't know anything about !"

'I can't bear it !' said Fatty, and let the last spoonful of ice-cream go down his throat.  Then he looked dismayed.  'Oh I say—do you know, I was so puzzled about Old Clear-Orf and his mystery that I ate that ice-cream without tasting it.  What a fearful waste.  I'll have to have another.'

The others looked at him.  'There's no more money,' said Pip.  'We spent it all.'

'I've got some,' said Fatty, and dug his hand into his pocket.  He always had plenty of money, much to the envy of the others, who had pocket-money each Saturday and had to make that do for the week, like most children.  But Fatty had plenty of rich relations, who seemed to pour money into his pockets in a most lavish way.

'Mother says it's bad for you to have so much money,' said Pip.  'She's always saying that.'

'It probably is bad for me,' said Fatty, 'but I'm not going round telling my relations to stop giving me tips.  Now, who wants another ice-cream ? Bets ?'

'Oh, Fatty, I couldn't,' sighed Bets sadly. 'I'd love to, but I know I can't.   I feel a bit sick already.'

'Well, go outside,' said Pip unfeelingly.  'No

thanks, Fatty. I don't feel sick, but I shan't eat
any supper if I have another, and then Mother will
stop all ice-creams for a week, or something awful.'

Larry and Daisy said they couldn't possibly eat
another either, so Fatty had a second one all by
himself, and this time he said he tasted every
spoonful, so it wasn't wasted as the first one had been.

Mr. Goon came back on his bicycle, just as the
children left the shop. ' There he is again ! ' said
Fatty admiringly. ' I've never seen him move so
quickly. Good evening, Mr. Goon ! '

Mr. Goon was just getting off his bicycle to go
into the police-station again. He glanced at Fatty,
and took no notice of him. Fatty was annoyed.

' You seem extremely busy, Mr. Goon,' he said.
' Solving another mystery, I suppose ? Nice to
get the old brains to work, isn't it ? I could do with
a bit of that myself, after lazing away most of these
holidays.'

' Oh ? You got some brains then ? ' said Mr.
Goon sarcastically. ' That's good hearing, that is.
But I'm busy now, and can't stop to talk about
your brains, Master Frederick. There's Big Things
going on, see, and I've got plenty to do without
wasting my time talking to you.'

' Big Things ? ' said Fatty, suddenly interested.
' What, another Mystery, Mr. Goon ? I say—
that's . . .'

' Yes, another Mystery,' said Mr. Goon, almost
bursting with importance. ' And I'm IN CHARGE
of it, see ? I'm the one that's tackling it, not you
interfering kids. And not a word do I tell you about
it, not one word. It's Secret and Important, and it's
a Matter for the Police ! '

' But Mr. Goon—you know how we . . .'
began Fatty anxiously ; but the policeman, feeling

for once that he had got the better of Fatty, interrupted loftily.

' All I know about you is that you're a conceited,
interfering kid what ought to be put in his place
and kept there—you and your nasty barking dog !
This here case is mine, and I'm already getting on
with it, and what's more I'll get Promotion over
this as sure as my name is Theophilus Goon,' said
the policeman, marching up the steps to the police-
station. ' You clear-orf now ! '

' What a blow ! ' muttered poor, disappointed
Fatty, as Goon disappeared through the door. He
and the others walked home slowly, discussing all
that Clear-Orf had said.

' To think of that fat policeman at work on a
perfectly gorgeous new mystery that we don't know
a thing about ! ' said Fatty, looking so miserable
that Bets put her arm through his. ' It's maddening.
And the worst of it is that I simply don't see how
we are going to find out a thing, if Goon won't tell
us.'

' Even Buster's upset about it,' said Bets.
He's got his tail right down. So have you, poor
Fatty. Never mind—you're going to try out your
grown-up disguise to-morrow—that will be a bit of
excitement for you, Fatty. And for us too ! '

' Yes, it will,' said Fatty, cheering up a little.
' Well—I'll be getting back home now. Got to
practise my disguise a bit before I try it out on you
all to-morrow. So long ! '

NEXT morning Larry had a note from Fatty.

> ' Go down to the side-shows by the river this afternoon. I'll meet you somewhere in disguise. Bet you won't know me !
>
> ' Fatty.'

Larry showed the note to Pip and Bets when he went to see them that morning. Bets was thrilled. ' What *will* Fatty be dressed in ? I bet I'll know him ! Oh, I can't wait for this afternoon to come ! '

Larry's mother gave him some money to spend at the side-shows when she heard they were all going there that afternoon. They set off at two o'clock, ready to spot Fatty, no matter how well he was disguised.

As they walked down the village street an old bent man came shuffling up towards them. He stooped badly and dragged his feet, which were in old boots, the toes cracked and the heels worn down. He wore a straggly sandy-grey beard, and had shaggy grey eyebrows, and he looked extremely dirty. His coat sagged away from his bent shoulders, and his corduroy trousers were tied up with string at the knees.

His hat was too large for him and was crammed down over his head. He had a stick in his hand and used it to help himself along. He shuffled to a bench and sat down in the sun, sniffing loudly.

' That's Fatty ! I know it is ! ' said Bets.

' It's just the sort of disguise he'd put on.  Isn't he clever ? '

The old man took a pipe out of his pocket and began to stuff it with tobacco.

' Fancy Fatty even thinking of bringing a pipe ! ' said Pip.  ' I bet he's watched his father stuffing tobacco into his pipe.  Golly—don't say he's even going to smoke it ! '

Apparently he was !  Great puffs of rather evil-smelling, strong smoke came wafting out from the old man.  The children stared.  ' I shouldn't have thought Fatty *could* smoke,' said Larry.  ' He oughtn't to.  He's not old enough.  But I suppose if he's in disguise . . .'

The old fellow sniffed loudly and then wiped his hand across his nose.  Bets giggled.  ' Oh dear !  Fatty is really simply marvellous.  I do think he is.  He must have been practising that awful sniffle for ages.'

Larry went over to the old man and sat down beside him.  ' Hallo, Fatty ! ' he said.  ' Jolly good, old boy !  But we all recognized you at once ! '

The old man took absolutely no notice at all. He went on puffing at his pipe and clouds of the smoke floated into Larry's face.

' Fatty !  Stop it !  You'll make yourself sick if you smoke like that ! ' said Larry.  The others joined him and sat there, giggling.  Pip gave the old man a punch in the ribs.

' Hey, Fatty !  You can stop pretending now. We know it's you ! '

The old man felt the punch and looked round indignantly, his eyes almost hidden under his shaggy eyebrows.  He moved a little way away from Larry and Pip and went on smoking.

' Fatty !  Shut up smoking and talk to us, idiot ! '

said Pip. The old man took his pipe out of his mouth, put his hand behind his ear, and said ' Wassat ? '

' He's pretending to be deaf now ! ' said Bets, and giggled again.

' Ah ? ' said the old man, looking puzzled. ' Wassat ? '

' What does " Wassat " mean ? ' asked Bets.

' It means " What's that " of course,' said Larry. ' Hey, Fatty, stop it now. Give up, and tell us we're right. We all spotted you at once.'

' Wassat ? ' said the old man again, and put his hand behind his ear once more. It was a very peculiar ear, large and flat and purple red. Bets gazed at it and then nudged Daisy.

' Daisy ! We've made a frightful mistake ! It's not Fatty. Look at his ears ! '

Every one gazed at the old fellow's ears. No —not even Fatty could make his ears go like that. And they were not false ears either. They were quite real, not very clean, and remarkably hairy. In fact, they were most unpleasant ears.

' Golly ! It *isn't* Fatty ! ' said Pip, gazing at the ears. ' What *must* the old man think of us ? '

' Wassat ? ' said the old man again, evidently extremely puzzled at the children's familiar behaviour towards him.

' Well, thank goodness the poor old thing is deaf,' said Daisy, feeling ashamed of their mistake. ' Come on, Larry, come on, Pip. We've made an idiotic mistake ! How Fatty would laugh if he knew ! '

' He's probably hiding somewhere around and grinning to himself like anything,' said Pip. They left the puzzled old man sitting on his bench and went off down the street again. They met the baker, and Bets gave him a long and piercing stare, wondering if he could by any chance be Fatty. But he wasn't. He was much too tall.

Then they met the window-cleaner, and as he was rather plump, and just about Fatty's height, they all went and pretended to examine his barrow of ladders and pails, taking cautious glances at him to find out whether or not *he* could be Fatty in disguise.

' Here !   What's the matter with you kids ? ' said the window-cleaner.  ' Haven't you ever seen ladders and pails before ?   And what are you giving me them looks for ?   Anythink wrong with me to-day ? '

' No,' said Larry hurriedly, for the window-cleaner sounded rather annoyed.  ' It's just that—er —these sliding ladders—er—are rather interesting ! '

' Ho, *are* they ? '  said  the  window-cleaner disbelievingly.  ' Well, let me tell you this . . .'

But the children didn't listen to what he had to tell them.  They hurried off, rather red in the face.

' I say !  We shall get into trouble if we go squinting at every one to find out if they really are Fatty,' said Larry.  ' We'll have to look at people a bit more carefully—I mean, without them knowing it.'

' There  he  is—I'm  sure  of  it ! '  said  Bets suddenly, as they went over the level-crossing to the river-side, where the side-shows were.  ' Look —that porter with the moustache.  That's Fatty, all right ! '

The porter was wheeling a barrow up the plat-form, and the others stood and admired him.  ' He wheels it exactly like a *real* porter,' said Bets.  ' Why do porters always wear waistcoats and no coats at railway stations ?  I'm sure that's Fatty.  It's just the way he walks. And he's plump like Fatty too.'

She raised her voice and hailed the porter. ' Hey, Fatty ! Fatty ! '

The porter turned round. He set his barrow down on the ground and walked towards them looking angry.

' Who are you calling Fatty ? ' he demanded, his face red under his porter's cap. ' You hold your tongue, you cheeky kids ! '

The children stared at him. ' It *is* Fatty,' said Bets. ' Look, that's just how his hair sticks out when he wears a hat. Fatty ! We know it's you ! '

' Now you look here ! ' said the porter, coming nearer, ' if you wasn't a little girl I'd come over and shake you good and proper. Calling me names ! You ought to be ashamed of yourself, you did ! '

' It *isn't* Fatty, you idiot,' said Pip angrily to Bets. ' Fatty isn't as short in the arms. *Now* you've got us into trouble ! '

But very luckily for them, a train came thundering in at that moment and the porter had to run to open and shut doors and see to luggage. The children hastily left the level-crossing and ran down to the river.

' You *stupid*, Bets ! You'll get us all into trouble if you keep on imagining every one is Fatty,' said Pip. ' Calling out " Fatty " like that—especially as the porter *was* fat. He must have thought you were disgustingly rude.'

' Oh dear—yes, I suppose it did sound awfully rude,' said Bets, almost in tears. ' But I did think it was Fatty. I'll be more careful next time, Pip.'

They came to the side-shows, which made a kind of Fair alongside the river road. There was a Roundabout, the Hoopla game, the Bumping Motor-

Cars, and the Waxwork Show. The children looked
at the people crowding in and out of the Fair, and
tried to see anyone that might be Fatty.

Bets was scared now to recognise any one as
Fatty. She kept seeing people she thought might
be Fatty and followed them around till she knew they
weren't. The others did the same. Some people
saw that they were being followed and didn't like
it. They turned and glared.

' What you doing, keeping on my heels like
this ? ' one man snapped at Larry. ' Think I'm
going to give you money for the Roundabout ? '

Larry went red and slipped away. He imagined
Fatty somewhere near, tickled to death to see the
Find-Outers trying in vain to spot him. Where
*could* he be ?

' I think I've found him ! ' whispered Bets to
Pip, catching hold of his arm. ' He's the man
selling the Roundabout tickets ! He's just like
Fatty, only he's got a black beard and thick black
hair, and gold ear-rings in his ears, and an almost
black face.'

'Well, he doesn't sound " just like Fatty " to
*me* ! ' said Pip scornfully. ' I'm tired of your
spotting the wrong people, Bets. Where's this
fellow ? '

' I told you. Selling Roundabout tickets,' said
Bets, and though Pip felt quite certain that not even
Fatty would be allowed to sell Roundabout tickets,
he went to see. The man flashed a grin at him and
held up a bunch of tickets.

' A lovely ride ! ' he chanted. ' A lovely ride on
the Roundabout. Only sixpence for a lovely ride ! '

Pip went and bought a ticket. He looked hard
at the man, who gave him another cheeky grin.
Pip grinned back.

*Pip gave the roundabout man a cheeky grin*

' So it *is* you ! ' he said.  ' Jolly good, Fatty ! '

' What you talking about ? ' said the Roundabout-man in surprise.  ' And who are you calling Fatty ? '

Pip didn't like to say any more somehow, though he really was quite certain it was Fatty.  He got on the Roundabout, chose a lion that went miraculously up and down as well as round and round, and enjoyed his ride.

He winked at the ticket-man as he got off and the man winked back.  ' Funny kid, aren't you ? ' said the man.  Pip went to the others.  ' I've found Fatty,' he said.  ' At least, I suppose it was Bets who did, really.  It's the man who sells the tickets for the Roundabout.'

' Oh no it isn't,' said Larry.  ' Daisy and I have found Fatty too.  It's the man who stands and shouts to people to come and have a go at the Hoopla.  See—over there ! "

' But it *can't* be ! ' said Pip.  ' He'd never be allowed to have a job like that.  No, you're wrong.  I don't think *that* can be Fatty."

' Well, and *I* don't think the Roundabout ticket-man is right, after all,' said Bets unexpectedly.  ' I know I *did* think so.  But I don't any more.  His feet are much too small.  He's got silly little feet.  Fatty's got enormous feet.  However much you disguise yourself you can't make big feet into small ones ! '

' I bet Fatty could ! ' said Daisy.  ' He's a marvel.  But I still think Fatty's the Hoopla-man —the one who shouts to people to come and try."

' And *I* think he's the ticket-man at the Round-about,' said Pip obstinately.  ' Well—we'll see. We'll have some fun, get tea over there, and wait for Fatty to show himself in his own good time ! '

HAVING more or less decided the question of Fatty's disguise, though Bets was very doubtful indeed, the four children had some fun.

Bets bought some of the wooden Hoopla rings from the man that Larry and Daisy were certain was Fatty in disguise, and managed to ring a dear little clock. She was really delighted. She held out her hand for the clock, her eyes shining with joy. ' It will do nicely for my bedroom mantel-piece,' she said happily.

' Sorry,' said the Hoopla-man. ' The ring didn't go quite over the clock, Miss.'

' But it *did*,' said poor Bets. ' It did. It didn't even touch the clock. It was the best throw I've ever done ! '

' You didn't ring it properly, Miss,' said the man. The other Hoopla-man, that Larry and Daisy thought was Fatty, looked on, and said nothing. Daisy, certain that it *was* Fatty, appealed to him, sorry to see little Bets being cheated out of the cheap little clock.

' She *did* win it, didn't she ? Make this man let her have it ! '

' Sorry, Miss. She didn't ring it properly,' said that man too. And then Bets walked off, dragging the others with her. ' *Now* do you think that man is Fatty ? ' she said fiercely. ' *He* would have let me have the clock at once ! Fatty is never unkind. He can't be Fatty ! '

' Well—he might *have* to say a thing like that,

argued Larry. 'The other man might have got angry with him and given him a punch. I still think it's Fatty.'

They went on the Roundabout, and in the Bumping Cars. Pip took Bets, and Larry went with Daisy, and with many squeals and yells they crashed into one another, and shook themselves and the little cars almost to pieces. It really was fun.

'Now let's go into the Waxwork Show,' said Larry.

'Oh, it's too hot,' said Daisy. 'Really it is. Besides, I don't much like waxwork figures—they scare me a bit—they look so real, and yet they never even blink!'

'*I* want to see them,' said Bets, who had never been inside a Waxwork Show in her life, and was longing to. 'They've got Queen Elizabeth in there, all dressed up beautifully, and Napoleon, with his hand tucked into his waistcoat, and Nelson with one arm and one eye, and . . .'

'Oh well, let's go in and see all these wonderful persons,' said Daisy. 'But it's a marvel to me they don't all melt in this weather. I feel as if I'm melting myself. We'd better have ice-creams after this.'

They paid their money and went in. The show was in a small hall. A red-headed boy took their money, scratching his head violently with one hand as he handed them tickets with the other. Bets stared at him. Could *he* be Fatty? Fatty had a red-headed wig and eye-brows, and he could put freckles all over his face, just like the ones this boy had. But Fatty had said he would be in a *grown-up* disguise—so he couldn't be this dirty-looking boy. Still—Bets couldn't help staring hard at him. The boy put out his tongue at her.

' Stare away ! ' he said. ' Never seen red hair before, I suppose ! '

Bets went red and joined the others. All round the little hall, arranged on steps that raised each row of figures up behind the others, were the wax people. They stood there, still and silent, fixed looks on their pink faces, staring without blinking.

Pip and Larry liked them, but the two girls felt uncomfortable to have so many strange figures looking at them.

' There's Queen Elizabeth ! ' said Pip, pointing to a very grand-looking wax figure at the end of the little hall. ' And there's Sir Walter Raleigh putting down his cloak for her to walk on. They're jolly good.'

' What grand clothes she wears,' said Bets, ' and I like her big ruff. And look at all her beautiful jewellery. I'm surprised people don't steal it ! '

' Pooh ! All bought at Woolworth's ! ' said Pip. ' I say—here's Nelson. I didn't know he was such a little chap.'

' Oh—and here's Winston Churchill,' said Bets in delight. She had a terrific admiration for this great statesman, and kept a photo of him on her mantelpiece. ' With his cigar and all. He looks the best of the lot ! '

' Look—there's a girl selling sweets,' said Larry suddenly, winking at Pip.' Here, Bets, go and buy some chocolate for us.' He gave the little girl some money and she went to the sweet-girl, who stood nearby with a tray of bags and boxes.

' I'll have some chocolate, please,' said Bets, and held out her money. The girl didn't take it. She looked steadily over Bets' head and said nothing.

' SOME CHOCOLATE, PLEASE,' said Bets loudly, thinking that perhaps the girl was deaf. The girl took absolutely no notice at all, and Bets was puzzled.

Then she heard the others exploding behind her, and guessed in a flash the trick they had played. ' Oh ! This girl is a waxwork too ! You beasts ! I've been trying to buy chocolate from a waxwork figure.'

' Oh, Bets ! Anyone can take you in, simply anyone ! ' said Pip, almost crying with laughter. ' To think you're one of the Find-Outers, too ! Why, you can't even spot when somebody is a waxwork ! '

Bets hardly knew whether to cry or to laugh, but fortunately she decided to laugh. ' Oh dear ! I really did think she was a proper person. Look at that horrid red-headed boy over there laughing at me ! '

They examined all the wax figures closely. There were a good many of them. Among them was a policeman rather like Mr. Goon, but taller and not so fat.

' I'd like to stand Old Clear-Orf in here ! ' said Pip, with a giggle. ' He looks just about as stolid and stupid sometimes. And I say—look at this postman. He's quite good, except for his idiotic grin.'

It was really very hot in the Waxwork Show and the children were glad to go out. The red-headed boy at the entrance put out his tongue at Bets again, and she tried not to look.

' What a horrid boy ! ' she said. ' I can't think how I thought he could be Fatty. Fatty wouldn't behave like that, even in disguise.'

' Let's go and have some tea,' said Daisy. ' Look, this place has got ices and home-made cakes.'

' Cakes and an iced lemonade for me,' said Pip. ' I'll have an ice later if I can manage it. I wish

old Fatty could join us. Wonder if he's looking
on at us, in his disguise. I'm sure he's the ticket-man
at the Roundabout. That man's mop of curly black
hair is too good to be true.

They had a very nice tea, and ate twenty-four
cakes between them. They finished up with ices,
washed down by a rather sweet lemonade, and then
felt able to go out into the sun once more.

' Let's go and sit down by the river,' said Bets.
' It will be cooler there. There's always a breeze
by the water ! '

They made their way out of the Fair. Bets
suddenly caught sight of a lovely patch of gay colour,
and she stopped. ' Pip ! Look at those air-balloons !
I do love a balloon. Have you got enough money
to buy me one ? '

' Don't be a baby,' said Pip. ' Fancy wanting
a balloon like any three-year-old kid ! '

' Well, I do,' said Bets obstinately. They all
went over to where the old woman sat, holding her
bunch of gay balloons. She was a shapeless old
dame, with a red shawl over her shoulders and head,
though the day was hot. Untidy hair hung in wisps
over her brown, wrinkled face, but she had surprisingly bright eyes.

' Balloon, young sir ? ' said she to Pip, in a
cracked old voice.

' No thanks,' said Pip. But Bets pulled his
arm.

' Oh, do buy me one, Pip. Oh, I wish Fatty was
here. He'd buy me one. They're so pretty ! '

' Well, but they're sixpence each ! ' said Pip,
looking at the price label hanging from the string
of balloons. ' Sixpence ! It's robbery. No, I
can't lend you sixpence for that. Mother would
think I was mad.'

' She can have one for half-price,' croaked the old woman kindly. Bets looked at Pip.

' Oh, all right,' he said, and pulled out three pennies. ' But mind you give me the money back when you get home, Bets.'

' Oh thank you, Pip,' said Bets, and took the money. She looked at all the gay balloons, swaying gently in the breeze, and couldn't make up her mind which one to buy. The reds were so nice and bright, the greens were so pretty, the blues were like the sky, the yellows were like sunshine—oh, which should she have ?

' Well, come on after us when you've made up your mind,' said Pip impatiently. ' We're not going to stand here all evening waiting for you, Bets.'

The others went off to the river-bank. Bets stared at the lovely balloons.

' Pretty, aren't they, young miss ? ' said the old woman. ' You take your time in choosing. I don't mind ! '

Bets thought what a kind old woman she was. ' It was so nice of you to let me have one at half-price,' she said. ' Really it was. Do you make a lot of money, selling balloons ? '

' Not much,' said the old dame. ' But enough for an old lady like me.'

Bets chose a blue balloon and the old woman held out her hand for the money. It was a very dirty hand, and it closed over the money quickly. Bets wondered why all the Fair people had such dirty hands and faces.

Then she noticed something that made her stare. The old woman's hand was certainly extremely dirty —but the nails on it were remarkably clean ! Much cleaner than Bets' own nails !

'How queer!' thought Bets, still staring at the clean, well-kept nails. 'Why should this old woman keep her nails so clean, and her hands so dirty?'

Bets then looked hard at the old woman's dirty brown face, all wrinkled up. She looked into the surprisingly bright, twinkling eyes—and she saw that they were Fatty's eyes! Yes, there wasn't an atom of doubt about it—they were Fatty's own bright, intelligent eyes!'

'Oh, Fatty!' whispered Bets. 'Oh, it really is you, isn't it? Oh, do say it is?'

The old woman looked round quickly to make sure no one was listening.

'Yes. It's me all right,' said Fatty, unwrinkling his face as if by magic, and straightening his bent back. 'Jolly good disguise, isn't it? But HOW did you know it was me, Bets? You're too cute for anything!'

'Sh! There's somebody coming,' whispered Bets. 'I'll go. Where will you meet us?'

'Go home at six and I'll meet you somewhere,' said Fatty hurriedly, and screwed his face up into all kinds of wrinkles again. Bets saw that he had cleverly painted the places where the wrinkles came, so that no one could possibly see that they were not always there. Fatty was simply marvellous!

'Don't tell the others!' said Fatty. 'Keep it dark for a bit.' Then he raised his voice and, in a feeble croak, called 'Balloons! Sixpence each! Fine strong balloons!'

Bets went off, her eyes shining. She had found Fatty—and oh, *wasn't* he clever! He really, really was.

BETS went to join the others, very pleased with herself. Her blue balloon floated behind her, tugging at its string.

'Here she is at last!' said Pip. 'We thought you were never coming, Bets. What's up with you? You look bursting with something.'

'Do I?' said Bets. 'Fancy that! By the way, I've a message from Fatty. We're to go home at six and he will meet us somewhere.'

'Who gave you that message?' said Pip, at once.

'That's *my* secret,' said Bets annoyingly.

'Did you speak to Fatty himself?' demanded Larry. 'Is he the Hoopla-man?'

'I shan't tell you,' said Bets. 'I'm going to keep my secret for a bit!'

And she wouldn't say another word, which annoyed the others very much. Fancy young Bets knowing something *they* didn't know!

At six o'clock they made their way back through the Fair, across the level-crossing, and up the lane from the river. Sitting on a bench, with her balloons, was the old Balloon-woman, waiting for them. She got up as they came.

'Balloons!' said she. 'Strong balloons!'

'No thanks,' said Pip, and walked on. The old woman walked with him. 'Buy a balloon!' she said. 'Just to help me, young sir!'

'No thanks,' said Pip again, and walked a little faster. But the old dame could walk surprisingly fast too. She kept up quite easily with Pip!

' *Do* buy a balloon ! ' she said, her voice cracking queerly.

How long she would have pestered Pip nobody knew—but Bets suddenly exploded into a series of helpless giggles that took the others by surprise. They stared at her.

' What *is* the matter ? ' said Pip, exasperated.

' Oh dear ! ' gasped Bets. ' Oh dear—I'm sorry. But I can't help it. It's all so f-f-f-funny ! '

' *What's* funny ? ' shouted Pip. And then he stared—for the old Balloon-woman, pulling her skirts above her knees, and showing sand-shoes and bare legs, was doing a lively jig in front of him and round him, making peculiar noises all the time.

' Don't, Fatty, don't ! I shall die of laughter ! ' said Bets, holding her aching sides.

The others stared as if their eyes were about to fall out. ' What—it's *Fatty* ? ' said Pip. ' *Fatty !* It isn't. I can't believe it ! '

But it was, of course. As soon as Fatty ' unscrewed ' his face, as Bets called it, and got rid of his lines and wrinkles, every one could see quite well it was Fatty.

Larry and Daisy were speechless. So Fatty hadn't been the Hoopla-man, or the Roundabout-man either. He was the old Balloon-woman instead. Trust Fatty to think out a disguise that nobody would guess !

Or had little Bets guessed it ? The others looked at her smiling face. Larry dragged the Balloon-woman to a wayside seat, and they all sat down.

' Is it really you, Fatty ? ' said Larry. The old woman nodded.

' Of course ! Golly, this disguise must be super if I could take you all in as well as that ! '

' Did Bets guess ? ' demanded Pip.

'She did,' said Fatty. 'She suddenly guessed when she was buying her balloon, and you had all gone off without her.'

'But how did she guess ? ' said Pip, annoyed.

'Goodness knows ! ' said Fatty. 'How *did* you guess, young Bets ? '

'Oh, Fatty—it was such a silly thing—I don't really like to tell you,' said Bets. 'I'm sure you'll think it was a silly way to guess.'

'Go on—tell me,' said Fatty, with much interest.

'Well, Fatty—you see, you had very dirty hands, like all the rest of the Fair people,' said Bets. 'But I couldn't help seeing that you had nice, clean nails—and it did seem to me a bit funny that somebody with dirty hands should bother to keep their nails so clean.'

'Well, I'm blessed ! ' said Fatty, looking down at his dirty hands, and examining the well-kept nails. 'Who would have thought of any one noticing that ? Very very careless of me not to get some dirt into my nails when I made my hands filthy. I never thought of it. Bets, you are very clever. Most intelligent.'

'Oh, Fatty—not really,' said Bets, glowing all over her face at such generous praise.

'Well, I must say I think it was jolly cute of young Bets to notice a thing like that,' said Larry. 'I really do. We all had a chance of noticing, because we all stood in front of you. But it was Bets who spotted it. Jolly good, Bets ! '

'She wins my second-best propelling pencil,' said Fatty. 'I'll give it to you when I get home, Bets. In fact I'm not sure that I oughtn't to give you my best one. That was a really smart bit of work. Bright enough for a first-class detective ! '

Daisy praised Bets too, but Pip was rather sulky.

He was afraid his little sister would get swollen-headed. ' If you say much more, Bets will want to be head of the Find-Outers,' he said.

' Oh no, I shan't,' said Bets happily. ' I know it was only a bit of luck, really, Pip. You see, I actually put the pennies into Fatty's hands, and that's how I noticed the clean nails. Pip, I'll lend you the propelling pencil *whenever* you want it. See?'

That was so like Bets. Not even a cross elder brother like Pip could sulk for long with Bets. He grinned at her.

' Thanks, Bets. You're a good Find-Outer, and a good little sport too!'

' I say—look out—here's Goon!' suddenly said Larry, in a low voice. ' Better pretend we're not with Fatty, or Goon will wonder why we are hob-nobbing with an old Fair woman!'

So they all got up, and left Fatty behind on the seat, with his string of balloons bobbing over his head. Mr. Goon was on his bicycle as usual. He pretended not to notice the children at all. He always seemed busy and important these days!

But he got off his bicycle when he saw the old woman. Fatty was drooping over, pretending to be asleep.

' Here, you!' said Goon. ' Move on! And where's your licence to sell balloons?'

The others heard this, and looked alarmed. Did you have to have a licence to peddle balloons? They were sure Fatty hadn't got one.

Fatty took no notice, but gave a gentle snore. Mr. Goon shook the shoulder of the Balloon-woman, and Fatty pretended to awake with a jerk.

' Where's your licence?' said Goon. He was always rude and arrogant to people like the old Balloon-woman.

' What did you say, sir ? ' said Fatty, in a whining
voice. ' Want to buy a balloon, sir ? What colour
do you fancy ? '

' I don't want a balloon,' said Goon angrily. ' I
want to see your licence.'

' Oh, ah, my licence ? ' said Fatty, and began to
pat all over his extremely voluminous skirts, as if
to find where a licence could possibly be hidden.
' Somewhere about, sir, somewhere about. If you
can just wait a few minutes, kind sir, I'll find it in
the pocket of one of my petticoats. An old woman
like me, sir, she wants plenty of petticoats. Sleeping
out under hedges is cold, sir, even on a summer night.'

' Gah ! ' said Goon rudely, mounted his bicycle
and rode off, ringing his bell furiously at a small dog
that dared to run across the road in front of him.
Was he, the Great Goon, in charge of a First-Class
Case, going to wait whilst an old pedlar-woman
fished for ages in her petticoats for a licence he
didn't really want to see ? Gah !

When Goon was safely out of sight the others
went back to Fatty, amused and half-alarmed.
' Oh, Fatty ! How *can* you act like that with Goon ?
If only he'd known it was really you ! '

' I enjoyed that,' said Fatty. ' Good thing
Goon didn't wait to see my licence though, because
I haven't got one, of course. Come on—let's get
back home. I'm dying to take off these hot clothes.
I've got layers of petticoats on to make me fat and
shapeless ! '

On the way up the village street they passed the
bench where they had spoken to the old man on
their way to the Fair that afternoon. Bets pointed
him out to Fatty.

' Fatty. Do you see that old fellow, sleeping on
that bench over there ? Well, we thought he was

*you* ! And we went and called him Fatty, and Pip
gave him a poke in the ribs ! '

Fatty stood and looked at the old chap. ' You
know, it would be quite easy to disguise myself like
him,' he said. ' I've a good mind to try it. Honestly,
I believe I could.'

' But you couldn't make your ears like his,' said
Bets. ' He's got awful ears.'

' No, I couldn't. But I could pull my cap down
lower than he does, and hide my ears a bit,' said
Fatty. ' Yes, that would be a very good and easy
disguise indeed. I'll try it one day. Did Pip really
poke him in the ribs ? '

' Yes. And the old fellow kept on saying, ' Wassat ? Wassat ? ' said Pip, with a giggle. ' He's
deaf, poor old thing."

The old man suddenly opened his eyes and saw
the children looking at him. He thought they must
have spoken to him. He cupped one of his ears
in his hand and croaked out his favourite word,
' Wassat ? '

The old Balloon-woman winked at the children
and sat down beside the old fellow. ' Fine evening,'
she said, in the cracked voice the children were
beginning to know well.

' Wassat ? ' said the old man. Then he sniffed,
and wiped his nose deftly with the back of his hand.
Fatty did exactly the same, which made Bets giggle
in delight.

' FINE EVENING,' said Fatty. ' AND A
FINE MORNING TOO ! '

' Don't know nothing about mornings,' said the
old man surprisingly. ' Always sleep till midday,
I do. Then I gets up, has my bit of dinner, and
comes out into the sun. Mornings don't mean
nothing to me.'

He sniffed again, and then took out his pipe to fill it. Fatty watched all he did. Yes, it would be a marvellous thing to do, to disguise himself as this old fellow. Pipe, sniffs, deafness, and all—Fatty could do it !

' Come on, Fatty ! ' said Pip, in a low voice. ' We really will have to get back. It's getting late.'

Fatty got up and joined them. They soon parted and went their different ways—Pip and Bets down their lane, and Larry and Daisy up theirs. Fatty went in at his back gate, and his mother caught sight of the old Balloon-woman, as she stood in the garden, cutting sweet-peas for the table.

' A friend of Cook's, I suppose,' she thought ; ' or is she trying to sell balloons here ? '

She waited for the Balloon-woman to come back again, but she didn't. So, rather curious, Mrs. Trotteville went to the kitchen door and looked in. There was no Balloon-woman to be seen—only Cook, red in the face, cooking the dinner.

' Where did that old Balloon-woman go ? ' said Mrs. Trotteville, in wonder. But Cook didn't know. She hadn't seen any old woman at all. And no wonder—for at that moment the old Balloon-woman was stripping off layers of petticoats down in the shed at the bottom of the garden—to come forth as a very hot and rather untidy Fatty.

' What a peculiar thing for a Balloon-woman to vanish into thin air ! ' thought Mrs. Trotteville. And so it was.

FATTY had much enjoyed his fun as the old Balloon-woman, and so had the others.  He gave Bets the silver propelling pencil and she was really delighted.

'I've never had such a lovely pencil,' she said. 'It writes in red and blue, as well as in ordinary lead.  Thank you awfully, Fatty.'

'The holidays are going too fast,' said Pip, rather gloomily.  'And we still haven't got a mystery to solve, though we know that Goon has.'

'Yes, I know,' said Fatty, looking worried.  'I can't bear to think of Goon getting busy on his mystery, and we haven't the least idea what it is. Though it *may* be all those burglaries that are cropping up all over the place, you know—I expect most of the police are keeping their eyes skinned for the gang that is operating such big thefts.'

'Can't we keep our eyes skinned too?' said Bets eagerly.  'We might see the gang some-where.'

'Idiot!  Do you suppose they go about in a crowd together, all looking like burglars?' said Pip scornfully.  'They're too jolly clever.  They have their own meeting-places, their own way of passing on messages, their own ways of disposing of the jewels they steal—haven't they, Fatty?  And they are not ways *we* would be likely to find out, even if we did keep our eyes skinned!'

'Oh,' said Bets, disappointed.  'Well—can't we ask Inspector Jenks if there really *is* a mystery here, and ask him to let us help?'

' Yes—why can't we ? ' said Daisy. ' I'm sure
he'd tell us. We've helped him such a lot before.'

Inspector Jenks was their very good friend. He
was what Bets called ' a very high-up policeman,'
and he belonged to the next big town. In the four
mysteries the children had solved before, Inspector
Jenks had come in at the end, and been very pleased
indeed at all the children had found out. Mr. Goon,
however, had not been so pleased, because it was
most annoying to him to have those ' interfering
children messing about with the Law '—especially
when they had actually found out things he hadn't.

' I think it's a very good idea of Bets,' said
Fatty. ' Very good indeed. If he knows what the
mystery is that Goon is working on—and he's sure
to—I don't see why he can't tell us. He knows
we'll keep our mouths shut and do all we can to
help.'

So the next day the Five Find-Outers, with
Buster in Fatty's basket, rode on their bicycles to
the next big town, where Inspector Jenks had his
headquarters. They went to the police-station there,
and asked if they might see him.

' What ! See the Inspector himself ! ' said the
policeman in charge. ' Kids like you ! I should
think not. He's a Big Man, he is, too busy to bother
with kids. Sauce, I call it ! '

' Wait a bit,' said another policeman, with a
nice face, and very bright blue eyes. ' Wait a bit—
aren't you the kids that helped with one or two
difficult cases over in Peterswood ? '

' Yes, we are,' said Fatty. ' We wouldn't want
to bother the Inspector if he's busy, of course—but
we would like to ask him something rather important. Important to us, I mean.'

' Shall I go in and tell the Inspector then ? '

said the first policeman to the other one. ' Don't
want my head bitten off, you know, for interrupting
without due cause.'

' *I'll* tell him ! ' said the blue-eyed policeman.
' I've heard him talk about these kids.' He got up
and went out of the room. The children waited as
patiently as they could. Surely their old friend
would see them !

The policeman came back. ' He'll see you,' he
said. ' Come on in.'

The children followed him down a long stone-
floored passage, and then down another. Bets
looked about her half-fearfully. Was she anywhere
near prisoners in their cells ? She hoped not.

The policeman opened a door with a glass top
to it, and announced them. ' The children from
Peterswood, sir.'

The Inspector was sitting at an enormous desk,
piled with papers. He was in uniform and looked
very big and grand. His eyes twinkled, and he
smiled his nice smile.

' Well, well, well ! ' he said. ' The whole lot of
you at once—and Buster too, I see ! Well, how are
you ? Come to tell me you've solved the mystery
that's been worrying us for months, I suppose ! '

He shook hands with them all, and put Bets on
his knee. She beamed at him. She was very fond
of this big High-Up Policeman.

' No, sir, we haven't come to tell you we've
solved any mystery, unfortunately,' said Fatty.
' These are the first hols for ages that we haven't
had a mystery to solve. But sir, we know that
Mr. Goon has got one he's working on, and we
thought perhaps we could work on it too. But we
don't know what it is.'

' Yes, Goon's on it,' said the Inspector. ' In

fact, most of the police force of the country seem to be on it too ! But it's not one that you can be mixed up in. I don't think you could help at all, first-rate detectives though you are ! '

' Oh ! ' said Fatty, disappointed. ' Is it—is it all these big burglaries, sir ? '

' Yes, that's right,' said the Inspector. ' Very clever, they are. The thieves know just what jewels to steal, when to get at them, and lay their plans very carefully. And we don't know one single one of the men ! Not one. Though we have our suspicions, you know ! We always have ! '

He twinkled at the listening children. Fatty felt desperate. Surely the Inspector could tell them more than that. Surely Goon knew more ? Else why was he so busy and important these days ?

' Mr. Goon looks as if he knew quite a lot, sir,' said Fatty. ' Is there anything going on in Peters-wood at all ? '

The Inspector hesitated. ' Well,' he said at last, ' as I said, this is not a thing for children to be mixed up in. Definitely not, and I am sure you would agree with me if you knew what I know. Peterswood is not exactly mixed up in it—but we suspect that some of the gang go there—to meet perhaps—or to pass on messages—we don't know.'

The children's eyes brightened immediately. ' Sir ! ' said Fatty, at once, ' can't we just keep our eyes open, then ? Not snoop round too much, if you don't want us to—but watch and see if we hear or spot anything unusual. Children can often see and hear things that grown-ups can't, because people suspect other grown-ups, but they don't notice children much.'

The Inspector tapped with his pencil on his desk. Fatty knew that he was weighing up whether

or not to let them keep a watch on things in Peterswood, and his heart beat anxiously.  How he hoped
they would be allowed just to have a little hand in
this Mystery !  It seemed a pretty hopeless one, and
Mr. Goon was sure to do better than they could,
because he knew so much more—but Fatty simply
couldn't *bear* to be left out of it altogether !

'All right,' said the Inspector at last, and put
his pencil down.  'You can keep your eyes open
for me—but don't plunge headlong into anything
foolish or dangerous.  Just keep your eyes open.
It's barely possible you children might spot something, simply *because* you're children.  Report to
me if you find anything suspicious.'

'Oh, *thank* you !' said every one at once,
delighted.

'It's jolly good of you, sir,' said Fatty.  'We
will find out something !  And we'll be as careful
as Mr. Goon !'

'Well, I'm afraid he will come out on top this
time,' said the Inspector, his eyes twinkling.  'He
knows so much more than you do.  But I can tell
you no more than I have done.  Good-bye—and
it's been so nice to see you !'

The children went.  They got on their bicycles
and rode back home, thrilled and pleased.  They all
went to Pip's garden, and sat down importantly in
his summer-house, right at the top of the garden.

'Well—we've got a Mystery after all !' said
Fatty.  'Who are the gang that steals all these
jewels ?  Goon's on the job, and he's got a flying
start—and now we'll be on it too.  Has anybody
noticed anything suspicious in Peterswood lately ?'

They all thought hard.  But nobody could
think of anything in the least suspicious.  Things
seemed to be pretty much as usual, except that the

hot weather had brought crowds of people into the little riverside village.

' I can't think of a thing,' said Larry.

' It's not a very *easy* Mystery,' said Daisy, frowning. ' There doesn't seem anywhere to begin.'

' Can't we do it the usual way—find clues, and make a list of Suspects ? ' said Bets.

' Right ! ' said Pip scornfully. ' You tell us what clues to look for, and who to put down on a list of Suspects ! '

' There are no clues to look for, and we don't even know where to look for Suspects,' said Larry mournfully. ' I wonder what Goon knows.'

' He's probably got a list of men he's suspicious of,' said Fatty thoughtfully. ' And he's also probably got all details of all the burglaries committed lately. I'd better get some back numbers of the newspapers and read them up. Not that it will help us very much, really.'

There was a long pause. ' Well,' said Pip, at last. ' What's the plan ? What are we going to do ? '

There simply didn't seem *any*thing to do ! All they knew was that it was possible that the thieves sometimes met in Peterswood.

' I think it wouldn't be a bad idea for me to disguise myself as that old deaf fellow, who sits on that sunny bench in the middle of the village,' said Fatty. ' We know he isn't there in the mornings, so that would be the time for me to go and sit there. I might be able to spot something suspicious. Men passing notes to one another as they meet— or making remarks in low voices—or even sitting on that bench and talking.

Every one looked doubtful. It didn't seem at all

likely, really. Bets guessed that Fatty wanted the
fun of disguising himself again. ' You had certainly
better not be there in the afternoon ! ' she said.
' People would begin to wonder, if they saw *two*
old fellows, exactly alike, sitting on the same
bench ! '

' Yes. Goon would have a fit ! ' said Larry, and
every one laughed.

' Don't you think it would be better if you chose
some other disguise, not disguise yourself like that
old fellow ? ' said Pip. ' Just in case you did both
wander along at the same time ? There doesn't
really seem any point in dressing up like that dirty
old man.'

' There isn't, really. I just feel I'd like to, that's
all,' said Fatty. ' You know, if you're as good an
actor as I am, there are certain parts or characters
that appeal to you much more than others. I loved
being that old Balloon-woman—and I shall love to
be that old man. I can act him exactly right.'

He gave a realistic sniff and wiped his nose with
the back of his hand. The others laughed, and did
not tease him over his boasting of being such a good
actor.

' You're disgusting ! ' said Daisy. ' Don't for
goodness sake start doing that sort of thing in front
of your parents ! They'll have a fit ! '

Fatty got up and hobbled out into the garden,
shuffling like the old man. He bent his back and
dropped his head. He really was an extremely good
actor.

Then he gave another frightful sniff and wiped
his nose on his sleeve.

A horrified voice spoke to him. ' Frederick !
Haven't you a handkerchief ? What disgusting
behaviour ! '

And there was Pip's mother, come to fetch them in to a meal, as they all seemed completely deaf to the gong.  Poor Fatty !  He went red to the ears, and produced an enormous handkerchief at once. How the others laughed !

WITH the help of the others, Fatty managed to get together some old clothes very like the old man on the bench had worn. Pip produced a very old gardening hat belonging to his father. Larry found an old coat hanging in the garage.

'It's been there for years, as far as I remember,' he said. 'Nobody ever wears it. You might as well have it. It's got mildew inside the pockets, so be careful how you put your hands in them!'

It was easy to get an old shirt and muffler. Fatty produced a torn shirt of his own, and found a muffler down in the garden shed, which he must have left there months before.

He dragged the shirt in the dirt, and it was soon as filthy as the old man's. He dirtied the muffler a little more too.

'What about the shoes?' he said. 'We want frightfully old ones. That old man's were all cracked open at the toe.'

The shoes were a real problem. Nobody's father had shoes as old as that. The children wondered if they could buy a pair from some tramp, but when they went out to find a tramp, the only one they met had perfectly good shoes on.

Then Daisy had a brain-wave. 'Let's look in all the ditches we pass!' she said. 'There are always old boots and shoes in ditches, I don't know why. We might find some there.'

Sure enough they did! Larry came across a dirty, damp old pair, open at the toes and well worn at the heels. He tossed them to Fatty.

' Well, if you think you really do want to wear such horrible things, there you are ! But you'll have to dry them or you'll get awfully damp feet, and have a streaming cold.'

' He'll be able to sniffle properly then,' said Bets. She too had been practising the old man's sniff, much to her mother's annoyance.

' I'll put them under the tank in the hot cup- board,' said Fatty. ' They'll soon dry there. They'll about fit me. I don't at all like wearing them, but, after all, if it's important to solve the Mystery, it's important to put up with little things like this ! '

The trousers seemed quite impossible to get. Nobody's father wore the kind of coarse corduroy that the old man wore. Could they possibly buy a pair in the village shop and make them torn and dirty for Fatty to wear ?

' Better not buy them in Peterswood, in case the news gets round,' said Fatty. ' I wouldn't want old Goon to know I'd bought workman's corduroys —he'd be sure to snoop round and find out why. He's got more brains lately, somehow.'

' We'll walk across the fields to Sheepridge,' said Daisy. ' We might buy a pair there.'

Half-way across the fields Pip gave a shout that made every one jump. He pointed to an old scare- crow standing forgotten in a field. It wore a hat without a brim, a ragged coat—and a pair of dreadful old corduroy trousers !

' Just what we want ! ' said Fatty joyfully, and ran to the scarecrow. ' We'll give them back to him when we've finished with them. Golly, aren't they holey ? I hope they'll hang together on me.'

' I'd better give them a wash for you,' said Daisy. ' They really are awful. If you wear your pair of brown flannel shorts under them, Fatty, the

'*Just what we want,*' said Fatty

holes won't show up so much. There are really too many to mend.'

Joyfully the Find-Outers went back to Larry's. Daisy washed the trousers, but not much dirt came out of them because the rain had washed them many a time. Bets couldn't imagine how Fatty could bear to put on such horrid old clothes.

'Duty calls!' said Fatty, with a grin. 'Got to do all kinds of unpleasant things, Bets, when duty calls. And a really good detective doesn't stick at anything.'

The next day they held a dress rehearsal and dressed Fatty up in the old clothes. He had already got a ragged, sandy-grey beard, which he had cut more or less to the shape of the old man's. He had shaggy grey eyebrows to put on too, and wisps of straggly grey hair to peep out from under his hat.

He made himself up carefully. He put in some wrinkles with his grease-paints, and then screwed up his mouth so that it looked as if he hadn't many teeth.

'Oh, Fatty—you're marvellous!' cried Bets. 'I simply can't bear to look at you, you look so awful. Don't stare at me like that! You give me the creeps! You're an old, old man, not Fatty at all!'

'Wassat?' said Fatty, putting his hand behind his ear. He had very dirty hands indeed—and this time he had remembered to blacken his nails too. He really looked appalling.

'What's the time?' he asked, for he had taken off his wrist-watch, in case it showed. 'Oh, twelve o'clock. Well, what about shuffling off for a snooze in the sun, on that bench? My double won't be there, because he said he never goes out till the afternoon. Come on. I'll see if I can play my part all right!'

' We'll all come,' said Pip. ' But we'll not sit near you. We'll go and have lemonade in that little sweet-shop opposite the bench. We can keep an eye on you then, and see what happens.'

Fatty, after sending Larry down his garden path to the back gate, to see if the coast was clear, shuffled down, hoping that nobody in his house would spot him. He didn't want his mother to get curious about the odd old men and women that seemed to haunt her back-entrance.

Once out in the road, the other four children kept near to Fatty, but not near enough to make any one suspect they were with him. He shuffled along, dragging his feet, bent and stooping, his hat well down over his ears.

' He's just *exactly* like that old fellow we saw ! ' whispered Bets to Daisy. ' I'd never know the difference, would you ? '

Fatty did a loud sniff and the others grinned. He came to the sunny bench and cautiously sat himself down, giving a little sigh as he did so. ' Aaaah ! '

He was certainly a marvellous actor. He sat there in the sun, bending over his stick, the very picture of a poor old man having a rest. The others made their way to the little lemonade shop, and sat down at the table in the window to watch him.

Just as they were finishing their lemonade a man came by on a bicycle, whistling. He was a perfectly ordinary man, in a perfectly ordinary suit and cap, with a very ordinary face. But, when he caught sight of the old man, he braked very suddenly indeed, and looked at him in some astonishment.

He got off his bicycle and wheeled it over to the bench. He leaned it against the seat and sat down by Fatty. The children, watching from the shop opposite, were surprised and rather alarmed. Had this man seen something queer about Fatty's disguise ? Had he guessed it was somebody pretending ? Would he give Fatty away ?

Fatty, too, felt a little alarmed. He had been enjoying himself thoroughly, getting right ' under the skin ' of the old man, as he put it to himself. He had seen the look of surprise on the man's face. Now here he was sitting beside him. Why ?

' What you out here for, in the morning ? ' said the man suddenly, in a very low voice. ' Thought you never came till the afternoon. Anything up ? Expecting any one ? '

Fatty was taken aback to hear this low and confidential whisper. Obviously the man thought him to be the old fellow, and was amazed to see him out in the morning. But what did all the questions mean ?

Just in time, Fatty remembered that the old man was deaf. He put his hand to his ear and put his ear towards the man, so that he should not look directly into his face. He was afraid that he might be recognized as a fraud if the man looked into his eyes.

' Wassat ? ' said Fatty, in a croaking old voice. ' Wassat ? '

The man gave an impatient exclamation. ' Of course—he's deaf ! ' He gave a quick look round as if to see if any one was near. Then somebody else cycled slowly by and the man sidled a little way away from Fatty, and took out a cigarette to light.

The cyclist was Goon, perspiring freely in the hot sun. He saw the two men at once, and got off his bicycle. He pretended to adjust the chain. The four children in the shop watched him with

interest, hoping that he wouldn't go and say anything to Fatty.

Buster saw Goon, and with a delighted yelp he
tore out of the sweet-shop, and danced round the
policeman's feet. Larry rushed after him, afraid
that Buster would go and lick Fatty's face, and give
the show away to Goon. But Buster was fully engaged with the angry policeman, and was having a
perfectly lovely time, dodging kicks, and getting in
little snaps and snarls whenever he could.

Fatty got up hurriedly and shuffled away round
the nearest corner without being noticed by Mr.
Goon, who was rapidly losing his temper. All the
others, seeing that Fatty wanted to get away before
Goon noticed he was gone, began to join in the fun,
pretending to call Buster off, but only succeeding in
exciting the little Scottie more than ever !

When at last Buster was safely in Larry's arms,
and Goon could look round at the bench, it was
empty ! Both the men had gone. Mr. Goon looked
extremely angry.

' That there dog ! ' he said, dusting his trousers
down violently. ' I'll report him, I will. Interfering with me doing my duty, that's what he did.
And now where are them two fellows gone ? I
wanted to put a few questions to them ! '

' They've disappeared,' said Daisy. Mr. Goon
did one of his snorts.

' No need to tell me that. I've got eyes in my
head, haven't I ? I may have lost a Most Important
Clue ! See ? Where's that fat boy that's always
with you ? I bet he's at the bottom of this ! '

' He isn't here,' said Larry truthfully. ' You'll
probably find him at home if you badly want to see
him, Mr. Goon.'

' I wouldn't care if I never set eyes on him again,

the cheeky toad!' said Mr. Goon, mounting his bicycle rather ponderously and wobbling a little. 'No, nor any of you neither. As for that dog!'

He was about to ride off, when he stopped, wobbled again, and spoke to Larry.

'Where were you just now?'

'In the sweet-shop, having lemonade,' said Larry.

'Ho,' said Mr. Goon. 'And did you see that old fellow sitting on that bench?'

'Yes, we did,' said Larry. 'He seemed half-asleep and quite harmless.'

'And did you see that other fellow talking to him?' demanded Mr. Goon.

'Well—he may have spoken to him. I don't know,' said Larry, wondering why the policeman was asking all these questions.

'You'd better come alonga me,' said Mr. Goon, at last. 'I'm going to call on that old fellow, see, and I want you to back me up when I tell him I want to know about the other fellow.'

The children felt distinctly alarmed. What! Mr. Goon was going to visit the *real* old man—who would probably be in bed—and ask him questions about the other man, whom he hadn't been there to see! Whatever would the poor old fellow say? He wouldn't in the least know what Mr. Goon was talking about!

## 8  THE FIRST CLUE—AND A PLAN

'I DON'T think we've got time to . . .' began Larry. But Mr. Goon pooh-poohed him.

'It's my orders,' he said pompously. 'You may be witnesses. You come alonga me.'

So the children went with Mr. Goon, Buster struggling wildly against the lead to get at the policeman's ankles. They turned one or two corners and came to a dirty little pair of cottages at one end of a lane. Mr. Goon went to the first one and knocked.

There was no answer at all. He knocked again. The children felt uncomfortable and wished they were at home. No answer. Then Mr. Goon pushed hard at the door and it opened into a room that was plainly half sitting-room and half bedroom. It was very dirty and smelt horrid.

In the far corner was a small bed, piled high with dirty bedclothes. In it, apparently asleep, his grey hairs showing above the blanket, was the old man. His clothes were on a chair beside him— old coat, corduroy trousers, shirt, muffler, hat, and shoes.

'Hey, you!' said Mr. Goon, marching in. 'No good pretending to be asleep, see? I saw you a few minutes ago in the village street, on the bench.'

The old man awoke with a jump. He seemed to be extremely surprised to see Mr. Goon in his room. He sat up and stared at him. 'Wassat?' he said. It really did seem to be about the only thing he could say.

'It's no good pretending to be in bed and asleep,' roared Mr. Goon. 'You were on the bench in the middle of the street just now. I saw you!'

'I ain't been out of this room to-day!' said the old man, in a cracked voice. 'I always sleeps till dinner, I do.'

'You don't,' shouted Mr. Goon. 'You didn't to-day. And I want to know what that fellow said to you when he came and sat beside you on the bench. Now you tell me, or it'll be the worse for you!'

Bets felt sorry for the old man. She hated it when Mr. Goon shouted so. The old fellow looked more and more puzzled.

'Wassat?' he said, going back to the word he loved.

'See these children here?' said Mr. Goon, beside himself with annoyance at the old man's stupidity. 'Well, they saw you there too. Speak up now you, kids. You saw him, didn't you?'

'Well,' said Larry, hesitating. 'Well . . .' He really didn't know what to say. He knew quite well it hadn't been the old man on the bench—and yet how could he say so without giving Fatty away?

Pip saw his difficulty and rushed in with a few clever words. 'You see, Mr. Goon, it's difficult to say, isn't it, because an old man in bed and an old man dressed don't look a bit the same.'

'Well, look at his clothes then,' said Mr. Goon, pointing to the clothes. 'Aren't those the very clothes he was dressed in?'

'They might not be,' said Pip. 'Sorry, Mr. Goon, but we can't help you in the matter.'

Larry thought it was about time to go, for Mr. Goon's face was turning a familiar purple. So he

and the others hurriedly went back up the lane
and made their way to Fatty's, longing to tell him
all that had happened.

They found Fatty in the wood-shed at the
bottom of his garden, trying to make himself a bit
respectable. All his old-man clothes were in a sack,
ready for use again. He was just smoothing down
his hair when the others poured in.

' I say ! ' began Fatty, his eyes bright. ' That
was a bit queer, wasn't it ? I mean—that man
being so surprised to see me—and sitting down and
saying things to me. I almost forgot I was deaf
and shouldn't hear them ! '

' What did he say ? ' asked Pip, and Fatty told
him. The others listened breathlessly.

' And then up comes Goon, spots this fellow,
and makes an awful to-do about adjusting his bike-
chain, in order to have a good squint at the chap,'
said Larry. ' Looks suspicious to me. I mean—it
looks as if Goon knew the fellow and wanted to
know what he was up to.'

' Is it a clue ? ' asked Bets eagerly.

' You and your clues ! ' said Pip scornfully.
' Don't be silly, Bets.'

' I don't think she *is* silly,' said Fatty thoughtfully. ' I think it *is* a clue—a clue to something
that's going on—maybe even something to do with
the Mystery. You know what the Inspector said—
that it is thought that Peterswood may be the
meeting-place of the thief-gang—the place where
messages are passed on, perhaps, from one member
to another."

' And perhaps the old man is the fellow who
takes the messages and passes them on ! ' cried
Daisy. ' Oh, Fatty ! Is he the chief burglar, do
you think ? '

' Course not,' said Fatty. ' Can you imagine a
poor feeble old thing like that doing anything
violent ? No, he's just a convenient message-bearer,
I should think. Nobody would ever suspect him,
sitting out there in the sun, half-asleep. It would
be easy enough for any one to go and whisper
anything to him.'

' But he's deaf,' objected Daisy.

' So he is. Well then, maybe they slip him
messages,' said Fatty. ' Golly—I feel we're on to
something ! '

' Let's think,' said Larry. ' We shall get somewhere, I feel, if we think ! '

They all thought. Bets was so excited that not a
single sensible thought came into her head. It was
Fatty as usual who came out with everything clear
and simple.

' I've got it ! ' he said. ' Probably Peterswood
*is* the headquarters of the gang, for some reason or
other, and when one member wants to get into
touch with another, they don't communicate with
each other directly, which would be dangerous, but
send messages by that old fellow. And, Find-
Outers, if I go and sit on that bench day in and day
out, I've no doubt some of the members of the
gang will come along, sit by me, and deliver messages
in some way, and . . .'

' And you'll learn who they are, and we can tell
the Inspector, and he'll have them arrested ! ' cried
Bets, in great excitement.

' Well, something like that,' said Fatty. ' The
thing is—the old man always sits there in the
afternoon, and that's really when I ought to sit
there, because it's then that any messages will come,
But how can I sit there, if *he's* there ? "

' That's why that man was so surprised this

morning,' said Daisy. 'He knew the old man never *was* there in the mornings—and yet it seemed as if he was, this morning! He never guessed it was you. Your disguise must have been perfect.'

'It must have been,' said Fatty modestly. 'The thing is—can we possibly stop the old fellow from going there in the afternoons? If we could, I could sit on that bench, and you could all sit in the sweet-shop and watch."

'We can't drink lemonade for hours,' said Bets.

'You could take it in turn,' said Fatty. 'The thing is, we *must* take notice of what the messengers are like, so that we should recognise them again. I shan't dare to look at them too closely, in case they suspect something. So you would have to notice very carefully indeed. I shall take whatever messages they pass on to me, and leave it to you to see exactly what the men are like that come to see me on that bench.'

'What about that one this morning?' said Larry suddenly. 'That must have been one of them. Now—what exactly was he like?'

Every one frowned and tried to remember. 'He was simply too ordinary for anything,' said Larry at last. 'Ordinary face, ordinary clothes, ordinary bicycle. Wait though—I'm remembering something about that bicycle. It had a—it had a hooter on it, instead of a bell!'

'So it had!' said Pip, remembering too. Daisy and Bets hadn't noticed that. In fact, they couldn't remember a thing about the man at all.

'A hooter,' said Fatty thoughtfully. 'Well, that might be a bit of a help in tracing the man. We'll keep a look-out for bikes with hooters. But the thing that's really worrying me *is*—how can we stop that old man from sitting on the bench in the afternoons, so that *I* can go instead ? '

Nobody knew. ' The only thing is,' said Fatty at last, ' the absolutely only thing is—for me to slide down on the bench beside him, and pretend to be one of the messengers myself— and tell him not to sit out there for two or three days ! '

' Ooooh yes ! ' said Pip. ' Because Mr. Goon may be watching. You could say that.'

' I could. And it will probably be quite true,' said Fatty, with a groan. ' Old Goon has got his suspicions too, and is on the right track. We've tumbled on it by accident. There I shall sit, under Goon's eye all the afternoon ! I bet no messenger will come if they know that he's watching.'

' If we see a likely-looking stranger hanging about, we could get Goon away for a bit,' said Larry. ' And I know how we could do it too ! We could go round a corner and toot a hooter ! Then Goon would think to himself, " Ha, hooter on a bike ! Maybe the man I want ! " and go scooting round the corner.'

' Yes, that's quite well worked out,' said Fatty. ' The thing is—Goon probably hasn't noticed the hooter on the man's bike.'

' Well, tell him then,' said Larry. ' He'll be awfully bucked at that. Let's go and tell him now.'

' Come on then. We'll go and look for him,' said Fatty. But just then Larry looked at his watch and gave an exclamation. ' Golly ! We'll be *fright*fully late for lunch ! We'll have to tell Goon this afternoon.'

' I will,' said Fatty. ' See you later ! '

That afternoon Mr. Goon, enjoying a brief after-dinner nap, was surprised to see Fatty coming in at the door, and even more surprised when the boy presented his bit of information about the hooter on the bicycle.

'I don't know if it will be of any use to you, Mr. Goon,' he said earnestly. 'But we thought you ought to know. After all, it's a clue, isn't it?'

'Ho! A clue to what?' demanded Mr. Goon. 'You aren't interfering again, are you? And any-way, I noticed that there hooter myself. And if I hear it tooting, I'll soon be after the cyclist.'

'What do you want him for?' asked Fatty innocently.

Mr. Goon stared at him suspiciously. 'Never you mind. And look here, how is it you know all about this here hooter, when you wasn't with the others? You tell me that.'

'Oh, *they* told me,' said Fatty. 'I'm afraid you're angry with me for trying to give you a clue, Mr. Goon. I'm sorry. I didn't know you had already noticed the hooter. I won't trouble you with any of our information again.'

'Now look here, there's no harm in . . .' began Mr. Goon, afraid that perhaps Fatty might withhold further information that might really be of use. But Fatty was gone. He visited a shop on the way home and bought a very nice little rubber hooter. Mr. Goon was going to hear it quite a lot! In fact, he heard it a few minutes later, just outside his window, as he was finishing his nap. He shot upright at once, and raced to the door.

But there was no cyclist to be seen. He went back slowly—and the hooter sounded again. Drat it! Where was it? He looked up and down the road once more but there really was no sign of a bicycle.  There was only a boy a good way down, sauntering along.  But he hadn't a bicycle.

He had a hooter, though, under his coat, and his name was Fatty !

THE next afternoon Fatty did not dress up as the old man, but instead, put on his Balloon-woman's petticoats and shawl again. The others watched him, down in the shed at the bottom of Fatty's garden. Bets thought she could watch him for days on end, making himself up as different people. There was no doubt at all that Fatty had a perfect gift for dressing up and acting.

' I'll go and sit on the seat beside the old man,' said Fatty. ' He's sure to be there this afternoon, waiting for any possible messages—and you can snoop round and see if Goon is anywhere about. If he isn't, I'll take the chance of telling the old man not to appear for a few afternoons as the police are watching. That should make him scuttle away all right if he's in with the gang ! '

' I'll come and buy another balloon from you,' said Bets eagerly. ' That will make it all seem real.'

' Oh, it'll be real enough,' said Fatty. ' All I hope is that Goon won't come and ask me for my licence again.'

' He won't, if you are sitting in the middle of the village street, and he thinks you've got to hunt all through your petticoats for it, and make him look silly,' said Larry. ' He can't bear to be made to look silly. And anyway, he won't want to draw attention to himself if he's watching for any possible gang members. He won't think *you're* one.'

' Quite right,' said Fatty. ' Well reasoned out, Larry. Now—am I ready ? '

' You look simply marvellous,' said Bets admiringly. ' You really do. I can't think how you
manage to make your face go so different, Fatty. It
doesn't look a bit like you.'

' Oh, I practise in front of a mirror,' said Fatty.
' And I've got some marvellous books about it. And,
of course, I've got the *gift*—you see . . ."

' Oh, shut up, Fatty,' said Larry good humour-
edly. ' We all know you're marvellous, without *you*
telling us ! '

The Balloon-woman suddenly screwed up her
face, and her mouth went down at the corners in a
most pathetic manner. She fished out a big red
handkerchief, decidedly dirty, and began to weep
most realistically.

' Don't be so unkind to me,' she wept, and the
others roared with laughter. Fatty peeped out at
them from the corner of his hanky. ' A pore old
woman like me ! ' he wept. ' Sleeping out under
hedges at night . . .'

' With layers of petticoats to keep you warm ! '
chuckled Larry. Then he stopped and looked
quickly out of the window of the shed.

' Quick ! There's your mother, Fatty. What
shall we do ? '

There wasn't time to do anything. Mrs. Trotteville was even then looking in at the door. She
had come to speak to the children, but when she
saw the old Balloon-woman, she was very much
astonished.

' What are you doing here ? ' she asked sharply.
' I saw you going down the garden-path the other
day.'

Bets spoke up before Fatty could answer.

' She sells lovely balloons,' she said. ' I want to
buy one, Mrs. Trotteville.'

'There's absolutely no need to buy one in the garden-shed,' said Mrs. Trotteville. 'You can buy one in the street. I don't want pedlars or tramps in the garden. I am surprised that Buster did not bark.'

Buster was there, of course, sitting at the Balloon-woman's feet. He looked as if she was his best friend—as indeed she was, if only Mrs. Trotteville had known it.'

'Where's Frederick?' asked Mrs. Trotteville, looking all round for Fatty.

'Er—not far away,' said Larry truthfully. 'Er —shall I go and look for him, Mrs. Trotteville?'

'Oh no. I suppose you are all waiting for him,' said Mrs. Trotteville. 'Well, I'm afraid this woman and her balloons must go—and please do not come into the garden again!'

'No, Mum,' said the Balloon-woman, and bobbed a funny little curtsey that nearly sent Bets into fits of laughter. They all went out of the shed and up the path to the front gate.

'That was a narrow squeak,' said Larry, when they were safely out in the road.

'Narrow squeaks are exciting!' said Pip.

They made their way to the main street of the village. There, on the sunny bench, was the old man as usual, bent over his stick, looking half-asleep.

'I'll go and sit down by him,' said Fatty, swinging his voluminous skirts out round him as he walked. 'You walk behind me now, and keep a watch out for Goon. Bets can tell me if he's any-where about when she comes to buy a balloon. You can all go and have lemonade in that shop, to begin with.'

The Balloon-woman sat down on the bench with

her bunch of gay balloons. The old man at the end of the seat took no notice of her at all. The balloons bobbed in the wind, and passers-by looked at them with pleasure. A mother stopped to buy one for her baby, and the four watching children giggled as they saw Fatty bend over the baby in the pram and tickle its cheek.

' How does he know how to do things like that ? ' chuckled Larry. ' I'd never think of those things.'

' But it's those little touches that make his disguises so real,' said Daisy, in admiration. They went into the lemonade shop and sat down to have a drink. A man was sitting at a table nearby, lost in a big newspaper. Larry glanced at him, and then gave Pip a kick under the table. Pip looked up and Larry winked at him, and nodded his head slightly towards the man.

The others looked—and there was old Clear-Orf, in plain clothes, pretending to read a newspaper, and keeping an eye on the bench across the road, just as they too intended to do !

' Good morning, Mr. Goon,' said Larry politely. ' Having a day off ? '

Mr. Goon grunted bad-temperedly. Those children again ! They seemed to turn up everywhere.

' You having a lemonade too ? ' said Pip. ' Have one with us, Mr. Goon. Do.'

Mr. Goon grunted again, and returned to his newspaper. He was in plain clothes and looked rather strange. The children couldn't remember ever having seen him in anything but his rather tight-fitting uniform before. He wore flannel trousers, a cream shirt open at the neck, and a belt that he had pulled too tight. Bets thought he didn't look like Mr. Goon at all.

She finished her lemonade. ' I'm going to buy a balloon,' she said. ' The one I bought at the Fair has gone pop. Order me an ice, Pip, and I'll be back to have it soon. We *are* all going to have ices, aren't we ? '

' Where's that fat boy ? ' asked Mr. Goon, as Bets got up.

' Fat boy ? What fat boy ? ' said Larry at once, pretending to be puzzled.

Mr. Goon gave a snort. ' That boy Frederick. Fatty, you call him. You know quite well who I mean. Don't act so daft.'

' Oh, *Fatty* ! He's not far off,' said Larry. ' Do you want to see him ? I'll tell him, if you like.'

' *I* don't want to see him,' said Mr. Goon. ' But I know he's always up to something. What's he up to now ? '

' *Is* he up to something now ? ' said Larry, a surprised look on his face. ' How mean of him not to tell us ! '

Bets giggled and went out. She crossed the road to where the old Balloon-woman sat, her skirts almost filling half of the bench.

' May I have a blue balloon, please ? ' she said. She bent over the bunch of balloons and whispered to Fatty. ' Mr. Goon is in the lemonade shop—in plain clothes. He looks so funny. I think he's watching the old man. You'll have to watch till you see Mr. Goon go off, and then give your message.'

' Have *this* balloon, little Miss ! ' said the Balloon-woman, winking at Bets to show that her message had been heard. ' This is a fine strong one. Last you for weeks ! '

Bets paid for it, and went back to the shop.

Larry had just ordered ices. He raised his eyebrows at Bets to ask her if she had delivered the message all right. She nodded. They began to eat their ices slowly, wondering if the policeman meant to stay in the shop all the afternoon.

They had almost finished their ices when the telephone went at the back of the shop. The shop-woman answered it. 'For you, please, Mr. Goon,' she said.

Mr. Goon got up, went to the dark corner at the back of the shop, and listened to what the telephone had to say. Larry took a look at him. Goon could not possibly see across the street to the bench from where he stood. Now would be Fatty's chance to give his message to the old man!

'It's hot in here,' said Larry, suddenly standing up. 'I'm going out for a breath of air. You come when you've finished your ices.'

He went out of the shop and shot across to the bench. He sat down beside the Balloon-woman. 'Goon's telephoning,' he said. 'Now's your chance. He can't see across the street from where the telephone is.'

'Right,' said Fatty. He moved nearer to the old man and nudged him. The old fellow looked round at once. Fatty slipped a note to him and then moved back to his end of the bench.

The old man deftly pocketed the note and sat for a few minutes more. Then, with a grunt, he got up and shuffled off round the corner. Larry followed him, at a sign from Fatty. As soon as he was safely round the corner the old fellow opened the slip of paper and looked at it. Then he took a match, lighted the paper, and let it drop to the ground, where it burnt away.

He did not go back to his bench. Instead, he shuffled off in the direction of his home. Larry went back to the bench and stood beside the old Balloon-woman, pretending to choose a balloon.

' Did he read the note ? ' said Fatty, in a low voice.

' Yes. And he's gone off home now, I think,' said Larry. ' What did you put in the note ? '

' I just put that he'd better not come to this seat for three afternoons as the police were watching it.' said Fatty. ' He'll think it was from a member of the gang, I expect. He will think they'd asked me to pass the message to him, as they wouldn't want to be seen doing it themselves, if the seat was watched. Well, let's hope we've got him out of the way for a few days ! '

' I'll have this balloon,' said Larry, as some people passed. ' How much ? '

Taking the balloon with him, he went back to the door of the shop. Mr. Goon was still telephoning. Good ! The others got up and went out. They all sauntered down the road, thinking how cross Mr. Goon would be when he stopped telephoning and found that the old man was gone.

The Balloon-woman went too. It had been decided that she should go to Pip's garden, in case Mrs. Trotteville, Fatty's mother, should spot her again, going down her garden-path, and make trouble. Pip's mother was out for the day, so it would be safe for Fatty to go there and change back to himself.

Soon all the Find-Outers, and Buster, were in Pip's summer-house. Fatty changed as quickly as he could.

' I shan't use this disguise more than I can help,' he said, pushing all the petticoats and skirts into the sack he kept them in. ' It's too hot. I shall get as thin as a rake if I keep getting so melting-hot ! '

' Oh, don't do that ! ' said Bets, in alarm. ' You wouldn't be Fatty any more, if you were thin. And I do like you just exactly as you are ! '

PLANS were laid for the next few days. 'These may be very important days,' said Fatty. 'We may be able to learn a lot—right under Goon's nose, too, if he's going to do this watch-dog act of his !'

'What exactly are we going to do ?' said Daisy, thrilled. 'You're going to disguise yourself as that old man, we know, and take his place, hoping for a message from one of the gang. But what are *we* to do ? We must have something interesting so that we can do our share as Find-Outers.'

'Woof,' said Buster.

'He wants a job too,' said Bets, with a laugh. 'Poor Buster ! He can't understand why you have to dress up as somebody different, Fatty. You don't look or sound the same to him—you only *smell* the same. And when you go out as the Balloon-woman or the old man, we have to lock Buster up and leave him behind, and he hates that.'

'Poor old Buster-Dog,' said Fatty, and at once Buster rolled himself over on his back to be tickled. His tongue came out, and his tail wagged so violently that it wagged his whole body and made it shake from end to end.

'Now,' said Fatty, taking out his note-book and opening it. 'Let's just have a look at what we know. Then we'll make our plans—and you shall each have something to do.'

'Good,' said Larry. 'I know you've got to do all the important work, Fatty, because you really

are a born detective—but we do want something
as well.'

'We don't know very much yet,' said Fatty,
looking at his notes. 'We know that Goon is
watching the old man because he suspects what we
do—that he receives messages to pass on—and we
feel certain that for some reason or other the headquarters are here in Peterswood. We have also seen
one of the members of the gang—the fellow with a
hooter on his bike—but that's about all we *do* know.'

'It's not very much,' said Larry. 'Not a scrap
more than we knew the other day.'

'We also know that the old fellow is likely to
keep away from that seat for a while,' said Fatty.
'Goon doesn't know that. We're ahead of him
there. *We* know that the old man who will be
sitting on the bench this afternoon, and to-morrow
and probably the next day too, will be *me*—and not
that old fellow.'

'Yes, that's one up to us,' said Pip.

'Now,' said Fatty, shutting his note-book and
looking round, ' to-morrow afternoon—in fact, each
afternoon that I sit out on that bench, one or more
of you must be in that sweet-shop, watching carefully to see if any one gives me a message—and it's
your job to notice every single detail about him very
carefully indeed. See? That's most important.'

'Right,' said Larry.

'And the other thing for you Find-Outers to do
is to try and discover which cyclists have hooters on
their bikes, instead of bells,' said Fatty. 'It would
be a help if we could discover who that man was
that came and spoke to me on the bench the other
morning. We could watch him, and find out who
his friends were, for instance.'

'I don't see how we can possibly find out who

has a hooter on his bicycle,' said Pip. ' We can't go and look into every one's bicycle sheds ! '

' You could go to the shop that sells hooters and get into talk with the shopkeeper, and ask him if he sells many hooters, and maybe even get him to tell you the names of the buyers,' said Fatty.

' Oh yes,' said Pip. ' I hadn't thought of that.'

' I thought of it the other day when I went to buy that hooter,' said Fatty. ' But I hadn't time to talk to the man then—well, actually it's a boy in the shop I went to. I should think he'd love to have a good old jaw with you.'

' I'd like to go and talk to him,' said Bets. ' With Daisy.'

' You and Daisy and Pip can go, if you like,' said Larry. ' And I'll watch the seat from the sweet-shop. Then, when you come back with all the information you can get you can take your turn at sitting in the shop and having lemonade, and I'll go and try and find out something else.'

' Buster can go with the ones who are going to the hooter-shop,' said Fatty. ' But he mustn't go to the sweet-shop. He would smell me all across the road, and come bounding out, barking. Goon would soon think there was something funny about Buster making up to a dirty old man ! '

The next afternoon Larry went to the sweet-shop opposite the bench, and ordered a lemonade. Mr. Goon was there again, reading his newspaper. He was once more in plain clothes, and he scowled at Larry when he came in.

' Why, Mr. Goon ! Here again ! ' said Larry, pretending to be most surprised. ' You *are* having a nice holiday ! Do you spend all your time in here ? '

Mr. Goon took absolutely no notice. He felt very angry. Here was he, forced to spend his afternoons in a hot, smelly, little shop, watching a bench out there in the sun—and he couldn't even have peace! Those children had got to come and poke fun at him. Mr. Goon eyed Larry's back grimly, and thought of all the things he would like to do to him and the other Find-Outers.

Then Mr. Goon straightened up a little, for the old man was coming shuffling along to his bench. Larry watched him. He knew it was Fatty, of course, but Mr. Goon didn't. Larry marvelled at the way Fatty lowered himself slowly down on to the bench. That was just exactly the way bent old people did sit down! Fatty never made a mistake in his acting.

Fatty took out a pipe and began slowly to fill it. Then he coughed. It was a horrible, hollow cough, and bent him double. Larry grinned. The cough was new. He supposed Fatty must have heard the old man, and had practised the cough till it was quite perfect.

The old man put his pipe away without smoking it. Evidently he was afraid of its making him cough too much! Larry turned to Mr. Goon.

' There's that old man you made us go and see the other day, Mr. Goon. Funny about him, wasn't it ? Did you ever find out what you wanted to know ? '

Mr. Goon again took no notice, but rustled the paper noisily. Larry winked at the shop-woman. ' Must have got a cold,' he said sympathetically. ' Gone quite deaf ! '

' Now, you look 'ere ! ' said Mr. Goon, going red and rising quite suddenly, ' if you don't . . .'

But just then two men came along, stopped by the bench and sat down. At once Mr. Goon subsided, and began to watch the men with much concentration. So did Larry. Were they going to pass a message to Fatty ?

The men had papers. They opened them and began to discuss something. One of them lighted a pipe. They stayed there for quite a time, but neither Goon nor Larry could spot any message being given or received. The old fellow at the end of the bench still leaned over his stick, his head nodding occasionally.

Then he sat upright, gave a loud sniff and wiped the back of his hand across his nose. Larry was amused to see the two men give him a disgusted look. They folded their newspapers, got up, and, still talking, walked off down the street.

Mr. Goon leaned back and wrote down a few notes. Larry wondered if he thought they were the members of the gang. He was certain they weren't. For one thing he was sure that one of them was a friend of his father's.

Larry began to be bored. He had finished his lemonade. He really didn't want another, and he felt that he couldn't possibly eat an ice at that moment. The shop-woman came up to him.

' Anything else, sir ? ' she asked. Larry said no thank you.

' Well, you go, then,' said Mr. Goon's voice. ' No need for you to hang about here if you've finished your everlasting lemonade, see ? '

This was awkward. Larry was supposed to watch the bench and Fatty until the others came back. He couldn't very well leave his post. But just at that moment the others *did* come back ! They clattered in, chattering.

Larry stood up at once. ' Hallo, you others !
I'm glad you've come for me.  I suppose Pip
wants to stay and have a lemonade as usual.
Well, you girls and I will go off and leave
him guzzling ! '

For a wonder even Bets sensed that Larry wanted
to leave only one of them behind.  So the girls
went off with Larry, and left Pip to seat himself
at the window-table, with a glowering Mr. Goon
nearby.  Was he *never* going to get rid of these
children !

Larry took the girls off, and when they were
safely round the corner, he told them how Mr. Goon
had ordered him to go.  ' So I thought we'd better
only just leave Pip behind,' he said, ' and then that
still leaves two more of us to go in singly and drink
lemonade or eat ices.  I think Goon is getting
suspicious of us ! '

' Larry !  We had a most interesting time at
the shop where the hooters are sold,' said Bets.
' Listen ! '

She told Larry all about it.  She and Pip and
Daisy had gone into the shop, which sold bicycles,
tyres, pumps, bells, hooters, torches, toys, prams,
and many other things.  There was a cheeky-looking
boy in charge.

' Afternoon,' he said, when they all trooped in.
' And what may I do for *you* ?  Want a pram,
perhaps ? '

Bets giggled.  ' No,' she said.  ' We want a
hooter.  My bell isn't very good, and I thought a
hooter would make quite a change.'

' Well, you're lucky,' said the boy, going over to
a shelf and getting down a rubber hooter.  ' We
only had these in last week.  First we've had for
months ! '

The children tried it. It hooted very nicely indeed. Parp-parp ! Parp-parp !

' Do you sell many ? ' asked Pip, whilst the two girls ambled round the shop, pretending to look at everything.

' Only sold three this week,' said the boy.

' All to cyclists ? ' asked Pip.

' How should I know ? ' said the boy. ' The customers don't wheel their bikes into the shop with them ! '

Pip didn't quite know what to say next. He joined the girls, and they all examined the contents of the rather interesting shop.

' You've got an awful lot of things here,' said Daisy. ' Do you remember all the prices and everything ? '

' 'Course. I've got a good memory,' said the boy. ' At the end of the day I remember every blessed thing I've sold ! '

' Gracious ! ' said Daisy admiringly. ' I bet you don't remember every customer too ! '

' Oh yes, I do,' said the boy proudly. ' Never forget a thing, I don't ! '

' Well—I bet you don't remember the customers who bought the three hooters ! ' said Daisy, quick as a flash. Pip and Bets thought how clever she was !

' 'Course I do,' said the boy. ' One was the fellow that lives down the road at Kosy-Kot. The second one was a fellow with rather queer eyes—one blue and one brown—I don't know his name and never saw him before. But I'd know him again all right. And the third one was a fat boy who seemed in a bit of a hurry.'

' That was Fatty,' thought the three children. Daisy smiled at the shop-boy. ' What a memory

you've got ! ' she said.  ' You really are a marvel.
Well, we must be going.  Got your hooter, Bets ?
Well, come on, then ! '

They hurried out of the shop, rejoicing.  The
man at Kosy-Kot—and a man with odd eyes.  They
might be Clues, they really might !

PIP was having a boring time in the sweet-shop. There was nothing to see outside, except the old man on the bench. Nobody went near him at all. Mr. Goon breathed heavily behind Pip, evidently finding the shop a very hot place to be in on this blazing day. Pip made his lemonade last out a long time and then, to Mr. Goon's annoyance, asked for an ice.

' You children seem to live here,' said Mr. Goon, at last.

' You seem to, as well,' said Pip. ' Nice shop, isn't it ? '

Mr. Goon didn't think so at all. He was sick and tired of the shop—but it was the best place to watch that old man from, no doubt about that !

' You look hot,' said Pip sympathetically. ' Why don't you go for a row on the river, Mr. Goon ? It would be cool there. Seems a pity to spend all your holiday cooped up here.'

Mr. Goon gave one of his snorts. He wasn't on holiday. He was on a case, a most important case. And for reasons of his own he had to wear plain clothes. But he couldn't explain all that to this irritating boy. Mr. Goon wished Pip was a mosquito. Then he would slap at him, and finish him off.

Bets came in next, and Pip was very glad to see her. ' Going to have an ice ? ' he said. ' Well, sorry I can't wait with you, Bets. So long ! '

He went out and, to Mr. Goon's annoyance, yet

another of those children, Bets this time, settled down at the window-table, obviously intending to be there for some time. Bets was afraid of the policeman, so she kept her back to him and said nothing at all, but kept a sharp eye on the old man opposite on the bench. She thought how bored poor Fatty must be !

Fatty had a coughing fit, and Bets watched in alarm. The cough seemed so very real that she felt sure poor Fatty must be getting a terrible cold.

Then Fatty had a fit of the sniffles, and hunted all over himself for a handkerchief, at last producing a violent red one. Then he got up and hobbled round a bit, as if he had got stiff with sitting. Nobody in the world would have guessed he was anything but a poor, stiff old man.

Bets enjoyed the performance immensely. She knew that Fatty was putting it on for her benefit. Fatty liked little Bets' admiration, and he was pondering whether or not he should actually light the pipe he had filled, and try smoking it. That would send Bets into fits !

But he didn't dare to. He had tried already and it had made him feel very sick. So he contented himself with putting the filled pipe in his mouth unlighted, and keeping it there.

All the Find-Outers were glad when that day was over. It really began to be very boring, taking turns at sitting in the sweet-shop, and watching for something that didn't happen. As for Fatty, he was terribly bored.

' To-morrow I'm going to supply myself with plenty of newspapers to read,' he said. ' I simply can't spend hours filling pipes and coughing and sniffing. And all for nothing too. Not a soul passed me a message or anything.'

'We found out something interesting at the hooter-shop, though,' said Bets, and she told Fatty about the two men who had bought hooters that week.

'One who lives at Kosy-Kot, and one man with odd eyes,' she said. 'The boy didn't know where he lived. And the third person who bought a hooter was you, of course.'

'Has that shop only sold three hooters all these months, then ? ' said Fatty, surprised.

'Well, they've only just got them in,' said Pip. 'That's why. So, if that fellow who spoke to you the other day on the bench *is* a member of the gang, he's either living at Kosy-Kot—or he's wandering about somewhere with odd eyes—one blue and one brown ! '

'We'd better try Kosy-Kot first,' said Fatty, pleased. 'You did well, Find-Outers. How did you get all this information ? '

'Well, Daisy did, really,' said Pip, and he told Fatty how it had happened. Fatty banged Daisy on the back.

'Jolly good,' he said. 'Very quick-witted. Now—who's going to tackle Kosy-Kot ? '

'Isn't it a frightful name ? ' said Pip. 'Why do people choose names like that ? Can't we go down into the village and find it to-morrow morning ? It's too late now.'

'Right,' said Fatty. 'We will. I shan't have to masquerade as that old fellow till the afternoon, so I can come with you. Meet at Pip's to-morrow morning, ten o'clock sharp.'

So, at ten o'clock, they were all there, Buster too. They set off to find Kosy-Kot. They met a postman and he told them where it was.

They soon found it. It was a little bungalow

set in a trim little garden. At the back was a shed.

'I bet that's where they keep the bicycles,' said Fatty. 'Now—how can we get a peep inside ?'

'I know !' said Pip. 'I've got a ball. I could chuck it into the garden, and then we could go and ask if we might get it back—and you could peep into the shed, Fatty. If a bike is there with a hooter on, we'll wait about for the man who lives here, and see if we recognize him as the one who spoke to you, and had a bike with a hooter. We might recognize the bike too, if we see it.'

This seemed a good and simple plan. So Pip proceeded to carry it out. He threw the ball wildly, and it flew into the garden of Kosy-Kot, actually hitting against the bicycle-shed.

'Blow !' said Pip loudly. 'My ball's gone into that garden.'

'We'll go and ask if we may get it,' said Daisy. So into the gate they went and up to the front door.

A woman opened it. 'Please, our ball has gone into your garden,' said Pip. 'May we get it ?'

'Yes, but don't tread on any of the beds,' said the woman, and shut the door. The children went round to the back of the house. To their annoyance they saw a man there, digging. He stared at them.

'What do you kids want ?'

'Oh—excuse us, please, but your wife said we might come and get our ball,' said Fatty, politely. 'I hope you don't mind.'

'Well, get it, then,' said the man, and went on digging. Fatty made for the shed and pretended to hunt round about. The door was open and he looked inside. It was full of garden tools and old sacks—but there was no bike there at all. How annoying !

' Haven't you found it ? ' said the man, and came over to look too. Then Fatty gave an exclamation and picked up the ball. He looked at the neat little shed.

' Useful sheds those, aren't they ? ' he said. ' Jolly good for bikes. Wish I had one like that.'

' Oh, I don't use it for bikes,' said the man. ' We haven't any. I use it for my garden tools.'

' Oh,' said Fatty. ' Well—thank you for letting us get our ball. We'll be going now.'

They went out into the road and crossed over to talk. ' Hasn't got a bike ! But that boy at the shop distinctly said that the man at Kosy-Kot bought a hooter,' said Bets indignantly. ' He *must* have got a bike. Why should he pretend he hasn't got one ? '

' It's a bit suspicious,' said Pip. They walked on, puzzled. Suddenly, round the corner, they heard the noise of a hooter ! Parp-parp ! Parp-parp ! The children clutched at one another, thrilled. A hooter ! Perhaps it belonged to the man with odd eyes ! Perhaps it would be his bicycle coming round the corner !

But, round the corner, ridden at a tremendous pace, came a child on a tricycle. He ran right into Fatty, who gave a yell, and hopped round on one leg, holding his right foot in his hand.

' You little idiot ! What did you come round the corner like that for ? ' yelled Fatty.

' Well, I hooted ! ' said the little boy indignantly. ' Didn't you hear me ? I hooted like this.'

And he pressed the rubber hooter on his tricycle and it parp-parped loudly. ' It's a new hooter,' he said. ' My Daddy bought it for me. You should have got out of the way when you heard me coming round the corner.'

' We weren't expecting a tricycle,' said Pip.

*' You're all right, aren't you? '*

We thought the hooter was on a bike, coming along
the road, not on the pavement.'

' Well, I'm sorry,' said the little boy, beginning
to pedal again. ' But I did hoot. I hoot at every
corner. Like this.'

Parp-parp went the hooter and the five children
watched the little boy pedal swiftly down the pavement, then cross the road, and disappear into the
gate of Kosy-Kot.

' I feel like saying " Gah ! " ' said poor Fatty.
' Wasting our time looking for a hooter that's on a
child's tricycle—and getting my foot run over ! '

' Never mind,' said Bets consolingly. ' You'll
be able *really* to limp this afternoon, when you're
the old man again.'

They all went back to Pip's. It didn't seem any
use trying to find the owner of the other hooter.
They couldn't possibly go round looking at every
one in Peterswood to see who had odd eyes. It was
very disappointing about the tricycle.

' I think this is a very *slow* sort of mystery,' said
Bets. ' It will be time to go back to school again
before we've even *begun* to solve it ! '

' What's the date ? ' said Pip. ' Let me see—it
must be the seventh of September—no, the eighth.
Gracious, we really haven't much more time ! '

' Perhaps something will happen soon,' said
Larry hopefully. ' You know how sometimes
things sort of boil up and get terribly exciting all
of a sudden.'

' Well, it's time this one did,' said Fatty. ' It's
been in the refrigerator long enough ! '

Every one laughed. ' I wouldn't mind sitting in
a frig myself,' said Daisy. ' Let's get our bathing
things and go and bathe in the river. I'm so awfully
hot.'

So down to the river they went, and were soon splashing about happily. Fatty, of course, was a very fine swimmer, and could swim right across the river and back. Bets splashed happily in the shallow water. The others swam about lazily just out of their depth.

Bets thought she would swim out to them. So off she went, striking out valiantly. She didn't see a punt coming smoothly through the water, and before she could save herself, she felt a sharp blow on her shoulder, and screamed.

The punt slid on, unable to stop, but a boat following behind, swung round, and a man caught hold of her and held her.

' You're all right, aren't you ? ' he said, bending over her. ' Can you swim ? '

' Yes,' gasped Bets, striking out again. ' Fatty ! Fatty ! Come here quickly ! '

The others swam over to the frightened little girl. They helped her to the shore and she gazed after the distant boat, and gulped.

' Oh,' she said, ' oh, I've missed the most wonderful Clue ! But I couldn't help it ! Oh, Fatty, the man in that boat had odd eyes—one blue and one brown. I couldn't help noticing them when he caught hold of my shoulder. And now the boat is gone—and I never even noticed its name ! '

' Oh, *Bets* ! ' said every one, and Bets looked ready to cry. ' Didn't you notice what colour it was, or anything ? ' asked Larry.

Bets shook her head. ' No—I suppose I was too frightened. Oh, I'm so sorry. It was such a wonderful Clue—and a Suspect, too—and I've lost them both ! '

THAT afternoon things really began to happen. Fatty disguised himself once more as the old man (who was keeping remarkably well out of the way), and went to the bench in the village street as usual. He limped most realistically this time, because his foot had swollen up from being run over by the tricycle.

He had provided himself with plenty of news-papers to read, and he sat down as carefully as ever, letting out a little groan as he did so.

In the sweet-shop opposite sat Mr. Goon, clad as usual in flannel trousers and a cream shirt open at the neck. He looked extremely hot, and was beginning to long for some bad weather—frost and snow if possible! Mr. Goon had never felt so hot in his life as in this blazing summer.

Larry went into the shop and sat down to order lemonade. Mr. Goon was getting used to the fact that one or other of the Find-Outers always seemed to be there. He took no notice of Larry. He just propped his paper up in front of him, and kept a watchful eye on the old fellow nodding on the bench across the street.

It looked as if Fatty had gone sound asleep. Larry yawned and wished he could go to sleep too. Then he noticed something. A man was standing in the shady doorway of a near-by shop, and he seemed to be watching the old man. Was he thinking of giving him a message?

Mr. Goon also spotted the man, and sat up

straight. The man looked up and down the street, and lighted a cigarette, puffing hard at it.

The village was empty and deserted on this hot afternoon. A car drove by and disappeared. A dog ambled round a corner, lay down, and fell asleep. Larry and Mr. Goon watched the silent man breathlessly.

The man sauntered across the road and stood for a few minutes looking in the window of a wireless shop. Then he strolled over to the bench and sat down near the old man.

Fatty was pretending to be asleep, but he spotted the man out of the corner of his eye, and something told him that the man was no chance companion. He was there for a purpose. Fatty jerked himself upright as if he had suddenly awakened, and sniffled loudly. He wiped his nose with his sleeve and then leaned over his stick again. Then he coughed his dreadful cough.

' Awful cough you've got ! ' said the man. Fatty took no notice, remembering that he was deaf. He coughed again.

' AWFUL COUGH YOU'VE GOT ! ' repeated the man. Fatty turned, put his hand behind his ear and croaked out a familiar word, ' Wassat ? '

The stranger laughed. He took out his cigarette case and offered the old man a cigarette. There was only one left in the case. As soon as Fatty had taken it, the man filled his case from a packet.

' Thank you, sir,' croaked Fatty, and put the cigarette into his pocket. His heart beat fast. He felt sure that there must be some kind of message in the cigarette. What would it be ? He did not dare to look closely at the man, but hoped that Larry was taking note of all his clothes and everything.

Larry was. And so was Mr. Goon! Both were mentally repeating the same things. ' Grey flannel suit. Blue shirt. Black shoes. No tie. Grey felt hat. Moustache. Tall. Slim. Long nose. Small eyes.'

The man got up to go. He disappeared quite quickly round a corner. Fatty thought that he, too, had better disappear quickly, before Mr. Goon could get hold of him and get the cigarette-message, whatever it was, away from him. So he, too, got up, and with most surprising agility in such an old man, he shot round another corner.

And then he saw something most aggravating! Coming towards him was the *real* old man, corduroy trousers, dirty muffler and all! He was out for a walk, though he did not mean to go and sit on the bench.

Fatty could not risk being seen by the old man, for he guessed he would be amazed and alarmed at the sight of his double. So he popped into the nearest gate and hid himself under a bush.

He was only just in time! Mr. Goon came round the corner with a rush—and almost bumped into the real old man! He clutched him tightly.

' Ha! Got you! Now you give me that cigarette right away! '

The old man looked most alarmed. He shrank away from the red-faced Mr. Goon, not in the least knowing who he was, for he did not recognize the policeman dressed in plain clothes.

' Where's that cigarette? ' panted Mr. Goon.

' Wassat? ' croaked the old man. Goon heard footsteps behind him and saw Larry. Larry was horrified to see what he thought was Fatty in the clutches of the policeman. He stayed nearby to see

what was going to happen. The old man tried
feebly to get away from Goon, but the policeman
held on grimly.

' You let go,' said the old fellow. ' I'll get the
police, see ?   Catching hold of me like this !   I'll
get the police ! '

' It's the police that have got *you*,' said Goon,
shaking him.   ' I'm GOON ! GOON the POLICE-
MAN ! And I want that CIGARETTE ! '

This was too much for the poor old man.   He
almost fell down in fright.   He hadn't the faintest
idea what Goon wanted him for, nor did he know
why Goon kept on shouting for a cigarette.

' Have my pipe,' said the old fellow, trying to
get it out of his pocket.   ' Have my pipe and let me
go.   I ain't done nothing.'

Mr. Goon snorted, caught hold of the old fellow
by the collar of his coat and marched him down the
street.   ' You can come to the police-station with
me,' he said.   ' And I'll search you there and get
that cigarette !   See ! '

Larry watched them go, feeling rather scared,
for he still thought it was Fatty that Mr. Goon had
got.   He had the fright of his life when he suddenly
saw another old man peering out from under a bush
at him !

' Larry !   Have they gone ? ' said this old man,
in Fatty's voice.   Larry almost jumped out of his
skin.

' *Fatty !*   I thought it was *you* that Goon was
taking away !   Golly, I'm glad it wasn't.'

Fatty came out from under the bush.   ' The
real old man happened to come walking up here
just as I was hurrying to get away from Goon ! '
said Fatty, with a grin.   ' So I hopped in at this
gate and hid, and Goon grabbed the old fellow and

ordered him to give up the cigarette he hadn't got
Phew ! That was a jolly narrow shave ! '

' Fatty ! Is there a message in that cigarette ? '
said Larry eagerly. ' Can we find out ? I saw that
fellow give you one. I watched him for a long time.
So did Goon.'

' Let's go to Pip's,' said Fatty. ' We're safer
there than anywhere, because his garden is so big.
Don't walk with me. Go in front, and when you
come to a corner, whistle if you want to warn
me.'

Larry walked on in front. He did not whistle
at any of the corners, because there seemed to be
nobody about in Peterswood at all that hot September afternoon. In ten minutes Fatty was safely
in Pip's summer-house. He did not strip off his
old clothes, because he had no others to change into.
He waited there whilst Larry went off to collect
the others, and he hoped that no grown-ups would
think of poking their noses into the summer-house
that afternoon. They would not be pleased to find
a dirty old tramp there !

Fatty longed to examine the cigarette and see
what was inside it. But he waited patiently till the
others came tearing up the path, pouring into the
little summer-house with excited faces.

' Fatty ! Larry's told us all about it ! What's
the message ? Is there one in the cigarette ? Have
you looked ? '

' Of course not. I waited for you all,' said Fatty.
He took the cigarette from his pocket. It was rather
a stout, fat one. It had tobacco at each end—but
when Fatty had scraped out as much tobacco as he
could, he found that the middle of the cigarette
was not made of tobacco at all—but was stuffed with
a tight roll of paper !

' Oh ! ' said Bets, almost too excited to breathe.
' A secret message !  Oh, Fatty ! '

Fatty unrolled the paper.  He flattened it with
his hand.  The five of them leaned over it, their
breaths hot against one another's cheeks.  Buster
tried in vain to see what all the excitement was about,
but for once in a way nobody took the slightest
notice of him !

The message proved to be very puzzling and
disappointing.  All it said was :

> ' One tin black boot-polish.
> One pound rice.
> One pound tea.
> Two pounds syrup.
> One bag flour.'

' Why !  It's only a grocery list ! ' said Daisy.
' Just like Mother often gives me and Larry when we
go shopping for her.  Whatever does it mean,
Fatty ? '

' I don't know,' said Fatty.  ' It must mean
something.  I hope it's not in a secret code.'

' What's a secret code ? ' asked Bets.

' Oh, a way of writing messages so that only the
persons receiving them know what they mean,' said
Fatty.  ' But somehow I don't think this is a code.
After all, that old man had got to read it and understand it, and I'm quite sure he hasn't brains enough
to understand a code.'

' Then could there be another message, but
written in secret ink ? ' said Pip suddenly.  ' You
know how you taught us to write secret messages,
in between the lines of an ordinary letter, don't
you, Fatty ?  Well, could there be a message written
between these lines, in secret ink ? '

'Yes, there could,' said Fatty. 'And that's what I think we shall find! Good for you, Pip. Can you go and get a warm iron? If we run it over the paper, the secret message will show up.'

Pip ran off. Gladys was actually ironing in the kitchen, and though she was very surprised to think that Pip should want to borrow the warm iron to take into the garden for a minute, she let him. He came tearing up to the summer-house with it in his hand.

'I've got it!' he said. 'Here you are. Put the paper out flat on the wooden table. That's right. Now I'll run the iron over it.'

He ran the warm iron over the spread-out bit of paper. Then he lifted it off and looked at the message. 'There's another one coming up, look—between the lines of the other!' squealed Daisy, in excitement. 'Iron it again, Pip, quick! Oh, this is too thrilling for words!'

Pip ironed the paper again—and this time another message showed up very clearly indeed. The words came up, looking a queer grey-brown colour, and began to fade almost as soon as the children had made them out.

'Tell Number 3. Waxworks, Tuesday,
nine p.m.—Number 5.'

'Golly!' said Pip. 'Look at that! Tell Number 3—that must be one of the gang. And Number 5 must be another.'

'Waxworks, Tuesday, nine p.m.' said Fatty, and his eyes gleamed. 'So that's one of their meeting-places. Down in the Waxworks Hall, where all those figures are. *Now* we know something!'

' We really do,' said Bets. ' What are they meeting about, Fatty ? '

' I don't know—but I shall find out,' said Fatty. ' Because—I shall be there on Tuesday night ! '

THE children were full of excitement when they heard Fatty say this. 'What! Go down to the Waxworks, and attend the gang meeting!' said Larry. 'You wouldn't dare! You'd be discovered, however well you hid yourself!'

'It's the only way of finding out who all the gang are,' said Fatty. 'I shall see them, hear them talk and plan—my word, this *is* a bit of luck!'

'No wonder Goon wanted to get hold of that cigarette from the old man,' said Daisy. 'He would give anything to have this message!'

'He'll wonder what the old chap's done with it!' said Fatty, with a grin. 'He'll have searched him from top to toe—but he won't have found that cigarette!'

They talked excitedly for some time and then Fatty said he really must go home and get out of his hot, smelly old-man clothes. The others walked down to the gate with him, leaving an angry Buster tied up in the summer-house.

Meanwhile Mr. Goon had had a most disappointing time. He had found no cigarette at all on the old man. He was angry and puzzled, and he shouted at the old fellow, getting redder and redder in the face.

'You can stay here till you tell me what you did with that cigarette, see?' he yelled. 'I'll lock you up till you do. Now then—are you going to tell me?'

The old chap had turned sulky. He knew nothing

of any cigarette, he hadn't been sitting on the bench,
he didn't know what the bad-tempered policeman
was talking about. So he sulked and said nothing
at all, which made Goon madder than ever.

'Right!' said Goon at last, getting up. 'I'll
talk to you some more to-morrow.'

He went home and changed into his uniform.
Then he decided to go and see 'that boy Larry'
and ask him if he, too, had noticed the man giving
the old fellow a cigarette that afternoon. Mr. Goon
couldn't help being puzzled by the old chap's firm
denials of any knowledge of a cigarette. But Larry
must have seen the gift, and would bear witness
to it.

But Larry was out. 'Try at the Hilton's,'
said Larry's mother. 'Oh, I do hope the children
haven't been misbehaving themselves, Mr. Goon.'

'Er, no—for a wonder, no, Mam,' said Mr. Goon,
and went off majestically.

He arrived at Pip's just as the children were
escorting Fatty, still disguised as the old man, out of
the front gate. Fatty stared at Goon, and Goon
stared back disbelievingly. What! Hadn't he
just locked that old man up? And here he was
again, free, and walking about! Mr. Goon began to
feel as if he was in a peculiarly unpleasant dream.

'Er—good evening, Mr. Goon,' said Larry.
Mr. Goon took no notice of him.

'Here, you!' he said, grabbing at Fatty's arm.
'How did you get out? Haven't I just locked you
up? What are things a-coming to, I'd like to know!
Here I've just locked you up and I meet you walking
into me, bold as brass!'

Mr. Goon looked so amazed and disbelieving
that Fatty badly wanted to laugh. He was at a loss
to know what to say.

'Wassat ?' he said at last, putting his hand behind his ear.

That was too much for Mr. Goon. He caught hold of Fatty's collar and marched him quickly up the lane.

'You've been 'wassating' me long enough!' said the annoyed Mr. Goon. 'I don't know how you got out—but I do know you're going in again— and this time I'll lock the door on you meself!' And there you'll stay till you see sense if it takes you a month!'

Fatty didn't like this at all. He debated whether or not to let Mr. Goon into the secret of his disguise. But before he had made up his mind, he was at the police-station. Mr. Goon was unlocking a door, and Fatty was being pushed into the dark, narrow little room behind.

And in it was the real old man! He stared at Fatty and Fatty stared at him. The old chap let out a howl. He was beginning to feel he must be mad. Why, here was himself staring at him! What was happening ?

Mr. Goon heard the howl and looked into the room—and then he saw the *two* old men! Exactly alike. As like as peas in a pod. Mr. Goon sat down heavily on a chair and mopped his forehead with a big handkerchief. He felt dazed. What with vanishing cigarettes, men that got locked up and then got out—and now two old men exactly alike— well, Mr. Goon began to feel that he must be lying asleep and dreaming in his own bed at home, and he fervently hoped that he would soon wake up.

'Lemme get out of here!' said the real old man, and tried to push past Mr. Goon. But the policeman caught hold of him. He wasn't going to have any more disappearings. He was Going to Get to the Bottom of Things.

Fatty saw that things had gone far enough, and he did not like the thought of his parents knowing that he was locked up at the police-station. So he spoke to Mr. Goon in his ordinary voice, and gave that poor man another terrible shock.

' Mr. Goon ! I'm not really an old man. I'm Frederick Trotteville.'

Mr. Goon's mouth fell open. He gulped once or twice, staring at Fatty as if he couldn't believe his eyes. Fatty twitched off his beard, and then Mr. Goon did indeed see that it was Fatty. He dragged him out of the dark little room, slammed and locked the door, and took Fatty into an office.

' Now you just tell me the meaning of all this here ! ' he said.

' Well,' said Fatty, ' it's a long story, but I'll tell you everything, Mr. Goon,' and he launched into the tale of all that the Find-Outers had done, and how he had disguised himself as the old man, and sat there to trap a message from the gang.

' What about that cigarette ? ' said Mr. Goon when he had got his breath back a bit. ' What about that ? That's a most important thing ! '

' Is it really ? ' said Fatty, in pretended surprise. ' Well, we undid the cigarette, of course, Mr. Goon, and inside we found nothing of importance at all, really—just a silly grocery list. We were terribly disappointed.'

Fatty did not mean to tell Mr. Goon what he and the others had discovered in the message—the few lines in secret ink. No, he would keep that to himself, and go to the meeting on Tuesday night, and see what he could find out. *He* wanted to solve the Mystery, he, Fatty, the chief of the Find-Outers.

He did not stop to think whether it was dangerous or not.

Mr. Goon grabbed hold of the message. He spread it out. He frowned. He read it through two or three times. 'Must be a code,' he said. 'I'll look up my code-book. You leave this to me.'

' Er—well—I'll be going now,' said Fatty, after watching Mr. Goon frowning at the list of groceries for a few minutes.

' If you hadn't given me this here bit of paper, I'd have locked you up,' said Mr. Goon. 'Interfering with the Law. That's what you're always doing, you five kids. Ho, yes, I know you think you've got a fine friend in Inspector Jenks, but one of these days you'll find he's fed up with you, see ? And I'll get my promotion and be a Big Noise, and then just you look out ! '

' Oh, I *will* look out,' said Fatty earnestly. ' Thanks for warning me, Mr. Goon. Er—what about that old fellow ? Are you still going to keep him locked up ? '

' Yes, I am,' said Mr. Goon. 'And your own common sense will tell you why—that's always supposing you've got any, which I very much doubt —I don't want him warning the gang that I'm on their track. If he's here, under my nose, he can't do much warning.'

' I think you're quite right, Mr. Goon,' said Fatty solemnly. ' I couldn't agree with you more. I think——'

' I'm tired of you,' said Mr. Goon. 'You clear-orf double-quick, before I change my mind about locking you up. I'm Right Down Tired of you. Messing about—interfering—dressing up— Gah ! '

Fatty scuttled off. He went home and quickly

changed out of his old-man clothes, and then shot up to Pip's to tell every one what had happened.

'I had to give him the cigarette message, worse luck,' he said. 'It was the only thing to keep him quiet. But I don't believe he'll make head or tail of it, and I bet he won't test it for a secret message as we did. You should have seen his face when he pushed me into the same room as the real old man, and saw two of us there! I thought he would go up in smoke!'

The others roared. They were most relieved to see Fatty back safe and sound. Bets had been imagining him locked up in a dreary cell, with only bread and water.

'He's keeping the old man under his eye for a few days,' said Fatty, 'in case he gets the wind up about all this, and warns the other members of the gang. I'm pleased he's doing that. I expect the Meeting will wonder why Number 3 doesn't turn up on Tuesday, whoever he is. Well, they'll have to wonder!'

'I think it's awfully dangerous for you to go down to the Waxworks on Tuesday,' said Daisy. 'I do, really. I think you ought to go and tell the Inspector about it, Fatty.'

'Oh no,' said Fatty. 'I want us to solve this Mystery before we see the Inspector again. I shall be quite safe.'

'I don't see how you can say that,' said Larry, who agreed with Daisy that it might be dangerous. 'The men will surely not be fools enough to hold their Meeting without being certain there's no spy there.'

'They won't discover *me*,' said Fatty. 'I shall wear a disguise!'

'I don't see how that will help you,' said Larry.

' Even if you are in disguise, you'll be a stranger
to the men, and they'll want to know who you
are.'

' I shan't be a stranger to them,' said Fatty,
exasperatingly. ' Nor to you, either.'

The others stared at him. ' What do you
mean ? ' said Pip at last. ' What are you getting
at ? '

' I shall be somebody the gang have seen often
enough before, if they have held their other meetings
in the Waxworks Hall. They'll know me so well
they won't even look at me ! '

' What do you *mean* ? ' said Daisy, getting
annoyed. ' Don't talk in these silly riddles.'

' Well,' said Fatty, and he lowered his voice to
a mysterious whisper, ' well—I shall be disguised as
one of the waxworks, silly ! Napoleon, I think,
because I'm pretty plump, and so was he ! '

There was a complete silence. All the Find-
Outers stared at Fatty in the greatest admiration.
What an idea ! No member of the gang would
suspect any of the waxwork figures ! Bets could
just imagine Fatty standing stiff and straight as
the waxwork Napoleon, staring fixedly in front of
him—seeing and hearing everything.

' What a really marvellous idea ! ' said Larry, at
last. ' Oh, Fatty—I should never have thought of
that if I'd thought for a month. You'll be right in
the lions' den—and they won't even *smell* you ! '

' It *is* rather a good idea, isn't it ? ' said Fatty,
swelling up a little. ' That's one thing about me,
you know—I've always got plenty of ideas. My
form-master said only last term that my imagination
was . . .'

But the others didn't in the least want to hear
what Fatty's form-master had said. They wanted

to talk about Tuesday night and what Fatty was going to do.

Tuesday night! Bets thrilled every time she thought of it. This Mystery was really getting too exciting for words. Oooh—Tuesday night!

THAT week-end dragged along very slowly indeed. Tuesday was such a long time in coming ! The only thing that enlivened it at all was that on the two or three occasions when the children met Mr. Goon, Fatty had his hooter tucked under his coat, and sounded it as soon as they had passed the policeman.

This made him jump, and he looked round in hope of seeing the cyclist who had once stopped and spoken to the old man. But he never did, of course. He hailed the children suspiciously the third time it happened.

' Did you hear that hooter ? ' he asked. They all nodded vigorously.

' Did you see a bike going by then ? ' said the policeman.

' A bike ? All by itself with a hooter ? ' asked Pip, and the others grinned.

' Gah ! ' said Mr. Goon, enraged as usual. ' You clear-orf ! I wouldn't put it past you to carry one of them hooters about, just to annoy me, like ! '

' He's getting quite bright, isn't he ? ' said Larry, as they walked off. ' I shouldn't be surprised if he does get promotion one of these days. He's really trying to use those brains of his a bit. We'd better not hoot any more when we pass him. He's quite likely to go and complain about us if we do— and ever since he went up to my house and asked for me the other day, Mother's been warning me not to get into trouble.'

Fatty was preparing himself very earnestly for Tuesday night. He knew how important it was, and he also knew that, unless all his details were absolutely perfect, he might be in considerable danger.

He and the others spent a long time in the Waxworks, much to the surprise of the red-headed boy, for it was very hot in there, and not many people visited the little hall these blazing days.

But Fatty had to study the figure of Napoleon very carefully indeed. He meant to get into the hall somehow on Tuesday evening, and dress himself up in Napoleon's clothes. Would they fit him? He asked Daisy what she thought.

'Yes, I should think they'd fit you very well,' she said, considering first Napoleon and then Fatty. 'You had better take a few safety-pins in case something doesn't quite meet. The hat will be fine—just your size, I should think. What about hair, Fatty?'

'I can manage that all right,' said Fatty. 'I rather think my own will do, if I smarm it down a bit, and pull a few pieces out in front, like old Napoleon has got. And, er—I don't know what you think—but—er—I'm not really *unlike* Napoleon in features, am I?'

The others stared at him. 'Well,' said Pip honestly, 'I can't see any likeness at *all*. Not the slightest.'

'Except that you're both fat,' said Daisy.

'Do you *want* to look like Napoleon?' said Bets in surprise. 'I don't think he looks very nice, really. And I don't like those men that go about thinking they want to conquer the whole world. Napoleon must have been very brainy, of course, and *you're* brainy, Fatty. But, except that you're fat and brainy, I don't see that you're very like Napoleon.'

Fatty gave it up. He stared once more at the figure of Napoleon, in its grand uniform, cocked hat, medals, epaulettes, and stars. It was a fine uniform and Fatty was longing to get into it. Well, he hadn't got long to wait now.

He tried to memorize exactly at what angle Napoleon wore his hat, exactly how he held his hands, exactly how he stared so blankly in front of him. Napoleon fortunately stood in the very front row of figures, so Fatty, as Napoleon, would be able to hear and see everything very well indeed. A little shiver went down his back when he thought of standing there, perfectly still, listening to the plans of the gang, and memorizing their appearance.

It was a very bold idea indeed. Not one of the other Find-Outers would have dared to do it. But Fatty, of course, would dare anything. Bets thought that he wouldn't even turn a hair if he met a roaring lion, the kind she met in her bad dreams, and which scared her terribly. Fatty would probably speak to it kindly and pat it, and the lion would lie down and roll over for Fatty to tickle it on its tummy—like Buster did !

The red-headed boy, curious at their sudden intense interest in Napoleon, came over and joined them.

' What's exciting you about *him* ? ' he said. ' Who is he ? Oh—Napoleon. What was he ? Some sort of soldier ? '

' Don't you *know* ? ' said Bets, in astonishment. ' Didn't you learn history at school ? '

' I've never been to school,' said the red-headed boy. ' I belong to the Fair, and us kids hardly ever go to school unless we have to. We move about from place to place, you see, and before we're popped into some school, we've moved on again. I can read, but I can't write.'

' Why are you in the Waxwork Show ? ' asked Fatty. ' Does this hall belong to the Fair people ? '

' Oh no—they've only hired it,' said the boy. ' The Waxworks belong to my uncle. He's the fellow that runs the Hoopla. I used to help him with that, but now I have to do the Waxworks, and it's jolly dull.'

Fatty wondered if any of the Fair people were in the gang of thieves. It seemed very likely. Well, he would know on Tuesday night.

The children went and studied other figures carefully too, so that the red-headed boy wouldn't get suspicious about their sudden interest in Napoleon. They had a good look at the wax figure of the policeman as well. He really did look a bit like Mr. Goon ! There he stood, on the second step, not far from Napoleon, his helmet on perfectly straight, the strap round the chin, and the belt a little tight.

The red-headed boy disappeared out-of-doors for a minute. Fatty at once went back to Napoleon and studied the clothes well, to make sure that he could take them off the wax figure fairly easily.

' Hope they're not *stuck* on in any way,' he said to the others anxiously. Daisy pulled at them.

' Oh no,' she said. ' They are put on just like ours—and look, the trousers are held up by braces. You'll be all right, Fatty. But you'll have to be here long before nine, or you'll never have time to undress yourself *and* Napoleon and then dress yourself up again.'

' I wish you wouldn't, really, Fatty,' said Bets, looking up at him with scared eyes. ' I shall hate

*Fatty examined Napoleon very carefully*

to think of you standing so near the gang—whatever would they do to you if they discovered you ? '

' They won't,' said Fatty. ' I shan't give myself away, you may be sure of that. I've already been practising standing still for ages, in my bedroom, in exactly that position. Buster simply can't understand it. He does all he can to make me move ! '

The others laughed. They could quite well picture Fatty standing solemnly in his room, perfectly still, with a most astonished Buster trying in vain to get a movement or a sound out of him !

' Come on—let's go now,' said Fatty. ' It's most frightfully hot in here. Hallo—there's Goon —and in uniform again ! He looks better in uniform than in plain clothes, I must say. Not that he's much to look at in either ! '

Mr. Goon was standing just outside the Waxworks Hall, apparently about to go in. He scowled when he saw the children. Funny how those kids always seemed to turn up everywhere !

' What you doing here ? ' he asked, in a suspicious voice.

' Passing the time away, Mr. Goon, just passing the time,' said Fatty airily. ' What are *you* doing here ? Is your holiday over ? You must miss your little trips to the sweet-shop.'

Buster was on the lead, or he would certainly have darted at his enemy. But Fatty, seeing the black look on Mr. Goon's face, hastily dragged him away.

' Wonder what he's done with that grocery list ! ' said Daisy, with a giggle. ' Put it with his Clues, I expect. Well, we know more about that than he does ! '

Bets wanted to go down by the river, so the others went, too, meaning to walk home by the

river-path.  Bets stared hard at every one in boats,
and Pip noticed her.

'Why ever are you glaring at every one who's in
a boat?' he asked.

'I'm not glaring,' said Bets.  'I'm just looking
to see if I can spot any one with odd eyes, that's all.
I did see the odd-eyed man in a boat, you know,
when that punt knocked against me—and I might
quite well see him again.

'What would you do if you did?' demanded
Pip.  'Jump in and arrest him?'

'It's quite a good idea of Bets,' said Fatty,
always quick to defend the little girl.  'After all, if
the man was in a boat once, he might be again.
And if we saw him on the river we could get the
name of the boat, and, if it was privately owned,
we could find out the name of the owner.'

'The only thing is—people go by so quickly
that it's difficult to see if their eyes are odd or not,'
said Bets.

'I say, Fatty, how are you going to get your
face all pink like Napoleon's?' asked Larry, looking
at Fatty's very brown face.

'Easy,' said Fatty.  'I shall put a little layer of
pink wax all over my face and let it set.  I know
how to do it.  It's in a book I've got.'

Fatty had the most extraordinary collection of
books.  He seemed to be able to find out from them
anything he wanted.

'You'll have to do that before you set out, won't
you?' said Daisy.  Fatty nodded.

'Yes.  Larry will have to go with me if the night
isn't dark enough to hide me, and warn me if any
one is coming who might be likely to spot me.  But
now that there's no moon, I ought not to be
noticed much in the twilight.'

' I do want Tuesday to come!' said Bets. ' I really can hardly wait! I wish I was going to see you all dressed up as Napoleon, Fatty. You'll look simply grand. Oh, Tuesday, hurry up and come!'

TUESDAY night did come at last. For once in a
way it was a cloudy night, and it almost looked as
if the longed-for rain was coming. It was a little
cooler, and every one was thankful.

' How are you going to manage about your
father and mother to-night ? ' asked Pip. ' I mean
—you want to set off about 7.30, don't you ? And
that's the time you have dinner with them.'

' They're away for a couple of nights,' said
Fatty. ' Bit of luck, that. Larry, you come to
dinner with me, and we'll have it at seven, together.
Then you can walk down with me to the Hall, to
make sure no one will see me.'

' Right,' said Larry. ' I will. Wish I was going
to come into the Hall with you, too, and see everything. Will you come back and tell us what's
happened, Fatty, even if it's awfully late ? I'll
keep awake.'

' All right. But I'd better not go to Pip's,' said
Fatty. ' Mrs. Hilton is sure to hear me if I call up
to Pip. Her room is just nearby.'

' Oh, *Fatty* ! We can't possibly wait till the
morning ! ' cried Bets.

' You'll have to,' said Fatty. ' I can't go round
to you all and tell you what's happened. Anyway,
you'll be fast asleep, little Bets ! '

' I shan't. I shan't sleep a wink all night,'
said Bets.

The day dragged by very slowly. At half-past
six Fatty left Pip's, with Larry, and the two of them

went to Fatty's house. They were to have dinner early, at seven—then their adventure would begin. All the children felt excited, but only Fatty did not show it. He appeared to be as calm as ever.

The two boys made a very good meal indeed. Then Fatty put the pink stuff on his face and after that they set out to go down to the river. They meant to take the path over the fields, then go by the water-side, and so come to the Fair without meeting a lot of people.

They arrived at the Waxworks Hall. ' How are you going to get in ? ' whispered Larry, suddenly seeing that the place was shut and in darkness.

' Didn't you spot me undoing the catch of one of the windows when we were here this morning ? ' whispered Fatty. ' I'm going to get in there. I say—what about you coming in too, in case I get into difficulties over dressing ? You can easily hop out of the window afterwards.'

' Yes, I will,' said Larry, pleased at the idea of watching Fatty dress himself as Napoleon. ' Where's the window ? '

' It's this one,' said Fatty, and looked cautiously round. ' Anyone about ? Not a soul ! Here goes, then ! '

He opened the window quietly, hauled himself up and dropped down into the hall. Larry followed. The boys shut the window carefully, in case any one noticed that it was open.

The hall wasn't dark, because a lamp from the Fair nearby shone into it, and gave a faint and rather eerie light to the still waxworks.

The boys looked round them. The figures somehow seemed more alive than in the daytime, and Larry gave a little shiver. Silly fancies crept into his head. Suppose wax figures came alive at

night and walked and talked ! What a dreadful
shock it would give him and Fatty !

'They all seem to be looking at us,' whispered
Larry. 'They make me feel quite creepy. Look at
Nelson—he's watching us all the time ! '

'Idiot ! ' said Fatty, walking over to Napoleon.
' Come on—help me to undress him, Larry.'

It was a queer business, undressing the rather
plump figure of the wax Napoleon. It wasn't easy,
either, because Napoleon didn't help in any way !
In fact, it almost seemed as if he quite deliberately
tried to make things difficult for the two boys !

' If only he'd raise his arms a bit, or give a
wriggle, or something,' whispered Larry. ' We could
get his things off easily then. But he just makes
himself as stiff as possible ! '

Fatty chuckled. ' I'd get a shock if he *did* raise
his arms or wriggle ! ' he said. ' I'd just as soon he
didn't. There—his coat's off, thank goodness—
but I've torn his high collar a bit. Now for his
trousers.'

Soon poor Napoleon stood stiff and straight
in nothing but some kind of shapeless under-
garment. The boys lifted him up and carried him
to a cupboard. They put him inside and shut the
door. Then Fatty proceeded to undress himself
very quickly. He stuffed his own clothes into the
cupboard with Napoleon.

Then, with Larry's help he put on Napoleon's
clothes. They fitted him quite well, and he only
had to use one of Daisy's safety-pins. He pulled
on the coat, and the medals made a little jingling
noise.

' Fatty ! You look marvellous in that uniform ! '
said Larry, in admiration. ' You honestly do ! Now
the hat—golly, it fits as if it was made for you ! '

Fatty made Larry hold up a small mirror and looked at his face in it. It was all covered with pink, and looked very like the faces of the wax figures around. Fatty pulled a strand of hair on to his forehead, just like the one the wax Napoleon had had. Then he put his hand under his coat, stood absoutely still and stiff, and stared straight in front of him.

Larry couldn't find enough words of praise. ' Nobody, *nobody* could possibly guess you weren't a wax figure ! ' he said. ' You're marvellous, Fatty ! Honestly, you're more of a wax figure than Napoleon was before ! I wish you could see your-self, I really do. Golly, it's wonderful ! '

Fatty was pleased. He beamed modestly at Larry, but not too broadly in case the wax on his face cracked a bit.

' It's only your eyes that are different from the other wax figures,' said Larry. ' They've got a proper light in them—the others haven't. Yours shine.'

' Well, I hope they won't shine too much ! ' said Fatty. ' Now, you'd better go, Larry, old boy. It's about half-past eight, isn't it ? The men might be here early.'

' Right,' said Larry—and then he suddenly stood stock-still in fright. It sounded as if some one was fumbling at the door of the hall !

' Go, quickly ! ' said Fatty, in a whisper, and Larry fled, threading his way carefully between the silent figures till he came to the window at the back of the hall. He opened it cautiously, climbed up and dropped out, shutting it again at once. He dived under a bush and sat there, hardly daring to breathe, mopping his forehead with his handkerchief.

He pictured the gang walking in silently, and he

felt glad he was not Fatty, all alone there, hidden in the rows of waxwork figures.  Golly, he'd only got out just in time !

Fatty was waiting in the greatest excitement for the hall door to open.  Who would come in ?  The leader of the gang ?  All the men ?  Would he know any of them ?

The fumbling at the door went on.  Somebody seemed to be having difficulty with the key.  But at last it turned and the door opened quietly.  Somebody stepped in, and shut the door—and locked it !  Why lock it ?  Fatty was puzzled.  Weren't the others coming in too, then ?

The silent-footed person moved down the hall, and the light from the Fair lamp outside shone down on him.  Fatty got a most tremendous shock.

It was Mr. Goon !

' Goon ! ' thought Fatty, and he almost fell off his step.  ' Old Clear-Orf !  *Goon !*  But—is he one of the gang then ?  Goon here, with the thieves ! What's it all mean ? '

Mr. Goon proceeded to do a few very peculiar things.  He walked behind Fatty, until he came to one of the wax figures.  Fatty did not know which one, for he dared not move or turn round to see what Goon was doing.

Mr. Goon then lifted up the figure, and, panting noisily, carried it to a big window, where a voluminous curtain hung.  Then Fatty was able to see which figure Mr. Goon was carrying.

It was the wax policeman !  Mr. Goon carefully placed him behind the curtain, and then creaked back to the place where the wax figure had stood.

And, in a flash, Fatty understood everything. He almost groaned in disappointment.

' Of course—Goon has read the secret message

in that grocery list after all—he found out, as we did, that a meeting of the Gang will be held here to-night—and he got the same brain-wave too. He thought he'd come and be one of the wax figures, and listen in to everything! Golly—he's got more brains and pluck than I'd have thought he had!'

Poor Fatty! It was a great shock and dis-appointment to him to know that the policeman would hear everything, and be able to solve the Mystery after all. He would know the Gang—and their plans—and would be able to arrest the whole lot of them at once!

But surely he wouldn't dare to tackle the whole gang single-handed? No—that couldn't be his plan. Then what was it? Fatty stood and puzzled his brains, angry and miserable to think that Goon should have been clever enough to think of exactly the same idea as the Find-Outers.

'But it was much more difficult for *me*,' thought Fatty. 'I had to undress the figure of Napoleon and dress myself up again—Goon only had to go and stand in the place of the wax policeman. We always did think that that wax figure was like Goon! Blow! Everything's spoilt.'

Fatty would have given anything to turn round and see what Goon looked like, standing stiffly there some way behind him. Goon was breathing very heavily, as he always did when he was excited. Fatty wondered if he would remember to breathe quietly when the Gang came in! Then Goon did a little cough, and cleared his throat.

'Of course, he thinks there's nobody here at all,' thought Fatty. 'So it doesn't matter what noises he makes. I want to cough, myself—but I daren't, because Goon would be very suspicious at once. What a shock it would give him, to hear one of the waxworks cough. I wonder if he'd get scared and go flying out of the hall at once! No, I don't think he would!'

Mr. Goon shuffled his feet a little and sniffed. Then he got out his handkerchief and blew his nose.

Fatty immediately wanted to blow his too! It was most irritating wanting to sniff and cough and blow his nose when he dared not make a single movement. Fatty disliked Mr. Goon intensely at that moment. Spoiling everything! Enjoying himself sniffing and coughing. Waiting for his Big Moment—and thinking of Promotion!

There came the sound of voices outside. Then a key was put into the door, and it opened. 'Ho!' thought Fatty, 'Mr. Goon had a duplicate key, had he? He made his plans well. Locked the door after him, too, so that the men shouldn't get suspicious, as they would have if the door had been unlocked!'

Four men came in. Fatty strained his eyes to try and see what their faces were like. But one and all wore soft hats pulled well down over their foreheads. They did not light a lamp, nor did they even use torches. The faint light from the Fair lamp outside seemed to be enough for them.

They got chairs and sat down. They waited for a while, saying nothing. Fatty wondered why. Then he knew.

'Where's Number Three?' said one of the men impatiently. 'He ought to be here. Didn't you warn him, Number Five?'

'Yes, I sent him a message,' said another man. 'In a cigarette I gave to old Johnny. He'll turn up soon.'

They waited in silence again. One of the men pulled out a watch and looked at it.

'Can't wait any longer,' he said. 'The job's on to-night.'

'To-night?' said another man. 'Where? All of us in it this time, or not?'

'All of us,' said the first man. 'Except Number Three, as he's not here. It's the Castleton pearls to-night.'

'Whew!' said two of the men. 'Big stuff!'

'Very big,' said the first man. 'Now see here— these are the plans. You, Number Two, have got to drive the car, and you . . .'

Fatty and Mr. Goon watched and listened intently. Mr. Goon remembered not to breathe loudly, and as for Fatty, he was so excited that he hardly breathed at all. They heard all the details of the new robbery to be pulled off that night. But try as he would Fatty could not see clearly the face of any of the men at all.

He began to think hard. The men would soon be gone. Once they were gone he would get to the telephone and tell the Inspector all he knew—and the robbery could be stopped. Then he remembered Mr. Goon. Blow! Goon would be in charge of this, not Fatty.

Poor Mr. Goon was not feeling very happy just at that moment. He wanted to sneeze. He could feel it coming quite distinctly. He swallowed violently and wriggled his nose about. No—that sneeze meant to come. Whooosh-ooo!

IT wasn't a very big sneeze, because Mr. Goon had tried most valiantly to stop it, and it came out in quite a gentlemanly manner. But it was enough to startle all the men, and Fatty too, almost out of their skins !

The men sprang to their feet at once, and looked all round the hall. 'What was that ? There's somebody here ! Somebody spying on us ! '

Fatty was suddenly frightened. The men's eyes gleamed under their hats, and he could hear a savage tone in the voice of the man who spoke. The boy kept absolutely still. Silly, idiotic old Goon, to give the game away like that !

' There's somebody here ! Who is it ? Show yourself ! ' shouted one of the men. Neither Goon nor Fatty made any movement, and all the wax figures stared stolidly at the group of men.

' It's creepy in here, with all those figures looking at us,' said the first man. ' But one of them's real ! No doubt about that ! Come on—we'll soon find out. I've got a torch.'

Fatty's heart beat fast. He hoped and hoped that the men would find Goon before they found him. But most unfortunately Fatty was in the front row, and Goon wasn't.

One of the men had a powerful torch. He walked over to Nelson and flashed it in his face. Nelson stared unblinkingly in front of him. ' He's wax all right,' said the man, and passed to the next figure, a tall soldier. He flashed the torch in his face.

The soldier didn't make a movement at all.   It was obvious that he was wax, for there was a little crack down one cheek, where he had once struck his face, when being carried from one place to another.

One after another the wax figures had the torch flashed into their faces, and one after another they stared unblinkingly past the man's head.   Fatty began to tremble a little.   Would he be able to stare without blinking too ?   He hoped so.

His turn came.   The torch was flashed suddenly in his face, and the boy could not help a sudden blink.   His eyes did it automatically, although he did his best not to.   He hoped the man hadn't noticed.   But there was something about Fatty's bright, shining, living eyes that caught the man's attention at once, as well as the blink.   He grabbed at Fatty's arm, and felt it to be warm and soft.

' Here he is ! ' he said.   ' Here's the spy. Standing here staring at us, listening to everything ! '

Poor Fatty was dragged down off his step and pulled into the middle of the hall.   He was frightened, but he meant to put a bold face on it.

' Who are you ? ' said the first man, and shone his torch into Fatty's face.

' Napoleon,' said Fatty, trying to brave things out.   ' Just doing it for a joke ! '

' He's only a boy,' said one of the men, pulling off Napoleon's hat.   ' How old are you ? '

' Fourteen,' said Fatty.

The men stared at him.   ' What are we going to do with him ? ' said one.   ' Can't take him off in the car with us—too risky.   And we can't waste time dumping him anywhere, because if we're not on time with this job, we'll fail.   What he wants is a

jolly good questioning and a good thrashing, and
he'll get it—but not now.  It's time we went.'

'We'll be back here again to-night with the
stuff,' said another man.  'We'll tie him up, gag
him, put him into the cupboard over there, and
lock him in.  He can't give the game away then.
We'll deal with him when we come back.  He
can't know anything about the job to-night, except
what he's just heard, so he won't have warned
any one.'

'Right,' said the other men, and then began
a bad time for poor Fatty.  He was rolled up
in a curtain, with his hands and feet tied, and
a big handkerchief was bound across his mouth.
Then he was popped into the cupboard with
Napoleon, and the door was shut and locked on
him.

His only comfort was that Mr. Goon was still
there, posing stolidly, quite unsuspected.  As soon
as the men had got away, Goon would surely come
to his rescue and untie him.  Then he, Fatty, would
be in at the last, after all.

He could hear nothing in the cupboard.  He
did not hear the men go out of the hall and lock
the door.  He did not see Goon wait on his step
for a few moments and then relax and give a deep
sigh.  Mr. Goon had had a most surprising and
unpleasant time himself from the moment he
had sneezed to the moment the men had at last
gone.

When he had sneezed, he had felt certain that
the men would search the figures and find him.  He
had no idea at all, of course, that Fatty had been
one of the figures too.  When the boy had been
found and hauled off his stand, Mr. Goon's eyes
had almost fallen out of his head.  What—somebody

else in the hall—somebody who must have been there when Mr. Goon himself had come in and changed places with the wax policeman? Who was it!

Mr. Goon recognised Fatty's voice as soon as the boy had spoken. He went purple with rage. That interfering boy again! So he, like Goon himself, had read the secret message—and he hadn't told the police. The bad, wicked . . . well, words failed Mr. Goon as he stood there thinking about Fatty.

The policeman shook when he thought that the men would probably find him next. When they did not think of looking any further, his heart beat a little less fast. Well, serve that boy right, if he got caught! He deserved to! Keeping information from the police! Mr. Goon's face went red again.

He had been so very pleased with himself at thinking of this idea—posing as the wax policeman, and listening in to the gang and their plans. Well, he knew a lot now, he did—and if only those men would go off to the job and leave him alone, he'd soon do a spot of telephoning, and arrange to catch them all neatly—red-handed, too! Mr. Goon glowed when he thought of it.

But the men hadn't gone yet. They were tying up that fat boy—hadn't even given him a clip over the ear, as Mr. Goon would himself have very much liked to do. The policeman watched with pleased eyes the efficient way in which the men rolled Fatty up in the curtain, his hands and legs well and truly bound, and a handkerchief over his mouth. Ha! That was the way to treat people like Fatty!

Mr. Goon watched the men pop Fatty into the

cupboard and turn the key on him. Good! Now
that boy was properly out of the way. If only the
men would go, Mr. Goon could step down and get
busy. He smiled as he thought of how busy he
would get. Inspector Jenks would be surprised at
his news. Yes, and pleased, too.

The door closed and the men were gone. Mr.
Goon heard the sound of a car starting up. He
thought it would be safe to step down into the hall,
and he stood there, looking round, feeling extremely
pleased with himself.

Fatty was struggling hard in the cupboard. He
had read books that told him the best way to wriggle
free of bonds, but, except that he had managed to
get his mouth away from the handkerchief, he wasn't
having much luck with his hands and feet! He
did all the things the books had advised him to,
but it was no good. He couldn't get his hands
free.

In his struggles, he fell against Napoleon, and
that gentleman over-balanced, and struck his head
against the back of the cupboard. He then rolled
on to Fatty, who yelled.

Mr. Goon, about to open the door and go out,
heard the yell. He paused. He didn't mean to
set Fatty free. Not he! That boy had got what
he deserved, at last, and he, Mr. Goon, wasn't
going to rob him of it. No—let him stay in the
cupboard and think about things. Maybe he'd
think it was best not to interfere with the Law
again.

But when Napoleon fell with such a crash, Mr.
Goon felt a stirring of his conscience. Suppose that
boy was being suffocated? Suppose that handkerchief stopped his breathing? Suppose he'd
wriggled about, and fallen and hurt himself? He

was a friend of the Inspector's, wasn't he, though
goodness knew why the Inspector should bother
himself with a boy like that. Still. . . .

Mr. Goon thought he might spare half a minute
to investigate. But he wasn't going to unlock that
cupboard. No, not he! He wasn't going to have
that there boy rushing out on him, all untied, and
playing some more of his tricks. No, Fatty was
safer locked up in a cupboard.

So Mr. Goon went cautiously to the cupboard
and knocked smartly on the door. Fatty's struggles
ceased at once.

'Who's that?'

'Mr. Goon,' said the policeman.

'Thank goodness!' said Fatty fervently. 'Unlock the door and untie me, Mr. Goon. We've
work to do! Have those men gone?'

Mr. Goon snorted. Did this fat boy really
think he was going to let him help him! After he
had deliberately not told him about that secret
message, too!

'You're all right in there,' said Mr. Goon, 'you
don't want to come messing about with thieves and
robbers, you don't!'

Fatty couldn't believe his ears. Did Mr. Goon
really mean he was going to leave him there, in
the cupboard, when all the fun was going on? He
wriggled about in agony at the thought, and spoke
beseechingly.

'Mr. Goon! Be a sport! Unlock the door and
let me out!'

'Why should I?' demanded Mr. Goon. 'Did
you tell me about that secret message? No, you
didn't. And I know your parents wouldn't want
you mixed up in this business to-night, see?
They'll thank me for leaving you here. I'll come

and get you later, when we've done all the arresting and everything.'

Fatty was desperate. To think of Goon doing it all, whilst he was shut up in this smelly cupboard !

'Mr. Goon ! Don't be mean. It was *your* sneeze gave the show away—and instead of catching *you*, they caught *me*. It's not fair.'

Mr. Goon laughed. It was rather a nasty laugh. Fatty's heart sank when he heard it. He knew then that the policeman meant to leave him where he was. He could make all kinds of excuses for it—that he hadn't time to free Fatty—that he meant to come back almost at once—anything would do. Blow Mr. Goon !

'Well—see you later,' said Mr. Goon, and he walked over to the door. Fatty groaned. Now he would have to stay in the cupboard till the fun was over. It was too bad. After all his fine plans, too ! What would Inspector Jenks say ? He would be very pleased with Goon, who certainly had used his brains in this Mystery, and worked hard on it.

Poor Fatty ! He lay in the cupboard in great discomfort, with rope biting into his wrists and ankles. It was all Goon's fault. What did he want to go and sneeze like that for, and give the game away ? He had come out of it very well himself—but he had messed everything up for poor old Fatty.

Suddenly Fatty heard a slight sound and he pricked his ears up. It sounded like the window opening. Was there somebody coming in ? Was one of the gang coming back ?

Then Fatty heard a low voice—a voice he knew very well indeed.

'Fatty ! Are you here anywhere ? Fatty !'

It was Larry ! Fatty's heart beat for joy and he struggled to a sitting position in the cupboard ' Larry ! I'm locked up in the cupboard where we put Napoleon ! Let me out ! Quick, let me out ! '

LARRY rushed over to the cupboard. The key was still in the lock. He turned it and the door opened. And there was poor Fatty, still wrapped up in the curtain.

'Fatty! What's happened?' cried Larry. 'Are you hurt?'

'Not a bit—except that my wrists and ankles are aching with the rope round them,' said Fatty. 'Got a knife, Larry? Cut the rope.'

Larry cut the ropes, and soon Fatty was unwrapping himself from the curtain. He tossed it into a corner with the cut ropes. He took off Napoleon's uniform, and put on his own clothes. Then he shut and locked the cupboard door.

'Oh Larry!' he said, 'wasn't I glad to hear your voice! But don't let's talk in here. Let's get back home, quick!'

'My people think I'm in bed,' said Larry. 'I'll come to your house, if you like. Your people won't be there, will they? Come on.'

'Right. We'll tell about everything when we get back,' said Fatty.

They made their way back over the fields as fast as they could, though poor Fatty's ankles were painfully swollen now, through being so tightly bound. They soon got to Fatty's house and let themselves in cautiously. They went up to his room and Fatty flung himself on the bed, rubbing his ankles ruefully.

'Larry! How did you manage to come back

and rescue me ? ' he asked. ' I'd have been there for hours, if you hadn't. That beast Goon wouldn't let me out. Now—you tell me your story first.'

' There isn't really anything to tell,' said Larry. ' I went back home and told Daisy all we'd done. And then, about half-past nine, when I was in bed, Pip turned up, and threw stones at my window.'

' Whatever for ? ' said Fatty.

' Well, Bets sent him,' said Larry. ' Pip said she was awfully upset, and wouldn't go to sleep, and kept crying and saying she knew you had got into danger. You know the silly feelings Bets gets sometimes. She's only a baby.'

' So Pip, thinking it would be fun to hear how you'd got on, dressing me up as Napoleon, told Bets he'd go round and see you,' said Fatty. ' It would make Bets feel better, and be a bit of excitement for old Pip. I see that—but what made you come along down to the Waxwork Hall ? '

' I don't exactly know,' said Larry. ' You know, once before Bets got the idea that you were in danger, and it turned out she was right. And I just thought—well, I thought it might be a good idea if I slipped down to the Waxwork Hall and just had a snoop round to see what was happening.'

' Golly ! I'm glad Bets had one of her feelings,' said Fatty thankfully. ' And I'm glad you came down, Larry, old boy.'

' So am I,' said Larry. ' When I got there, the Hall was in darkness and there was nobody about at all. So I opened that window, got in, and called your name. That's all.'

There was a silence. Fatty suddenly looked extremely gloomy. ' What's up ? ' said Larry.

You haven't told me what happened yet—or why you got locked up. Were you discovered after all ? '

Fatty began his tale. Larry listened in astonishment. So Goon had been there too ! When Fatty came to Goon's sneeze, and related how he, Fatty, had been caught because of it, and not Goon, Larry was most sympathetic.

' Poor old Fatty ! So Goon got all the information, left you there, the beast, and has gone to do the arresting and reporting. Quite a busy evening for him ! '

' He said he'd come back and let me out of that cupboard when the fun was over,' said Fatty, beginning to grin. ' He'll be surprised to find I'm gone, won't he ? '

' He will,' said Larry. ' He won't know what's happened. Let's pretend to him that we don't know where you are, shall we ? We'll go and ask him about you to-morrow—he'll have twenty fits if he thinks you've vanished. He won't know *what* to think ! '

' And he'll feel most uncomfortable because he'll know he jolly well ought to have let me out,' said Fatty. ' Well, I'm going to bed, Larry. You'd better go and get some sleep too. Oh, I do feel so disappointed—after all our work and disguises and plans—for Goon to solve the Mystery and get all the credit ! '

The boys parted and Larry ran swiftly home. He wondered what Goon was doing. He thought about the Castleton Mansion and wondered if the thieves were at work — if the house was being quietly surrounded—if Goon was doing some arresting. Well, maybe it would all be in the papers to-morrow.

Goon had certainly done some good work that night. He had surrounded the mansion with men whilst the thieves were actually inside. He had arrested all four of them—although one, alas, had got away in the struggle—and Goon was feeling very pleased with himself indeed. The escaped thief would soon be caught. Not a doubt of that.

It wasn't until past midnight that Mr. Goon suddenly remembered that he had left Fatty locked up in the cupboard in the Waxworks Hall.

' Drat that boy ! ' he thought. ' I could go to bed now, and sleep easy, if it wasn't for getting him out of that cupboard. He's had a nice long time there to think over all his misdeeds, he has. Well, I'd better get along and let him out—and give him a few good words of advice too. He's missed all the fun this time—and I've solved this Mystery, not him ! Ha ! '

Mr. Goon cycled down to the Waxworks Hall and, leaving his bicycle outside, went into the Hall. He switched on his torch and walked to the cupboard. He rapped smartly on it.

' Hey, you ! ' he said. ' Ready to be let out yet ? We've done everything, and now that the fun's over, you can come along out ! '

There was no answer. Mr. Goon rapped loudly again, thinking that Fatty had gone to sleep. But still there was no answer. A little cold feeling crept round Mr. Goon's heart. Surely that boy was all right ?

Hurriedly Mr. Goon turned the key in the lock and opened the door. He shone his light into the cupboard. Napoleon looked back at him, standing there in his under-garment—but no Fatty ! Mr. Goon's hands began to tremble. Where was that

boy ? He couldn't get out of a locked cupboard !
Or could he ? Mr. Goon remembered how Fatty
had apparently passed mysteriously through a
locked door in the last Mystery.

Mr. Goon poked Napoleon in the ribs to make
sure he was wax, and not Fatty. Napoleon did not
flinch. He looked straight at Mr. Goon. Yes, he
was wax all right.

Mr. Goon shut the door, puzzled and upset.
Now where was that boy ? Had somebody carried
him off ? He had seen him bound and gagged, so he
couldn't have escaped by himself. Well then, what
had happened ?

Mr. Goon went home slowly, pedalling with
heavy feet. He ought to have let that boy free
before he had gone after the gang. Suppose he
didn't turn up in the morning ? What explanation
could he give to the Inspector ? He was seeing him
at ten o'clock.

Mr. Goon gave a heavy sigh. He had been
looking forward to that interview—now he wasn't
so sure. That fat boy was very friendly with the
Inspector. If it came out that anything had happened to him, Inspector Jenks might ask some very
very awkward questions. Drat the boy !

Fatty slept soundly that night, tired out with his
adventures. Mr. Goon slept too, but not so soundly.
He dreamt about his great success in arresting the
gang—but every time he was about to receive words
of praise from the Inspector, Fatty came into the
dream, tied up, begging for help. It was most
disturbing, because he woke Mr. Goon up each
time, and then he found it hard to go to sleep
again.

At nine o'clock the Five Find-Outers were all
together in Pip's garden, going over and over the

happenings of the night before. All of them were most indignant with Goon for leaving Fatty in the cupboard.

'We're going to make him think Fatty's been spirited away,' said Larry, with a grin. 'We'll wait about the village for him, and each time he passes any of us we'll ask him if he's heard anything of Fatty.'

So, at half-past nine, the children, with the exception of Fatty, of course, hung about near Goon's house, waiting for him to come out. Larry was at the corner, Pip was near the house, and Daisy and Bets were not far off.

Larry gave a whistle when he saw Goon coming out, wheeling his bicycle, ready to ride over to see the Inspector. He looked very smart indeed, for he had brushed his uniform, cleaned his belt and helmet and shoes, and polished his buttons till they shone. He was the very picture, he hoped, of a Smart Policeman Awaiting Promotion.

'I say, Mr. Goon!' called Pip, as the policeman prepared to mount his bicycle. 'Do you know where our friend, Frederick, is?'

'Why should I?' scowled Mr. Goon, but his heart sank. So that boy had vanished!

'Well, we just wondered,' said Pip. 'I suppose you haven't seen him at all?'

Mr. Goon couldn't say that. He mounted his bicycle and rode off, his face red. He hoped that boy Fatty wasn't going to cause a lot of trouble, just as he, Goon, had got things going so very nicely.

He passed Daisy and Bets. Daisy called out 'Oh, Mr. Goon! Have you seen Fatty? Do tell us if you have!'

'I don't know where he is,' said Mr. Goon

desperately, and cycled on. But at the corner, there was Larry !

' Mr. Goon ! Mr. Goon ! Have you seen Fatty ? Do you know where he is ? Do you think he's disappeared ? Mr. Goon, do tell us where he is. Have you locked him up ? '

' Course not ! ' spluttered Mr. Goon. ' He'll turn up. He'll turn up like a bad penny, you may be sure ! '

He rode on, feeling most uncomfortable. Where *could* the boy be ? Had that thief who escaped gone back to the Hall, and taken Fatty ? No, that couldn't be, surely. But WHERE WAS that boy ?

The Inspector was waiting for Mr. Goon in his office. On his desk were various reports of the happenings of the night before, sent in, not only by Mr. Goon, but by two other police-two men who had helped in the arrests, and by plain-clothes detectives who had also been on the case.

He also had reports on what the three prisoners had said when questioned. Some smart work had been done, there was no doubt about that—but something was worrying the Inspector.

Mr. Goon saw it as soon as he got into the office. He had hoped and expected to find his superior officer full of smiles and praise. But no—the Inspector looked rather solemn, and a bit worried. Why ?

' Well, Goon,' said the Inspector, ' some good work appears to have been done on this case. But it's a pity about the pearls, isn't it ? '

Mr. Goon gaped. ' The pearls, sir ? What about them ? We've got them, sir—took them off one of the gang.'

'Ah, but you see—they are not the stolen pearls,' said the Inspector gently. 'No, Goon—they are just a cheap necklace the man was going to give his girl! The *real* pearls have vanished!'

MR. GOON's mouth opened and shut like a goldfish.
He simply couldn't believe his ears.

' But, sir—we got the thieves red-handed.  And
the one that escaped was only the one on guard in
the garden, sir.  He hadn't anything to do with the
thieving.  It was the three upstairs who did that
—and we've got them.'

' Yes, you've got them, and that was a very good
bit of work, as I said,' said the Inspector.  ' But
I'm afraid, Goon, that one of the upstairs thieves,
when he knew the game was up, simply threw the
pearls out of the window· to the man below.  He
must have pocketed them, and then, when he was
arrested, struggled so violently that he managed to
escape—*with* the pearls.  Pity, isn't it ? '

Mr. Goon was most dismayed.  True, they had
got three of the gang—but the pearls were gone.
He had waited to catch the men red-handed—had
actually let them take the pearls, because he felt so
certain he could get them back, when the men were
arrested—and now, after all, the robbery had been
successful.  One of the gang had got them, and
would no doubt get rid of them in double quick
time.

' It's—it's most unfortunate, sir,' said poor
Mr. Goon.

' Well—let's hear your tale,' said the Inspector.
You only had time to send in a very short report—
what's all this about posing as a waxwork ? '

Mr. Goon was proud of this bit, and he related it all in full to the interested Inspector. But when he came to the part where he had sneezed, and the men had caught Fatty, instead of himself, Inspector Jenks sat up straight.

'Do you mean to tell me that Frederick Trotteville was there?' he said. 'Posing too? What as?'

'Napoleon, sir,' said Goon. 'Interfering as usual. That boy can't keep his nose out of things, he can't. Well, sir, when the men had gone to do the robbery, I crept out after them, and I went to the telephone box and . . .'

'Wait a bit, wait a bit,' said the Inspector. 'What happened to Frederick?'

'Him? Oh well—nothing much,' said Goon, trying to gloss over this bit as quickly as possible. 'They just tied him up a bit, sir, and chucked him into a cupboard. They didn't hurt him. Of course, if they'd started any rough stuff with him, I'd have gone for them, sir.'

'Of course,' said the Inspector gravely. 'Well I suppose you went and untied him and let him out of the cupboard before you rushed off to telephone.'

Mr. Goon went rather red. 'Well, sir—to tell you the truth, sir, I didn't think I had the time— and also, sir, it was a dangerous business last night, and I didn't think that boy ought to be mixed up in it. He's a terror for getting into the middle of things, sir, that boy is, and . . .'

'Goon,' said the Inspector, and the policeman stopped abruptly and looked at his superior. He was looking very grave. 'Goon. Do you mean to say you left the boy tied up in a locked cupboard? I can hardly believe it of you. What time did you let him out?'

Mr. Goon swallowed nervously. ' I went back, sir, about midnight—and I unlocked the cupboard door, sir—and—and the cupboard was empty.'

' Good heavens ! ' said the Inspector, startled. ' Do you know what had happened to Frederick ? '

' No, sir,' said Mr. Goon. The Inspector reached out for one of his five telephones.

' I must ring his home to see if he is all right,' he said.

Mr. Goon looked more downcast than ever. ' He's—well, he seems to have vanished, sir,' he said. The Inspector put down the telephone, and stared at Mr. Goon.

' Vanished ! What do you mean ? This is very serious indeed.'

' Well, sir—all I know is that the other kids—the ones he's always with—they keep on asking me if I know where their friend is,' said Mr. Goon desperately. ' And if they don't know—well, he might be anywhere ! '

' I must look into the matter at once,' said the Inspector. ' I'll get into touch with his parents. Now finish your story quickly, so that I can get on to this matter of Frederick Trotteville at once.'

So poor Mr. Goon had to cut short his wonderful story, and blurt out quickly the rest of the night's happenings. He felt very down in the mouth as he cycled back home. The pearls had gone after all ! What a blow ! And now this wretched boy had disappeared, and there would be no end of a fuss about him. Privately Mr. Goon thought it would be a very good thing if Fatty disappeared for good. Oh, why hadn't he let him out of that cupboard last night ? He had known that he ought to—but it had seemed such a very good way of paying out that interfering boy !

Where could Fatty be? Mr. Goon pondered the matter deeply as he turned into the village street. Had the escaped thief gone back to the Hall, and taken Fatty prisoner, meaning to hold him up for ransom, or something? Mr. Goon went cold at the thought. If such a thing happened, he would be held up to scorn by every one for not having freed Fatty when he could.

He was so deep in thought that he did not see a small dog run at his bicycle. He wobbled, and fell off, landing with a bump on the road. The dog flew round him in delight, barking lustily.

'Clear-orf!' shouted Mr. Goon angrily, and suddenly recognised Buster. 'Will you clear-orf!'

He looked round to see who was in charge of Buster—and his mouth fell wide open. He was so astonished that he couldn't get up, but went on sitting down in the road, with Buster making little darts at him.

Fatty was standing there, grinning down at him. *Fatty!* Mr. Goon stared at him. Here he'd been reporting to the Inspector that Fatty had vanished —and the Inspector had gone all hot and bothered about it—and now here was that same boy, grinning down at him, large as life and twice as natural.

'Where've you been?' said Mr. Goon at last, feebly pushing Buster away.

'Home,' said Fatty. 'Why?'

'*Home?*' said Mr. Goon. 'You've been at home? Why, the others kept asking me where you were, see? And I reported your disappearance to the Inspector. He's going to start searching for you.'

'But Mr. Goon—why?' asked Fatty innocently. 'I'm here. And I got home all right last night, too. All the same, it was jolly mean of you to leave

*'Hallo, Fatty! Jolly good, old boy'*

me in that cupboard. I shan't forget that in a hurry.'

Mr. Goon got up. 'How did you get out of that there cupboard?' he asked. 'All tied up you were, too. Do you mean to say you untied yourself, and unlocked that cupboard and got out all by yourself?'

'You never know, do you?' said Fatty. 'Well so long, Mr. Goon—and do telephone the Inspector to tell him not to start searching for me. I'll be at home if he wants me!'

He went off with Buster, and poor Mr. Goon was left to cycle home, his head spinning. 'That boy! First he's locked up, then he disappears, then he comes back again—and nobody knows how or when or why.' Mr. Goon couldn't make head or tail of it.

He didn't enjoy ringing up the Inspector and reporting that he had just met Fatty.

'But *where* had he been?' said the Inspector, puzzled. 'Where was he last night?'

'Er—at home, sir,' said poor Mr. Goon. 'It was the other children put me off, sir—asking me if I knew where he was, and all that, sir.'

The Inspector put down his receiver with an impatient click. Really, Goon was too idiotic at times! The Inspector sat looking at his telephone, thinking deeply. He had had reports from all kinds of people about this Case—but not from one person, who appeared to know quite a lot about it—and that was Master Frederick Trotteville! The Inspector made another telephone call. Fatty answered it.

'I want you to cycle over here this morning and answer a few questions, Frederick,' said the Inspector. 'Come straight along now.'

So, with Buster in his basket, Fatty rode off
to the next town, wondering a little fearfully what
the Inspector wanted to know. Would he think he
had been mixing himself up in this Mystery a bit
too much? He had warned the Find-Outers not
to get mixed up, because it might be dangerous.

The Inspector was friendly, but business-like,
and he listened to the whole of Fatty's tale with the
greatest interest, especially to the tale of Fatty's
various disguises.

' Most interesting,' he said. ' You've got a gift
for that kind of thing, I can see. But don't over-do
it. Now — you've heard all about the arrests, I
suppose? '

' I only know what's in the paper this morning,
sir,' said Fatty. ' I knew it was no good asking
Mr. Goon anything. I'm a bit fed up that he
managed the Mystery after all, whilst I was locked
up in the cupboard.'

' He should have let you out,' said the Inspector
shortly. ' Very remiss of him. Not the kind of
thing I expect from a police officer. Well, Frederick,
three arrests were made, as you know—but the
man on guard in the garden below escaped. And,
most unfortunately, he appears to have escaped
with the Castleton pearls! '

' But the papers said they were found in one of
the arrested men's pockets! ' said Fatty.

' We've got later news,' said Inspector Jenks.
' Those pearls were only cheap ones, bought by
one of the men as a gift for his wife—or stolen
from somewhere else probably. They're only worth
a few pounds. The real pearls have gone.'

' I see,' said Fatty, and he cheered up considerably. ' So—the Mystery isn't quite over, sir.
We've got to find out where the pearls are? Can

you find the man who escaped, do you think ?   He might split, and tell where he put the pearls.'

'We *have* got him,' said the Inspector grimly. 'The news came in ten minutes ago.   But he hadn't got the pearls, and won't say where he's put them. But we happen to know that Number Three of the gang is usually the one who disposes of the stolen jewels—and it's likely that this fellow we've just arrested has put the pearls in some agreed place, for Number Three, whoever he is, to fetch, when all the hue and cry dies down.'

'You don't know who Number Three is, do you, sir ? ' asked Fatty.

'Haven't any idea,' said the Inspector.   'We more or less had our suspicions of the other four— but Number Three we've never been able to guess at.   Now, Frederick, I'm not altogether pleased at the way you mixed yourself up in all this, when I warned you not to, because it was dangerous—now you just see if you can't solve the rest of the Mystery, and find those pearls before Number Three does. There's no danger now—so you Five Find-Outers can go ahead.'

'Yes, sir,' said Fatty, looking rather subdued. 'We'll do our best.   We've got just a few things to go on.   I'll work them out and see what can be done.   Thanks for giving us a chance to solve the Mystery of the Missing Pearls !   Good-bye, sir ! '

ғ ATTY went straight to Pip's. He felt sure he would find the rest of the Find-Outers there, waiting for him. They were outside the summer-house, making Larry tell them over and over again all that had happened.

'Here's Fatty!' cried Bets. 'What did the Inspector say, Fatty? Wasn't he angry with Goon for leaving you in that cupboard?'

'He wasn't very pleased with him—at least he didn't *sound* very pleased,' said Fatty. 'He didn't sound very pleased with me either! Seemed to think I oughtn't to have got so mixed up in this Mystery. But how *could* I keep out of it?'

'I expect he thought it was dangerous,' said Bets, 'and so it was, last night. Oh, Fatty, I knew you were in danger. I really, really did.'

'Good old Bets!' said Fatty, giving her a hug. 'I'm jolly glad you had one of your funny feelings about me—if you hadn't sent Pip to Larry, and Larry hadn't come along to the Waxworks Hall, goodness knows how long I'd have been shut up in that cupboard. By the way—the Mystery is still not *quite* ended!'

Every one sat up at once. 'What do you mean?' said Daisy.

Fatty explained about the missing pearls and Number Three. 'The Inspector thinks that Number Five, who escaped with the pearls last night, had time to put them in some safe place, before he was caught this morning. He will

probably try and get a message to Number Three—
the gang member who wasn't there last night and
so is still at large — and till Number Three gets
that message about the pearls and finds them,
*any* one might find them! And it's up to us
to do it!'

'I see,' said Larry slowly. 'But how in the
world can any one find them if they don't even
know where to look? It's impossible.'

'Nothing's impossible to a really good detective,'
said Fatty. 'I agree that it's a frightfully difficult
mystery to solve—but I think if only we can get
hold of Number Three somehow, and shadow him,
he might lead us to the necklace!'

'What do you mean—shadow him?' asked
Bets.

'Follow him, silly—always keep him in sight,'
said Pip. 'Spot where he goes, or where he hangs
about. He's sure to hang about the place where
the pearls are, waiting for a chance to get them.'

'That's right,' said Fatty. 'The thing is—
*who* is Number Three and how can we get hold of
him?'

There was a silence. Nobody knew the answer.

'What do we know about Number Three?'
said Fatty, considering. 'We know he rides a
bike that has a hooter on it. We know he has odd
eyes, one blue and one brown. And we know he
rows a boat. I rather think, as we've seen him in
Peterswood twice that he must live here.'

There was another silence. None of the things
they knew about the odd-eyed man seemed to be
of any help in finding him. Then Pip suddenly
gave an exclamation.

'I think I know what to do!'

'What?' said every one eagerly.

' Well, we're sure that Number Five hid the pearls somewhere, and we're pretty certain he'll get a message to Number Three, *some*how—has probably sent one already, in case he himself got caught by the police and put into prison. Now who would he send that message to, to deliver to Number Three ? '

' The old man, Johnny, of course ! ' said Fatty. ' He's the one they always use, apparently, when they want to send messages to one another. So—if we watch old Johnny again—sooner or later we'll see Number Three go quietly up to him. . . . '

' Sit down beside him—and receive the message ! ' said Larry. ' And if we shadow him, after that, we shall spot where he goes. Maybe he'll lead us straight to the necklace ! '

Every one felt much more cheerful and hopeful. ' That's a brain-wave of yours, Pip,' said Fatty. ' I'm surprised I didn't think of it myself. Very good.'

All the Find-Outers loved a word of praise from their leader. Pip went quite red with pleasure.

' I suppose that means we must go and sit in that smelly little lemonade shop again,' said Daisy. Fatty considered.

' Only one of us had better shadow Number Three closely,' he said. ' If he sees five of us tailing him he's bound to get a bit suspicious. I'll do the shadowing—if you don't mind, Pip, though it *was* your idea—and you can all follow me at a safe distance.'

' I don't mind a bit,' said Pip generously. ' I'm sure you'll be much better at shadowing than I shall. Where will you wait ? And shall we have bikes or not ? '

'Better have bikes,' said Larry. 'He was on a bike last time he went up to the old man. If he's walking we can always leave our bikes somewhere, and walk after him.'

'Yes, that's a sound idea,' said Fatty. 'What's the time? Almost dinner-time. The old fellow doesn't come out till the afternoon, so we'll meet just before two, at the bottom of my lane, with bikes.'

'But, Fatty, do you think the old man will come out and sit on your seat, after your warning, and after what he will have read in the papers to-day?' asked Larry. 'Won't he be afraid?'

'Yes, probably he will,' said Fatty. 'But if he has a message to deliver, I think he'll risk it. I bet the gang pay him well for this go-between business.'

Now that there was something to do again the Find-Outers felt very cheerful. They went to their dinners pleased that there was still a Mystery to solve. If only they could find those pearls before Goon did!

Mr. Goon, of course, was exercising his mind too, about the missing pearls. He too knew that if only he could spot Number Three, he might be led to the pearls. But he had not got as far as reckoning out that it would be a good idea to watch old Johnny again, to see if Number Three came to receive a message!

That afternoon four of the Find-Outers sat in the little sweet-shop, on the opposite side of the road to the bench where the old man so often sat. Fatty was not with them. He was leaning against a tree not far off, apparently deep in a paper, his bicycle beside him. He was watching for the old man to come. How he hoped he would!

The bicycles belonging to the others were piled against the side of the sweet-shop. The four children in the shop were eating ices, and watching the bench opposite as keenly as Fatty was.

Some one came shuffling round the corner. Hurrah ! It was the old man, complete with sniffle and pipe and cough. He sat himself down gingerly on the bench with a little groan, just exactly as Fatty used to do.

Then he bent himself over his stick-handle and seemed to go to sleep. The children waited, whilst their ices melted in the saucers. Had Johnny got a message to deliver from Number Five to Number Three ?

A noise made them jump violently. It was the sound of a hooter ! Fatty jumped too. He lifted his head cautiously from his paper, and saw a man riding down the High Street on a bicycle. It had a hooter instead of a bell.

The man rode to the bench, hooted, and got off his bicycle. He stood his machine against the kerb and went to sit down on the bench close to the old man.

The old fellow did not even look up. How would he know if it was Number Three or not then ? He was deaf and would not hear a whisper. Fatty puzzled his brains to think.

' Of course ! ' he thought suddenly. ' That loud hooter always tells the old man when Number Three is coming to sit on the bench beside him. Of course ! Gosh, that's clever.'

The old man took absolutely no notice of the other man. Fatty watched very carefully, but he could not see any movement of the old man's mouth, nor could he see the giving of any paper-message.

For a few moments the two men sat together, and then old Johnny sat up a little straighter, and began to draw patterns in the dust with the end of his stick. Fatty watched more carefully to see if the old man was talking, under cover of his movements. But he could not make out that he was—unless he could talk without moving his lips, as a ventriloquist can !

After a minute or two the other man got up and went to his bicycle. He got on it, hooted, and rode slowly over to the sweet-shop. The four children in there stiffened with excitement. What was he coming over there for ?

Bets gave a gasp as he came in, and Pip kicked her under the table, afraid she might give them away. Bets took one look at the man and then began to finish her ice, making rather a noise with her spoon.

'Box of matches, please,' said the man, and put a penny down on the counter. Nobody liked to look at him in case he became suspicious of them.

He went out, lighting a cigarette. '*He's got odd eyes !*' said Bets. 'He's the one ! Hooter on his bike—and odd eyes ! Oooh—it's getting exciting.'

Fatty, waiting by the tree outside, saw the man go in and out of the shop. The boy folded up his paper quickly, and mounted his bike as the man went swiftly by him. He followed him at a discreet distance, wondering if he had had any message, and if he was going to lead him to the pearls !

'Come on,' said Larry, going out of the shop quickly. 'We've got to follow too.'

The man rode down to the Fair. He wandered round a bit and then went to the Hall of Waxworks.

But he only just put his head inside, and came out.

Fatty popped his head inside too, but except that it was full of people looking at the waxworks, there was nothing different to see. Napoleon was dressed and back in his place, and the red-haired boy was relating an extraordinary tale of how, in the night, Napoleon had apparently got out of his place, undressed and put himself to bed in a cupboard.

' Story-teller ! ' said some listening children. ' What a fib ! '

' And what's more,' said the red-headed boy, thoroughly enjoying himself, ' that wax policeman over there—do you see him ? Well, *he* got up in the night and went and stood himself behind that curtain. Such goings-on ! '

Fatty longed to hear more of this, but the man he was following had gone, and Fatty had to go too, or lose him. The man had put his bicycle beside the hedge and padlocked the back wheel, so Fatty knew he meant to stay around for a while.

The other Find-Outers came up, and Fatty winked at them. ' Looks as if we're going to spend an hour or two in the Fair ! ' he said.

The man wandered about most aimlessly. He didn't even have a ride on the Roundabout, or try for a Hoopla gift, or go in a Bumping Car—he just trailed about. Every now and then he passed the Waxworks Hall, and looked inside. But he didn't go in at all. Fatty wondered if he was waiting for somebody to meet him there.

' I don't believe he knows where the pearls are ! ' thought Fatty. ' Or surely he'd go straight to them ! My word what a crowd there is at the Fair to-day ! '

The man evidently thought the same. He asked a question about it of the man at the Hoopla stall. ' Quite a crowd to-day ! What's up ? '

' Oh, it's a trip from Sheepsale, a kind of outing,' said the man. ' They're going at four o'clock, then the place will empty a bit. Good trade for us, though ! '

The man nodded. Then he made his way through the crowd to his bicycle, and unpadlocked it. Fatty followed him. It was clear that the man couldn't do whatever he wanted to do, because the place was too crowded. Probably he would be coming back. It was up to Fatty to follow him. He would leave the others down in the Fair, because he was sure that he and the man would be back there sooner or later, when the trippers had gone.

He had time to give a quick message to Larry. Then off he went over the level-crossing on his bicycle, following the man as closely as he dared. Round the corner they went, the man hooting with his little hooter—parp-parp.

And round the corner on *his* bicycle came Goon ! The two almost collided. Goon, who had heard the hooter, glued his eyes on the man at once. Was he Number Three ? He must be ! He seemed to be the only man within miles who had a hooter on his bicycle, instead of a bell, for some peculiar reason that Goon couldn't guess.

Goon made up his mind to follow Number Three at once, and keep him in sight. Visions of pearl necklaces floated in front of his eyes. Number Three knew where those pearls were, Goon was sure of it. Off he went after Number Three.

And behind him went Fatty, annoyed and angry.

Was Goon going to get in first *again* !  Goon heard some one behind him and turned.  He scowled.

That fat boy again !  Was *he* after Number Three too.  ' Gah ! ' said Goon to himself.  ' The interfering Toad ! '

AND now, of course, Mr. Goon spoilt simply everything ! Number Three couldn't possibly help
guessing that he was being shadowed by the fat,
panting policeman ! For one thing, Goon didn't
keep a fair distance away, but pedalled closely to
Number Three's bicycle—so close to it that if
Number Three had to brake suddenly, his ' shadow '
would almost certainly bump into him !

Fatty cycled on, some way behind the other
two, thinking hard. It was too bad of Old Clear-Orf
to butt in like this, just as the Find-Outers had
really got going again. For one moment Fatty
knew what Mr. Goon felt like, when others interfered ! He, Fatty, had often interfered with the
policeman's working out of a mystery—and now
here was Goon doing the same thing. And he'd
done it the evening before, too, in the Waxworks
Hall. It was most exasperating.

Number Three, giving occasional scowling
glances behind him, saw that Goon was hot on his
trail. He didn't really need to look round him to
see the policeman, because he could hear him well
enough too—Goon's puffs and pants were terrific.

A little grin curled the corners of Number
Three's lips. Goon wanted a bicycle ride, did he ?
All right then, he could have it, with pleasure.
Number Three would take him for a long, long ride
through the countryside, on this hot, sultry after-
noon !

Fatty soon began to have an inkling of the way

in which Number Three's mind was working, for the man suddenly seemed to have a tremendous desire to cycle up all the steep hills it was possible to find.

He was a strong, muscular fellow, and he sailed up the hills easily enough—but poor Goon found it terribly hard work, and Fatty wasn't very happy either. He began to puff too, and to wish that he had given Larry or Pip the job of shadowing this extremely active fellow.

' The wretched man knows that Goon is following him because he suspects him of knowing where the pearls are, and he's going to lead him a fine old dance, up hill and down dale ! ' thought Fatty, his legs going round and round furiously, and the perspiration dripping into his eyes. ' He's either going to tire old Goon out, and make him give up—or else he's going to give him the slip somehow.'

Still the three went on and on, and Fatty's clothes stuck to him horribly, he was so hot. Number Three didn't seem to tire in the least, and had a most uncanny knowledge of all the nasty little hills in the district. Poor Mr. Goon went from red to scarlet, and from scarlet to purple. He was in his hot uniform, and even Fatty felt a bit sorry for him.

' He'll have a fit if he goes up any more hills at top speed,' thought Fatty, wiping his forehead. ' So shall I ! Golly, I'm absolutely melting. I shall have lost pounds and pounds in weight soon. Phew ! '

Mr. Goon was absolutely determined that he wasn't going to be shaken off by Number Three. He knew that Fatty was behind him, and that if he, Mr. Goon, failed in the chase, Fatty would go triumphantly on. So Mr. Goon gritted his big teeth and kept on and on and on.

A big hill loomed up in front. Mr. Goon groaned from the bottom of his heart. Number Three sailed up as usual. Mr. Goon followed valiantly. Fatty, feeling that this was absolutely the last straw, went up it too.

And then he felt a peculiar bumping from his back tyre. He looked down in alarm. Blow, blow, blow ! He'd got a puncture !

Poor Fatty ! He got off and looked at his tyre. It was absolutely flat. No good pumping it up, because it would be flat again almost at once—and, in any case, if he stopped to pump it up he would lose Number Three and Mr. Goon.

If he had been Bets he would have burst into howls. If he had been Daisy he would have sat on the bank and shed a few quiet tears. If he had been Larry he would have shaken his fist at the tyre and kicked it. If he had been Pip he would probably have yelled at it and then jumped on it in fury. But being Fatty, he did none of these things at all.

He took a quick look up the hill and caught sight of a triumphant Mr. Goon looking back at him with a grin on his face. Then he and Number Three disappeared over the top of the hill. Fatty waved to Goon.

' I wish you a nice long ride ! ' he said pleasantly, and mopped his forehead. Then he waited for a car to come along over the top of the hill.

It wasn't long before he heard one. It was a lorry, driven by a young man with a cigarette hanging out of the corner of his mouth. Fatty hailed him.

'Hie! Stop a minute, there's a good chap.'

The lorry stopped. Fatty took a half-crown out of his pocket. 'Would you mind stopping at the next garage and asking them to send out a taxi for me?' he said. 'I've got a puncture, and I'm miles from anywhere, and don't want to have to walk home.'

'Bad luck, mate,' said the driver. 'Where do you live?'

'Peterswood,' said Fatty. 'I don't know how far I've ridden this afternoon, but I imagine it must be about twenty miles away!'

'Oh, not so far as that, mate!' said the driver. 'I'm going near Peterswood. Chuck your bike in the back of the lorry, climb up here beside me—and put your money away! I can give a chap a lift without being paid for it!'

'Oh, thanks awfully,' said Fatty, and put away his half-crown. He lifted his bicycle into the lorry, and then climbed up beside the driver. He was very hot and tired, and terribly thirsty, but he chatted away in a friendly manner, glad to have this unexpected lift back.

'Here you are,' said the driver, when they had rattled through the countryside for about twenty minutes. 'Peterswood is not above a mile from here. You can walk that.'

'Very many thanks,' said Fatty, and jumped down. He took his bicycle and waved to the departing lorry. Then he walked smartly off in the direction of Peterswood. He went home and put away his punctured bike. His father's bicycle was in the shed, so Fatty borrowed that, and off he went, quite cheerful, on his way to the Fair to see what the others were doing.

They were wondering what had happened to

Fatty. They hadn't liked to leave the Fair, so they had had tea there, and were now conversing with the red-headed boy at the Waxworks, hearing for the twentieth time, the extraordinary tale of Napoleon's escapade in the night.

' Oh, *Fatty* ! ' cried Bets, when she saw him. ' You've come back at last ! Whatever happened ? And how frightfully hot you look ! '

Buster welcomed Fatty uproariously. He had been left behind with Larry, in case Fatty had to do some quick shadowing. Fatty looked at him.

' I feel as if *my* tongue's hanging out like Buster's, I'm so hot and thirsty,' he said. ' I must have an iced gingerbeer. Come and sit with me whilst I have it, and I'll tell you what's happened ! '

' Did Number Three lead you to the missing pearls ? ' asked Bets excitedly, as Fatty went to the gingerbeer stall. He shook his head.

' Come on over to the grass here,' he said, and led the way. He flung himself down and drank his gingerbeer in long, thirsty gulps. ' Golly ! This is the very best drink I've ever had in my life ! '

Soon he was telling the others about the wild-goose chase that Number Three had led both him and Mr. Goon. They listened eagerly. How annoying of Goon to butt in like that ! They laughed when they thought of the poor, hot, fat policeman pedalling valiantly up hill and down after Number Three.

' What a shame you had a puncture,' said Bets. ' Still, Fatty, I'm sure Number Three would never lead you or Goon to where the pearls were, once he knew he was being followed ! He might not have known that *you* were shadowing him—but he simply couldn't *help* knowing that Goon was ! '

Fatty finished his iced gingerbeer and ordered

another. He said he had never been so thirsty in his life. ' When I think of poor, hot Goon, pedalling away still for dear life, and feeling as thirsty as I am—well, all I can say is that I'm jolly glad I got a puncture ! ' said Fatty, drinking again. ' I should think Goon will end up somewhere in Scotland, by the time he's finished this bike-ride ! '

' All the same,' said Larry, ' it's a bit sickening that we aren't any nearer solving the mystery of where those pearls are hidden. Instead of the man leading us *to* them—he seems bent on going as far from them as he can ! '

' I wonder if that old fellow *did* give him a message,' said Pip, frowning. ' You're sure you didn't see any sign of a message at all ? Let's think now. All that old Johnny did was to mess about in the dust, drawing patterns with his stick. Nothing else.'

Fatty was drinking his gingerbeer as Pip said this. He suddenly choked and spluttered, and Bets banged him on the back. ' Whatever's the matter ? ' she said.

Fatty coughed, and then turned a pair of bright eyes on the Find-Outers. ' Pip's hit it ! ' he said. ' What a lot of blind donkeys we are ! Of course— *we saw that old chap giving the message to Number Three under our very noses*—and we weren't smart enough to spot it ! '

' What do you mean ? ' said every one, in surprise.

' Well—he must have been writing some kind of message with his stick, in the dust, of course, for Number Three to read ! ' said Fatty. ' And to think it was there for us to read, too, if only we'd gone over and used our eyes. We're bad Find-Outers. Very bad indeed.'

The others looked excited. Pip slapped Fatty on the shoulder. ' Well, come on, let's go and see if the message is still there, idiot ! It might be ! '

' It might. But it's not very likely now,' said Fatty, getting up. ' Still, we'll certainly go and see. Oh—to think we never thought of this before. Where are my brains ? They must have melted in this heat ! '

The Find-Outers, with Buster in Fatty's basket, set off back to the village street. They came to the bench. It was empty—but obviously people had been sitting there, for there were paper bags strewn about. The children looked eagerly at the dust in front of the seat. Would there still be a message they could read ?

THERE were certainly some marks in the dust, but not many, for somebody's feet had evidently scuffled about just there. Fatty sat himself down in exactly the same place in which the old man had been. He stared hard at the dust.

So did the others. 'That looks like a letter W,' said Fatty, at last, pointing. 'Then there's a letter half rubbed out. And then that looks like an X. Then all the rest of the letters have been brushed out where people have walked on them. Blow !'

'W—something—X,' said Larry, who was good at crosswords, with their missing letters. 'W—A —X—it might be that.'

And then exactly the same thought struck all the Find-Outers at the same moment.

'WAXworks ! That's what the word was !'

They stared at one another in the greatest excitement. Waxworks ! Were the pearls hidden somewhere in the Waxworks Hall ? It was a very likely place, a place that all the gang knew well. And Number Three had kept looking in at the door that afternoon.

'He kept peeping in—but he couldn't go and get the pearls, because there were too many people there !' said Fatty. 'Golly, we've got the idea now ! That's the hiding-place—in the Waxworks Hall ! Now we've only got to go there and hunt, and we'll find the pearls somewhere—in the cupboard, perhaps, or under a floor-board.'

' Let's go and look for them straightaway,' said
Larry, getting up. ' Come on.'

' We can't very well, under the nose of that
red-haired boy,' said Fatty. ' Still, we'll go down to
the Hall anyway.' They set off and soon came to
the Fair again.

' There's the red-headed boy over there—he's
gone to his tea or something,' said Bets, pointing.
' Has he left the Hall empty for once ? '

They hurried to see. There was a badly written
notice stuck on the locked door. ' Gone for tea.
Back soon.'

' Aha ! ' said Fatty, his eyes gleaming. ' This
couldn't be better for us. We'll get in at that
window, Larry. It's sure to be open still.'

It was still unfastened, and the children climbed
in excitedly, almost tumbling on to the floor in their
eagerness to go hunting for the pearls.

' Behind the curtains, in the cupboards, up the
chimney, every place you can think of ! ' said Fatty,
in a thrilled voice. ' Go to it, Find-Outers. Solve
the mystery if you can ! '

Then such a hunt began. Every cupboard,
every shelf, every nook and cranny in that Hall
were searched by the bright-eyed Find-Outers.
Buster, eager to help, though without the faintest
idea of what they were looking for, scrabbled
about too, having a vague hope that it might be
rabbits.

Fatty even examined the floor-boards, but none
of them was loose. At last, when it seemed as if
every single place had been searched, the five children
sat down to rest and discuss the matter.

' I suppose it *is* here, that necklace ! ' said Daisy.
' I'm beginning to think it isn't.'

' *I* feel as if I'm playing Hunt-the-Thimble,'

said Bets. ' Where *is* the thimble ? It must be in some jolly good place, that necklace ! '

Fatty stared at Bets. ' Bets,' he said, ' supposing we went out of the room, and you had to hide a pearl necklace somewhere here, what difficult place would you think of ? '

Bets looked round the Hall and considered. ' Well, Fatty,' she said, ' I've always noticed that when people play Hunt-the-Thimble, the most difficult hiding-places to find are the easiest ones really.'

' What do you mean ? ' demanded Pip.

' Well,' said Bets, ' I remember looking *every-* where for the thimble once—and nobody found it— and yet where do you think it was ? On Mother's finger ! '

Fatty was listening hard to Bets. ' Go on, Bets,' he said. ' Suppose you had to hide that pearl necklace here, in this Hall—where would *you* hide it ? It would have to be a good place, easy to get at —and yet one where ordinary people would never dream of looking for a valuable necklace.'

Bets considered again. Then she gave a little smile. ' Well, *I* know where I'd put it ! ' she said. ' Of course I'd know ! And it would be under the noses of every one, and yet nobody would notice it ! '

' Where ? ' cried every one.

' I'll tell you,' said Bets. ' See Queen Elizabeth over there, in her grand clothes and jewels, standing looking so proud and haughty ? Well, I'd put the pearl necklace round her neck with all the other necklaces, of course—and nobody would ever guess that among the false Woolworth ones there was a REAL one ! '

Fatty leapt to his feet. ' Bets, you're right. I'd got that idea half in my own mind, and now you've

said all that, I'm sure you're right ! I bet the necklace is there ! Clever old Bets ! '

They all ran to the stately wax figure of Queen
Elizabeth whose neck was hung with brilliant
necklaces of all kinds. Among them was a double
necklace of beautifully graded pearls, with a diamond
clasp—at least, the children felt sure it was a diamond
one. Fatty lifted the necklace carefully off the
figure's neck, undoing the clasp first.

The pearls shone softly. It was clear even to
the children's eyes that they were not cheap ones,
bought at a store. They were lovely, really lovely.

' These must be the missing pearls ! ' said Fatty,
exultantly. ' They really must ! Golly, we've found
them. *We've* solved that mystery ! What will the
Inspector say ? Let's go and ring him up.'

They climbed out of the window and hurried to
their bicycles. Fatty had the wonderful necklace
safely in his pocket. He couldn't believe that they
really had found it—and in such an *easy* place too !

' But a jolly clever one,' said Fatty. ' To think
it was under the eyes of scores of people to-day—and
nobody guessed ! It was safer on Queen Elizabeth's
neck than anywhere else ! '

' Look out—there's Goon ! ' said Larry.

' And Inspector Jenks with him ! ' cried Bets in
delight. ' Shall we tell him ? '

' Leave it to me,' ordered Fatty. ' Good
evening, Inspector. Come to hunt for the necklace
too ? '

' Frederick,' said the Inspector. ' I believe you
were bicycling after the member of the gang called
Number Three this afternoon, weren't you ? '

' Yes, sir,' said Fatty. ' With Mr. Goon, as
well, sir.'

' Well, unfortunately he gave Mr. Goon the

slip,' said the Inspector. 'Mr. Goon rang me up, and I came over, because it is imperative that we keep an eye on Number Three, if we can, owing to his knowledge of where the pearls are hidden. Did you by any chance see the man, after you had got your puncture?'

'No, sir,' said Fatty. 'Haven't set eyes on him.'

The Inspector gave an annoyed exclamation. 'We *must* get Number Three. We've found out that he is the ring-leader, the man we want most of all! And now if he gets those pearls, wherever they are, and clears off, sooner or later these burglaries will start all over again. He will find it quite easy to start a new gang.'

Mr. Goon looked very down in the mouth. He also looked hot and tired.

'He's a clever fellow, sir,' he said to the Inspector. 'Very clever. I don't know how he managed to give me the slip, sir.'

'Never mind, Mr. Goon,' said Fatty comfortingly. '*I* can tell the Inspector where the pearls are, and how you can catch Number Three if you want to.'

Mr. Goon stared disbelievingly at Fatty. 'Gah!' he said. 'You make me tired. Talking a lot of tommy-rot! I don't believe a word of it!'

'What do you mean, Frederick?' said the Inspector, startled.

Fatty drew the pearl necklace out of his pocket. Mr. Goon gasped and his eyes bulged more than ever. The Inspector stared in amazement too. He took the pearls from Fatty. All the children crowded round in excitement.

'Frederick! These *are* the missing pearls! A double row of the very finest graded pearls there are,' said the Inspector. 'My dear boy—where *did* you get them ! '

'Oh—we played a little game of Hunt-the-Thimble with Bets—and she told us where they were,' said Fatty, and Mr. Goon gave a disbelieving snort. 'They were round Queen Elizabeth's neck, in the Waxworks Hall, Inspector—a very clever place—and Bets thought of it ! '

'Certainly a very clever place,' said the Inspector,' and a very clever thought of yours, little Bets, if I may say so ! ' he said, turning to the delighted little girl. 'They must have been shining there under the noses of hundreds of people to-day—and nobody so much as guessed ! But now, Frederick—how do you propose that we lay hands on Number Three ? '

'Well, sir—he knows that the pearls were hidden in the Waxworks Hall,' said Fatty, ' and maybe knows too that they were on Queen Elizabeth's neck—so he's bound to go back for them, sir, when everyone has gone, and the Hall is dark and empty. Oh, sir—could I come and hide in the Hall to-night when you do your spot of arresting ! '

'No,' said the Inspector. 'I'm afraid not. I'll have three men posted there. See to that straight-away, please, Goon. Er—I'm sure we can congratulate the Find-Outers on solving our problems for us in such a praiseworthy way—don't you think so, Goon ? '

Goon murmured something that sounded sus-piciously like ' Gah ! '

'What did you say, Goon ? ' said the Inspector. ' You were agreeing with me, I imagine ? '

' Er—yessir, yessir,' said Goon hurriedly, and turned a familiar purple. ' I'll get the men now, sir.'

' And now to think we've got to help with our packing and go back to school ! ' said Pip, in disgust. ' After all our fine detective work, we've got to go and learn the chief rivers of the world, and the date when Queen Elizabeth came to the throne, and how much wheat Canada grows, and . . .'

' Never mind—we'll have another Mystery to solve next hols,' said Bets happily. ' Won't we, Fatty ? '

Fatty grinned at her. ' I hope so, little Bets,' he said. ' I really do hope so ! '

I hope so too. It would be *most* disappointing if they didn't !

BOOK THREE

# The
# Mystery
## of the
# Hidden
# House

# 1  THE FAT BOY AT THE STATION

' IT's to-day that Fatty's coming back, ' said Bets to Pip. ' I'm so glad. '

' That's the sixth time you've said that in the last hour, ' said Pip. ' Can't you think of something else to say ? '

' No I can't, ' said Bets. ' I keep on feeling so glad that we shall soon see Fatty. ' She went to the window and looked out. ' Oh Pip—here come Larry and Daisy up the drive. I expect they will come to the station to meet Fatty too. '

' Of course they will, ' said Pip. ' And I bet old Buster will turn up as well! Fancy Fatty going away without Buster-dog ! '

Larry and Daisy walked into Pip's play-room. ' Hallo, hallo ! ' said Larry, flinging his cap on a chair. ' Won't it be nice when Fatty's back? Nothing ever seems to happen unless he's around. '

' We aren't even the Five Find-Outers without him, ' said Bets. ' Only four—and nothing to find out ! '

Larry, Daisy, Fatty, Pip and Bets called themselves the Five Find-Outers (and Dog, because of Buster). They had been very good indeed at solving all kinds of peculiar mysteries in the various holidays when they came back from boarding-school. Mr. Goon, the village policeman, had done his best to solve them too, but somehow the Five Find-Outers always got a little ahead of him, and he found this very annoying indeed.

' Perhaps some mystery will turn up when Fatty comes, ' said Pip. ' He's the kind of person that things always happen to. He just can't help it. '

'Fancy him being away over Christmas!' said Daisy.
'It was queer not having Fatty. I've kept him his presents.'

'So have I,' said Bets. 'I made him a note-book with
his full name on the cover in beautiful lettering. Look,
here it is—Frederick Algernon Trotteville. Won't he be
pleased?'

'I shouldn't think he will,' said Pip. 'You've got it all
dirty and messy, carrying it about.'

'I bought him this,' said Daisy, and she fished a box
out of her pocket. She opened it and brought out a neat
little black beard. 'It's to help him in his disguise.'

'It's a lovely one,' said Pip, fingering it, and then
putting it on his chin. 'How do I look?'

'Rather silly,' said Bets, at once. 'You look like a boy
with a beard—but if Fatty wore it he would look like an
elderly man at once. He knows how to screw up his face
and bend his shoulders and all that.'

'Yes—he's really most frightfully clever at disguises,'
said Daisy. 'Do you remember how he dressed up as
Napoleon Bonaparte in the waxwork show last hols?'

They all laughed as they remembered Fatty standing
solemnly among the waxworks, as still as they were,
looking exactly like one.

'That was a super mystery we solved last hols,' said
Pip. 'I hope one turns up these hols too. Any one seen
Mr. Goon lately?'

'Yes, I saw him riding his bicycle yesterday,' said Bets.
'I was just crossing the road when he came round the
corner. He almost knocked me down.'

'What did he say? Clear orf?' said Pip, with a grin.

Clear-Orf was the nickname that the children gave to
Mr. Goon the policeman, because he always shouted that
when he saw them or Buster, Fatty's dog.

'He just scowled like this,' said Bets, and screwed up
her face so fiercely that every one laughed.

Just then Mrs. Hilton, Pip's mother, put her head in at the door. 'Aren't you going to the station to meet Frederick?' she said. 'The train is almost due!'

'Gosh! Yes, look at the time!' cried Larry, and they all sprang to their feet. 'He'll be there before we are if we don't hurry.'

Pip and Bets dragged on coats and hats, and the four of them went thundering down the stairs like a herd of elephants. Crash, went the front door, and Mrs. Hilton saw them racing down the drive at top speed.

They got to the station just as the train was pulling in. Bets was terribly excited. She hopped about first on one foot, then on the other, waiting for Fatty's head to pop out of a carriage window. But it didn't.

The train stopped. Doors were flung open. People jumped down to the platform, some with bags that porters hurried to take. But there was no sign of Fatty.

'Where is he?' said Bets, looking upset.

'Perhaps he's in one of his disguises, just to test us,' said Larry suddenly. 'I bet that's it! He's dressed himself up and we've got to see if we can spot him. Quick, look round and see which of the passengers he is.'

'Not that man, he's too tall. Not that boy, he's not tall enough. Not that girl, because we know her. Not those two women, they're friends of mother's. And there's Miss Tremble. It's not her. Golly, which can he be?'

Bets suddenly nudged Larry. 'Larry, look—*there's* Fatty! See, that fat boy over there, pulling a suit-case out of the very last carriage of all.'

Every one stared at the fat red-faced boy at the end of the train. 'Yes! That's old Fatty! Not such a good disguise as usual, though—I mean, we can easily spot him this time.'

'I know! Let's pretend we *haven't* spotted him!' said Daisy, suddenly. 'He'll be so disgusted with us. We'll let him walk right by us without saying a word to him. And then we'll walk behind him up the station slope and call to him.'

'Yes—we'll do that,' said Larry. 'Here he comes. Now—pretend not to know it's Fatty, every one!'

So when the plump boy walked down the platform towards them, carrying his bag, and a mackintosh over his arm, the others didn't even smile at him. They looked right through him and beyond him, though Bets badly wanted to run up and take his arm. She was very fond of Fatty.

The boy took no notice of them at all. He marched on, his big boots making a clattering noise on the stone platform. He gave up his ticket at the barrier. Then he stopped outside the station, put down his bag, took out a red-spotted handkerchief and blew his nose very loudly.

'That's how Mr. Goon blows his!' whispered Bets in delight. 'Isn't Fatty clever! He's waited for us to go up to him now. Don't let's! We'll walk close behind him, and when we get out into the lane, we'll call to him.'

The boy put his handkerchief away, picked up his bag and set off. The four children followed closely. The boy heard their feet and looked back over his shoulder. He scowled. He put down his bag at the top of the slope to rest his arm.

The four children promptly stopped too. When the boy picked up his bag and walked on again, Larry and the others followed at his heels once more.

The boy looked back again. He faced round, and said, 'What's the big idea? Think you're my shadows, or somethink?'

Nobody said anything. They were a little taken-aback. Fatty looked so very spiteful as he spoke. 'You clear-orf,' said the boy, swinging round again and going on his way.

'I don't want a pack of silly kids following me all day long.'

'He's better than ever!' whispered Daisy, as the four of them walked on at the boy's heels. 'He quite scared me for a minute!'

'Let's tell him we know him,' said Pip. 'Come on! We can help to carry his bag then!'

'Hey! Fatty!' called Larry.

'Fatty! We came to meet you!' cried Bets and caught hold of his arm.

'Hallo, Fatty! Have a good Christmas?' said Daisy and Pip together.

The boy swung round again. He put down his bag. 'Now, look here, who do you think you're calling Fatty? Downright rude you are. If you don't clear-orf straight away I'll tell my uncle of you. And he's a policeman, see?'

Bets laughed. 'Oh, Fatty! Stop being somebody else. We know it's you. Look, I've got a note-book for your Christmas present. I made it myself.'

Looking rather dazed, the boy took it. He glanced round at the four children. 'What's all this, that's what I want to know!' he said. 'Following me round—calling me names—you're all potty!'

'Oh, Fatty, *please* be yourself,' begged Bets. 'It's a wizard disguise, it really is—but honestly we knew you at once. As soon as you got out of the train, we all said, 'That's Fatty!'

'Do you know what I do to people who call me names?' said the boy, looking round fiercely. 'I fight them! Any one like to take me on?'

'Don't be silly, Fatty,' said Larry, with a laugh. 'You're going on too long. Come on, let's go and find Buster, I bet he'll be pleased to see you. I thought he'd be at the station to meet you with your mother.'

He linked the boy's arm in his, but was shaken off roughly. 'You're potty,' said the boy again, picked up his bag and walked off haughtily. To the surprise of the others he took the wrong road. The way he went led to the village, not to his mother's house.

They stared after him, shaken and puzzled. A little doubt crept into their minds. They followed the boy at a good distance, watched him go to the village, and then, to their enormous surprise, he turned in at the gate of the little house where Mr. Goon, the policeman, lived.

As he turned in, he saw the four children at a distance. He shook his fist at them and went to knock at the door. It opened and he went in.

'It *must* be Fatty,' said Pip. 'That's exactly the way he would shake his fist. He's playing some very deep trick on us indeed. Gosh—what's he doing going to Mr. Goon's house?'

'He's probably playing a trick on Mr. Goon too,' said Larry. 'All the same—I feel a bit puzzled. We didn't get even a wink from him.'

They stood watching Mr. Goon's house for a little while and then turned to go back. They hadn't gone very far before there was a delighted barking, and a little black dog flung himself on them, licking, jumping and barking as if he had suddenly gone mad.

'Why, it's Buster!' said Bets. 'Hallo, Buster! You've just missed Fatty. What a pity!'

A lady was coming down the road, and the two boys raised their caps to her. It was Fatty's mother, Mrs. Trotteville. She smiled at the four children.

'I thought you must be somewhere about when Buster suddenly tore off at sixty miles an hour,' she said. 'I'm going to meet Frederick at the station. Are you coming too?'

'We've already *met* him,' said Larry, in surprise. 'He

was in a frightfully good disguise, Mrs. Trotteville. But we spotted him at once. He's gone to Mr. Goon's house. '

'To Mr. *Goon's* house,' said Mrs. Trotteville, in amazement. ' But whatever for ? He telephoned me to say he had just missed the train, but was getting one fifteen minutes later. Did he catch the first one then ? Oh dear, I wish he wouldn't start putting on disguises and things— and I *do* hope you won't all begin getting mixed up in something horrid as soon as Frederick comes home. *Why* has he gone to Mr. Goon ? Surely something odd hasn't turned up already ? '

This was an idea. The children stared at one another. Then they heard the whistle of a train. ' I must go, ' said Mrs. Trotteville. ' If Frederick isn't on that train, after telephoning me he'd missed the other, I shall be very angry indeed ! '

And into the station she went, with all the children following.

## 2  HULLO, FATTY!

THE train drew in. People leapt out—and Bets suddenly gave a shriek that made every one jump in fright.

'There *is* Fatty! Look, look! And he isn't in disguise either. Fatty! Fatty!' Fatty swung little Bets off the ground as she and Buster flung themselves on him. He grinned all over his good-natured face. He kissed his mother and beamed round at every one. 'Nice of you to come and meet me. Gosh, Buster, you've made a hole in my trousers. Stop it!'

Mrs. Trotteville was very pleased to see Fatty, but she looked extremely puzzled. 'The children said they had already met you once—in some disguise or other,' she said.

Fatty was astonished. He turned to Larry. 'What do you mean? I haven't arrived till now!'

The four children looked very foolish. They remembered all they had said to the other boy. Was it possible that it hadn't been Fatty after all—well, it couldn't have been of course, because here *was* Fatty, arriving on the next train. He couldn't possibly be on two trains at once.

'We've made complete idiots of ourselves,' said Larry, going red. 'You see ...'

'Do you mind walking out of the station before the porters think we are waiting for the next train?' said Mrs. Trotteville. 'We're the last on the platform as it is.'

'Come on,' said Fatty, and he and Larry set off with his bag between them. 'We can talk as we go.'

Bets took his mackintosh. Pip took a smaller bag and Daisy took a parcel of magazines. They were all extremely glad to see the real Fatty, to hear his determined voice, and see his broad grin.

' You see, ' began Larry again, ' we didn't know you'd missed the first train so we came down to meet you—and we thought you might be in disguise—so when a plumpish boy got off the train, we thought he was you ! '

' And we didn't say anything at first, just to puzzle you, as we thought, ' said Pip. ' We followed this boy out of the station and he was frightfully fed up with us. '

' And then we called to him, and said, " Fatty ! " ' said Bets. ' And you see, he *was* fat—and he swung round and said he fought people who called him rude names. '

' Golly ! I wonder he didn't set on you all ! ' said Fatty. ' You might have known I wouldn't say things like that to you, even if I *was* disguised. Where does he live ? '

' He went to Mr. Goon's house, ' said Daisy. ' He said Old Clear-Orf was his uncle. '

' Gracious ! You've put your foot in it properly ! ' said Fatty. ' Goon *has* got a nephew—and I bet he's asked him to stay with him. Won't he be wild when he knows how you greeted him ! '

' It's a great pity, ' said Mrs. Trotteville, who had been listening to all this with astonishment and dismay. ' He must have thought you were very rude. Now Mr. Goon will probably complain about the behaviour of you children again. '

' But, Mother—can't you see that ... ' began Fatty.

' Don't begin to argue, please, Frederick, ' said Mrs. Trotteville. ' It seems to me that you will have to go and explain to Mr. Goon that the others thought his nephew was you. '

' Yes, Mother, ' said Fatty in a meek voice.

' I do want you to keep out of any mysteries or problems these holidays, ' said Mrs. Trotteville.

' Yes, Mother, ' said Fatty. Mrs. Trotteville heard a

suppressed giggle from Bets and Daisy. They knew perfectly well that Fatty didn't mean a word he was saying. Who could keep him out of a mystery if he even so much as smelt one? Who could imagine that he would go and explain anything to Mr. Goon?

'Don't say "Yes, Mother," and "No, Mother" like that unless you mean it,' said Mrs. Trotteville, wishing she didn't feel annoyed with Fatty almost as soon as she had met him.

'No, Mother. I mean, yes, Mother,' said Fatty. 'Well—I mean whatever you want me to say, Mother. Can the others come to tea?'

'Certainly not,' said Mrs. Trotteville. 'I want to have a little chat with you and hear all your news—and then you have your bag to unpack—and soon your father will be home, and ...'

'Yes, Mother,' said Fatty, hastily. 'Well, can the others come round afterwards? I haven't seen them at all these hols. I've got presents for them. I didn't send them any at Christmas.'

The mention of presents suddenly made Bets remember that she had given her precious notebook to the fat boy. She bit her lip in horror. Gracious! He had put it into his pocket! She hadn't asked for it back, because she had been so scared when he had offered to fight them all, that she had forgotten all about the note-book.

'I gave that boy the present I had made for you,' she said, in a rather shaky voice. 'It was a note-book with your name on the front.'

'Just what I want!' said Fatty, cheerfully, and gave Bets a squeeze. 'I'll get it back from that boy, don't you worry!'

'Now, just remember what I say,' warned Mrs. Trotteville, as they came to her gate. 'There's to be no silly feud with that boy. He might be very nice.'

Every one looked doubtful. They were as certain as they could be that any nephew of Mr. Goon's must be as awful as the policeman himself. Buster barked loudly, and Bets felt sure he must be agreeing with them in his doggy language.

'Mother, you haven't said if the others can come round this evening,' said Fatty, as they went in at the gate.

'No. Not this evening,' said Mrs. Trotteville, much to every one's disappointment. 'You can meet them tomorrow. Good-bye children. Give my love to your mothers.'

Fatty and Buster disappeared up the path with Mrs. Trotteville. The others outside the gate looked gloomily at one another and then walked slowly down the road.

'She might have let us have just a *little* chat with Fatty.' said Larry.

'We made an awful noise last time we went to Fatty's,' said Bets, remembering. 'We thought Mrs. Trotteville was out, do you remember—and played a dreadful game Fatty made up, called Elephant-Hunting ...'

'And Mrs. Trotteville was in all the time and we never even heard her yelling at us to stop because we were making such a row,' said Pip. 'That was a good game. We must remember that.'

'I say, do you think that boy *was* Mr. Goon's nephew?' said Daisy. 'If he tells Mr. Goon all we did we'll get a few more black marks from him!'

'He'll know who we are,' said Bets dolefully. 'That boy's got the note-book I made—and there's Fatty's name on it. And, oh dear, inside I've printed in my best printing, headings to some of the pages. I've printed "CLUES," "SUSPECTS," and things like that. So Mr. Goon will know we're looking out for another mystery.'

'Well, silly, what does that matter?' demanded Pip. 'Let him think what he likes!'

' She's always so scared of Old Clear-Orf, ' said Daisy.
' I'm not ! We're much cleverer than he is. We've solved
mysteries that he hasn't even been able to *begin* solving. '

' I hope Mr. Goon won't come and complain to our
parents about our behaviour to that boy, ' said Pip.
' Honestly, we must have seemed a bit dotty to him.
Goon will probably think we did it all on purpose—made
a set at the boy just because he was his nephew. '

Pip's fear of being complained about was very real. He
had strict parents who had very strong ideas about good
and bad behaviour. Larry and Daisy's parents were not
so strict and Fatty's rarely bothered about him so long as
he was polite and good mannered.

But Pip had had some angry tickings-off from his father
and two or three canings, and he and Bets were always
afraid of Mr. Goon coming to complain. So, when they
arrived home that afternoon to tea, they were horrified to
hear from their maid, Lorna, that a Mr. Goon had been
ringing up their mother ten minutes before.

' I hope as how you haven't got into mischief, ' said
Lorna, who liked the children. ' He says he's coming to
see your Ma to-night. She's out to tea now. I thought I'd
just warn you in case you've gone and got yourselves into
trouble. '

' Thank you awfully, Lorna, ' said Pip and went to have
a gloomy tea in the play-room alone with Bets, who also
looked extremely down in the dumps. How *could* they
have thought that boy was Fatty ? Now that she came to
think of it Bets could quite clearly see that the boy was
coarse and lumpish—not even Fatty could look like that !

The two children decided to warn Larry and Daisy, so
they rang them up.

' Gosh ! ' said Larry. ' Fancy listening to tales from that
clod of a nephew about us ! I don't expect my mother will
pay much attention to Mr. Goon—but yours will ! Horrid

old man. Cheer up. We'll meet to-morrow and discuss it all. '

Pip and Bets waited for their mother to come in. Thank goodness their father was not with her. They went down to greet her.

' Mother, ' said Pip, ' We—er—we want to tell you something. Er—you see ... '

' *Now*, what mischief have you got into ? ' said Mrs. Hilton impatiently. ' Have you broken something ? Tell me without all this humming and hawing. '

' No. We haven't broken anything, ' said Bets. ' But you see, we went to meet Fatty at the station ... '

' And there was a fat boy we thought was Fatty in one of his disguises, ' went on Pip, ' so we followed him up the road, pretending not to know him ... '

' And then we called out "Fatty" to him, and told him we knew him—and he was angry, and ... '

' And what you mean is, you made a silly mistake and called a strange boy Fatty, and he was annoyed, ' said Mrs. Hilton, making an impatient tapping noise on the table. ' Why *must* you do idiotic things ? Well, I suppose you apologized, so there's not much harm done. '

' We didn't actually apologize, ' said Pip. ' We really thought he *was* Fatty. But he wasn't. He was Mr. Goon's nephew. '

Mrs. Hilton looked really annoyed. ' And now I suppose I shall have that policeman here complaining about you again. Well, you know what your father said last time, Pip—he said ... '

The door opened and Lorna came in. ' Please Madam, there's Mr. Goon wanting to see you. Shall I show him in ? '

Before Mrs. Hilton could say yes or no, the two children had opened the French windows that led to the garden and had shot out into the darkness. Pip wished he hadn't gone, as soon as he was out there, but Bets clutched him so desperately that he had shot off with her. A great draught of icy air blew into the sitting-room behind them.

Mrs. Hilton closed the garden door, looking cross. Mr. Goon came into the room, walking slowly and pompously. He thought Mr. and Mrs. Hilton were proper parents— they listened to him seriously when he made complaints. Well, he was going to enjoy himself now.

'Sit down, Mr. Goon,' said Mrs. Hilton, trying to be polite. 'What can I do for you?'

## 3  ERN

PIP and Bets went round to the kitchen door and let themselves in. The cook was out and Lorna was upstairs. They fled past the big black cat on the hearthrug and went up to their play-room.

'I should have stayed,' said Pip. 'I haven't done anything wrong. It was silly to run away. It will make Mother think we really are in the wrong.'

'Hark! Isn't that Daddy coming in?' said Bets. 'Yes, it is. He'll walk straight in on top of them, and hear everything too!'

Mr. Goon seemed to stay a long time, but at last he went. Mrs. Hilton called to Pip.

'Pip! Bring Bets down here, please. We have something to say to you.'

The two children went downstairs, Bets quite plainly scared, and Pip putting on a very brave face. To their surprise their parents did not seem angry at all.

'Pip,' said his mother, 'Mr. Goon came to tell us that he has his nephew staying with him. He says he is a very nice lad indeed, very straightforward and honest— and he says he would be glad if none of you five led him into trouble. You know that every holidays you seem to have been mixed up in mysteries of some kind or other— there was that burnt cottage—and the disappearing cat— and ...'

'And the spiteful letters, and the secret room, and the missing necklace,' said Pip, relieved to find that apparently Mr. Goon hadn't done much complaining.

'Yes. Quite,' said his father. 'Well, Mr. Goon doesn't want his nephew mixed up in anything like that. He says

he has promised the boy's mother to look after him well
these holidays, and he doesn't want you dragging him
into any mystery or danger ... '

'As if we'd *want* to do that!' said Pip, in disgust. 'His
nephew is just a great clod. We don't want to drag him
into anything—we'd like to leave him severely alone.'

'Well, see you do,' said his mother. 'Be friendly and
polite to him, please. Apparently you were very rude and
puzzling to him to-day—but as Pip had already explained
to me the mistake you made, I quite saw that you didn't
really mean to be rude. Mr. Goon was very nice about
that.'

'We won't drag his nephew into anything,' said Pip.
'If we find a mystery we'll keep it to ourselves.'

'That's another thing I want to say to you,' said his
father. 'I don't like you being mixed up in these things.
It is the job of the police to solve these mysteries and to
clear up any crimes that are committed. It's time you five
children kept out of them. I forbid you to try and solve any
mysteries these holidays.'

Pip and Bets stared at him in the greatest dismay. 'But
I say—we belong to the Five Find-Outers,' stammered
Pip. 'We *must* do our bit if a mystery comes along. I
mean, really ... why, we couldn't possibly promise to ... '

'Mr. Goon has already been to see Larry and Daisy's
parents,' said Mrs. Hilton. 'They have said that they too
will forbid their children to get mixed up in any mysteries
these holidays. Neither you nor they are to look for any,
you understand?'

'But—but suppose one comes—and we're mixed up in
it without knowing?' asked Bets. 'Like the missing
necklace mystery.'

'Oh, one won't come if you don't look for it, said Mr.
Hilton. 'Naturally if you got plunged into the middle of
one without your knowledge nobody could blame you—

but these things don't happen like that. I just simply forbid you to look for any mystery these holidays, I forbid you above all to allow Mr. Goon's nephew to get mixed up in anything of the kind.'

'You can go now,' said Mrs. Hilton. 'Don't look so miserable! Any one would think you couldn't be happy without some kind of mystery round the corner!'

'Well,' began Pip, and then decided to say no more. How could he explain the delight of smelling out a mystery, of making a list of Clues and Suspects, of trying to fit everything together like a jigsaw puzzle till the answer came, and the picture was complete?

He and Bets went out of the room and climbed up the stairs to their play-room. 'Fancy Larry and Daisy being forbidden too,' said Pip. 'I wonder if Mr. Goon went to Fatty's people too?'

'Well, I shouldn't think it would be any good forbidding Fatty to get mixed up in anything,' said Bets.

Bets was right. It wasn't any good. Fatty talked his mother and father over to his point of view under the very nose of Mr. Goon.

'I've been very useful indeed to Inspector Jenks,' he told his parents. 'You know I have. And you know I'm going to be the finest detective in the world when I'm grown up. I'm sure if you ring up the Inspector, Mother, he will tell you not to forbid me to do anything I want to. He trusts me.'

Inspector Jenks was a great friend of the children's. He was chief of the police in the next town, head of the whole district. Mr. Goon was in great awe of him. The children had certainly helped the Inspector many times in the way they had tackled various mysterious happenings.

'You ring up the Inspector, Mother,' said Fatty, seeing that the policeman didn't want Mrs. Trotteville to do this at all. 'I'm sure he'll say Mr. Goon is wrong.'

'Don't you bother the Inspector, Mrs. Trotteville;
*please,*' said Mr. Goon. 'He's a busy man. I wouldn't
have come to you if it hadn't have been for this young
nephew of mine—nice fellow he is, simple and innocent—
and I don't want him led into all sorts of dangers, see?'

'Well, I'm sure Frederick will promise not to lead him
into danger,' said Mrs. Trotteville. 'It's the last thing he
would want.'

Fatty said nothing. He was making no promises. He
had a kind of feeling that it would be good for Mr.
Goon's nephew to be led into something if he was as
simple and innocent as the policeman made out. Anyway,
all this was just to make sure that the Five Find-Outers
didn't solve another mystery before Mr. Goon did! Fatty
could see through *that* all right! Mr. Goon, not feeling
very satisfied, departed ponderously down the garden-
path, annoyed to find that his bicycle had suddenly
developed a puncture in the front tyre. It couldn't possibly
have been anything to do with That Boy, who had been
in the room all the time—but Mr. Goon thought it was a
very queer thing the way unpleasant things happened to
him when he was up against Frederick Algernon
Trotteville!

The Five Find-Outers met at Fatty's the next day.
Buster gave every one a hilarious welcome. 'Now!' he
barked. 'We are all together again. That's what I like
best.'

But four of them, at least, looked gloomy. 'That spoil-
sport of a Goon,' said Larry. 'We were just waiting for
you to come home and find another mystery to solve,
Fatty. Now we're forbidden even to look for one.'

'All because of that goofy nephew of Mr. Goon's,' said
Daisy.

'Well—*I'm* going to do exactly as I've always done,'
said Fatty. 'Look out for a mystery, find my clues and

suspects, fit the pieces together—and solve the whole thing before Mr. Goon even knows there's anything going on. And I'll tell you exactly what I'm doing the whole time!'

'Yes—but we want to *share* it,' said Pip. 'Share it properly, I mean—not just look on whilst you do it all. That's no fun.'

'Well, I don't suppose anything will turn up these hols at all,' grinned Fatty. 'Can't expect something *every* time, you know. But it would be rather fun to pretend we're on to something and get Goon's nephew all hot and bothered about it, wouldn't it? He'd say something to Goon, who wouldn't know whether to believe it or not—and he'd get into a mighty stew, too.'

'That's a wizard idea,' said Larry, pleased. 'Really wizard. If we can't find a mystery ourselves, we'll make up one for that boy. That'll serve Goon right for trying to spoil our fun!'

'Let's come and see if we can find the boy.' said Fatty. 'I'd be interested to see what sort of a fellow you mistook for me in disguise! Must be jolly good-looking, that's all I can say!'

They all went to the village. They were lucky, because just as they came in sight of Mr. Goon's house his nephew came out, wheeling his uncle's bicycle, having been ordered by Goon to take it to the garage and get the puncture mended.

'There he is!' said Bets excitedly. Fatty looked and an expression of deep disgust came over his face. He gazed at the Find-Outers in disappointment.

'Well! *How* you could think that boy was me—even in *disguise*, I really don't know! He's an oaf! A clod! A lump! Not a brain in his head. Good gracious, surely I don't look in the *least* like him?'

Fatty looked so hurt that Bets put her arm in his and

squeezed it. 'Fatty! Don't be upset. We thought it was one of your clever disguises.'

The boy wheeled his bicycle towards them. He stopped when he saw them, and to their surprise he grinned.

'Hallo! I know all about your mistake yesterday. You got me properly hot and bothered. I told my uncle and he spotted it was you. Said you called yourself the Find-Outers, or some such thing. He said you were a set of cheeky toads.'

'What's your name?' asked Pip.

'Ern,' said the boy.

'*Urn*?' said Bets in surprise, thinking of the great tea-urns her mother had at mothers' meetings.

'SwatIsaid,' said Ern.

Nobody understood the last sentence at all. 'I beg your pardon? What did you say?' asked Larry politely.

'I said "SwatIsaid," ' said Ern, impatiently.

'Oh—he means "It's what I said," ' explained Daisy to the others.

'Course it is—short for Ernest, see?' said Ern. 'I got two brothers. One Sid, short for Sidney the other's Perce, short for Percy. Ern, Sid and Perce—that's us.'

'Very nice,' murmured Fatty. 'Ern suits you marvellously.'

Ern looked pleased. 'And Fatty suits you,' he said, handsomely. 'Right down to the ground it does. And Pip suits him too—bit of a pipsqueak, isn't he? Wants to grow a bit, I'd say.'

The Find-Outers thought these remarks were out of place from Ern. He was getting a bit too big for his boots.

'I hope you'll have a nice holiday with your uncle,' said Bets, suddenly very polite.

Ern made a curious chortling noise. 'Oooh! My uncle! His high-and-mighty-nibs! Says I mustn't get led into

danger by you! Well, you see here—if you get hold of any
mysteries you just tell me, Ern Goon. I'd like to show my
uncle I've got better brains than his.'

'That wouldn't be very difficult,' said Fatty. 'Well,
Ern—we'll certainly lead you to any mysteries we find. I
expect you know that your uncle has forbidden us to solve
any ourselves these hols—so perhaps you could take our
place and solve a mystery right under his nose?'

Ern's rather protruding eyes nearly fell out of his head.
'Jumping snakes! Do you mean that? Lovaduck!'

'Yes. We'll provide you with all sorts of clues,' said
Fatty, solemnly. 'But don't you go and tell your uncle in
case he gets angry with us.'

'You bet I won't,' said Ern.

'Oh, Ern—can I have back that note-book I gave you
by mistake yesterday?' said Bets, suddenly. 'It wasn't
meant for you, of course. It was meant for Fatty.'

'I was going to use it for my portry,' said Ern, looking
disappointed. He took it out and held it for Bets to take.
'I love portry.'

'What's portry?' asked Bets, puzzled.

'Portry! Lovaduck, don't you know what's portry. It's
when things rhyme, like.'

'Oh—you mean poetry,' said Bets.

'SwatIsaid,' said Ern. 'Well, I write portry.'

This was so astonishing that nobody said anything for
a moment.

'What sort of poetry—er, I mean portry?' asked Fatty.

'I'll recite you some,' said Ern, looking very pleased
with himself. 'This here one's called "The Pore Dead
Pig." He cleared his throat and began:

> 'How sad to see thee, pore dead pig,
> When all ...'

'Look out—here's your uncle!' suddenly said Larry,

*Ern chatted to the others*

as a large dark-blue figure appeared in Mr. Goon's little front garden. A roar came from him.

'What about my BIKE! Didn't I tell you I wanted it right back?'

'So long!' said Ern, hurriedly, and shot off down the street at top speed. 'See you later!'

## 4   FATTY IS MYSTERIOUS

ERN soon became a terrible bore. He lay in wait for the Find-Outers every day, and pestered them to tell him if they had smelt out any mystery yet. He kept wanting to recite his 'portry.' He shocked the five children by his very low opinion of his uncle, Mr. Goon.

'We've got a low opinion of Old Clear-Orf ourselves,' said Larry, 'but really, to hear Ern speak of his uncle any one would think he was the meanest, slyest, greediest, laziest policeman that ever lived!'

Ern was always bringing out dreadful tales of his uncle. 'He ate three eggs and all the bacon for his breakfast, and he didn't leave me nothing but a plate of porridge,' said Ern. 'No wonder he's bursting his uniform!'

'My uncle isn't half lazy,' he said another time. 'He's supposed to be on duty each afternoon, but he just puts his head back, shuts his eyes and snores till tea-time! Wouldn't I like the Inspector to come along and catch him!'

'My uncle says you all want locking up for a few days, you're just a set of cheeky toads,' said Ern, yet another time. 'He likes *your* mother and father, Pip—but he says Fatty's people are just the ...'

'Look here, Ern—you oughtn't to repeat what your uncle says about us or our people,' said Fatty. 'It's a rotten trick. You know jolly well Mr. Goon wouldn't tell you all these things if he thought you were going to repeat them.'

Ern gave one of his chortles. 'Lovaduck! What do you suppose he says them for? 'Course he wants me to tell you them! Nice easy way for him to be rude to you.'

' Really ? ' said Fatty. Well, two can play at that game. You tell your uncle we think he's a ... '

' Oh don't, Fatty, ' said Bets, in alarm. ' He'll only come round and complain again. '

' He can't complain to *your* parents about what *I* say, ' said Fatty.

' Oh yes, he can, ' said Pip. ' You should just see him walking into our house like a flat-footed bull-frog, as pompous as a ... '

Ern gave such a loud chortle that every one jumped. Pip stopped in a hurry.

' That's a good one, that is ! ' said Ern. ' Lovaduck, I'd like to see Uncle Theophilus when I tell him that ! '

' If you repeat that I'll fight you ! ' said Pip, furious with himself for saying such a silly thing in front of Ern. ' I'll knock your silly nose off, I'll ... '

' Shut up, Pip, ' said Fatty. ' You can't even box. You ought to learn boxing at school like I do. You should just see me box ! Why, last term I fought a chap twice my size, and in five minutes I ... '

' Had him flat on his back ! ' finished Larry ' with a couple of black eyes and a squashed ear. '

Fatty looked surprised. ' How do you know ? ' he said. ' Have I told you before ? '

' No, but your stories always end in some way like that, ' grinned Larry.

' Found any mystery yet ? ' inquired Ern, who didn't like to be left out of the talk for long. Fatty at once looked secretive.

' Well, ' he said, and hesitated. ' No, I don't think I'd better tell you, Ern. You'd only split to your uncle. You just can't keep your mouth shut. '

Ern began to look excited. ' Come on ! You've got something, I know you have. You said you'd tell me if you was on to a mystery. Lovaduck ! Wouldn't it be a sell for

Uncle if I got on to a mystery and solved it before he got a sniffofit. '

'What was that last word?' asked Fatty. Ern had a curious habit of running some of his words together. ' Sniffofit? What sort of a fit is that? Does your uncle go in for fits?'

'Sniffofit!' repeated Ern. ' Can't you understand plain English? Sniffofit. '

'He means "sniff of it" said Daisy.

'SwatIsaid, ' said Ern, looking sulky.

'Swatesaid, ' said Fatty at once to the others. They giggled. Ern scowled. He didn't like it when the others made fun of him. But he soon cheered up.

'Go on—you tell me about this mystery you've got, ' he begged Fatty.

Fatty, of course, knew of no mystery at all. The holidays, in fact, stretched dull and drear in front of him, with not a hint of any mystery anywhere. Only Ern promised a little fun and excitement. Fatty looked mysterious.

He began to speak in a whisper. 'Well, ' he said, ' it's like this. ' He stopped and looked over his shoulder as if there were people listening. Ern began to feel thrilled.

Then Fatty shook his head firmly. 'No, Ern. I can't tell you yet. I don't think I'd better. I'm only at the beginning of things. I'll wait till I know a little more. '

Ern could hardly contain his excitement. He clutched Fatty's arm. 'Look here, you've *got* to tell me!' he hissed. 'I won't breathe a word to Uncle. Go on, Fatty, be a sport. '

The others watched Fatty, trying not to laugh. They knew he hadn't anything to tell. Poor old Ern—he just swallowed everything he was told.

'I'll wait till I've a bit more to tell, ' said Fatty. 'No, it's no good, Ern. Not even the others know anything yet. The time hasn't come yet to develop the case. '

' Lovaduck! That sounds good, ' said Ern, impressed. ' All right, I'll wait. I say—do you think I ought to get a note-book and write down in it the things young Bets here wrote down in yours—the one she gave you for a present? '

' It wouldn't be a bad idea, ' said Fatty. ' You've a note-book in your pocket, I see—bring it out and we'll show you what to write. '

' No. That's my portry note-book, ' said Ern. ' Can't write nothing in that except portry. ' He took it out and flicked over the pages. ' Look—I wrote a pome last night—proper good pome it was too. It's called "The Pore Old Horse." Shall I read it to you? '

' Well, no—not now, ' said Fatty, looking at his watch and putting on a very startled expression. ' My word—look at the time. Sorry, old horse—pore old horse—but we can't stop to-day. Another time perhaps. Get a note-book, Ern, and we'll set down in it all you ought to have in a proper mystery note-book. '

The five went off with Buster, grinning. Ern went back to his uncle, pondering whether to repeat Pip's words to his uncle—what were they now? Flat-footed bull-frog. That was good, that was. Good enough to put into a pome!

' Ern and his pomes and portry! ' giggled Daisy. ' I wish I could get hold of that portry book—I'd write a poem in it that would make Old Clear-Orf sit up! '

' Quite an idea! ' said Fatty, and put it away in his mind for future use. ' Now, Find-Outers, we'd better plan what sort of wild-goose chase we're to send Ern on! We can't possibly disappoint him. We've got to give him a bit of excitement. '

They went to Pip's play-room and began to plan. ' It

wouldn't be a bad idea to practise a few disguises,' said Fatty thoughtfully. 'It doesn't look as if we're going to have much fun these hols, so we might as well make our own.'

'Oh, yes—*do* let's practise disguises,' said Bets, thrilled.

'We're going to have a good time with old Ern,' chuckled Fatty. 'Now, let's plan. Anybody got any ideas?'

'Well—what about a mystery kidnapping or something like that?' said Larry. 'Men who kidnap rich men's children and keep them prisoner. We might get Ern to try and rescue them.'

'Or we might have mysterious lights at night flashing somewhere, and send Ern to see what they are,' said Bets.

'Go on. We're getting some good ideas,' said Fatty.

'Or what about a robbery—with the loot hidden somewhere—and Ern has to find it?' suggested Daisy.

'Or a collection of clues to puzzle Ern. You know how we once put a whole lot of clues down for Clear-Orf,' said Pip. 'My word—I'll never forget that.'

Every one laughed. Fatty tapped his knee thoughtfully with his pencil. 'Jolly good ideas, all of them,' he said. 'Super, in fact. I vote we try and use all of them. Might as well give Ern good measure. And if old Goon gets excited about it too, so much the better. I bet Ern won't be able to keep it dark. Goon will know there's something up—but he won't know how much is pretence and how much isn't. We'll have them both on a string!'

'It won't be as good as a real mystery, but it will be great fun!' said Bets, hugging herself. 'It will serve Mr. Goon right for coming to complain to Daddy and Mother! And for trying to do *us* out of a mystery these hols.'

'Not that there's even a shadow of one at the moment,' said Daisy.

'Well, now, let's get down to it,' said Fatty. 'Ern will come complete with his note-book next time we see him, I'm sure of that. We'll put down the usual headings— Clues, Suspects, Progress and so on. Then we'll begin providing a few clues. We'd better let him find them. He'll get awfully bucked if he thinks he's better at spotting things that we are. I'll make up some kind of story, which I won't tell you now, so that it will seem quite fresh to you. You can listen with large eyes and bated breath!'

'What's bated breath?' asked Bets. 'Do we breathe fast, or something?'

'No—we just hold it, silly,' said Pip. 'And don't you go and give the game away, Bets. It would be just like you to do that!'

'It would *not*,' said Bets, indignantly. 'Would it, Fatty?'

'No. You're a very good little Find-Outer,' said Fatty, comfortingly. 'I bet you'll bate your breath best of any one. Hallo, what's that?'

'The dinner-bell,' said Pip, gloomily. 'It always goes when we're in the middle of something.'

'Spitty,' said Fatty, and got up.

'What do you mean—*spitty*?' said Larry.

'He means "It's a pity!"' said Bets with a giggle.

'SwatIsaid,' said Fatty, and got up to go.

## 5   IN FATTY'S SHED

THE next day Ern got a message that filled him with excitement. It was a note from Fatty.

'Developments. Must talk to you. Bottom of my garden, twelve o'clock. F.T. '

Mr. Goon saw Ern goggling over this note and became suspicious at once. 'Who's that from ? '

'One of my friends. ' said Ern haughtily, and put it into his pocket.

Mr. Goon went a purple-red. 'You show it to me, ' he said.

'Can't, ' said Ern. 'It's private. '

'What do you mean—*private* ! ' snorted Mr. Goon. 'A kid like you don't know what private means. You give me that note. '

'But Uncle—it's only from Fatty to say he wants to see me, ' protested Ern.

'You show that note to me ! ' shouted Mr. Goon, and Ern, scared, passed it over. Mr. Goon snorted again as he read it.

'Gah ! All a lot of tommy-rot ! Developments indeed ! What does he mean by that ? '

Ern didn't know, and he said so several times, but his uncle didn't believe him. 'If that there cheeky toad is up to his tricks again, I'll skin him ! ' said Mr. Goon. 'And you tell him that, see ? '

'Oh, I will, Uncle, ' said Ern, trying to edge out of the room. 'I always tell them what you say. They like to hear. But it's not right of Pip to say you're a flat-footed bull-frog, I did tell him that. '

Before the purple Mr. Goon could find his tongue to say what he thought of this, Ern was out of the house and away. He mopped his forehead. Lovaduck—his uncle was a hot-tempered chap all right. Anyway, he hadn't forbidden him to go ; that was something !

He arrived at the bottom of Fatty's garden and heard voices in the shed there. It was Fatty's work-room and play-room. He had made it very comfortable indeed. On this cold winter's day he had an oil-stove burning brightly and the inside of the shed was warm and cosy. A tiger-skin was on the floor, old and moth-eaten but looking very grand, and a crocodile skin was stretched along one side of the shed-wall. The Five Find-Outers were trying to roast chestnuts on top of the oil-stove. They had a tin of condensed milk and were each having a dip in it with a spoon as they talked.

Ern looked in at the window. Ha ! They were all there. Good ! He knocked at the door.

'Come in !' called Fatty, and Ern went in. An icy draught at once came in with him.

'Shut the door,' said Daisy. 'Oooh ! What a draught. Hallo, Ern. Did you enjoy your egg for breakfast ? '

Ern looked surprised. 'Yes. But how did you know I had an egg for breakfast ? '

'Oh—we're doing a bit of detecting for practice this morning, ' said Daisy. The others tried not to laugh. Ern had spilt a good bit of his egg down the front of his jacket at breakfast, so it was not a difficult bit of detecting !

'Sorry you had to leave in such a hurry to come here, ' said Fatty, solemnly.

Ern looked even more surprised. 'Lovaduck ! Is that another bit of detecting ? How'd you know I left in a hurry ? '

Ern had no hat and no coat, so *that* wasn't a very difficult bit of detecting either. Nobody explained to Ern how they knew about his breakfast or his hurry, and he sat down feeling rather puzzled.

'Perhaps you'd like to tell me what *I* had for breakfast,' said Fatty to Ern. 'Go on—do a bit of detecting too.'

Ern looked at Fatty's solemn face, but no ideas about breakfast came into his mind. He shook his head. 'No. I can see this sort of thing wants a lot of practice. Coo, I wasn't half excited when I got your note this morning. My uncle saw me reading it.'

'Did he really?' said Fatty with interest. 'Did he say anything?'

'Oh, he got into a rage, you know, but I soon settled *that*.' said Ern. 'I just told him what I thought of him. "Uncle," I said, "this is a private note. It's none of your business, so keep out of it." Just like that.'

Every one looked at him admiringly but disbelievingly. 'And what did he say to that?' asked Pip.

'He began to go purple,' said Ern, 'and I said "Now calm yourself, Uncle, or you'll go pop. And don't go poking your nose into what I do with my friends. It's private." And then I walked out and came here.'

'Most admirable!' said Fatty. 'Sit down on the tiger-skin rug, Ern. Don't be afraid of the head and the teeth. He's not as fierce now as he was when I shot him in the Tippylooloo Plain.'

Ern's eyes nearly fell out of his head. 'Lovaduck! You been tiger-shooting? What about that thing up on the wall? Did you shoot that too?'

'That's a crocodile skin,' said Bets, enjoying herself. 'Let me see, Fatty—was that the third or fourth crocodile you shot?'

Ern's respect for Fatty went up a hundredfold. He gazed about him with the greatest awe. He looked at the fierce head of the tiger-rug, and felt a bit scared of it, even though it was no longer alive. He moved a little way from the snarling teeth.

'You said in your note there were developments,' said Ern, eagerly. 'Are you going to tell us anything to-day?'

'Yes. The time has come for us to ask you to do something,' said Fatty, in a solemn voice that sent a thrill down Ern's spine. 'I am uncovering a very mysterious mystery.'

'Coo,' said Ern, in a hushed voice. 'Do the others know?'

'Not yet,' said Fatty. 'Now listen all of you. There are strange lights flashing at night over on Christmas Hill!'

'Oooh,' said Ern. 'Have you seen them?'

'There are rival gangs there,' said Fatty, in a grave voice. 'One is a kidnapping gang. One is a gang of robbers. Soon they will get busy.'

Ern's mouth fell open. The others, although they knew it was all Fatty's make-up, couldn't help feeling a bit thrilled too. Ern swallowed once or twice. Talk about a mystery! This was a whacker!

'Now the thing is—can we get going, and find out who they are and their plans, before they start their robbing and kidnapping?' said Fatty.

'*We* can't,' said Bets, in a dismal voice. 'We've been forbidden to get mixed up in an mystery these hols.'

'So have we,' said Larry and Daisy together. 'Yes, it's bad luck,' said Fatty. 'I'm the only one who can do anything—but I can't do it alone. That's why I've got you here this morning, Ern. You must help me.'

Ern took in all this rather slowly, but with the utmost excitement and delight. He swelled out his chest proudly.

'You can count on me,' he said, and made his voice deep and solemn. 'Ern's with you! Coo! I feel all funny-like. I bet I'd write a good pome with this sort of feeling inside me!'

'Yes. It could begin like this,' said Fatty, who could reel off silly verse by the mile.

> 'There's a mystery a-moving
> Away on Christmas Hill,
> Where kidnappers and robbers
> Are waiting for the kill.
> But when kidnappers are napping
> And robbers are asleep,
> We'll pounce on them together
> And knock them in a heap!'

Every one laughed. No one could reel off verse like Fatty. Ern gaped and couldn't find a word to say. Why, that was wonderful portry! To think Fatty could say it all off like that!

He found his voice at last. 'Lovaduck! Did you make all that up out of your head just this minute? It takes me hours to think of a pome—and even when I do, it won't rhyme for ages. You must be one of them queer things—a genius.'

'Well—you never know,' said Fatty, trying to look modest. 'I remember having to write a poem—er, I mean pome—for class one day, and forgetting all about it till the master pounced on me and asked for mine. I looked in my desk, but of course it wasn't there because I had forgotten to write one. So I just said 'Sorry, sir, it seems to be mislaid—but I'll recite it if you like.' And I stood up and recited six verses straight off out of my head. What's more, I got top marks for it.'

'I don't believe you,' said Pip.

'Well, I'll recite it for you now if you like,' said Fatty, indignantly, but the others wouldn't let him.

'Stop boasting,' said Larry. 'Let's get down to work. How did we get on to this poem-business anyway? You'll have Ern wanting to recite next!'

Ern would have been only too willing to oblige, but most unfortunately in his hurried departure from his uncle's house he had left his portry note-book—a very grand one, with black covers, and elastic band, and a pencil down the back.

'Mr. Goon's got one like that,' said Bets. 'Did he give you that?'

Mr. Goon would not even have dreamed of giving his nephew one of his precious note-books, provided for him by the Inspector. Ern licked the end of the pencil and looked round triumphantly. 'Give it me! I should think not! I pinched it out of his drawer.'

There was a horrified silence. 'Then you'll jolly well give it back,' said Fatty. 'Or *you'll* be pinched one day. You're disgusting, Ern.'

Ern looked hurt and astonished. 'Well, he's my uncle, isn't he? It won't hurt him to let me have one of his note-books—and I'm going detecting, aren't I? You're very high-and-mighty all of a sudden.'

'You can think us high-and-mighty if you like,' said Fatty, getting up. 'But we think *you're* very low-down to take something out of your uncle's drawer without asking him.'

'I'll put it back,' said Ern, in a small voice. 'I wouldn't have taken it for my portry—but for detecting, well, somehow I thought that was different. I kind of thought I *ought* to have it.'

'Well, you think again,' said Fatty. 'And put it back before you get into trouble. Look—here's a note-book of mine you can have. It's an old one. We'll tell you what to write in it. But mind—you put that black one back as soon as ever you get home!'

'Yes, I will, Fatty,' said Ern, humbly. He took the old note-book Fatty held out to him, and felt about in his pocket for a pencil, for he did not feel he dared to use the one in the black note-book now. Fatty might get all high-and-mighty again.

'Now,' said Fatty, 'keep this page for clues. Write the word down—Clues.'

'Clues,' said Ern, solemnly, and wrote it down. The word 'Suspects' came next. 'Coo,' said Ern, 'do we have Suspects too? What are they?'

'People who *might* be mixed up in the mystery,' said Fatty. 'You make a whole list of them, inquire into their goings-on, and then cross them off one by one when you find they're all right.'

Ern felt very important as he put down the things Fatty told him. He licked his stump of a pencil, and wrote most laboriously, with his tongue sticking out of the corner of his mouth all the time.

Buster suddenly growled and cocked up his ears. Fatty put his hand on him. 'Quiet, Buster,' he said. He winked at the others. 'I bet it's Old Clear-Orf snooping round,' he said. Ern looked alarmed.

'I wonder he dares to come snooping after Ern, considering the way he got ticked off by Ern himself this morning,' said Fatty, innocently. 'If it *is* your uncle, Ern, you'd better send him off at once. Bit of cheek, tracking you down like this!'

Ern felt even more alarmed. A shadow fell across the cosy room, and the Find-Outers and Ern saw Mr. Goon's head peering in at the window. He saw Ern with a note-book. Ern looked up with a scared face.

'You come on out, Ern,' boomed Mr. Goon. 'I got a job for you to do!'

Ern got up and went to the door. He opened it and out shot Buster in delight. He flew for Mr. Goon's ankles at once, barking madly.

'Clear-orf!' yelled Mr. Goon, kicking out at Buster. 'Here you, call off your dog! Ern, hold him! He'll take a bit out of my ankle soon! Clear-orf, you pestering dog!'

But it was Mr. Goon who had to clear-orf, with Buster barking at him all the way, and Ern following in delight. 'Go on, Buster!' he muttered under his breath. 'Keep it up! Good dog then. Good dog!'

## 6  ERN GETS INTO TROUBLE

THE Five Find-Outers were very pleased with their little bit of work that morning. 'We'll keep Ern busy,' said Fatty. 'And as I'm pretty sure he'll let everything out to Goon—or Goon will probably dip into Ern's note-book—we shall keep *him* busy too!'

'It's a pity Mr. Goon came and interrupted our talk this morning,' said Bets, getting up to go. 'We were just getting on nicely. Fatty, what's the first clue to be?'

'Well, I told Ern that this morning,' said Fatty. 'Mysterious lights flash on Christmas Hill at night! Ern will have to go and find out what they are.'

'Will you go with him?' asked Bets.

'No. I'll be flashing the lights,' said Fatty with a grin. The others looked at him enviously.

'Wish we could come too,' said Larry. 'It's maddening to be forbidden to do anything these hols.'

'Well, you're not forbidden to play a trick on somebody,' said Fatty, considering the matter. 'You're forbidden to get mixed up in any mystery or to go and look for one. You're not looking for a mystery, and there certainly isn't one, so I don't see why you and Pip can't come.'

The others' faces brightened. But Bets and Daisy were soon disappointed. 'The girls can't come out these cold nights,' went on Fatty. 'We'll have to find something else for them to do. Look here—I'll do a bit of disguising the first night Ern goes mystery hunting—and you two boys can do the light-flashing. I'll let Ern discover me crouching in a ditch or something, so that he really will think he's happened on some robber or other.'

' Yes—that would be fine ! ' said Larry. ' When shall we do it ? '

' Can't do it to-night, ' said Fatty. ' We may not be able to get in touch with Ern in time. Tomorrow night, say. '

' Wasn't Ern funny when you spouted all that verse, ' said Larry, with a grin. ' I don't know how you do it Fatty, really I don't. Ern thinks you're the world's wonder. I wonder if Sid and Perce are just as easy to take in as Ern. Are we going to meet again to-day ? '

' If I can get my mother to say you can all come to tea, I'll telephone you, ' said Fatty. ' I don't see why I can't go and buy a whole lot of cakes, and have you to tea down here in the shed. We'd be nice and cosy, and we could make as much noise as we liked. '

But alas for Fatty's plan, an aunt came to tea, and he was made to go and behave politely at tea-time, handing bread and butter, jam and cakes in a way that Ern would have admired tremendously.

Ern was not having a very good time with his uncle. He had tried in vain to replace the note-book he had taken, but Mr. Goon always seemed to be hovering about. Ern didn't mean to let his uncle see him put it back !

He kept trying to go into his uncle's office, which was next to a little wash-place off the hall. But every time he sauntered out into the hall, whistling softly as if he hadn't a care in the world, his uncle saw him.

' What you want ? ' he kept asking. ' Why are you so fidgety ? Can't a man have forty winks in peace without you wandering about, and whistling a silly tune ? '

' Sorry, Uncle, ' said Ern, meekly. ' I was just going to wash my hands. '

' What, *again* ? ' said Mr. Goon, disbelievingly. ' You've washed them twice since dinner already. What's this new idea of being clean? I've never known you wash your hands before unless I told you. '

' They feel sort of—sticky, ' said Ern, rather feebly. He went back into the kitchen, where his uncle was sitting in his arm chair, his coat unbuttoned, and his froggy eyes looking half-closed and sleepy. Why didn't he go to sleep as he usually did?

Ern sat down. He picked up a paper and pretended to read it. Mr. Goon knew he was pretending, and he wondered what Ern was up to. He didn't want to wash his hands! No, he wanted to go into his uncle's office. What for? Mr. Goon thought deeply about the matter.

A sudden thought came into his mind. Aha! It was that cheeky toad of a boy, Frederick Trotteville, who had put Ern up to snooping about his office to see if any mystery was afoot. The sauce! Well, let him catch Ern snooping in his desk, and Ern would feel how hard his hand was! He began to hope that Ern *would* do a bit of snooping. Mr. Goon felt that he would quite like to give somebody a really good ticking-off! He was in that sort of mood, what with that dog snapping at his ankles and making him rush off like that in front of Ern.

He closed his eyes. He pretended to snore a little. Ern rose quietly and made for the door. He stopped in the hall and looked back. Mr. Goon still snored, and his mouth was half open. Ern felt he was safe.

He slipped into the office, and opened the drawer of the desk. He slid the note-book into the drawer—but before he could close it a wrathful voice fell on his ears.

' Ho! So that's what you're doing—snooping and prying in my private papers! You wicked boy—my own nephew too, that ought to know better. '

Ern felt a sharp slap across his left cheek, and he put up his hand. ' Uncle! I wasn't snooping! I swear I wasn't. '

' What were you doing then? ' demanded Mr. Goon.

Ern stood and stared at his uncle without a word to say. He couldn't possibly own up to having taken the note-book—so he couldn't say he was putting it back! Mr. Goon slapped poor Ern hard on the other cheek. 'Next time I'll put you across my knee and deal with you properly!' threatened Mr. Goon. 'What are you snooping for? Did that cheeky toad of a boy tell you to hunt in my desk to see what sort of a case I was working on now? Did he tell you to find out any of my clues and give them to him?'

'No, Uncle, no,' said Ern beginning to blubber in fright and pain. 'I wouldn't do that, not even if he told me to. Anyway, he knows the mystery. He's told me about it.'

Mr. Goon pricked up his ears at once. What! Fatty had got hold of another mystery! What could it be? Mr. Goon could have danced with rage. That boy! A real pest he was if ever there was one.

'Now, you look here,' he said to Ern, who was holding his hand to his right ear, which was swollen with the slap Mr. Goon had given it, 'you look here! It's your duty to report to me anything that boy tells you about this mystery. See?'

Ern was torn between his urgent wish to be loyal to Fatty, the boy he admired so tremendously, and his fear that Mr. Goon might really give him a thrashing if he refused to tell anything Fatty told him.

'Go on,' said his uncle. 'Tell me what you know. It's your bounden duty to tell a police officer everything. What's this here wonderful mystery?'

'Oh—it's just lights flashing on Christmas Hill,' stammered poor Ern, rubbing his tear-stained face. 'That's about all I know, Uncle. I don't believe Fatty knows much more. He's given me a note-book—look. You can see what's written down in it. Hardly anything.'

Mr. Goon frowned over the headings. He began to plan. He could always get this note-book from Ern—and if the boy refused to give it to him, well then, as an officer of the law he'd get it somehow—even if he had to do it when Ern was asleep. He gave it back to Ern.

'I've got a good hard hand, haven't I, Ern?' said Mr. Goon to his nephew. 'You don't want to feel it again, do you? Well, then, you see you report to me all the goings-on that those kids get up to.'

'Yes, Uncle,' said Ern, not meaning to at all. He backed away from his uncle. 'There aren't any goings on just now. We hadn't planned anything, Uncle. You came and interrupted us.'

'And a good thing too,' said Mr. Goon. 'Now you can just sit down at the kitchen table and do some holiday work, see? Time you did something to oil those brains of yours. I'm not going to have you tearing about with those five kids and that dog all day long.'

Ern went obediently to the kitchen and settled down at the table with an arithmetic book. He had had a bad report from his school the term before, and was supposed to do a good bit of holiday work. But instead of thinking of his sums he thought about the Find-Outers, especially Fatty, and the Mystery, and Flashing Lights, and Kidnappers and Robbers. Lovaduck! How exciting it all was.

Ern was worried because his uncle wouldn't let him go out. He couldn't get in touch with the others if he didn't go out. Suppose they went to look for those flashing lights and didn't let him know? Ern felt he simply couldn't *bear* that.

All that day he was kept in the house. He went to bed to dream of tigers, crocodiles, Fatty reciting verse and somebody kidnapping his uncle. When he awoke the next morning he began to plan how to get into touch with the others.

But Mr. Goon had other plans. ' You can take down all those files in those shelves, ' he said. ' And clean up the shelves and dust the files, and put them back in proper order. '

That took Ern all the morning. Mr. Goon went out and Ern hoped one of the Find-Outers would come, but they didn't. In the afternoon Mr. Goon settled himself down to go to sleep as usual. He saw Ern looking very down in the dumps and was pleased. ' He won't go snooping again ! ' he thought. ' He knows what he'll get if he does ! '

And Mr. Goon went peacefully off to sleep. He was awakened by a thunderous knocking at the door. He almost leapt out of his chair, and Ern looked alarmed.

' Shall I go, Uncle ? ' he said.

Mr. Goon did not answer. He went to the door himself, buttoning up his uniform. That knocking sounded official. It might be the Inspector himself. People didn't usually hammer on the door of a police officer like that. They'd be afraid to !

Outside stood a fat old woman in a red shawl. ' I've come to complain, ' she began, in a high, quavering voice. ' The things I've put up with from that woman ! She's my next-door neighbour, sir, and she's the meanest woman you ever saw. She throws her rubbish into my garden, sir, and she always lights her bonfire when the wind's blowing my way, and ... '

' Wait, wait, ' said Mr. Goon, annoyed. ' What's your name and where do ... '

' And only yesterday she called me a monster, sir, that was the very word she used, oh, a wicked woman she is, and it's myself won't stand it any longer. Why, last week her dustbin ... '

Mr. Goon saw that this would go on for ever. ' You can

put in a written complaint,' he said. 'I'm busy this afternoon,' and he shut the door firmly.

He settled himself down in his chair again, but before two minutes had gone, there came such a knock at the door that it was a wonder it wasn't broken down. Mr. Goon, in a fury, leapt up again and almost ran to the door. The woman was there again, her arms folded akimbo over her chest.

'I forgot to tell you, sir,' she began, 'when I put my washing out last week this woman threw a pail of dirty water over it, and I had to wash it all again, and ...'

'Didn't I tell you to put in a written report?' roared Mr. Goon. 'Do as you're told, woman!' And again he shut the door, and stamped into the kitchen, fuming.

No sooner had he sat down than the knocker sounded again. Mr. Goon looked at Ern. 'You go,' he said. 'It's that woman again. Tell her what you like.'

Ern went, rather scared. He opened the door and a flood of words poured over him. 'Och, it's you this time, is it? Well, you tell your uncle, what's the good of me putting in a written report, when I can't read nor write? You ask him that. You go in and ask him that!'

And then, to Ern's enormous astonishment, the red-shawled woman dug him in the chest, and said in a whisper, 'Ern! Take this! Now, tell me to go away, quick!'

Ern gaped. that was Fatty's voice, surely. Coo, was this Fatty in one of his disguises? Wonderful! Fatty winked hugely, and Ern found his voice.

'You clear-orf!' he cried. 'Bothering my uncle like this! I won't have it! Clear-orf, I say!'

He slammed the door. Mr. Goon, in the kitchen, listened in astonishment. Why, Ern had been able to get rid of the woman far more quickly than he had. There must be something in the boy after all.

Ern was quickly reading the note Fatty had pushed into his hand :

'To-night. Watch for lights on Christmas Hill. Hide in ditch by mill. Midnight. Report tomorrow. '

Ern stuffed the note into his pocket, too thrilled for words. It was beginning ! He was plunging into a Mystery ! And he wouldn't tell his uncle a single word. That Fatty ! Fancy having the cheek to dress up like that and come thundering on his uncle's front door. Ern went into the kitchen, quite bemused.

' So you got rid of that woman ? ' said his uncle. ' Well, let's hope she won't come hammering again. '

She didn't. She went home to Fatty's house, slipped out of her things in Fatty's shed—and there was Fatty himself, taking off the woman's wig he wore, and rubbing away the wrinkles he had painted on his face. He chuckled. ' That took Goon in properly ! My word, Ern 's face was a picture when he saw it was me ! '

## 7   MYSTERIOUS HAPPENINGS ON CHRISTMAS HILL

ERN was in such a state of excitement all the rest of the day that his uncle couldn't help noticing it. He stared at Ern and wondered. What was up with the boy? He hadn't seen or heard from the others. Then why was he so excited? He couldn't keep still for a minute.

'Stop fidgeting, Ern!' said Mr. Goon sharply. 'What's the matter with you?'

'Nothing, Uncle,' said Ern. Actually Ern was a bit worried about something. He knew Christmas Hill all right—but he didn't know where this mill was that Fatty had written of in his letter. How could he find out? Only by asking his uncle. But would his uncle smell a rat if he began talking about the mill?

He decided to get a map of the district out of the book-case and study it. So when Mr. Goon was answering the telephone, Ern slid the map from the shelf, opened it and looked for the mill. Oh yes—there it was—on the right of the stream. If he followed the stream he couldn't help coming to the mill. Ern shivered in delight when he thought of creeping out all by himself that night. He marked where the mill was, and then with his pencil followed the way he would go, right up to the mill.

Mr. Goon's eyes looked sharply at the map as he came back into the room. 'What you studying? he asked.

'Oh—just looking at a map of this district to see if I can go for a good walk somewhere,' said Ern. He put the map back, and felt the little note in his pocket. Nothing would make him show it to Mr. Goon. Ah, that was a clever trick of Fatty's getting him a message through, right under Mr. Goon's nose!

Mr. Goon knew there was something up, especially when Ern said he would pop off to bed early. That wasn't like Ern! He watched him go, and then took out from the shelf the map that he had seen Ern using. He at once saw the pencilled path from the village of Peterswood to the old mill on Christmas Hill.

'So that's where something's going on!' said Mr. Goon to himself. 'Lights flashing on Christmas Hill—which means somebody's there that's got no business to be. And the person to look into this is P.C. Goon. There's no time like the present, either. I'll go to-night!'

Quite a lot of people were preparing to go to Christmas Hill that night! Pip and Larry were going, complete with torches, and red, blue and green coloured paper to slip over the beam now and again. Fatty was going, of course, to give Ern a fright. Ern was going—and so was Mr. Goon. A real crowd!

Mr. Goon didn't go to bed that night. It wasn't worth it. He planned to slip off at about half-past eleven, very quietly so as not to wake Ern.

Ern, as a matter of fact, was wide awake, listening to the church clock striking the half-hours. He shivered with excitement in his warm bed. He didn't hear Mr. Goon go quietly out of the front door and pull it to behind him. He quite thought his uncle was in bed and asleep, as he usually was at that hour.

About two minutes after Goon had gone from the house Ern got up. He was fully dressed. He took his torch and tried it. Yes, it was all right. Bit faint, but it would last. He pulled on a coat, stuffed a scarf round his neck, and put on his big cap. He trod quietly down the stairs, hoping not to wake up his uncle—who by this time was plodding softly up Christmas Hill.

Fatty was already by the mill, hidden safely under a bush. Larry and Pip were some distance away, each with a torch and directions to begin shining them here and there, to and fro, every few minutes, in the direction of the mill. The hill was a desolate, deserted place, and the wind was very cold as it swept across it that night.

Mr. Goon wished he was safe home and warm in bed. He plodded along quietly, thinking of comforting things like oil-stoves and hot cocoa and hot water-bottles. And quite suddenly he saw a light flashing not far from him!

Mr. Goon sank down on the hillside beside a hedge. So that toad of a boy was right. There *was* something going on after all on Christmas Hill! What could it be?

He watched intently, almost forgetting to breathe. A red light—flash-flash! A green one—flash-flash-flash! And gracious, there was another light farther up the hill— a blue one, flash!

Larry and Pip were enjoying themselves, flashing hard, hoping that Ern was seeing the flashes and marvelling. Fatty was waiting impatiently for Ern. Where was he? All this flashing was being wasted if Ern wasn't seeing it. Surely he hadn't gone to sleep in bed when he had been told to come to the mill?

The Fatty heard a sigh as if some one was letting out a big breath. Ah—that must be Ern. He must be hiding somewhere nearby. Perhaps he didn't quite know where the mill was.

Flash-flash-flash! The lights winked out over the hill. Mr. Goon wondered if they were being flashed in the Morse code, but after trying hard to puzzle out any letters being flashed he gave it up. Who were these signallers? Were they flashing to somebody in the old deserted mill? Mr. Goon thought about the mill. It was almost ruined. He was positive there was nothing to be found there but rats and owls.

Mr. Goon moved his cramped legs and a twig cracked sharply under him. He held his breath again ! Would any one hear that ? He listened and heard nothing. The lights went on and on flashing merrily. Most extraordinary. Mr. Goon debated whether or not to tell the Inspector about it. He decided not to. He 'd better get to the bottom of things before that cheeky Frederick Trotteville did.

The lights stopped flashing. They had been going strong for twenty minutes, and now Larry and Pip were so cold that they decided to make their way home. They would meet Fatty again in the morning, and hear what had happened to him and Ern. They chuckled as they thought of Ern, discovering Fatty crouching in a ditch, and wondered what he would do. Run away, probably.

When the lights stopped flashing Mr. Goon moved very cautiously from the hedge. He went down into some kind of ditch and tried to get a safe footing. Fatty heard him scraping about and had no doubt at all but that it was Ern, watching lights flashing with wonder and fear.

Well, if Ern wasn't going to discover *him*, he had better discover Ern ! He would leap on him and give him the fright of his life ! They would have a good old rough and tumble !

Fatty crept towards Mr. Goon. He decided to make a few noises first. So he made a mewing noise like a cat. Mr. Goon stopped, surprised. A cat ? Out here on Christmas Hill, with not a building near ! Poor thing !

'Puss, puss, puss !' he called. Then he heard an unmistakable clucking. '*Cluck*-luck-luck-luck-luck ! *Cluck*-luck-luck-luck-luck !'

A hen ! Who could it belong to ? Mr. Goon frowned. It must have escaped from somewhere—but where ? There was no farm for miles !

Fatty then mooed like a cow. He was a good mooer and could even startle cows. He startled Mr. Goon extremely, much more than he had ever startled cows. Mr. Goon almost jumped out of his skin. A cow now! Visions of Christmas Hill suddenly populated in the middle of night with cows, cats and hens came into Mr. Goon's mind. He couldn't understand it. For one moment he wondered if he could be dreaming.

But he was too cold to be dreaming. He scratched the side of his cheek and puzzled about the cow. He ought to take a cow away from this bitter-cold hill. He felt for his torch, and shone it all around, trying to find the cow. Fatty, crouched under a nearby bush, giggled. He thought it was Ern trying to see the cow, the cat and the hen. He debated whether to grunt like a pig or to wail like a baby.

He wailed, and Mr. Goon froze to his very marrow. He was petrified. What else was abroad on this dark hill to-night? Whatever there was he wasn't going to waste any more time looking for it. He turned to run, and another wail made him shake at the knees.

Fatty stood up when he heard the noise of somebody running away. He couldn't let Ern go like that! He must go after him, pounce on him and pummel him—and then he'd let him go—and perhaps Ern would spin such a wonderful tale to Old Clear-Orf about queer mysteries up on Christmas Hill that it would bamboozle the policeman completely.

So Fatty padded after Mr. Goon. The policeman was terrified to hear somebody after him. He caught his foot on a root and fell flat on his face. Fatty fell over him and began to pummel him. He was thoroughly enjoying himself.

But Ern seemed curiously strong! Fatty found himself heaved off, and a strong arm bent him back. A familiar voice grated in his ear. 'Ho, you would, would you? You comealonga me!'

Now it was Fatty's turn to get a shock. Gracious, it was

*Goon,* not Ern. Fatty freed himself as soon as he could and shot off down the hill, praying that Goon would not be able to put on his torch quickly enough to spot him.

His head was spinning. That was *Goon.* Why was *he* there ? Where was Ern ? He went cold when he thought of what Mr. Goon would say if he found out that it was Fatty who had leapt on him like that.

Mr. Goon fumbled for his torch, but it was broken in the rough and tumble. He was no longer frightened. He felt victorious. He had frightened off that fellow who had attacked him, whoever it was.

' He must have been a big chap, ' thought Mr. Goon, ' a big hefty strong chap. And I heaved him off as easy as winking. Flung himself on me, he did, like a ton of bricks ! And me down flat on my face, too. Not a bad night's work, really. '

He made his way cautiously down the hill. He heard no more curious noises. Nobody else attacked him. He puzzled over the night's happenings and tried to sort them out.

' Flashing lights—all colours—in two different places. A cat, a hen, a cow and something that wailed in a horrible manner. And a great giant of a fellow who attacked me out of the dark. That's something to go on ! Can't make head nor tail of it now, but I'll get to the bottom of it ! '

Fatty made his way home too. Larry and Pip were already home and in bed, hugging rather lukewarm hot-water bottles. They were longing to see Fatty in the morning and to know what had happened to Ern. Had he been frightened of the lights ? What did he do when he found Fatty crouching in the ditch ?

Where *was* Ern ? *He* was having a little adventure all on his own !

# 8 ERN HAS AN ADVENTURE TOO

ERN, most unfortunately, had followed the wrong stream, so that it did not, of course, lead him to the mill on Christmas Hill. It meandered through frosty fields, and didn't go anywhere near a hill at all. Ern was rather astonished that he had no climbing to do, but he clung to the stream, hoping that sooner or later it would take him uphill.

If he had cared to flash his torch on the water he would have seen that the stream was going exactly the same way as he was, and could on no account be expected to run uphill, but Ern didn't think about that. He just went on and on.

He felt that it must be past midnight, and still there was no sign of a mill, and no sign of Christmas Hill either. He couldn't imagine where he was. He stumbled on over the frosty bank beside the little stream, following its curves.

Soon it was about half-past twelve. Ern paused and considered things. He must be going the wrong way. The others wouldn't have waited for him. They would probably have gone home after watching for the lights.

' I'd better go back, ' said Ern, shivering. ' It's too cold. I don't care what the others say, I'd better go back. '

And then Ern suddenly saw a light! He was not expecting one and was extremely astonished. It suddenly shone out from some distance away and then faded. Could it possibly be part of the Mystery?

Then he heard a noise. He listened. It was a low purring noise, like a car. It came from the same direction as the light he had seen. He couldn't see the car at all, but it must have passed down some path or lane not very far from him, because the purring of the engine grew louder and then faded again as the car was driven farther and farther away.

'Why didn't it have lights?' wondered Ern. He stood there, waiting and listening and then decided to move on a little farther down the stream. He went cautiously, not liking to put on his torch.

Then he heard footsteps—soft footsteps walking nearby, crunching quietly over the frosty ground. Two pairs of footsteps—or was it three? No, two.

A voice spoke softly in the darkness. 'Goodnight, Holland. See you later.'

There was an answering mumble, and then no other noise except departing footsteps. It sounded as if the two men had gone different ways.

Ern shivered with excitement and cold. He wished the others were there. Why weren't they? This must be part of the Mystery Fatty had talked about. Then Fatty should have been there to share it with him. Were those men kidnappers or robbers or what?

Ern turned back. He put up his coat-collar and tightened his scarf, for now he was meeting the wind. He kept close to the stream and walked over the frosted grass as fast as he could. Ooooh! It was cold!

He came at last to the bridge he knew, that crossed the stream and led into a little lane. He went up the lane, turned into the village street and made his way quietly to his uncle's house. He had been wise enough to take the back-door key with him. He stole round to the back, and let himself in.

Mr. Goon was now in bed, fast asleep and snoring. He didn't even know that Ern was out! He had crept upstairs, undressed, and got into bed with hardly a sound, not wanting to let Ern know he had been out at midnight. He didn't want him to guess he had been up to Christmas Hill, probing the Mystery !

It took Ern a long time to go to sleep. To begin with he was very cold, and the bed wouldn't seem to warm up. And then he was puzzled by what he had seen and heard. It wasn't much—but it didn't make sense somehow. He thought he couldn't be a very good detective. That boy Fatty would have guessed a whole lot of things if he had been with Ern that night. Ern was quite sure of that.

Neither Mr. Goon nor Ern said a word to each other of their midnight escapades. Mr. Goon had a bruise on his cheek where his face had struck a stone when he had fallen. Ern had a scratch across his forehead where a bramble had scraped him. They both looked tired out.

' You do what you like to-day, Ern, ' said Mr. Goon, who felt that probably Ern might pick up a few Clues from Fatty about the Mystery, and pass them on to him— or if he wrote them down in his note-book he could get them when Ern was asleep and read them.

' Thanks, Uncle, ' said Ern, perking up at once. Now he would be able to go and see the others and hear what had happened.

He went round to Fatty's shed, but Fatty wasn't there. However, there was a message up on the door. ' Gone to Pip's. Join us there. '

Guessing correctly that the message was for him Ern went up to Pip's. Bets saw him from the window and waved to him.

She opened the window. ' Don't go to the front door. Come in the garden door at the side of the house, and wipe your feet for goodness' sake ! '

Ern did as he was told. He forgot to take off his cap when he got into the house, and when he met Pip's mother she stared at him disapprovingly and said, ' Please take your cap off. Where are your manners ? '

Ern blushed bright red and fled upstairs. He pulled his cap off so hurriedly that his hair stood straight up.

'Hallo,' said Fatty, when he came in at the play-room door. 'You saw the message then. What happened to you last night? You went to sleep and didn't wake up in time to come, I suppose?'

'I didn't go to sleep at all!' said Ern, indignantly. 'I got up and followed the stream—but it didn't lead me to Christmas Hill, or to any mill. I don't know where it led me to. But I saw the mysterious light all right.'

'You didn't,' said Larry. 'Pip and I and Fatty were up on the hill and saw them. You couldn't *possibly* have seen any flashing lights if you weren't up on the hill.'

'Well, I did then,' said Ern, looking annoyed. 'You weren't with me. You don't know *what* I saw!'

'Did you tell your uncle that we had told you to go to the mill on Christmas Hill last night?' demanded Fatty.

''Course I didn't,' said Ern, even more annoyed. 'He was in bed and snoring!'

'He wasn't,' said Fatty. 'He was up on Christmas Hill.'

Ern didn't believe him at all. 'Oh, goanborlyered!' he said in a disgusted voice.

The Find-Outers looked inquiringly at him. What did this peculiar word mean? 'What did you say then?' asked Fatty, interestedly. 'Is it Spanish or something?'

'I said "Goanborlyered,"' repeated Ern. 'And fry your face too!'

The second part of what he said threw light on the first part. 'Oh! he said "Go and boil your head!"' explained Daisy.

'SwatIsaid,' said Ern looking sulky.

'Swatesaid,' said Fatty. 'What's the matter, Ern? Why don't you believe me when I say your uncle was up on the hill last night?'

' Because I heard him snoring like billyoh when I got in, that's all, ' said Ern.

' Did you hear snoring like billyoh when you went out ? ' asked Fatty. Ern considered, frowning hard.

' No. Can't say I did. He *might* have gone out without me hearing him, and come back before I did. '

' That's about what he did then, ' said Fatty. ' But what I can't make out is—why did he go up ? How did he know anything about meeting at the mill on Christmas Hill ? '

' He might somehow have got hold of the note you gave Ern when you disguised yourself as the red-shawled woman, ' said Daisy. ' He'd know then. '

' Yes. I suppose that's what he must have done—if Ern was silly enough to give him the chance, ' said Fatty.

' Well, I didn't, ' said Ern. ' What you all getting at me this morning for ? I got up, didn't I, and I tried to get to Christmas Hill ? I must have followed the wrong stream, that's all. I looked up the mill in the map and I saw that if I could follow the stream that runs down by it, I'd get there all right. But it was dark and I couldn't see anything. But I tell you I did see a light. ' Every one felt certain that Ern was making this up, just as they had made up their flashing lights ! Ern went on, trying to impress the others that he really was telling the truth.

' I was standing by the stream, see. And I saw this light. It just shone out once and then faded. Then I heard a purring noise and a car came by somewhere—and it hadn't any lights on. That was queer, and I thought maybe it was all part of the mystery too. '

The others were listening now. Ern went on, warming up a little. ' Well then, after the car had gone I heard footsteps—two pairs—and then I heard one man say to the other "Good-night, Holland. See you later" or something like that. And after that I turned back and went home. '

There was a silence. Every one believed Ern now. If he had been making up his tale he would have pretended that he had seen many lights, heard more than one car and more that two men. Because it was a simple story, it seemed as if it might be true.

'Have you told your uncle this?' asked Fatty at last.

'No,' said Ern. There was a pause. Then Ern remembered something. 'I put that note-book back,' he said, 'and Uncle found me just shutting the drawer. He said I was snooping round to find out things for you, and he hit me twice. See my ear?'

He showed the children his ear, which was still swollen. Bets felt very sorry for him. Horrible Mr. Goon!

'I'm not telling my uncle a thing now!' said Ern. 'Hitting me like that when I was doing something decent.'

'You shouldn't have taken the note-book in the first place,' said Fatty. 'Then you wouldn't have had to put it back and you wouldn't have been discovered and got those blows. You deserved what you got, in case you think you didn't.'

Ern scowled, partly because he knew Fatty was right and partly because he didn't like having it said to him in such a candid manner. But Fatty always did say what he thought, and nothing would stop him.

'Look here,' said Ern, suddenly, 'which mystery is the real one? The one you mean, with flashing lights on Christmas Hill—or mine, down by the stream? Or are they both real?'

Fatty rubbed his nose. He didn't quite know what to say. His had been made up, but he didn't want to admit that. Neither did he want Ern to think there might be any mystery in what *he* had seen and heard the night before, in case there really *was*. If there was, Fatty didn't want Ern blundering into it and telling his uncle everything.

' I suppose, ' said Ern, answering his own question, ' the mystery up on the hill's the real one—or else uncle wouldn't have gone up there, would he ? '

' He must have thought there was something going on there, ' agreed Fatty.

' And there was, ' said Pip, with a little giggle.

' Well, Ern, what about you going up on Christmas Hill to see if you can find a few clues in daylight, ' said Fatty. ' They would be a help. '

' What sort of clues ? ' asked Ern, looking cheerful again.

' Oh—cigarette ends, buttons, footprints, anything like that, ' said Fatty. ' You just never know. A real detective can usually find no end of clues. '

' I'll go up about three, ' said Ern. ' Uncle will be having his afternoon snooze then. Well—I'd better be going. I'll bring any clues to you if I find them. So long ! '

# 9  LOTS OF CLUES FOR ERN!

THE Find-Outers looked at each other when Ern had disappeared. 'What do you think, Fatty?' said Larry. 'Anything in what he said?'

'I don't know,' said Fatty slowly. 'It seems a bit queer, doesn't it—a light in the middle of the night—a car suddenly appearing without lights—and then voices. What did he say the one man said to the other?'

'"Good-night, Holland. See you later,"' said Larry.

'Yes, that's it. Wonder how Ern managed to remember the name Holland, and if he heard it right,' said Fatty.

'Any good having a snoop along the stream to see if we can spy anything?' asked Larry.

'Not allowed to,' said Pip at once.

'Well—it's not a mystery *yet*, and may never *be*,' said Larry. 'So I don't see why we shouldn't at least go for a walk along the stream.'

'With Ern?' asked Bets.

'I don't know,' said Fatty. 'He'll probably go and tell everything to Goon. Still, Goon has got plenty to think of at the moment. He's seen masses of lights on Christmas Hill, heard a cow, a hen, a cat and a baby up there, and struggled with an unknown attacker. Quite a nice little mystery for him to be getting on with!'

The others laughed. They had roared at Fatty's account of what had happened the night before, and his amazement at finding the person by the hedge was Goon, not Ern.

'I think one of the best things we can do is to go up to Christmas Hill before three o'clock, and drop a nice meaty lot of clues,' said Fatty. 'Ern will find them and glory in them—probably write some portry about them. And if he hands them over to Goon so much the better! '

So, in great glee, the Five Find-Outers and Buster set off up Christmas Hill, taking with what they thought would do for Clues. It was a fine sunny day, but cold, and they got nice and warm going up the hill. Their parents were pleased to see them going out. Nobody liked all the five indoors. Some noisy game always seemed to develop sooner or later.

' Here's where I fought Goon last night,' said Fatty, showing where he and Goon had rolled in the ditch. 'I got an awful shock when I found it was Goon. He's strong, you know. He almost caught me. What a row I'd have got in if he'd seen it was me! '

' Let's put a clue here, ' said Larry. 'A torn-off button with bit of cloth attached. Very good clue! '

' Where did you get it? ' said Daisy. 'You'll get into trouble if you tore it off one of your coats. '

' Idiot! I tore it off the old coat that's hung in the garage for ages, ' said Larry, and threw the brown button down, with its bit of brown cloth attached to it. ' Clue number one. '

' Here's Clue number two, ' said Pip, and put down a bit of paper, on which he had scribbled a telephone number. ' Peterswood 0160. '

' Whose number's that? ' asked Fatty at once.

' Oh, nobody's, ' said Pip. ' I just made it up. '

' Your finger-prints will be on it, ' said Fatty, who always thought of things like that.

' No they won't, ' said Pip. ' I tore it out of a new note-book, with gloves on my hands, and I've carried it in my gloved hands all the way. So there! '

' You're getting quite clever, ' said Fatty, pleased. ' Right. That's Clue number two. Here's Clue number three. '

He threw down a cigar-stump that he had taken from his father's ash-tray.

'That's a good clue,' said Larry. 'Robber smokes Corona cigars. Mr. Goon will love that if he gets it from Ern.'

'I've got a clue too,' said Bets. 'A red shoe-lace, broken in half and dirtied!'

'Yes. Very good, Bets,' said Fatty, approvingly. 'I like the way you've dirtied it. Ern will be thrilled to pick that up.'

They went on a little way farther, nearer the mill. Daisy still had her clue to dispose of. It was a very old ragged handkerchief with ' K ' embroidered in one corner.

'K,' said Fatty. I can't think of any one we know beginning with K. Whose was it?'

'Don't know,' said Daisy with a laugh. 'I picked it up by the hedge that runs by Pip's garden!'

'I hope the wind won't blow any of our clues away,' said Larry anxiously.

'I don't expect so,' said Fatty. 'It's a calm day. Come on, let's get back before we meet Ern coming up here.'

They ran down the hill. At the bottom they met Mr. Goon labouring along on his bicycle, very angry because his snooze had been interrupted by a call about a stolen dog. When he saw the children at the bottom of Christmas Hill, he stopped in suspicion.

'What you been doing up there?' he asked.

'Having a lovely walk, Mr. Goon,' said Fatty, in the polite voice that always sent Mr. Goon into a frenzy. Buster, who had been left some way behind, with his nose in a rabbit-hole, now came rushing up in delight.

'If you don't want that dog of yours kicked, you keep him off,' said Mr. Goon, fixing them all with a protruding eye. 'And if I was you—I'd keep away from Christmas Hill.'

'Oh, Mr. Goon but why?' asked Fatty, in such an innocent voice that Mr. Goon began to go purple. That cheeky toad!

'It's such a nice hill to run down,' said Pip.

'Now, don't *you* start!' said Mr. Goon, slowly swelling up in rage. 'And take my advice—don't you go up Christmas Hill again!'

'Can we come down it?' asked Larry, and the others went off into shouts of laughter to see Mr. Goon trying to work this out.

'Any more sauce from you,' he began, 'and ...'

At this moment Buster, who had been struggling for all he was worth in Fatty's arms, leapt right out of them almost on top of Mr. Goon. The policeman hurriedly got on his bicycle. 'You clear-orf!' he shouted to Buster and the children too. He kicked out at Buster and nearly fell off his bicycle. He rode up the lane at top speed, trying to shake him off, and almost collided with Ern, who was on his way to search for clues up Christmas Hill.

'Out of my way!' yelled Mr. Goon, nearly running over Ern's toes. Buster ran between Ern's legs and he fell over at once. In joy and delight Buster stopped to sniff round this fresh person, and found it was Ern. He leapt on him and began to lick him, whilst Mr. Goon pedalled thankfully up the road, getting redder and redder as he went.

'Your uncles's in a bit of a rage,' said Fatty. 'It's not good for him to ride a bike at such a speed. You ought to warn him. It must be bad for his heart.'

'It would be, if he had one,' said Ern. 'Well, I'm going to do what you said—hunt for clues. You coming too?'

'No, we've got to get home,' said Fatty. 'I hope you find a few, Ern. Let us know if you do. That's the sign of a good detective, you know, to be able to spot clues.'

Ern glowed. If there were any clues to be found on the

*Out of my way*

hill, he'd find them! He badly wanted Fatty to admire
him. He took out his note-book and opened it.

' I wrote a pome about last night, ' he said. ' It's called
"The Dark, Dark Night". '

' Fine ! ' said Fatty, hastily. ' Pity we can't wait and hear
it. Don't be too long before you go up the hill, Ern, or
you'll find yourself in the dark dark night up there again.
Follow the stream and you'll come to the mill. '

They parted, and Ern put his note-book away. He took
out his other note-book, the one Fatty had given him. He
opened it at the page marked ' CLUES. ' How he hoped
to be able to make a list there before the afternoon was
done.

The others went home. Fatty was rather silent. Bets
walked close beside him, not interrupting his thoughts.
She knew he was trying to puzzle out something.

' Pip, have you got a good map of the district? ' said
Fatty, as they came to Pip's house. ' If you have I'll just
come in and have a squint at it. Somebody's borrowed
ours. '

' Yes. Dad keeps one in the map-shelf, ' said Pip. ' But
for goodness sake put it back when you've finished with
it. '

' 'Course I will, ' said Fatty, and they went in. Pip
found the map and they took it upstairs. Fatty put his
finger on Peterswood, their village. He traced the way
up to the mill, up the stream on Christmas Hill. Then
he traced another way, alongside another stream, that
at first ran near the first one and then went across the
fields.

' I think this must be the stream Ern went by last night, '
he said. ' Let's see where it flows past. Nothing much,
look ! Just fields. '

The others all bent over the map, breathing down
Fatty's neck. They watched his finger go along the

stream. It came to where a thick wood was marked. In the middle of the wood some kind of building was shown.

'Now I wonder what building that is,' said Fatty, thoughtfully. 'Any one been along that way?'

Nobody had. Nobody even knew the wood very well, though they had sometimes passed it. Not one of them had known there was any building in the wood.

'We'll ask about it,' said Fatty, getting up. 'Golly, I must go. I'm supposed to be going out to tea with mother. Awful thought. You know, I do believe there may be something in Ern's story. Cars that leave a wood in the middle of the night without lights need a bit of looking into.'

The others looked excited. 'Is it a mystery, Fatty?' asked Bets eagerly. 'Do say it is! Wouldn't it be funny if we did tumble into the middle of a real mystery just because we invented one for Ern.'

'It would,' said Fatty. 'Well, we shall see. Won't Ern be thrilled when he finds all those clues? He'll come rushing along to-morrow!'

'I hope I shan't giggle,' said Bets.

'You dare!' said Pip. 'Good-bye, Fatty. Behave yourself at tea, and be a dear, well-mannered child!'

'Oh, goanborlyered!' said Fatty, rudely, and off he went, with shouts of laughter following him.

# 10  MR. GOON AND ERN

ERN had a simply wonderful time up on Christmas Hill, collecting clues. It was a lovely afternoon and he walked slowly up the hill, his eyes on the ground. He felt important. The beginnings of a 'pome' swam into his mind, as he looked up and saw the sun sinking redly in the west.

'Pore dying sun that sinks to rest,' thought Ern, and felt excited and pleased. That was a good line, a very good one indeed. Ern never wrote a cheerful 'pome'. They were all very very sad, and they made Ern feel deliciously sad too.

He walked on, his eyes on the ground, thinking about the dying sun. He suddenly saw a piece of rag fluttering and picked it up. Nobody could tell what colour it had been. Ern looked at it. Was it a clue? He pondered over it. He wished he was like Fatty, able to tell at a glance what things were clues and what weren't.

He put it into his overcoat pocket. Fatty would know. He cast his eyes on the ground again. Aha! What was this in the ditch? A button! Yes, with a bit of brown cloth attached to it. Surely that was a clue? Ern looked at the ground in the ditch, and noted the broken twigs and the way the frosty ground was rubbed and scraped. 'Been somebody here!' thought Ern in excitement. 'And this button's off his coat. That's a Fat Clue, a really Meaty One.'

He put that in his pocket too. He was feeling really thrilled now. Two clues already!

He found the broken shoe-lace. He found the cigar-end and sniffed at it in a very knowing manner. 'Ha! A

good cigar ! Whoever was here has money to spend. I'm
getting on. I see a man with a brown coat with brown
buttons, smoking a good cigar, and wearing reddish laces
in his shoes. I don't know about that bit of rag. That
doesn't fit in somehow. '

He picked up an empty cigarette packet. It had held
Players ' cigarettes. ' Coo ! He smokes cigarettes as well ! '
said Ern, feeling cleverer and cleverer. That went into his
pocket too. He was getting on ! Who would have thought
there were so many clues left carelessly lying about like
that ? No wonder detectives went hunting for them after
a robbery.

He picked up a broken tin next. It looked as if it had
possibly been a tin of boot polish, but it was so old and
rusty that there was no telling what it might have been.
Anyway it went into his pocket too.

Then he found Pip's bit of paper blowing about. Ern
picked it up. ' Lovaduck ! Now we're getting hot ! This is
somebody's telephone number—in Peterswood too. I'm
really getting hot ! Pity Fatty didn't come up with me—
we'd have had a fine time collecting clues ! '

He then found Daisy's ragged old handkerchief,
embroidered with ' K ' in the corner. This seemed a first-
class clue. ' K ! ' he thought. ' K for Kenneth. K for Katie.
Or it might be a surname of course. Can't tell. ' That went
into his pocket as well.

After that he only found two more things that seemed
worth picking up. One was a burnt match, the other was
the stub of a pencil. It had initials cut into it at the end.
E.H.

With a pocketful of interesting clues Ern went down
the hill again. It was getting dark. He would have liked to
stay longer and find more clues but he couldn't see clearly
any longer. Anyway he had done well, he felt.

When he got home his uncle was out. Ern got himself

some tea, then took out his note-book and opened it at the page marked 'Clues'.

He sharpened his pencil and set to work to put down a list of all the things he had found.

CLUES

1.   Piece of rag.
2.   Brown button with bit of cloth.
3.   Broken shoe-lace, reddish colour.
4.   End of good cigar.
5.   Empty cigarette packet (Players).
6.   Broken tin, very rusty.
7.   Bit of paper with telephone number.
8.   Ragged handkerchief, 'K' in corner.
9.   Burnt match.
10.  Pencil, very short, E.H. on it.

'Look at that', said Ern, in satisfaction. 'Ten clues already! Not a bad bit of work. I'd make a good detective. Lovaduck! Here's uncle!'

Mr. Goon could be heard coming into the little hall, and a familiar cough sounded. In haste Ern swept all the clues into his pocket, and was just stuffing his note-book away when his uncle came in. Ern looked so guilty that Mr. Goon was suspicious at once. Now what had that boy been up to?

'Hallo, Uncle,' said Ern.

'What you doing sitting at an empty table, doing nothing?' said Mr. Goon.

'I'm not doing anything,' said Ern. Mr. Goon gave a snort.

'I can see that. What you been doing this afternoon?'

'I've been for a walk,' said Ern.

'Where?' said Mr. Goon. 'With those five kids?'

'No. By myself,' said Ern. 'It was such a nice afternoon.'

Ern was not in the habit of taking walks by himself, and
Mr. Goon looked at him suspiciously again. What *was* the
boy up to? How much did he know?

'Where did you go?' he asked again.

'Up Christmas Hill,' said Ern. 'It—it was awfully nice
up there. The view, you know, Uncle.'

Mr. Goon sat down ponderously in his armchair and
gazed solemnly at Ern. 'Now, you look here, my boy,' he
said, 'you're Up To Something with those pestering
kids. Ho, yes, you are, so don't try to say you aren't. Now,
you and me, we must work together. We're uncle and
nephew, aren't we? In the interests of the Law we must
tell each other all the Goings-On.'

'What Goings-On?' asked Ern, in alarm, wondering
how much his uncle knew. He was beginning to feel
frightened. He put his hand into his pocket to feel the
clues there. He mustn't tell his uncle about them. He
must keep them all for Fatty and the others.

'You know quite well what the Goings-On are,' said
Mr. Goon, beginning to remove his boots. 'Up Christmas
Hill! Didn't you tell me about the lights flashing there?'

'Yes,' said Ern. 'But that's all I told you, Uncle. What
other Goings-On do you mean?'

Mr. Goon began to lose his temper. He stood up in his
stockinged feet and advanced on poor Ern, who hadn't
even a chance of getting up from his chair and backing
away.

'I'm going to lose my temper with you, Ern,' said Mr.
Goon. 'I can feel it. And you know what happened last
time, don't you?'

'Yes, Uncle. But please don't hit me again,' begged
Ern.

'I got a cane somewhere,' said Mr. Goon, suddenly,
and began to rummage about in a cupboard. Ern was
terrified. He began to cry. He was terribly ashamed of

himself, because he knew quite well that not even little Bets would give away her friends, but he knew he was going to. He was a coward! Poor Ern.

When he saw his uncle bringing out a very nasty-looking yellow cane, he blubbered even more loudly.

'Now, you stop that noise,' said Mr. Goon. 'You're not hurt yet, are you? You be a good boy, and work with me, and everything will be fine. See? Now you tell me what that boy, Frederick, told you.'

Ern gave in. He hadn't any courage at all. He knew he was a poor weak thing, but he couldn't seem to help it.

'He said there were two gangs,' blubbered Ern. 'Kidnappers was one gang. Robbers was the other.'

Mr. Goon stared at Ern in surprise. This was news! 'Go on!' he said disbelievingly. 'Kidnappers and robbers! What next!'

'And lights flashing on Christmas Hill,' went on Ern. 'Well, I don't know about that, Uncle. I haven't seen any lights there at all.'

Mr. Goon had though! He looked thoughtfully at Ern. That bit of the tale was true, anyway—about the lights flashing, because he had seen them himself the night before—so the other part might be true, too. Kidnappers and robbers! Now *how* did that boy Frederick get to know these things? He brooded about Fatty for a little while and thought of quite a lot of things he would like to do to him.

It was very very necessary to make sure that Ern told him everything in future. Mr. Goon could see that. He decided it would be best not to frighten Ern any more. He must win his friendship! That was the line to follow.

So, to Ern's enormous surprise, Mr. Goon suddenly patted him on the shoulder, and gave him his large handkerchief to wipe his eyes. Ern looked up in surprise and suspicion. Now what was Uncle up to?

'You were right to tell me, Ern, all that you've heard from those kids,' said Mr. Goon, in a kindly voice. 'Now you and me can work together, and we'll soon clean up this mystery—and we'll get no end of praise from Inspector Jenks. You've met him, haven't you? He said he thought you were a fine boy, and might help me no end.'

This wasn't true at all. Inspector Jenks had hardly glanced at Ern, and if he had he certainly wouldn't have said such nice things about him. Poor Ern didn't shine in public at all, but looked very awkward and stupid.

Ern was relieved to see that his uncle was going to be friendly after all. He watched him put away the cane. Lovaduck! That was a near squeak. All the same Ern was very much ashamed of giving away all that Fatty had told him. Now his uncle would solve the mystery himself, arrest all the men, and Fatty and the other Find-Outers wouldn't have any fun.

'Anything else you can tell me, Ern?' said Mr. Goon, putting on his enormous slippers.

'No, Uncle,' said Ern, wishing he hadn't got a pocketful of clues. He was glad he hadn't tried to wipe his eyes with his own handkerchief—he might have pulled out a whole lot of clues with it!

'What did you go up Christmas Hill this afternoon for?' asked Mr. Goon, lighting his pipe.

'I told you. For a nice walk,' said Ern, looking sulky again. When would his uncle stop all this?

Mr. Goon debated whether to go on cross-examining Ern or not. Perhaps not. He didn't want to make the boy obstinate. When he was safely asleep in bed that night he would get Ern's note-book out of his pocket and see if he had written anything down in it. Mr. Goon picked up the paper and settled down for a read. Ern heaved a sigh of relief, and wondered if he could slip out to see the others.

It was about six o'clock now—but Ern felt that he simply *must* tell Fatty all about the clues.

' Can I go out for a bit, Uncle ? ' he asked, timidly. ' Just to slip round and have a talk with the others ? They might have a bit of news for me. '

' All right, ' said Mr. Goon, turning a friendly face to Ern. ' You go. And get all you can out of them and then tell me the latest news. See ? '

Ern lost no time. He pulled on his coat, took his cap and scarf and fled out of the house. He made his way to Pip's, because he remembered that Fatty was going out to tea that day.

He was lucky enough to find all the Find-Outers gathered together in Pip's play-room, under strict instructions from Mrs. Hilton to take off their shoes if they wanted to play any games that meant running across the room. Fatty had just arrived, having dropped in on his way home with his mother, who was seeing Mrs. Hilton for a few minutes downstairs.

' I say ! ' said Ern, bursting in suddenly. ' I've got ten clues for you ! What do you think of that for a good day's work ! I've got them all here ! '

' Lovaduck ! ' said Fatty. ' Smazing ! Simpossible ! Swunderful ! Let's have a look, Ern, quick ! '

## 11   ERN'S CLUES

ERN pulled everything out of his pocket. When Bets saw all the things there that the Find-Outers had so carefully put on Christmas Hill for Ern to find, she wanted to giggle. But she saw Fatty's eye on her, and she didn't.

'See?' said Ern, proudly. 'Cigar-end. That means somebody with money. And look here—he smokes cigarettes too—see this empty packet? And look—we want to look for somebody with a brown coat. And ...'

'This is a very remarkable collection of clues, Ern,' said Fatty, solemnly. 'I can see that Mr. Goon's brains have been passed on to you. You take after him! A very remarkable afternoon's work.'

Ern was thrilled. Praise from Fatty was praise indeed. He showed every clue he had.

'Course, some of them mayn't be clues at all,' he admitted handsomely. 'I see that.'

'You're right,' said Fatty. 'You think of everything, Ern. This is all most interesting. It will help us tremendously.'

'Will it really?' said Ern, delighted. Then his face clouded over. 'I got something awful to tell you,' he said.

'What?' asked every one, curiously.

'I went and gave the game away to my uncle,' said Ern, dismally. 'He took a cane out of the cupboard and I could see he was gong to use it on me—so I went and told him about the kidnappers and the robbers up of Christmas Hill. You needn't call me a coward. I know that all right.'

He looked so completely miserable that the Five Find-Outers wanted to comfort him. Even Buster felt the same and put his front paws up on Ern's knee. Ern looked down at him gratefully.

'Well,' said Fatty, 'certainly it wasn't a brave thing to do, Ern, to give away somebody else's secret—but Mr. Goon and a cane must have been a very frightening pair. We won't tick you off.'

'He told me I must work with him,' said Ern, brightening up a little, as he saw the the Find-Outers did not mean to cast him off. 'He said we were uncle and nephew, and we ought to work together. I've got to tell him anything that happens.'

Fatty considered this. It suited him very well to have Goon told all the things that didn't matter. It would serve him right for threatening poor Ern with the cane. Fatty did not like the streak of cruelty in Mr. Goon.

'Well, there's something in that,' said Fatty. 'Yes, quite decidedly there's something in that. Families ought to work together. We shan't complain any more if you pass on any news to your uncle, Ern.'

'But I don't want to!' protested Ern at once. 'I want *you* to solve things, not uncle. I don't want to work with uncle.'

'Poor Ern!' suddenly said Bets. She could see very clearly how Ern was torn in two—he dearly wanted to work with the Find-Outers and be loyal to them—and he was terribly afraid he would have to help his uncle instead, because he was so frightened of him. All Ern needed was a little courage, but he hadn't got it.

'You'd better show these clues to your uncle,' said Fatty. 'Hadn't he, Larry? If they are going to work together, Goon had better know about these. He'll think that Ern has done a fine piece of work.'

'I don't want to show him the clues,' said Ern, desperately. 'I tell you, I found them for you, not for uncle.'

'Well, do what you like,' said Fatty. 'We shan't mind whether you show them or not. I suppose you wrote them all down in your note-book?'

'Oh yes,' said Ern, proudly, and showed his long list. Fatty nodded approvingly.

'You didn't tell your uncle about how you went out alone last night, did you?' he said. It was very important that Goon shouldn't know that. Ern shook his head.

'No. 'Course I didn't. I'm not telling him things he can't possibly guess. He'd be very angry if he knew I'd slipped out like that.'

'Tell us again about your little adventure,' said Fatty. So Ern obligingly told it. He used almost the same words as before, and all the Find-Outers felt that he was telling the exact truth.

'Are you certain that one man addressed the other as "Holland?"' asked Fatty.

'Oh yes. You see we did Holland in geography last term,' said Ern. 'So I knew the name all right.'

Well, that certainly seemed to fix the name. That might be very useful, thought Fatty. He got up to go, hearing his mother calling him from downstairs. Larry and Daisy got up too.

'There's mother ready to go,' said Fatty. 'Come on, Ern—you'd better go too.'

'I thought of a fine pome this afternoon,' said Ern, getting up. 'About the Dying Sun.'

'We haven't time to hear it now,' said Daisy.

'Spitty,' said Fatty. Every one but Ern knew what this meant. Ern looked at him in surprise.

'Spitty?' he said. 'What do you mean?'

'You heard me,' said Fatty. 'SPITTY!'

Bets went off into giggles. There came another call from downstairs. Fatty hurried to the door.

'He meant "It's a pity,"' giggled Bets.

'SwatIsaid,' said Fatty and disappeared with Larry and Daisy.

Ern, still rather bemused over the curious word Fatty had suddenly used, followed the three downstairs. He slipped out of the garden-door unseen. He didn't want to meet Mrs. Hilton, Pip's mother. He was scared of her in case she found fault with his manners again. He tore home to his uncle's house, hoping there was something nice for supper.

A delicious smell of bacon and eggs met him as soon as he got in. Ern stood and sniffed. Lovaduck! Uncle was doing himself proud to-night. Ern wondered if he was going to get any bacon and eggs, or whether he would have to sup on bread and cheese.

'Hurry up, young Ern!' called Mr. Goon, in a jovial sort of voice that Ern had never heard before. 'I've fried you an egg and a bit of bacon. Hurry up!'

Ern hurried up. There was not only bacon and eggs but a bowl of tinned peaches and creamy custard. Ern took his place hungrily.

'Well? Did you see those kids? Get any news from them?' inquired Mr. Goon, affably, piling egg, bacon and toast on to Ern's plate.

'No. There wasn't any news, Uncle,' said Ern.

'But you must have talked about something,' said Mr. Goon. 'What did they say to you?'

Ern racked his brains to think of something harmless to tell his uncle. He suddenly remembered something.

'I told them you said we were to work together,' he said.

'You shouldn't have told them that,' said Mr. Goon, crossly. 'Now they won't tell you a thing!'

'Oh yes they will. They said it was right that an uncle and nephew should work together,' said Ern, shovelling egg and bacon into his mouth. 'And what's more, Fatty said I took after *you*, Uncle. He said you'd passed your brains on to *me*. '

Mr Goon looked most disbelievingly at Ern. He felt certain that Fatty didn't think much of any brains he possessed, and if he did he certainly wouldn't say so. He was just pulling Ern's leg. Mr. Goon wished in exasperation that Ern wasn't so simple.

' He didn't mean that, see ? ' said Mr. Goon. ' He can't think much of *your* brains, Ern. You know you haven't got any to speak of. You think of your last school report. '

Ern thought instead of the remarkable set of clues he had found that afternoon. He smiled. ' Oh, I've got brains all right, Uncle. You wait and see. '

Mr. Goon felt that he was about to lose his temper again. He just simply couldn't be more than ten minutes with Ern without feeling annoyed and aggravated. His ears turned red, and Ern saw them and felt uncomfortable. He knew that was a danger sign. What *could* he have said now to annoy his uncle ?

He ate his peaches and custard in silence, and so did Mr. Goon. Then, still in silence, Ern did the washing-up and after that got out his books to do some work. Mr. Goon, trying to look pleased so as not to make Ern obstinate, sat reading his paper again. He looked up approvingly as Ern sat down to work.

' That's right, my boy. That's the way to get brains like mine. A bit of hard study will make a lot of difference to you. '

' Yes, Uncle, ' said Ern, resting his head on his hands as if he was learning something. But Ern was going over his clues, one by one. He was thinking of robbers and kidnappers. He was up on Christmas Hill, waiting for desperate men to do desperate deeds. Oh, Ern was far far away from his geography book on the kitchen table !

He went to bed early because he was tired. He fell

asleep at once, and did little snores like Mr. Goon's big ones. Mr. Goon heard them from downstairs and rose quietly. Now to get Ern's note-book and see what he had written in it! If Ern wouldn't tell him everything Mr. Goon meant to find it out. No harrassing thoughts of being mean or deceitful entered Mr. Goon's mind. He thought himself in duty-bound to sneak Ern's note-book from his pocket!

Ern did not stir when Mr. Goon tiptoed in. His uncle slipped his hand into the coat-pocket and found the note-book at once. He felt the trousers and decided to take them downstairs and see what was crowding up the pockets.

He sat down at the table to study Ern's note-book. It fell open at the page headed ' Clues. ' Mr. Goon's eyes grew round as they saw the long, long list.

' Look at that! All them clues and never a word to me about them. The young limb! I'd like to skin him! '

He read down the list. Then an idea occurred to him and he put his hand into Ern's trousers ' pocket. Out came the ten clues, tumbling on the table. Mr. Goon took a deep breath and stared at them.

A button and a bit of cloth! Now that was a very very important clue. And this cigar-end. Expensive! Mr. Goon sniffed it. He picked up the clues one by one and considered them carefully. Which of them would have any real bearing on the happenings up on Christmas Hill?

Should he tell Ern he had found the clues or not? No, better not. Ern might tell Fatty and the others, and they would have plenty to say about Mr. Goon's methods of getting hold of things. Mr. Goon took a little snipping of the cloth attached to the button so that he would have a piece to match up with the coat, should he be fortunate enough to meet any one wearing it. He took a note of the Peterswood number. Whose was it?

He rang up the telephone exchange to find out. The number belonged to a Mr. Lazarinsky. Ha—that sounded most suspicious. Mr. Goon made a mental note to keep an eye on Mr. Lazarinsky. So far as he knew, the man was a harmless old fellow who spent most of his time growing roses and chrysanthemums. But you never know. That might be a cover for all kinds of dirty work.

Mr. Goon replaced everything in Ern's pockets, the note-book as well. Ern didn't stir when he tiptoed out of the bedroom. Mr. Goon felt that he had done a good evening's work. He wondered how much Fatty knew about this curious mystery. It was funny that the Inspector hadn't sent him word of any possible goings-on in Peterswood.

Well, it would be a real pleasure to Mr. Goon to open the Inspector's eyes, and show him that dirty work could go on under his very nose, in his own district—without people guessing anything. But he, Mr. Goon knew! He'd soon clear everything up—and perhaps this time he really *would* get promotion.

But even Mr. Goon couldn't help feeling that this was rather doubtful!

## 12   A LITTLE INVESTIGATION

FATTY had been making a few inquiries. What was that
building in the middle of the little wood? He asked his
mother, who had never even heard of it. He asked the
postman, who said it wasn't on his round, but he thought
it was a ramshackle old place that had been used in the
last war.

He found a directory of Peterswood, but it did not
mention the building—only the wood, which it called
Bourne Wood. The little stream that flowed through
Peterswood was called the Bourne, so Fatty imagined the
wood was named after it.

He didn't seem to be getting very far. He decided that
it would be a very good idea to walk out to the wood and
have a look round. So, the next morning, he went round
to Larry and Daisy, collected them, and then went to
fetch Pip and Bets. Buster came, of course, full of delight
to think there was a walk for him.

'I thought we'd follow the stream, just like Ern did,'
said Fatty. 'Then, when we come to about where he
thought he was, we'll have a look round to see where that
light he saw could have come from.'

The others were thrilled. 'Now mind!' said Fatty,
'*you* are only going for a walk. Nothing to do with any
mystery, so keep your minds easy. I'm the one that is
mystery hunting!'

They all laughed. 'Right,' said Pip. 'But if we do
happen to spot anything we'll tell you, Fatty!'

Ern had not appeared so far, so they all set off without
him. Fatty thought it was best, anyhow. They didn't want
to let Ern think there was any real mystery in what he had

seen the other night, in case he said anything to Mr. Goon. Let Mr. Goon concentrate on Christmas Hill and the imaginary kidnappers and robbers!

They crossed the little bridge, and went along the bank beside the stream. It was still frosty weather and the grass crunched beneath their feet. The little stream wound in and out, and bare willow and alder trees grew here and there on its banks. The scene was a maze of wintry fields, dreary and desolate.

The stream wound endlessly through the fields. Here and there Fatty pointed to where Ern must have stumbled the other night, for marks were clearly to be seen on the frosty bank.

After some time Bets pointed to the left. 'Look! Is that the wood over there?'

'Can't be,' said Pip. 'It's on our left instead of straight ahead.'

'I expect the stream winds to the left then,' said Fatty. And so it did. It suddenly took a left-hand bend and ran towards the dark wood.

The wood was made up of evergreen trees, and stood dark and still in the wintry air. Because the fir and pine trees still kept their foliage, dark green and thick, the wood somehow looked rather sinister.

'The trees are crouched together as if they are hiding something!' suddenly said Bets. Every one laughed.

'Silly!' said Pip. But all the same they knew what Bets meant. They stood by the stream and looked at the wood. It did not seem very little now that they were near it. It seemed large and forbidding.

'I don't like it,' said Daisy. 'Let's go back.'

But she didn't mean that, of course. Nobody would have gone back just as they had got there. They were all filled with curiosity to know what was so well hidden in those trees!

They followed the stream again until they had almost reached the wood. Not far off was a narrow lane, almost a cart-track, it was so rough.

Fatty stopped. 'Now,' he said, 'we know that a car went by not far from Ern, when he stood by the stream. It seems to me that the car must have gone down that lane. It must lead to the road that goes to Peterswood. I saw it in the map.'

'Yes,' said Larry. 'And this little lane or track must come from the middle of the wood—from whatever building is there. Let's go to the track and follow it.'

'Good idea,' said Fatty. 'Hey, Buster, come along. There can't be any rabbits down that hole—it's far too small!'

Buster left the rat-hole he was scraping at and ran to join them. They all jumped across the little stream, Buster too, and went towards the narrow track. They squeezed through the hedge and found themselves in a very small lane indeed, hardly wide enough to take a full-sized car!

'There are car tracks each side of the lane,' said Fatty, and the others saw tyre marks—many of them, all running almost on top of one another because the lane was so narrow. Two cars could not possibly pass.

'Come on—we'll go up the lane,' said Fatty. Then he lowered his voice. 'Now, not a word about anything except ordinary things. And if we're stopped, be surprised, scared and innocent. Don't say anything we don't want people to hear—we don't know when we may be overheard.'

A familiar thrill went through the Find-Outers as they heard Fatty's words. The mystery was beginning. They were perhaps walking into it. They had been forbidden to—but how could they tell, until they had walked into one, that a mystery was really and truly there?

The track wound about almost as much as the stream had done. Buster ran ahead, his tail wagging. He turned a corner ahead and then the children heard him barking.

They ran to see why. All they saw was a big pair of iron gates set into two enormous stone posts. A bell hung at one side. On each side of the posts stretched high walls, set with glass spikes at the top.

'Gracious! Is this the building?' said Bets in a whisper. Larry frowned at her, and she remembered she mustn't say anything unless it was quite ordinary. So she began to talk loudly about a game she had had for Christmas. The others joined in. They came near to the gates and then saw that a small lodge was on the other side.

They went to the great gates and pressed their faces to the wrought-iron work. Beyond the gates lay a drive, much better kept than the lane outside. Tall, dark trees lined the drive, which swept out of sight round a bend. There was no sign of any building.

Fatty looked and looked. 'That building, whatever it is, must be jolly well hidden,' he thought. 'I wonder what it was used for in the last war. Some hush-hush stuff, I suppose. Well, it looks as if it's pretty hush-hush now, tucked away in this wood, guarded by this enormous wall, and these gates. I wonder if they're locked.'

He pushed against them. They didn't budge. The others tried too, but nobody could open them. Fatty thought they must be locked on the other side.

He glanced at the bell. Should he ring it? Yes, he would! He could always ask the way back to Peterswood, and make that the excuse for ringing. Somebody at the little lodge nearby would probably answer.

So, to the others' delight, Fatty pulled at the bell. A jangling noise came from above their heads, and they saw a bell ringing by one of the stone posts. Buster barked. He was startled by the bell.

' I'm going to ask the way, ' said Fatty. ' We're lost. See! '

Somebody peered out of one of the little windows of the dark lodge. Then the door opened and a man came out. He was dressed like a gamekeeper, and had on a corduroy coat, trousers tucked into boots and a belt round his waist. He looked surly and bad-tempered.

' What do you want? ' he shouted. ' You can't come in here. Go away! '

Fatty promptly rang the bell again. Bets looked scared. The man came striding to the gates, looking black as thunder.

' You stop ringing that bell! ' he shouted. ' What's the matter with you? This is private, can't you see that? '

' Oh! ' said Fatty, looking innocently surprised. ' Doesn't my uncle, Colonel Thomas, live here? '

' No, he doesn't, ' said the man. ' Go away, the lot of you, and take that dog with you. '

' Are you *sure* he doesn't live here? ' persisted Fatty, still looking disbelievingly. ' Well, who does then? '

' Nobody! The house is empty, as anybody knows. And I'm here to see the kids and tramps don't get in and spoil the place, see? So get away quickly! '

' Oh—couldn't we just see round the garden, ' begged Fatty, and the others, taking his cue, joined in. ' Yes, do let's, please! '

' I'm not going to stand here arguing all afternoon with a pack of silly kids, ' said the man. ' You clear off at once. Do you know what I keep for people that come here and pry? A great big whip—and maybe I set my dogs on them. '

' Aren't you afraid of living here all alone? ' said Bets, in an innocent voice.

' In one minute more I'll open these gates and come out and chase you with my whip, ' threatened the man—and he looked so terribly fierce that Fatty half-thought he might be as good as his word.

'Sorry to have bothered you,' he said, in his politest voice. 'Could you tell us the way back to Peterswood? We came over the fields, and we might lose our way going back. We haven't any idea where we are. What's this place called?'

'You just go and follow the lane, and you'll come to Peterswood all right,' said the man. 'And good riddance to you! Waking me up and bringing me out here for nothing. Be off with you!'

He turned to go back to his lodge. The children set off down the narrow track.

'What a very very sweet-natured fellow,' said Larry, and they all laughed.

'Pity we couldn't get in,' said Pip, in a low voice to Fatty. Fatty nudged him to keep quiet. Pip saw somebody riding up the track. It was a postman on his bicycle.

'Good afternoon,' said Fatty, at once. 'Could you tell us the time, please?'

The postman got off his bicycle, undid his coat and looked at a watch in his pocket.

'Stopped!' he said. 'Don't know what the matter is with this old watch of mine. Just won't go now!'

'It's a nice old watch, isn't it,' said Fatty. 'Are you going up to those iron gates? We've just been there too, but the man at the lodge won't let us in.'

'He's the caretaker,' said the postman, putting back his watch and buttoning up his coat. 'Proper bad-tempered fellow too. 'Course he wouldn't let you in! He's there to stop children and tramps and trippers from spoiling the place. It belongs to an old fellow who won't live there himself, and asks such an enormous price for the place that nobody will buy it.'

'Really?' said Fatty, with interest. 'Is he ever here?'

'Not that I know of,' said the postman. 'The only letters I ever take are for Peters the gate-keeper—the man you saw. He has too many for me! It's a job cycling out all this way each day to take letters to one man! Well—sorry not to be able to tell you the time. Bye-bye!'

He cycled off again, whistling. Fatty looked very pleased. 'Trust a postman for being able to tell you all you want to know!' he said, in a low voice. 'A queer story, isn't it? A great big place, apparently unlet and empty, surrounded by an enormous wall, with one surly man to guard the place—and *he* has a lot of letters! That last bit strikes me as queer.'

The children went down the lane, talking quietly. They all felt sure they had hit on their next mystery. But so far they couldn't make head or tail of it!

## 13   A LITTLE PORTRY

ERN was not told anything about the walk to the wood. He wanted to know, however, what were the steps that Fatty was going to take in the mystery of Christmas Hill.

'Well,' said Fatty, looking mysterious, 'word has come to me that a big robbery will be done in the next few days, and that the robbers on Christmas Hill will hide the loot in the old mill.'

Ern's eyes almost dropped out of his head. 'Coo!' he said, and couldn't say any more.

'The thing is—who's going to look for the loot after the robbery?' said Fatty, seriously. 'I can't let any of the others, because they're forbidden to do things like looking for loot—and at the moment I've got other things in hand—tracking down the kidnappers, for instance.'

'Coo,' said Ern again, in awe. An idea shone brilliantly in his mind. 'Fatty! Why don't you let *me* find the loot? I could go and search the old mill for you. Lovaduck! I'd be awfully proud to find the swag.'

'Well—I *might* let you,' said Fatty. He turned to the others. 'What about it, Find-Outers? Shall we let him in on this and give him a chance of finding the loot? After all, he did a lot of hard work finding those clues.'

'Yes. Let him,' said the others, generously, and Ern beamed and glowed. Whatever next! This was life, this was—creeping out at dead of night—hunting for clues up on the hill next day—and now searching for hidden loot. What exciting lives the Find-Outers led!

Ern felt honoured to belong to their company. He felt
he could write a 'pome' about it all. A line came into his
head.

'The dire dark deeds upon the hill.' What a
wonderful beginning to a 'pome.' Ern took out his
portry note-book and wrote down the line before he
could forget it.

'See that?' he said triumphantly to the others. 'The
dark dire deeds upon the hill. That's the beginning of a
new pome. That's real portry, that is.'

> 'The dark dire deeds upon the hill
> Strike my heart with a deadly chill,'

began Fatty.

> 'The robbers rob and the looters loot,
> We'd better be careful they don't all shoot,
> They're deadly men, they're fearful foes,
> What end they'll come to, nobody knows!
> Oooh, the dark dire deeds upon the hill
> Strike my heart with a deadly chill!'

This poem was greeted with shrieks of delighted
laughter by all the Find-Outers, even Buster joining
in the applause. Fatty had reeled it off without
stopping.

Only Ern didn't laugh. He listened solemnly, with
open mouth, to Fatty's recitation, admiration literally
pouring out of him.

'Fatty! You're a *reel* genius. Why, you took my first line
and you made up the whole pome without stopping. I'd
never have thought of all that, if I'd sat down the whole
day long.'

'Ah—that's the secret,' said Fatty, wickedly. 'You
don't sit down—you just stand up and it comes. Like
this :

' Oh have you heard of Ernie's clues,
Ernie's clues, Ernie's clues,
A broken lace, our Ernie found,
A smoked cigar-end on the ground,
A match, a packet, and a hanky,
Honest truth, no hanky-panky!
A rag, a tin, a pencil-end,
How very clever is our friend! '

Fatty couldn't go on because the others were laughing so much. Ern was even more impressed. But he felt down in the dumps too. He could never, never write pomes like that. How did Fatty do it? Ern determined to stand up in his bedroom that night when he was alone and see if portry rolled out of him as it did out of Fatty.

' You're marvellous, ' he said to Fatty. ' You ought to be a poet, you reelly ought. '

' Can't, ' said Fatty. ' I'm going to be a detective. '

' Couldn't you be both? ' said Ern.

' Possibly, but not probably, ' said Fatty. ' Not worth it! Any one can spout that sort of drivel. '

Ern was astonished. Could Fatty really think that was drivel? What a boy!

' Well, to come back to what we were talking about, ' said Fatty, ' we've decided, have we, to let our Ern look for the loot? '

' Yes, ' chorused every one.

' Right, ' said Fatty.

' When do I look for it? ' said Ern, almost quivering with excitement. ' To-night? '

' Well, it's not usual to look for loot before the robbery has been committed, ' said Fatty, his face very serious. ' But if you think there's a chance of finding it before it's put there, you go on and do it, Ern. '

Bets gave a giggle. Ern worked all this out and blushed. 'Yes. I see what you mean. I won't go looking till after the robbery. But when will the robbery be?'

'The papers will tell you,' said Fatty. 'You look in your uncle's papers each morning, and as soon as you see that the robbery has been done, you'll know it's time to hunt in the old mill. And if you want to tell your uncle about it, we've no objection.'

'I don't want to,' said Ern. 'Well, I must be going. Lovaduck! You're a one for spouting portry, aren't you? I can't get over it. So long!'

He went, and the others began to laugh. Poor old Ern. His was a wonderful leg to pull! Larry suddenly saw his 'portry note-book' left on the table.

'Hallo! He's left this. Fatty, write something in it! Something about Goon. Go on!'

'I'll write a "pome" about Goon himself, in Ern's handwriting,' said Fatty, beginning to enjoy himself. He could imitate any one's writing. Bets thought admiringly that really there wasn't anything that Fatty couldn't do— and do better than any one else too! She stood close beside him and watched him.

He found a page in the book, and borrowed a pencil from Pip. 'Ern will be simply amazed to find a poem about his uncle written in his own book in his own handwriting,' said Fatty. 'He'll certainly think he must have written it himself—and he won't know when! Golly, I wish I could be there when he finds it!'

He began to write. As usual the words flowed out straightaway. No puzzling his brains for Fatty, no searching for a rhyme! It just came out like water from a tap.

' TO MY DEAR UNCLE

' Oh how I love thee, Uncle dear,
Although thine eyes like frogs ' appear,
Thy body is so fat and round,
Thy heavy footsteps shake the ground.
Thy temper is so sweet and mild
' Twould frighten e'en the smallest child,
And when thou speakest, people say,
"Now did we hear a donkey bray?"
Dear Uncle, how ... '

' Fatty! Ern's coming back!' said Bets, suddenly. Her sharp ears had heard footsteps. ' Shut the book, quick. '

Fatty shut the book and slid it over the table. He picked up Buster and began to play with him. The others crowded round, laughing.

Ern's head came round the door. 'Did I leave my portry note-book here? Oh yes, I did. Silly of me. Goodbye all. '

He took his book and disappeared. ' What a pity you couldn't finish the poem, Fatty, ' said Daisy. ' It was such a good one—especially all the thees and thys. Just the kind of thing Ern would write. '

' And it was all in Ern's own writing too, ' said Bets. She gave Fatty a hug. ' Fatty, you're the cleverest person in the world. How do you manage to copy other people's writing?'

' Just a gift!' said fatty, airily. ' I remember once last term we had to write an essay—and I wrote a very long one in my form-master's own handwriting. My word— you should have seen his face when I gave it in!'

' And I suppose, as usual, you got top marks for it?' said Pip, who only believed half of the extraordinary stories that Fatty told. As a matter of fact most of them were perfectly true. The rest were almost true but rather exaggerated. Fatty certainly had a remarkable career at school, and had caused more laughter, more annoyance and more admiration than any other boy there.

'I say, Fatty—poor old Ern may have to wait weeks to look for his loot,' said Daisy.

'No, he won't,' said Fatty. 'Haven't you noticed that there's a robbery reported nearly every day in the paper? It's about the commonest crime there is. There'll be one to-morrow, or the next day, don't you worry?'

Fatty got out his own note-book, in which he kept particulars of whatever mystery the Find-Outers were trying to solve. He glanced down his notes.

'This is a very difficult case,' he said to the others. 'There doesn't seem much we can do to find out anything. I've hardly got anywhere. I've found out that that building in the wood is called Harry's Folly, but nobody seems to know why. And the name of the man who is supposed to own it is Henry White—a very nice, common, insignificant name. I can't find out where he lives—all I've heard is that he lives abroad—which doesn't help us much!'

'We know that one of the men who was near the place was called Holland,' suggested Bets.

'Yes,' said Fatty, giving Bets a pat on the shoulder. 'That's a good point. I was just coming to that. As the men were walking, it looks as if they lived in or near Peterswood—though according to Ern, they said good-night to one another near him and went different ways. So it's likely that one might have been the caretaker, and the other was Holland. In which case Holland was walking home.'

Every one sat and thought. 'Where's your telephone directory, Pip?' said Fatty. 'Let's see if there are any Hollands in it.'

Pip fetched it. They all crowded round Fatty as he

looked up the H's. 'Here we are,' he said. 'Holland. A.J. Holland. Henry Holland. W. Holland & Co., Garage proprietors, Marlow. Three Hollands.'

'Have to look them all up, I suppose,' said Larry. 'Lists of Suspects! Three Hollands and one caretaker, called Peters!'

'Correct!' said Fatty. He looked thoughtfully at the directory. 'We'd better begin a bit of detecting again,' he said.

'Well, we're in on this,' said Larry at once. 'We *still* don't know if it's a mystery, so there's no harm in asking about the Hollands.'

'I believe my mother knows some people called Holland,' said Pip suddenly. 'I'll find out. Where do they all live, by the way?'

'Two in Peterswood, and the garage fellow at Marlow,' said Fatty. 'Well, Pip, you be responsible for finding out about one lot of Hollands. Larry and Daisy find out about the other—and I'll bike over to Marlow and smell out the Hollands there.'

They all felt very cheerful now that there was something definite to do. 'I think I'll go in disguise,' said Fatty, who always welcomed a chance to put on one of his disguises. 'I'll go as Ern! I bet I could make myself up to be exactly like him, now I know him so well.'

'Why—you were quite annoyed with us for thinking Ern was you when we met him at the station,' said Daisy.

'I know. Still, I think I can put on a disguise that would deceive even old Goon, if he wasn't too near!' chuckled Fatty. 'Well, Find-Outers, we'll do a spot of work tomorrow. Come on Buster. Stop chewing the rug and come and have your dinner!'

## 14  SOME GOOD DETECTING

QUITE a lot things happened the next day. For one thing there was the report of a big robbery in the daily papers. Ern could hardly believe his eyes when he saw the headlines! Fatty was right. There was the robbery. Coo!

Mr. Goon was astonished to see Ern poring over the paper, reading details on the front page, and the back page too, quite forgetting his breakfast.

'What's up?' he said. 'Give me the paper. Boys shouldn't read at meal-times.'

Ern handed it over, his head in a whirl. It had happened! The robbery was committed. Soon the loot would be in the old mill—and he'd find it. He'd be a hero. His uncle would admire him tremendously and be very sorry indeed for all the hard things he had said. Ern sat in a happy dream all through his breakfast, much to the surprise of his uncle.

Mr. Goon read about the robbery too—but he didn't for one moment think it had anything to do with Ern or himself. Robberies didn't concern him unless they were in his own district. He wondered why Ern looked so daft that morning. Had he found any more clues, or got any more news?

No, said Ern—he hadn't. He felt guilty when he remembered how he was going to find the loot, without telling his uncle anything about it—but he wasn't going to split on Fatty any more. He was going to behave like a real Find-Outer!

The Find-Outers were busy that day. Pip and Bets had laid their plans very carefully, hoping not to arouse their parents' suspicions when they asked about the Hollands.

'We'll talk about people who have queer names,' decided Pip. 'I'll remind you of a girl you used to know whose surname is Redball—you remember her? Then you say "oh yes—and do you remember those people called Tinkle?" or something like that. And from that we'll go on to people with names of towns or countries—and when we get to the name Holland, I'll ask mother if she knows people of that name.'

'Yes, that would be a safe way of finding out,' said Bets, pleased. So they began at breakfast time.

'Do you remember that girl you used to know—she had such a funny name,' said Pip. 'Redball, I think it was.'

'Oh yes,' said Bets. 'That *was* a queer name. I remember somebody else with a funny name too—Tinkle. Don't you remember, Pip?'

'Yes. It must be queer to answer to a name like that,' said Pip.

'You get used to it,' said his mother, joining in unsuspectingly.

'Some people have names of countries and towns,' said Pip. 'There's a composer called Edward Germany, isn't there?'

'Edward *German*,' corrected his father, 'not Germany. Plenty of people are called England and I have known an Ireland and a Scotland too.'

'Have you known a Holland?' asked Bets. This was going much better than they had hoped!

'Oh yes,' said Mrs. Hilton at once. 'I know a Mrs. Holland quite well.'

'Is there a Mr. Holland?' asked Pip.

'Yes, I think so,' said Mrs. Hilton, looking rather surprised. 'I've never seen him. He must be an old man by now, because Mrs. Holland is a very old lady.'

'Did they have any children?' asked Pip, ruling out

old Mr. Holland at once, because it didn't seem very likely that he would be engaged in any sort of mystery if he was so old.

'Well—their children would be grown up by now,' said his mother.

'Was there a boy?' asked Bets. 'A boy who would be a man now?'

Mrs. Hilton felt surprised at these last questions. 'Why all this sudden interest in the Hollands?' she asked. 'What are you up to? You are usually up to something when you begin this sort of thing.'

Pip sighed. Mothers were much too sharp. They were like dogs. Buster always sensed when anything was out of the ordinary, and so did mothers. Mothers and dogs both had a kind of second sight that made them see into people's minds and know when anything unusual was going on. He kicked Bets under the table to stop her asking any more questions.

She understood the kick, though she didn't like it, and tried to change the subject. 'I wish I had another name, not Hilton,' she said. 'A more exciting name. And I wish people would call me Elizabeth, not Bets.'

'Oh *no*,' said her father. 'Bets suits you. You are a proper little Bets.'

So the subject was changed and nothing more was said about the Hollands. But Pip and Bets were rather downcast because they had't found out what Fatty would want to know.

They went up to the play-room. Lorna the maid was there, dusting. 'It's a pity we didn't find out anything more about the Hollands,' said Bets. 'Oh—hallo, Lorna.'

'The Hollands?' said Lorna. 'What do you want to know about them for? There's not much to know! My sister's in service with old Mrs. Holland.'

Well! Who would have thought that Lorna knew all

about the Hollands ! She told them in half a minute all they needed to know.

' Poor old Mrs. Holland, she's all alone now that her husband's dead, ' said Lorna. ' She had two daughters, but they're both living in Africa—and her son was killed in the last war but one. So she's nobody to care for her at all. '

Pip and Bets thought this was very sad. They also thought that their Mrs. Holland, at any rate, didn't belong to the family of Hollands that Fatty was looking for.

' I wonder how Larry and Daisy are getting on, ' said Pip.

They were getting on quite well ! They had decided to ask their postman if he knew of any Hollands. He was a great friend of theirs. So they swung on their front gate that morning and waited till he came.

' Well, aren't you cold, out here so early ? ' said the postman, when he came. ' Expecting something special ? '

' Only our circus tickets, ' said Larry, truthfully. ' Ah— I bet they're in this envelope. '

He and the postman then had a very interesting talk about the various circuses they had both seen. ' Well, I must be off, ' said the postman at last, and he turned to go.

As if he had only just thought of it, Larry called after him. ' Oh—half a minute—do you know any one called Holland in Peterswood ? '

' Holland—let me see now, ' said the postman, scratching his rough cheek. ' Yes, there are two. One's in Rosemary Cottage. The other's in Hill House. Which on do you want ? '

' One with a man in it, ' said Daisy.

' Ah—then you don't want old Mrs. Holland of Rosemary Cottage, ' said the postman. ' Maybe you want the Hollands of Hill House. There's a Mr. Holland

*Larry called after the postman*

there—but I did hear he's in America at the moment. Yes, that's right, he is. I keep taking post cards from America to the house for all the children. Five of them and little monkeys they are too ! '

' Thank you, ' said Larry, as a loud knocking came from behind him. It was his mother knocking on the window for him to come in to breakfast. He and Daisy fled indoors. It didn't look as if either of the Peterswood family of Hollands was the right one. Perhaps the Marlow Holland was the one they wanted !

Fatty was out on his bike when the other Find-Outers went to find him. ' Gone over to Marlow, I expect, ' said Larry. ' Well, we'll wait for him. He's left the oil-stove on in his shed. We'll wait there. '

So they sat down in the cosy shed. Buster was not there. He had gone with Fatty, sitting upright as usual in Fatty's bicycle basket. Fatty had set off soon after breakfast before his mother could plan any jobs for him to do. It was not very far to Marlow—hardly three miles. The wind was cold, and Fatty's cheeks grew redder and redder.

He had made himself up just like Ern, enormous cap and all ! Ern had teeth that stuck out, so Fatty had inserted his set of false celluloid teeth, which were very startling when displayed in a sudden grin. But they did make him look like Ern. He had put on a wig of rather untidy, coarse hair, very like Ern's, an old mack, and corduroy trousers. He wished the others could see him !

Buster was used to Fatty's changed appearances by now. He never knew when his master was going to appear as an old woman, a bent old man, an errand boy or a correct young man ! But Buster didn't mind. Fatty always smelt the same, whatever he wore, so Buster's nose told him the truth, even if his eyes didn't.

Holland's garage was in a road off the High Street. Fatty cycled to find it. He saw it from a distance and then dismounted. Taking a quick look round to make sure that nobody saw him, he let all the air out of one of his tyres, so that the wheel bumped dismally on the ground.

Fatty then put on a doleful expression and wheeled his bicycle to Holland's Garage. He turned in at the big entrance. There were a good many men working about on different cars, but nobody took any notice of him.

Fatty saw a boy about his own age washing down a car near the back of the garage. He went up to him.

' Hallo, chum, ' he said, ' any chance of getting my bike mended here. Got a puncture. '

' Not just now, ' said the boy. ' I do the punctures usually, but I'm busy. '

' Oh come on! Leave the washing alone, and do my bike for me, ' said Fatty. But the boy was keeping an eye on a little window let into the wall of the wooden office near him. Fatty guessed correctly that the Boss might be in there.

' Can't do it yet, ' said the boy, in a low tone. ' I say is that your dog in the basket! Isn't he good! '

' Yes. He's a fine dog, ' said Fatty. ' come on Buster, you can get down now! '

Buster leapt out of the basket, and ran to the hose. He barked at it and the boy gave him a spraying, which delighted Buster's heart.

' This is quite a big garage, isn't it? ' said Fatty, leaning back against the wall. ' And a lot of men working in it. You must be pretty busy. '

' We are, ' said the boy, still vigorously hosing the car. ' Busier than any other garage in the district. '

' I wouldn't mind taking a job in a garage myself, ' said Fatty. ' I know a bit about cars. Any chance of a job here? '

' Might be, ' said the boy. ' You'd have to ask Mr.

Williams there—he's the foreman. The Boss would want a look at you too.'

'Who's the Boss?' asked Fatty.

'Mr. Holland, of course,' said the boy, his eye still on the window nearby. 'He owns this garage and another one some miles away. But he's usually here. Slave-driver, I call him.'

'Bad luck,' sympathized Fatty.

At that moment another dog ran into the garage, and Buster darted at him. Whether Buster thought this was his own particular garage for the moment or not Fatty didn't know—but Buster certainly acted as if he thought it was! He caught the other dog by the back of the neck, and immediately a terrific howling, snarling and barking filled the place.

The little window near Fatty and the boy flew up at once. 'Who does that black dog belong to?' said a harsh voice.

'To this boy here, Mr. Holland, sir,' said the garage boy, scared.

'What's your name?' demanded Mr. Holland of Fatty, who was too surprised not to answer.

'Frederick Trotteville of Peterswood,' he said. 'What's the fuss about, sir?'

'I won't have dogs fighting in my garage,' snapped the man. 'I shall report your dog to the police if you bring him in here again. What have you come for? I've seen you chattering to this boy here for ages, making him do his work carelessly!'

'I came to ask if I could have my bike puncture mended,' said Fatty. He eyed Mr. Holland, wondering whether to take a shot in the dark. He decided that he would.

'I want to ride over to a place called Harry's Folly, sir. It's got some fine iron gates, I'm told, and I'm interested in them, sir. Do you happen to know the best way to get to Harry's Folly?'

Fatty paused for breath, watching Mr. Holland's face.

Mr. Holland had certainly heard of Harry's Folly! He started a little when Fatty mentioned it, and a peculiar expression came over his face. Then his face smoothed out, and he answered immediately.

'Harry's Folly! No, I've never heard of it. We can't mend your bike here now. We're too busy. Clear off and take your dog with you.'

Fatty winked at the boy, who was now hosing the wheels of the car very very well indeed. He called Buster. 'Hey, Buster! Come on!'

Buster left the fascinating hose and ran to Fatty's feet. Fatty wheeled his bike slowly out of the garage. He had a very satisfied expression on his face.

He was sure he had found the right Mr. Holland! He had seen the little start the man gave at the mention of Harry's Folly. He knew the house all right—then why did he deny all knowledge of it?

'Very very fishy,' decided Fatty, wheeling his bicycle into another side road. He pumped up the tyre swiftly, put Buster into the basket, and rode home, pleased with himself. Frederick Algernon Trotteville, you certainly are a good detective, Fatty told himself.

Back at the garage Mr. Holland sat in his office, quite silent. He took down a telephone directory and found the name Trotteville in it, and the address. He dialled a number and spoke to somebody.

'That you Jack? Listen—what was the name of that kid who cleared up the Missing Necklace affair? Smart lad, you remember? Ah, I thought so. It may interest you to know he's just been here—complete with a dog called Buster—and he told me he wanted to bike to a place called Harry's Folly! What do you make of that?'

Somebody evidently made a lot of it at the other end of the telephone, for Mr. Holland listened intently for a few minutes. Then he spoke in a low voice, very near the mouthpiece.

'Yes, I agree with you. Kids like that must be dealt with. Leave it to me!'

## 15   MR. GOON IS MYSTIFIED

FATTY cycled back to Peterswood, his mind hard at work. So Mr. Holland was connected with Harry's Folly—and something was going on there, though Fatty couldn't imagine what! And Mr. Holland didn't want people to know that he knew Harry's Folly—very peculiar altogether!

'Shall I ring up Inspector Jenks?' wondered Fatty. 'Or shall I just jog along on my own for a bit and try to solve the mystery? I'd like to do that. Funny to think of old Goon getting all excited about an imaginary mystery, and here are the Find-Outers on the edge of a real one again!'

He came to Peterswood. He stopped and put Buster down. The little Scottie bounded gleefully along by the bicycle.

In the distance Mr. Goon loomed up, on his way to talk severely to somebody who had let their chimney get on fire. To his enormous surprise he saw somebody he thought was Ern riding a bicycle not far off. Mr. Goon stopped and stared. He simply couldn't believe his eyes.

'I've left Ern at home, clearing out my shed,' he thought. 'And I told him to clean my bike too. And now there he is, riding my bike, calm as a cucumber. I'll tell him off! Can't trust that boy at all, not for one minute!'

He hurried towards Fatty. Fatty spotted him, and rode into a side-street, waving merrily. He couldn't help hoping that Mr. Goon would think he was Ern. Mr. Goon, of course, hadn't any doubt of it at all. He was feeling very angry.

'Ern!' he called. 'ERN!'

Fatty took no notice, but rode slowly. Mr. Goon
hurried after him, his face going purple. That boy!
Waving to him like that, cheeky as a monkey!

' ERN! YOU COME HERE!'

' Ern ' rode round the corner and Mr. Goon lost sight
of him. He almost burst with rage. He retraced his steps
and went back down the road, thinking of all the things
he would do to Ern when he next saw him. To his
astonishment Ern actually appeared before him again, at
the end of the street, and waved to him.

Mr. Goon nearly had a fit. Fatty, of course, was dying
of laughter at the sight of Mr. Goon's face, and could
hardly keep on his bicycle. He pedalled out of sight, tears
running down his cheeks, almost helpless with laughter.

Once more he cycled round the block of houses and
swam into Mr. Goon's sight and out again. Mr. Goon
had now reached the pitch of shaking his fist and muttering,
much to the amazement of all the passers-by. Fatty
decided that he really would fall off his bicycle with
laughing if he saw Mr. Goon again, and regretfully
pedalled home to tell the Find-Outers all that had
happened.

But Buster, having spotted Mr. Goon, thought it
would be much more fun to trot at his heels than to go
with Fatty. So he went behind him, sniffing at his trousers
till the policeman felt him and turned in aggravation.

' Now you clear-orf!' said Mr. Goon, exasperated.
' First it's Ern cheeking me, and now it's you! Clear-orf
I say, or I'll kick you into the middle of next week. '

Buster didn't clear-orf. He capered round Mr. Goon,
making playful little darts at his legs as if he wanted him
to have a game. Mr. Goon was so worked up that he
backed straight into a street-sweeper's barrow and almost
knocked it over.

The sweeper sent Buster away by frightening him with

his broom. Buster trotted down the street pleased with himself. He certainly was a dog worthy of a master like Fatty!

Mr. Goon finished his errand, gradually getting less purple, and then walked home. Now to deal with Ern!

Ern had done a remarkably good morning's work. He had cleaned out the shed thoroughly, and now he was just finishing cleaning Mr. Goon's bicycle. He was trying to think of some portry as he worked.

The next-door neighbour, Mrs. Murray, thought that Mr. Goon had a very hard-working boy for a nephew. Every time she hung out her washing, there he was, working away. She called over the fence.

'You're a good boy, you are! You haven't stopped working one minute since you began!'

Ern beamed. Mrs. Murray went indoors. Mr. Goon arrived, and walked down the little garden to where Ern was working by the shed, polishing the bicycle handles.

'Ho!' said Mr. Goon, in an awful voice, 'so you thought you could sauce me, did you? What do you mean by it, riding round the village on *my* bike, cheeking me like that?'

Ern couldn't make out what his uncle was talking about at all. He stared at him, puzzled.

'What do you mean, Uncle?' he said. 'I've been here all the time. Look, the shed is clean and tidy—and I've almost finished your bike.'

Mr. Goon looked. He was most surprised to see the shed so neat and tidy, and certainly his bicycle looked very spick and span.

'Ern, it's no good you denying it,' he said, his face going red, on its way to turning purple. 'I saw you—and you waved at me. I called you and you didn't come. What's more, you were riding my bike, and I don't allow that.'

'Uncle, I tell you I've been here all the morning,' said Ern, in an aggrieved voice. 'What's the matter with you? Haven't I done all you said? I tell you I didn't ride your bike. You've made a silly mistake.'

Mr. Goon was now purple. He raised his voice. 'I won't have you cheek me, Ern, see? You were out on my bike, and you cheeked me? I tell you ...'

Mrs. Murray popped her head over the fence. She had heard everything, and she meant to put in a word for that hard-working boy, Ern.

'Mr. Goon,' she said, and the policeman jumped. 'Mr. Goon! That boy hasn't left this garden. A harder-working boy I never did see in all my life. You ought to be proud of a boy like that instead of accusing him of things he never did. I say to you, Mr. Goon, that that boy hasn't budged from his place. I've been in and out with my washing, and I know. You leave that nephew of yours alone, or there's things I'll tell round to every one. Ah, you may be an officer of the law, Mr. Goon, but you don't deceive *me*! I remember when ...'

Mr. Goon knew that there was absolutely no way of stopping Mrs. Murray once she had begun. He was afraid of what she might say in front of Ern. So he put on a very dignified face, said 'Good morning to you, Mam,' and marched indoors. Retreat was always the best policy when Mrs. Murray was on the warpath!

'You stick up for yourself, lad,' said Mrs. Murray. 'Don't you let him go for you like that!'

A voice bellowed from the kitchen. 'ERN!'

Ern dropped his duster and ran. However mistaken his uncle might be, he was still an uncle with a cane in the cupboard, and Ern thought he had better keep on the good side of both.

Mr. Goon said no more about Ern riding his bike. An uncomfortable thought had come into his mind. He was wondering if that boy who looked like Ern could possibly have been Fatty up to his tricks. Ern must certainly have been in the garden all the time if Mrs. Murray said so. Her tongue was sharp and long but it told the truth.

'Have you seen those kids to-day yet?' asked Mr. Goon. 'Got any more news for me?'

'You know I haven't been out, Uncle. I've just told you so,' said Ern. 'I'd like to go and see them this afternoon though.'

Ern was longing to discuss the robbery with the Find-Outers. He had got the paper again as soon as his uncle had gone out, and read every single detail. The jewels those thieves had taken! Coo! There ought to be a fine bit of loot up at the old mill to-night! Ern was thrilled at the thought.

'How that boy Fatty knows these things just beats me,' thought Ern. 'He's a wonder, he is! I wish I could be like him. I'd do anything in the world for Fatty!'

A good many people felt like that about Fatty. However annoying, boastful or high-handed he was people always admired him and wanted to do things for him, especially other boys. He was head and shoulders above them in brains, boldness and courage, and they knew it.

Ern rushed round to the Find-Outers immediately after his dinner. They were at Fatty's down in the cosy shed. He had been telling them all his adventures of the morning. They had admired the things he had found out at Holland's garage and had roared with laughter at the way he had played a trick on Goon, pretending to be Ern.

'I expect Ern will be along soon,' said Fatty, opening a daily paper. 'Any one see the account of this big robbery? Ern will be sure to think it's the one we meant!'

Larry and Daisy had seen it, but not Pip or Bets. They all pored over it, and Ern chose a very good moment to come into the shed.

'Hallo! 'he said, beaming round. 'I say—you're looking at the story of the robbery! You're a marvel, Fatty, to know it was going to be done so soon. I can't think why you don't tell the police beforehand, when you know these things. '

'They wouldn't believe me, ' said Fatty, truthfully. 'Well, Ern— there should be plenty of fine loot up in the old mill soon! '

'I'm going to-night, ' said Ern, solemnly. 'It's awfully good of you to let me, Fatty. '

'Don't mention it, ' said Fatty. 'Spleshure. '

'Pardon? ' said Ern.

'SPLESHURE! ' said Fatty, loudly.

The others laughed. 'What's he say? ' said Ern, puzzled.

'He means, "It's a pleasure," ' explained Bets, giggling.

'Swatesaid! ' chorused the Find-Outers together.

'Funny way of talking you have sometimes, ' said Ern to Fatty, seriously. 'I say, my uncle wasn't half queer with me this morning. Said he saw me riding his bike and cheeking him when all the time I was cleaning out his shed. '

'Must be mad, ' said Fatty. 'Well, Ern—the best of luck to you to-night. I hope the swag won't be too heavy for you to carry. '

'Coo! ' said Ern, in alarm. 'I never thought of that! '

# 16   UNPLEASANT NIGHT FOR ERN

ERN passed the rest of the day in a state of excitement. His uncle couldn't think what was the matter with him.

'Thinking out some more of your wonderful portry, I suppose,' he said, scornfully.

'No, I'm not,' said Ern, and he wasn't. He was thinking of what he was going to do that night. There would be a small moon. That would help him to find the way properly this time without making a mistake. Would the loot be too heavy? Well, if it was he'd go twice to fetch it!

Ern went to bed early again. Mr. Goon felt that Something was Up. Ern knew something that he hadn't passed on to his uncle. Drat the boy!

He listened at Ern's door when he went up to bed himself. If Ern was asleep he'd creep in and get that note-book again. But Ern wasn't asleep. He was tossing and turning, because Mr. Goon could quite well hear the bed creak.

Mr. Goon undressed and got into bed, meaning to lie awake till Ern was asleep. But somehow he didn't. His eyes closed and soon Ern heard the familiar snores echoing through the little house.

Ern didn't want to go to sleep. He wanted to keep awake safely and leave for Christmas Hill about one o'clock when the moon would be up and giving a little light.

But it was hard to keep awake. Ern's eyes kept closing. He sat up straight. This wouldn't do. He'd be asleep in half a tick.

A thought came into his head. He remembered how

Fatty had said that portry would come pouring out of you if you stood up to say it. It would be a good chance to try it now—Uncle was asleep— there was no one to interrupt him. And it would stop him going off to sleep.

Ern got out of bed. It was cold and he shivered. He pulled on his overcoat and put a scarf round his neck. He got out his portry note-book, and his book of Clues and Suspects. He was proud of them both.

He read down his list of clues again. Then he took a pencil and wrote a few lines on the next page.

'Robbery committed January 3rd. Loot will be hidden in the old mill on Christmas Hill. Ern Goon detailed to find it on night of Jan. 4th.'

That looked good. Ern drew a line under it and thought with pleasure of what he might be able to write the next morning. 'Loot collected. Worth about ten thousand pounds.' How he hoped he would be able to write that down too!

Now for the portry. He read through his various 'poems' and decided that they were not nearly as good as the ones Fatty had made up out of his head on the spur of the moment. He didn't see the one that Fatty had written in the book about Mr. Goon. He didn't even know it was there.

Ern shut the portry note-book and put it on top of the other book. Then he stood up to begin saying portry straight out of his head like Fatty.

But somehow it wouldn't come. Ern stood there, waiting and shivering. Then suddenly a line came into his head. Ah—it was beginning!

Ern recited the line. 'The pore old man lay on the grass ...'

He stopped. Nothing else came. Now if only he were Fatty, he'd go on with another line and another and another—a whole poem, in fact, which he could remember and write proudly down.

He recited the line again, a little more loudly. 'The pore old man lay on the grass ... on the grass ... on the ... '

No, it wasn't any good. He couldn't think of another line to follow. But that was just it—Fatty didn't *have* to think. Portry just came out of him without stopping when he wanted it to ! Perhaps Fatty was a genius and Ern wasn't. Ern thought sadly about this for a moment.

Then he began again, reciting loudly, 'A pore old man lay on the grass, A pore old man lay on the grass, A pore old man ... '

Mr. Goon, in the next room, woke up with a jump. What was that peculiar noise ? He sat up in bed. A voice came to him from the bedroom next to his. Mr. Goon listened in amazement.

'A pore old man lay on the grass, A pore ... '

'It's *Ern* !' said Mr. Goon, really astonished. 'What's he doing, talking in the middle of the night about pore old men lying on grass ? He must be out of his mind !'

Mr. Goon put on a dressing-gown much too small for him and went majestically into Ern's room. The boy stood there in the dark, still reciting his one line desperately. 'The pore old man ... '

'Now what's all this ?' said Mr. Goon in a loud voice and Ern nearly jumped out of his skin. 'Waking me up with your pore old men ! What do you think you're doing, Ern ? I won't have this kind of behaviour, I tell you straight.'

'Oh, it's you, Uncle,' said Ern, weakly. Mr. Goon switched on the light. He saw Ern there in coat and scarf and he was even more astonished.

'You going somewhere ?' he inquired.

'No. I was cold so I put some things on,' said poor Ern,

getting into bed. 'I was only making up portry, Uncle. It comes better when you stand up.'

Mr. Goon caught sight of the two note-books on a chair. 'I'll teach you to wake me up in the middle of the night with portry!' he snorted, and picked up the two books to take back with him.

'Uncle! Oh Uncle, please don't touch those!' begged Ern, leaping out of bed and trying to take them from his uncle. But Mr. Goon held them all the more tightly.

'What's the matter? What are you so upset about? I'm not going to throw them into the fire,' said Mr. Goon.

'Uncle!' wailed Ern. 'They're private. Nobody is to read those but me.'

'Ho!' said Mr. Goon. 'That's what *you* think!' and he switched off the light and shut the door. Ern got into bed, shivering with fright. Now his uncle would read about the Loot—and the wonderful secret would be out! Ern shed a few tears on to the sheet.

Mr. Goon read through the portry note-book first. When he came to the poem about himself he could hardly believe his eyes. How could Ern write such a rude poem? Right down rude, it was. Talking about his uncle's eyes in that way, and his voice—and that bit about the donkey's bray! Mr. Goon felt himself swelling up with righteous rage.

He then read the other book. He only glanced at the Clues and other Notes which he had read before. But when he came to the bit Ern had written in that very night his eyes grew rounder than ever.

> 'Robbery committed January 3rd. Loot will be hidden in the old mill in Christmas Hill. Ern Goon detailed to find it on night of Jan. 4th.'

Mr. Goon read this several times. What an extraordinary thing! What robbery? And how did anybody know where the loot was ? And who detailed Ern to get it ? That boy Frederick, of course ! Mr. Goon gave one of his snorts. Then he sat and thought very deeply.

It was a real bit of luck that he had got Ern's note-books to-night ! Now *he* could go and find the loot instead of Ern. That would be a bit of a blow to that boy Frederick ! Aha ! He wouldn't like Mr. Goon turning up with the loot instead of Ern. And what would Inspector Jenks say to all this ? He wouldn't be pleased with anybody but Mr. Goon !

He read the bit of portry about himself again, and felt very angry indeed. Ungrateful boy Ern was ! He determined to give Ern something to remember. Where had he put that cane ?

Ern heard Mr. Goon go downstairs. He heard him come up again. He heard him open his door and switch on the light—and oh, what a horrible sight, there stood his uncle at the door with a cane in his hand !

' Ern, ' said Mr. Goon, in a sad voice, ' this is going to hurt me more than it hurts you. I've read that pome you wrote about me. It's wicked, downright wicked. '

Ern was astonished and alarmed. ' What pome, Uncle ? I haven't written anything about you at all. '

' Now don't you go making things worse by telling stories, ' said Mr. Goon. He opened the portry note-book at the right page and to Ern's consternation he saw, written in his own handwriting, a poem addressed to ' My Dear Uncle. ' He read it and quaked.

' Uncle ! I didn't write it. I couldn't. It's too good a pome for me to write ! '

' What do you mean, it's *"too good!"* ' demanded his uncle. ' It's a wicked pome. And how you can sit there and tell me you didn't write it when it's in your own handwriting, well it beats me ! I suppose you'll say next it isn't your writing ? '

Ern looked at the ' pome '. ' It *is* my writing, ' he said in a faint voice. ' But I don't understand it at all, Uncle, because honestly I don't remember writing it. I don't believe I *could* make up a pome as good as that. It's—it's like a dream, all this. '

' And there's another thing, Ern, ' said Mr. Goon, bending the cane to and fro in a very alarming manner, ' I've read what's in your other book too. That robbery— and the loot hidden in the old mill. You never told me nothing about that, nothing at all. You're a bad boy. And bad boys get the cane. Hold out your hand ! '

Poor Ern ! He began to cry again, but there was nothing to do but hold out his hand, or else be caned on other places that might be still more painful.

Swish ! ' That's for the pome, ' said Mr. Goon, ' and so is that ! And that's for not telling me about the robbery and so is that. '

Ern howled dismally and held his hand under his arm-pit. Mr. Goon looked at him grimly. ' And don't you think you're going loot-hunting to-night, because you're not ! I'm going to lock you in your bedroom, see ? And you can just spend the night thinking of what happens to bad boys who write rude pomes and don't tell their uncle the things they ought to know ! '

And with that Mr. Goon switched off the light, shut the door—and locked it ! Ern's heart sank. Now he was Properly Done. No going up to the old mill for him to-night. A horrid thought struck his head under the pillow and wept for his smarting hand, his locked door, and his lost hopes.

He heard Mr. Goon dress. He heard him go quietly out of the house. Ern knew he was going up to Christmas Hill. Now he'd find the loot. All Fatty's plans would come to nothing because of him, Ern Goon, and his silliness. Ern felt very small and very miserable.

Then a thought struck him. He remembered the rude 'pome' about his uncle. He got out of bed and switched on the light. His portry note-book was on the chair where his uncle had tossed it. Ern picked it up and found the page with rude 'pome' on it. *To My Dear Uncle.*

Ern read it through six times. He thought it was remarkably clever. And yes, it was certainly in his own handwriting, though he couldn't for the life of him remember when he had written it.

'I must have done it in my sleep,' said Ern, at last. 'Geniuses do queer things. I must have dreamt it last night, got out of bed in my sleep, and written it down. Coo! Fancy me writing a good pome like that. It's wonderful! It's better than anything Fatty could have done. Perhaps I'm a genius after all!'

He got into bed again, and put his note-book under his pillow. He recited the poem several times. It was a pity it wasn't finished. He wondered why he hadn't finished it. Funny he couldn't remember doing it at all! It showed how his brain worked hard when he was asleep.

Ern didn't mind his smarting hand now. He didn't even mind very much that his uncle was finding the loot. He was so very proud to think that he, Ern Goon, had written a first-rate pome—or so it seemed to Ern.

He fell asleep reciting the pome. He was warm and cosy in his bed. But Mr. Goon was not. He was far up on Christmas Hill, looking for loot that wasn't there!

# 17  UNPLEASANT NIGHT FOR MR. GOON

MR. GOON laboured up Christmas Hill in a cold wind. He kept a sharp eye for mysterious lights and noises and hoped fervently that cows and hens and cats wouldn't suddenly moo and cluck and yowl as they had done the time before.

They didn't. The night was very peaceful indeed. A little moon shone in the sky. No mysterious lights appeared. There were no noises of any kind except the little crunches made by Mr. Goon's big feet on the frosty hillside.

The old mill loomed up, faintly outlined in the darkness by the moonlight. Mr. Goon went cautiously. If the loot was there, the robbers might be about also. He felt for his truncheon. He remembered the man who had attacked him the other night, and once more thought proudly how he had sent him flying.

Everything was quiet in the old mill. A rat ran across the floor and Mr. Goon caught sight of its two eyes gleaming in the darkness. An owl moved up above, and then swept off on silent wings, almost brushing Mr. Goon's face, and making him jump.

After standing quite still for some time to make sure there was nobody there, Mr. Goon switched on his powerful torch. It showed a deserted, ruined old place, with holes in the roof and walls, and masses of old rubbish on the floor. There were holes in the floor too and Mr. Goon decided that he had better move cautiously or his feet would go through a rotten board.

His torch picked out what looked like a pile of rotten old sacks. The loot might possibly be hidden under those! Mr. Goon began to scrabble about in them, tossing them to one side. Clouds of dust choked him and a nasty smell rose around him.

'Pooh,' said Mr. Goon, and sneezed. His vast sneeze echoed round the old mill and would certainly have alarmed any robber within half a mile. Fortunately for him there was nobody about at all.

Mr. Goon then began on a pile of old boxes. He disturbed a nest of mice, and made a few rats extremely angry. One snapped at his hand and Mr. Goon hit at it with his torch. The torch missed the rat but hit the wall behind—and that was the end of the torch. It flared up once and then went out. No amount of shaking and screwing would make it light up again.

'Broken!' said Mr. Goon, and hurled the torch at the wall in anger. 'Drat that rat! Now I can't see a thing.'

He had some matches in his pocket. He got them out and struck one. He saw some sacks in another corner. The match went out and Mr. Goon made his way across the floor to the sacks. His foot sank into a hole in the boarding and he had a hard struggle to get it out again.

By this time Mr. Goon was feeling so hot that he considered taking off his top-coat. He reached the sacks and began feeling about in them. Any cases of jewels? Any cash-boxes? His fingers felt something hard, and his heart leapt. Ah—this felt like a jewel-case!

He pulled the box out of the sacks. He opened it in the dark and dug his fingers in. Something sharp pricked him. Mr. Goon lighted a match to see what was in the box.

Rusty tacks and nails lay there, and Mr. Goon felt his heart sink. Only an old box of nails! He licked his bleeding finger and thumb.

Mr. Goon worked very hard indeed for the next hour. He went through all the piles of dirty, dusty old rags and sacks and newspapers. He examined every old or broken box, and put his hand down every hole in the wall, disturbing various families of mice but nothing else. He had a most disappointing night.

He stood up and wiped his hot face, leaving smears of black all across it. His uniform was cloudy with the old fine dust of the mill. He scowled into the darkness.

'No loot here. Not a sign of it. If that boy Frederick has been pulling Ern's leg about this, I'll—I'll—I'll ...'

But before Mr. Goon could make up his mind exactly what he would do to Fatty, a frightful screech sounded just above his head.

Mr. Goon's heart stood still. The hair on his head rose up straight. He swallowed hard and stood absolutely still. Whatever could that awful noise be? Was somebody in pain or in terror?

Something very soft brushed his cheek and another terrible screech sounded just by his ear. It was more than enough for Mr. Goon. He turned and fled out of the old mill at top speed, stumbling and almost falling as his foot caught in the rubbish lying around.

The screech owl saw him go, and considered whether to go after him and do another screech near his head. But the movement of a mouse down below on the floor caught his eye, and he flew silently down to catch it.

Mr. Goon had no idea that the frightful noise had come from the screech owl that lived in the old mill. All kinds of wild ideas went through his mind as he stumbled down the hill, but not once did he think of the right one—the harmless old owl on the rafters in the ruined roof.

His heart beat fast, he panted loudly, and little drops of perspiration ran down his face. Mr. Goon made up his mind very very firmly that never again would he go looking for loot on Christmas Hill in the dark. He'd rather let Ern go, yes, a hundred times rather!

He steadied down a little as he reached the bottom of the hill. He had wrenched his right ankle, and it made him limp. He thought of Ern safe in his warm bed and envied him.

He walked home more slowly, thinking hard. He thought of the rude ' pome ' in Ern's book. He thought of all the clues and other notes he had read. He marvelled that Fatty should have let Ern go to look for the loot—if there *was* any loot. That boy Frederick was always at the bottom of everything !

Mr. Goon let himself into his house, went upstairs and switched on his bedroom light. He stared in horror at himself. What a sight he was ! Absolutely filthy. His face was criss-crossed with smears of dirt. His uniform gave out clouds of dust wherever he touched it. What a night !

Mr. Goon washed his face and hands. He took off his dirty uniform and put it outside on the little landing, because it smelt of the rubbish in the old mill. Ern found it there the next morning and was most astonished.

Mr. Goon got into bed tired out, and was soon snoring. Ern was asleep too, dreaming that he was broadcasting his poem about Mr. Goon. Lovaduck ! Fancy him, Ern Goon, at the B.B.C. !

In the morning Ern was sulky, remembering his smarting hand. He sulked too because he knew that his uncle had gone off to get the loot. Had he found it ? Would he tell him if he had ?

Mr. Goon was late down for breakfast. He was feeling very very tired. Also, in the bright light of morning, he couldn't help thinking that perhaps he had been rather foolish to rush off to Christmas Hill in the middle of the night like that. Loot in the old mill didn't seem nearly so likely now as it had seemed to him the night before.

Ern was eating his porridge when his uncle came down.

They both scowled at one another. Ern didn't offer to get his uncle's porridge out of the pan for him.

'You get my porridge, and look slippy about it,' said Mr. Goon. Ern got up, holding his caned hand in a stiff kind of way as if he couldn't possibly use it. Mr. Goon saw him and snorted.

'If your hand hurts you, it's no more than you deserve, you rude, ungrateful boy.'

'I don't see what I've got to be grateful to you for,' mumbled Ern. 'Hitting me and caning me and always ticking me off. Can't do anything right for you. Serve you right if I ran away!'

'Gah!' said Mr. Goon, and began to eat his porridge even more noisily than Ern.

'Locking me in my bedroom so that I couldn't do my bit,' went on Ern, sniffling. 'And *you* went off after the loot, so you can't pretend you didn't, Uncle. It was a mean trick to play. You wait till I tell the others what you did.'

'If you so much as open your mouth about anything I'll take that can and show you what it really *can* do!' said Mr. Goon. 'You just wait.'

Ern sniffed again. 'I'll run away! I'll go to sea! That'll make you sorry you treated me so crooly!'

'Gah!' said Mr. Goon again, and cut himself a thick slice of bread. 'Run away! Stuff and nonsense. A boy like you hasn't got the courage of a mouse. Run away indeed!'

Breakfast was finished in silence. 'Now you clear away and wash up,' said Mr. Goon at the end. 'I've got to go out for the rest of the morning. You get that pot of green paint out of the shed and paint the fence nicely for me. No running round to those kids, see?'

Ern said nothing. He just looked sulky. Mr. Goon, who had come down to breakfast in his dressing-gown, now put on his mackintosh and took his uniform into the garden to brush. Mrs. Murray next door was amazed to see the clouds of dust that came out of it.

'Been hiding in a dust-bin all night to watch for robbers?' she inquired, popping her head over the fence.

Mr. Goon would have like to say 'Gah!' but that kind of exclamation didn't go down very well with Mrs. Murray. He just turned a dignified back and went on brushing.

Ern collected the dirty breakfast things and took them into the scullery to wash. He brooded over his wrongs. Uncle was hard and unkind and cruel. Ern had hoped to have such a wonderful time with Mr. Goon, and had actually meant to help him with his 'cases'—and all that had happened was that he was always getting into some kind of trouble with his uncle. There was no end to it.

'As soon as he's gone out of the house I'll pop round to Pip's,' thought Ern. 'The Find-Outers said they'd be there. I'll tell them about last night and how Uncle caned me. And I'll show them that wonderful pome. They'll be surprised to think I can do things like that in my sleep. I hope Fatty won't be cross because I couldn't go and look for the loot.'

Mr. Goon went off on his bicycle at last. Ern slipped out of the back door and made his way to Pip's. With him he took his portry note-book. He read the rude pome again and again and marvelled. 'I reely am a genius!' he thought, proudly. 'That's a wonderful pome even if it's rude.'

# 18 THINGS HAPPEN TO ERN

THERE was nobody in Pip's play-room except Bets. She had a cold and was not allowed out. The others had gone on an errand for Pip's mother.

'Hallo!' said Bets. 'How did you get on last night, Ern? Did you find the loot?' She giggled a little as she asked Ern. Poor Ern! Had he gone loot-hunting all by himself? What a simpleton he was!

Ern sat down and poured out all the happenings of the night before. Bets soon grew serious as she heard how Mr. Goon had caned poor Ern. She examined his hand and almost cried over it. Bets was very tender-hearted and could never bear any one to be hurt.

'Oh, Ern, poor Ern! Does it hurt very much? Shall I put something on your hand to make it better? That horrid hateful Mr. Goon!' she said, and Ern glowed at having so much sympathy. He thought Bets was the nicest little girl he had ever met.

'You're nice,' he said to Bets. 'I wish you were my sister. I bet Sid and Perce would like you too.'

Bets felt very guilty when she thought of all the tricks that the Find-Outers had played on Ern. She wished they hadn't now. Especially that poem-trick! It was that poem, written in Ern's own handwriting by Fatty that had made Mr. Goon cane Ern. Oh dear! This was dreadful. They would have to own up to Ern and to Mr. Goon too. Fatty would hate that—but they couldn't go on deceiving Ern like that.

Ern opened his portry note-book. 'You know, Bets,' he said, 'I don't remember writing this pome at all. That's queer isn't it? But it's a wonderful pome and I'm

right-down proud of it. It was worth a caning! Bets, do
you think I can possibly be a genius, even a little one, if
I can write a pome like that and not know I'd written it?
I must have done it in my sleep. '

Bets didn't know what in the world to say. She looked
at Ern's serious face. Ern began to read the pome in a
solemn voice, and Bets went off into giggles. She really
couldn't help it.

' Don't you think it's a wonderful pome, Bets?' said
Ern, hopefully. Honestly, I didn't think I could write one
like that. It's made me feel all hopeful, like. '

' I don't wonder it made your uncle angry, ' said Bets.
' Poor Ern. I do hope your hand will feel better soon. Now
wouldn't you like to go and meet the others? They've
gone to Maylins Farm for mother. You'll meet them
coming back if you go now. '

' Right, ' said Ern, getting up. He buttoned his precious
note-book into his coat pocket. ' Do you think Fatty will
be annoyed about me not going to find the loot?' he
asked anxiously.

' Oh no. Not a bit, ' Bets assured him. Ern grinned at
her, put on his cap and started off downstairs. He saw
Mrs. Hilton crossing the hall below and hastily pulled off
his cap again. He waited till she had gone and then darted
out of the house.

He made his way through the village, keeping a sharp
eye out for his uncle. He went up the lonely lane that led
to Maylins Farm. It was a long and winding road, with
few houses. Ern went along with his head down, muttering
the first line of a new pome he was thinking of.

' The pore little mouse was all alone ... '

A car came down the lane. Ern looked up. A man was
at the wheel, and another man at the back. Ern stood
aside to let the car pass.

It went on a few yards and stopped. The man at the

back leaned forward and said something to the driver. The driver opened his window and shouted back at Ern.

'Hey, boy! Do you know the way to the post office?'

'Yes,' said Ern. It's down there a little way. Turn to the left, up the hill a little way, and you'll see a ...'

'Jump in and show us, there's a good lad,' said the driver. 'Save us a lot of time. We've lost the way two or three times already. Here's half-a-crown if you'll help us.'

He held out half-a-crown and Ern's eyes brightened. He only had threepence a week pocket-money and half-a-crown seemed riches to him. He hopped in beside the driver at once. The man at the back had his face buried in a newspaper.

The car started off again—but instead of going off at the turning to the post office it swept on past it, took a left-hand turn and then a right-hand one, and then shot off at a great speed towards Marlow.

Ern was astonished. 'Here! This isn't right!' he said. 'Where you going?'

'You'll see,' said the man at the back, in a nasty sort of voice that sent a horrid little thrill down Ern's spine. 'We're going to show you what we do with interfering boys.'

Ern stared at the two men in alarm. 'What do you mean? What have I interfered in? I don't understand.'

'You soon will,' said the man at the back. 'Always poking your nose into this and that, aren't you, Frederick Trotteville? You thought when you came along to the garage the other day you were being very clever, didn't you?'

Ern simply couldn't make head or tail of what the sour-faced man at the back was saying. He felt very frightened.

'I'm not Frederick,' he said. 'I'm Ern Goon. My uncle is the policeman at Peterswood.'

' Don't waste your breath telling those tales to us, ' said the driver, grimly. ' Trying to be so innocent! You certainly *look* a simpleton—but you can't put it across us that you are. We know you all right. '

Ern gave it up. What with mysterious, rude pomes, canings, a furious uncle, and now two men kidnapping him, he simply didn't know what to think.

Kidnappers! At that thought poor Ern shivered and shook. Fatty had said there were two gangs—one gang was kidnappers, the other robbers. Now he had got mixed up with the kidnappers! This was a simply frightful thought.

He didn't know why the men thought he was Fatty. But they, of course, had only seen Fatty disguised as Ern, the day he had cycled over to Holland's garage. When they had spotted the real Ern wandering up the lane, they had had no doubt but that it was Fatty, the same boy they had seen with the dog at the garage.

Ern was taken to a garage some miles from Marlow, owned by Mr. Holland. He was driven into a big shed, and made to get out. A door led from the shed up a ladder into a small room. The men pushed Ern there.

' If you shout you'll get a hiding, ' said Mr. Holland. You'll be here all day and if you're quiet you'll get food and drink. If you're not, you won't. We're going to take you somewhere else to-night where you can have a nice quiet time all by yourself till we decide what to do with you. It's time silly kids like you were stopped from poking your noses into other people's business. '

Ern was completely cowed. He sat down on some straw in the tiny room, and trembled till the men had gone out of the door and locked and bolted it. He looked for a window but there was none. The only light came in through a tiny skylight set in the roof.

Ern began to sniffle. He was no hero, poor Ern, and

*The man pushed Ern into the small room*

things were happening too fast for him. He sat there all the morning, miserable and frightened.

The door was unbolted and unlocked at half-past one, when Ern had begun to fear that he was going to be starved. A hand came in with a loaf of bread, a jar of potted meat and a jug of water. Nothing else. But Ern was so hungry that he ate the whole loaf, and the potted meat too, and drank the last drop of the water.

He was given no tea. At half-past four when it was almost dark, the door opened again and the men came in. ' Come on out, ' said one of them. ' We're going. '

' Where to ? ' stuttered Ern, afraid.

There was no answer. He was pushed down the ladder, into the shed, and into the back of the car. The two men got in at the front. The car backed out.

Ern was in despair. How could he let the others know anything ? He felt sure that if he were Fatty he would be able to find some way of telling the Find-Outers that something dreadful had happened to him.

He felt in his pocket. His clues were still there, all ten of them. Suppose he threw them out of the window one by one ? There *might* be a chance of one of the Find-Outers picking one of them up. They would recognize a clue immediately.

It was a very faint hope indeed, especially as Ern had no idea of where the car was going. He might be miles away from Peterswood. He peered out of the window to see if he could recognize anything at all in the darkness.

No, there was nothing to tell him where he was. But, wait a bit—wasn't that the post office in Peterswood ? Yes, it was ! They were actually going through Peterswood ! Ern wondered if he could let down the window far enough to throw out his clues one by one. He tried, but at once one of the men turned round.

'Don't you dare to open the window! If you think you're going to shout, you can think again!'

'I'm not going to,' protested Ern. Then a really brilliant idea struck him. 'I feel sick, see? I want air. Let me open the window a few inches. If you don't I'll be sick all over the car.'

The man gave an impatient exclamation. He leaned back and opened the window about two inches. Ern made a horrible noise as if he was on the point of being violently sick. He felt very clever indeed. The man opened the window a little more.

'If you dare to be sick in the car I'll box your ears!' he threatened.

Ern made a noise again, and at the same time threw out the button with the bit of cloth attached. Then he threw out the cigar-end. Next went the pencil-stub with E.H. on the end and then the rag.

Every now and again Ern made a horrible noise and the man glanced back anxiously. They were nearly there! That wretched boy. Mr. Holland made up his mind to give him a fine old hiding if he spoilt the car.

Out went the next clue—the hanky with 'K' on. Then the broken shoe-lace—then the empty cigarette packet. After that the tiny bit of paper with the telephone number went fluttering into the road, and then the rusty old tin. That was the lot.

Ern leaned back, feeling pleased. Aha! The clues he had found on Christmas Hill were going to be first-rate clues as to his whereabouts for all the Find-Outers. Ern was quite certain that people as clever as the Five Find-Outers would somehow find the clues and read them correctly.

The man looked round. 'Feel better?' he said.

'I'm all right now,' said Ern, and grinned to himself in the darkness. He *was* clever! He was surprised himself to think how clever he was. The man shut the window up again. The car was going slowly now, up a very narrow lane. The headlights were out. Only the side-lamps were on.

The headlights were flashed once as they came round a bend. The car slowed. Ern tried to see why but he couldn't. There came the creak and clang of gates, and the car moved on. It ran on to something smooth after a short while and stood still. Then, to Ern's terrific alarm the car suddenly shot straight downwards as if it were a lift ! Ern clutched the sides and gasped.

' Here we are, ' said Mr. Holland's voice. ' Out you get, Frederick Trotteville. This is the place you were inquiring about—but you'll soon wish you had never never heard about it in your life ! Welcome to Harry's Folly ! '

## 19   MR. GOON FEELS WORRIED

THE Find-Outers were very surprised when they got back
to Bets, to hear that Ern had been sent to meet them.

'We never saw a sign of him,' said Fatty. 'I suppose he
went home after all.'

They listened to Bets' account of what Ern had told
her of the night before. Their faces became serious. It was
one thing to pull Ern's leg to get a laugh out of him. It was
quite another to cause him to get a caning.

'Golly! And old Goon went loot-hunting on Christmas
Hill instead of Ern. Won't he be wild when he knows it
was a put-up job!' said Larry.

'We'll have to tell Ern—and Goon too—that I wrote
the poem,' said Fatty. He looked uncomfortable. 'Goon
will be furious. I shall get into a fine old row.'

'Yes, you will,' said Pip. 'He'll go round complaining
again.'

'Ern was terribly terribly proud of the poem,' said
Bets. 'He said that was the only thing that comforted him
last night—the thought that he had written a wonderful
poem like that, and hadn't even known he had. He
thought he must have written it in his sleep. I simply
couldn't bear to tell him he hadn't written it, Fatty.'

'It's a bit of a tangle, isn't it?' said Daisy. 'In order to
make Mr. Goon realize that he's caned Ern unfairly we've
got to disappoint Ern by telling him the poem isn't his!
Poor old Ern! I wish we hadn't pulled his leg so much.
He's awfully silly, but he's quite harmless and sometimes
very nice.'

'An awful coward, though,' said Pip. 'Look how he
keeps giving everything away! It's a good thing it wasn't

a *real* mystery we set him on. He'd have given absolutely every single thing away to Goon.'

'Yes. He can't really be trusted,' said Daisy. 'But I do feel sorry about this. I wonder what's happened to him now. I suppose he went home.'

But Ern hadn't gone home, as we know. He didn't appear at dinner-time, and Mr. Goon who had got quite a nice dinner of stew and dumplings, felt most annoyed.

That pestering boy! He hadn't painted the fence green as he had been told to. Now he was late for dinner.

'Well, I shan't wait—and if he doesn't come, I'll eat the lot!' said Mr. Goon. 'That'll learn him!'

So he ate the lot, and felt so very full afterwards that he sat down in his armchair by the kitchen fire, undid a few buttons and immediately fell sound asleep. Mr. Goon was tired after his night's hunting up on Christmas Hill. He slept and he slept. He slept the whole afternoon away. He didn't even hear the telephone ringing. He slept solidly all through the rrrrr-ring, rrrr-ring, his snores almost drowning the bell.

He awoke at half-past five. He yawned, sat up, stretched, and looked at the clock. He looked again. What! Almost half-past five! The clock couldn't be right! Mr. Goon took out his big watch and looked at that too. Why, that said the same!

'I've been asleep three solid hours!' said Mr. Goon, quite shocked. 'Shows how tired I was. Where's Ern? Why, he's almost let the fire out, and there's no kettle boiling for tea!'

He gave a loud yell, 'ERN! ERN!'

No Ern came. Mr. Goon frowned. Where was that boy? He hadn't come in to dinner! Now he hadn't come in to tea. Gone round to those kids, he supposed, and they'd kept him for meals. Spun a wonderful tale about

his crool uncle ! Ho, Mr. Goon would have something to
say about that.

Mr. Goon made himself a cup of tea very quickly. He
didn't stop for anything to eat. He suddenly remembered
that he was supposed to go along to Miss Lacey's and
hear about two of her hens being stolen. How could he
have forgotten that ? If he'd gone about half-past four he
could have had tea in the kitchen with Mrs. Tanner the
cook. Fine gingerbread she made every week, as Mr.
Goon very well knew.

Mr. Goon went off to Miss Lacey's. She was out. Mrs.
Tanner the cook told Mr. Goon that Miss Lacey was
annoyed because Mr. Goon hadn't come along
sooner. So the policeman didn't have a chance to sit
in a warm kitchen and have a piece of new
gingerbread. He was most annoyed, and went
pompously down the steps into the darkness of the
drive.

He wondered again where Ern was. Bad boy to stay
away like that. Pretending he had run away, perhaps ! Mr.
Goon gave a small snort. Ern would never have the spunk
to do a thing like that.

But a very small doubt crept into his mind at that
moment. Suppose Ern really *had* run away ? No, no, how
silly ! He must be somewhere with those kids.

Mr. Goon walked up the road that led to the post office.
It was dark and he shone his torch on the ground before
him. It suddenly picked up something in its beam. A
button !

Mr. Goon always collected any button or pin he found.
He picked this button up. It had a bit of cloth attached to
it. Why—he knew that button and bit of cloth ! It was one
of Ern's clues !

' So Ern's been along this way, ' thought Mr. Goon. He
picked it up. ' What's Ern doing, chucking his clues about

like this? At—here's a pencil-end! I bet it's the clue he found with E.H. at the end. Yes, it is!'

He missed the rag, which had blown under the hedge. He walked on some way and saw a ragged handkerchief. He had a feeling it would have 'K' on. So it had. Another of Ern's clues. How extraordinary, thought Mr. Goon. Then an idea came into his head.

'It's those kids again, playing a trick on me! They've spotted me walking down here, and they've got Ern to chuck down his clues to lead me on! They've spotted me walking down here, and they've got Ern to chuck down his clues to lead me on! They'll jump out at me round the corner or wet that pestering dog round my ankles. Well, I'm not going any farther! I'm going straight round to Mr. and Mrs. Hilton to complain!'

Mr. Goon made his way to Pip's house, filled with indignation. Getting Ern to throw down clues like that to lead him up the way just for a track! What did they take him for?

Mr. and Mrs. Hilton were out. 'But the five children are here,' said Lorna the maid. 'If it's them you're wanting to see, sir?'

'I'll see them,' said Mr. Goon. 'You go up the stairs first and tell Master Trotteville to keep his dog under control. Nasty snappy little beast that is.'

When Lorna appeared with her news the Find-Outers looked surprised and Bets felt alarmed. Oh dear—what had happened now?

Mr. Goon walked in. He put down the clues on the table. 'Another of your silly tricks, I suppose?' he said, glaring round. 'Getting Ern to chuck these about where you knew I'd find them. Ho—very childish, I must say!'

The Five Find-Outers gazed at the clues and recognized them. Fatty picked up the button. He was puzzled.

' Where is Ern ? ' he asked Mr. Goon. ' We haven't seen him all day. '

Mr. Goon snorted. ' Think I believe that ? Well, *I* haven't seen him all day, either ! But I bet he's hidden in this house somewhere ! That's called aiding and abetting somebody, see ? '

Fatty thought Mr. Goon was being rather silly. ' Mr. Goon. We—have—NOT seen Ern since early this morning when he came along here for a few words with Bets. Where *is* he ? '

Mr. Goon began to feel slightly alarmed. There was the ring of truth in Fatty's voice. If these kids hadn't seen Ern all day, where *was* he then ? Surely he couldn't have run away ? No, that wouldn't be in the least like Ern.

He stared at the silent children. ' How do *I* know where that dratted boy is ? ' he said, raising his voice a little. ' Worries the life out of me, he does—and you do your best to do the same. And let me tell you *I* know all about this mystery of yours ! Yes, I know more about robbers and kidnappers on Christmas Hill than *you* do ! '

' I'm so glad to hear it, ' said Fatty, in the very polite voice that made Mr. Goon go purple. ' Perhaps you can solve it more quickly than we can. The thing is— where is Ern ? He was very upset when he saw Bets this morning. Apparently you attacked him in the night, Mr. Goon. '

Mr. Goon could hardly speak. Then he stuttered with outraged feelings. ' Me ! *Attack* him ! I never heard of such a tale. I gave him the cane, see, for being rude. '

' Well, ' said Fatty, and hesitated. Should he tell Mr. Goon now about the poem—that *he* had written it and not Ern ? No, perhaps it would be best to tell Ern first. But where *was* Ern ?

Fatty felt really puzzled. The things Mr. Goon had put on the table were certainly Ern's ' clues'—the things he had picked up on Christmas Hill. They were not all there, though. Fatty inquired about the rest.

'Didn't you find any more clues, Mr. Goon? Are those all you picked up?'

'I don't know how many more you told Ern to put down for me to follow,' snorted Mr. Goon. 'But I wasn't going to go wandering over half the town to find any more!'

'Where did you find these?' asked Larry.

'As if you didn't know!' said Mr. Goon, sarcastically. 'Where you put them, of course—or where you told Ern to put them. Up Candlemas Lane.'

'What could Ern have been doing there?' wondered Bets.

'Don't you really know where Ern is?' said Mr. Goon, after a pause. Another little doubt was creeping in on him. Wouldn't it be awkward if Ern *had* run away because he, Mr. Goon, had caned him? Perhaps he had gone home to his mother. Mr. Goon decided to make inquiries when he got back, and find out. He could ring up a friend of his who knew Ern's mother, and get him to slip round quietly to Ern's home and find out if he was there.

'No. We don't know where he is,' said Fatty, impatiently. 'Haven't we kept telling you that? I shouldn't be surprised, Mr. Goon, if poor old Ern hasn't run away to sea, or something, after your cruel attack on him last night!'

Mr. Goon for once had nothing whatever to say. Fatty's suggestion, coming on top of his own fear that Ern might have run away, made him quite tongue-tied. It was all very very awkward. He began to wish he hadn't caned Ern the night before.

He went soon after that, much to Pip's relief. He and Bets were afraid that their parents might arrive home before Mr. Goon left, and they didn't want that to happen.

'It's very queer, ' said Fatty, letting Buster off the lead, where he had held him tightly for the last quarter of an hour. 'We haven't seen Ern at all to-day. Only Bets saw him this morning. And now here's this tale of clues scattered about in Candlemas Lane. Why should Ern do that?'

'Hole in his pocket, ' suggested Pip.

'Not very likely, ' said Fatty.

'Perhaps he got tired of his clues and just *threw* them away, ' said Bets.

'Silly idea, ' said Pip, scornfully.

'I'm going out with my torch to see if there are any more of Ern's clues scattered about, ' said Fatty. 'I feel as if there's something wrong somewhere. I'm worried about our Ern!'

He went off by himself with Buster, his torch shining its beam in front of him. He made his way to Candlemas Lane.

He saw nothing in the way of clues at first—but farther on, at the turning out of the lane into the track that ran across the fields for a mile or two to Harry's Folly, Fatty found three or four more of the clues. He stood thoughtfully in the track, puzzling things out in his mind. Where was Ern? What in the world could have happened to him?

## 20 FATTY ON THE TRACK

ERN didn't come home that night. By the time nine o'clock came Mr. Goon had worked himself into a terribly state of mind. He imagined all kinds of things happening to Ern. He had been run over. He had run off to sea and was already in a ship, being very seasick. He had gone home to his mother and Sid and Perce and told terrible tales about his uncle. All these things and many others flashed through Mr. Goon's worried mind.

He tried to find out if Ern had gone home, but no, he wasn't there. Whatever was Mr. Goon to do! He felt terribly guilty now. He, Ern's uncle, had driven him away! What would people think?

'I'll stay up till eleven to see if Ern comes,' thought Mr. Goon. 'I'll put some bacon and eggs ready to cook for him when he comes—and I'll hot up some cocoa. I'll go and put a hot-water bottle in his bed.'

Mr. Goon felt quite sentimental about Ern as the night wore on, and no Ern appeared. He remembered all Ern's good points and forgot the bad ones. He felt ashamed when he remembered how he had boxed Ern's ears and caned him.

'Oh Ern, you come back and we'll get on fine, thought Mr. Goon over and over again. Eleven o'clock struck. Mr. Goon made up the fire again. Then he loosened his clothes and settled down in the armchair. He would wait up for Ern all night.

But suppose he didn't come? Mr. Goon considered this with a very serious face. He'd have to ring up Inspector Jenks and report his disappearance—and the first question asked would be 'Was the boy in any trouble before he disappeared ? ' And what was Mr. Goon to say to that ?

He fell asleep about midnight. He slept soundly through the night, and awoke in the morning, very cold and stiff, with the fire out—and no Ern anywhere ! And now Mr. Goon really did begin to feel frightened. Something *had* happened to Ern !

The telephone bell rang, and Mr. Goon almost jumped out of his skin. He went to answer it. It was Fatty, asking if Ern had come back.

' No, ' said Mr. Goon. ' He hasn't. Have you heard anything about him. '

' Not a word, ' said Fatty. ' It's pretty serious, this, Mr. Goon. Looks as if your attack on Ern has sent him off. '

Mr. Goon was too upset even to get angry over Fatty's persistence in calling the caning an attack. ' What am I to do ? ' he said, in a dismal voice. ' You might not think it, Master Trotteville, but I'm very fond of Ern. '

' You hid your affection very well then, ' came Fatty's smooth voice over the telephone. Mr. Goon shook his fist at the receiver. That dratted cheeky boy ! But the policeman soon forgot his anger in his worries about Ern.

' I'd better go to Inspector Jenks, I suppose, ' said Mr. Goon, after a pause. ' Master Trotteville, do you think this here mystery on Christmas Hill's got anything to do with Ern's disappearance ? These kidnappers and what-nots ? '

' You never know, ' said Fatty, in a serious voice. ' Er— did you find the loot the other night, Mr. Goon ? '

' That's none of your business, ' said Mr. Goon, shortly. ' Well—I suppose I'd better go and see the Inspector. '

' Mr. Goon, I don't know if you'd like to wait till to-night, ' said Fatty, suddenly. ' I've got an idea at the back of my mind which might just be the right one. But I can't tell you any more than that. It's *possible* I should be able to tell you where Ern is if you like to wait another day before reporting that he's vanished. '

Mr. Goon was only too glad to clutch at any straw. He was dreading having to go to the Inspector. He didn't want to say how he'd caned Ern the night before he went—nor did he want to say anything about the rude ' pome. ' Why, the Inspector might even want to read it ! Mr. Goon's face burned at the very thought.

' Right, ' said Mr. Goon. ' I'll wait another day. I'll wait up to-night till I hear from you. Poor Ern—I do hope he's all right. '

' I'll give you a ring on the phone to-night, as soon as I know anything, ' said Fatty.

He rang off. He was at his own house, and the Find-Outers were due down at the shed at any moment. Fatty went with Buster down the garden, just in time to see the others coming in.

' No Ern yet, ' he said. ' Goon's getting all worked up about him. And so he should ! He doesn't like the thought of having to go and tell the Inspector how he whacked him in the middle of the night ! '

' What *has* happened to Ern ? ' said Pip. ' I could hardly get to sleep last night for worrying about him—and thinking about those clues Old Clear-Orf found in Candlemas Lane. '

' I found some more last night, ' said Fatty. ' And two of them were along the track that leads across the field to Harry's Folly ! I believe Ern's there. '

' But why ? Do you mean he went off across the fields to explore Harry's Folly, or something ? ' demanded Larry. ' But he doesn't know anything about *that* mystery ! '

' I know he doesn't, ' said Fatty. ' All the same I think he's there. I think he must have been *taken* there, but I can't imagine why. Even if Holland came along in his car and saw Ern, why should he take him away?'

'I expect he thought Ern was *you*,' said Bets, suddenly. 'After all, you were disguised as Ern when you went over there, weren't you—and you *might* have given the game away to him, Fatty, when you mentioned Harry's Folly. He might have been scared, thinking you knew something, and decided to capture you!'

Fatty stared at Bets, thinking hard. Then he banged the table and made them all jump. 'That's it. Bets has got it! They've kidnapped Ern thinking he was me—and they think I know too much about Harry's Folly, because I spoke about it as I did! Good old Bets. She's the best Find-Outer of the lot!'

Bets was thrilled at this unexpected praise. She blushed red. 'Oh—we'd all have thought of it soon!' she said.

'Yes—Bets is right. They must have mistaken Ern for me—and—and—yes, I wonder if Ern could have thrown away those clues to warn us something was up—even to show us the way to follow?'

'That's too clever a thing for Ern to do,' said Daisy.

'Yes. It is a bit clever,' said Fatty thoughtfully. 'But in desperation Ern might be cleverer than he usually is. Tell me, Bets—what time did Ern leave you?'

'About half-past ten,' said Bets. 'He said he was going off to meet you straightaway. He should have met you coming back about three quarters of the way there.'

'I'm going out to make a few inquiries,' said Fatty. 'Stay here, all of you. I'll be back.'

Fatty went into the village, and then turned up the way to Maylins Farm. He saw a small girl swinging on a gate and called to her.

'Hallo, Margery. Did you see Ern Goon here yesterday? You know Ern, don't you? The policeman's nephew.'

'Yes,' said Margery. 'I saw him going up this way

yesterday morning. He didn't see me because I was hiding.'

'Did you see him come back again?' asked Fatty. 'You saw us all walking back, didn't you, later on? Did you see Ern again?'

'No, I didn't,' said Margery. 'There was a big car came down a little while after, and nearly knocked me over. Then you came with the others. That's all. What's Ern done?'

'Nothing,' said Fatty. 'Here's a penny. Catch!'

He walked on up the road thinking hard. Ern had gone to meet them up there—but hadn't come back. But a car had come along soon after. Was it Holland's car, cruising round to snoop for Fatty, perhaps—and finding Ern instead, thinking *he* was Fatty.

Some way up, in a very lonely part of the road, Fatty saw where a car had suddenly put on its brakes and swerved a little to a quick stop. He looked at the marks on the road thoughtfully, his mind working. This was probably where the men in the car had met Ern, thought he was Fatty, stopped suddenly, asked Ern some question to get him into the car—and gone off with him.

The car wouldn't go to Harry's Folly in the daytime, that was certain. It was more likely it would have gone to Marlow or to the other garage Holland owned. the men would have locked Ern up somewhere for the day—and then perhaps they would have brought him back to Harry's Folly.

'And when Ern saw he was going through Peterswood he suddenly thought of chucking out all the clues he had, knowing we'd recognize them, and read them correctly!' said Fatty. 'Well! If Ern really did do that he's cleverer than we ever thought him!'

He went back to the others, Buster trotting soberly at

his heels. Buster always knew when his master was thinking hard, and never bothered him then.

Fatty told the others what he thought. They listened in silence. 'It was Bets' sudden idea that put me on to everything else,' said Fatty. 'Well—I've got to go and rescue Ern if I can—and perhaps I can solve this mystery at the same time! I'll go to-night.'

'Oh Fatty—don't do that!' begged Bets. 'Can't you ring up Inspector Jenks and tell him all you've said to us.'

'No,' said Fatty. 'Because I might be absolutely wrong in everything! Ern *might* be hiding in an old barn somewhere, sulking, to give Goon a fright. And what do we really know of this other mystery? Hardly anything! Not as much as Old Clear-Orf knows of the imaginary one!'

'We'll come with you then, Fatty, if you're going to-night,' said Larry.

'You can't. You're forbidden,' said Fatty. 'In any case I wouldn't let the girls come.'

'But we're not going to solve a mystery—we're going to rescue Ern,' protested Pip. 'That's quite different.'

'I'm going by myself,' said Fatty. 'I shall take a rope-ladder to get over the wall—and sacks to put on those spikes at the top so that I can climb over easily. Then—aha—there'll be dark dire deeds, as Ern would say!'

'Oh *don't*,' said Bets, with a shiver. 'I wish you wouldn't go, Fatty. Please don't!'

'Well, I feel rather bad about Ern,' said Fatty, seriously. 'I feel as if he's had very bad luck all round—what with us pulling his leg—and Goon caning him for what he hadn't done—and then getting kidnapped because I once disguised myself as Ern. It's up to me to do *some*thing. I really *must* go, Bets, old thing.'

'I suppose you must,' said Bets, with a sigh.

They hunted for the rope-ladder, which was at last

discovered on a shelf, neatly rolled up. Then they found sacks. Larry examined Fatty's torch to make sure the battery was all right. Bets slipped a bar of chocolate into his pocket. They all felt rather solemn, somehow, as if Fatty was going on a long long journey!

' I'll start about half-past eight, after I've had dinner with my mother and father, ' said Fatty.

They are going out to a bridge party afterwards, so I shall be able to slip out easily without any one knowing. '

' Half-past eight ? ' said Larry and Pip together. ' Sure you'll start then ? '

' Yes. The moon won't be up. I shan't be seen at all, ' said Fatty. ' I shall take the same path over the field by the stream as we did before. Sorry you can't come with me, Pip and Larry. '

They looked at him solemnly. ' Yes, ' said Pip. ' Spitty ! Well—good luck, Fatty ! '

## 21   INTO THE HEART OF THE MYSTERY

FATTY set out after dinner that night, exactly at half-past eight. He had with him the rope-ladder, and the sacks. Buster was left at home, whining and scratching at the shed-door. He was very angry that Fatty should have left him behind.

Fatty made his way to the little bridge across the Bourne. He then walked cautiously along on the frosty bank of the stream. Two shadowy figures came out from behind a tree and followed him quietly.

Fatty's sharp ears caught the soft crunch-crunch somewhere behind him. He stopped at once. He stiffened when he heard the footsteps coming quietly nearer. He saw the dim outline of a tree nearby and slipped behind it.

The footsteps drew nearer. He heard whispers. Two people then. Were they after him? What were they doing in the fields at that time of night?

Just as they passed, Fatty's sharp ears caught one word in the whispered conversation. 'Buster ... '

He grinned. He knew who it was following him now. It was Larry and Pip! They weren't going to be left out, whether they had been forbidden or not! Good old Larry and Pip!

He tiptoed after them. They soon stopped, not being able to hear Fatty in front of them any more. He spoke in a mournful voice just near them.

'Beware! Beware!'

Larry and Pip jumped violently. Then Pip stretched out his hand and touched Fatty. 'Fatty! It's you! Idiot! You did make us jump!'

'We *had* to come, Fatty,' said Larry. 'We couldn't let you go alone. We've decided that, mystery or not, we're all in it!'

Fatty gave Larry's arm a squeeze. 'Nice of you. Glad of your company, of course. Come on.'

They went on together, the three of them. After some time they came to where the narrow cart-track to Harry's Folly ran near to the stream. They left the bank and went into the little lane. They walked on steadily and silently in the darkness till they came to the iron gates. They were shut, of course. A light shone in the lodge nearby.

'We won't get over the wall here,' said Fatty. 'I don't think there *are* any dogs belonging to the lodge-keeper, but you never know. We'll walk round the wall a bit and choose a place some way off.'

They walked round the high wall. The sky was clearing now, and there was a fading starlight which helped them to see things better.

'This will do,' said Fatty. He hunted about and found a heavy stone. He tied it to the end of a rope he had, which, in its turn, was fastened to the top of the rope ladder.

'Help me chuck this stone over the wall,' said Fatty to Larry. The two boys took the stone between them. 'One, two, three, go!' said Fatty, and they heaved the stone up as hard as they could. It rose up and went neatly over the wall, dragging its short tail of rope behind it.

As the stone fell heavily to the ground on the other side, the rope-ladder was pulled up the wall by the rope attached to the falling stone. It rose up and stayed hanging on the wall. Fatty gave it a tug.

'Just right! Part of it's over the other side—and one of the rungs has got firmly held by the spikes at the top. Pip, you're the lightest. Shin up to the top, and we'll chuck the sacks for you to put on the spikes. Then sit on them, and make the ladder fast for us. Larry and I are heavy. '

Pip was light. The ladder shifted a little as he went up, but held firmly enough. The others threw him up the sacks. Pip arranged them on the top of the wall so that they lay like a cushion over the spikes, preventing them from using their sharp points.

Pip sat on the sacks, and made the ladder as firm as he could for the others. Fatty gave it a hard tug. Yes. It was all right.

He made Pip come down again. Then he himself went up, sat on the sacks, pulled up the rope-ladder so that half hung down one side the ground and half the other—made it fast so that it could not slip, and then went down the other side, into the grounds of Harry's Folly. The others followed, clambering up one side and down the other.

' Good ! ' said Fatty, in a whisper. ' Now, we'll find the house ! '

They made their way through thick trees. Fatty marked them with white chalk as he passed, for he was a little afraid that without some guide he might not be able to find his way back to the rope-ladder—and they *might* be in a hurry later on !

After quite a long walk the old house loomed up before them in the starlight. It looked forbidding in the dark night. Pip pressed close to the others, rather scared.

There was not a light to be seen anywhere. Fatty could dimly make out great shutters bolted across the windows. Then they came to a long flight of stone steps. The boys went up them silently. They led to a nail-studded front door, also tightly closed. The mansion seemed completely and utterly deserted.

' Do you think Ern is hidden somewhere here ? ' whispered Larry, his mouth close to Fatty's ear.

'Yes,' whispered back Fatty. 'There's some mystery about this place—it's used for something it shouldn't be used for, I'm sure, though I don't know what. And I'm certain Ern is here somewhere. Come on—we've still got a good way to go round the house.'

In the darkness the house seemed really enormous. The walls were endless to the boys as they walked cautiously beside them. There was no light anywhere and no noise at all.

They came to the back of the old house. A pond gleamed dully in the starlight, frozen over. Two big flights of steps led down to it.

'What an enormous place!' whispered Pip. 'I wonder what its history is.'

'Shhhhhh!' hissed Fatty, and they all stood like stone, pressing against one another. They had heard a noise—a very curious noise. It seemed to come from underground!

'What is it? It's like some great machine at work,' whispered Larry. 'Where is it?'

They went on round the house, and came to what must have been either stables or garages. These also were enormous. A small door stood open in one of the garages, for Fatty could hear it creaking a little as it swung in the cold night wind. He made his way to it, the others following.

'Come on. This door's open. Let's go into the garage,' whispered Fatty, and in they went. It was dark, and the boys could see nothing at all. The noise they had heard was now quite gone.

Fatty cautiously got out his torch and shone it quickly round. They saw a vast garage, with shadowy corners. In front of them was a smooth expanse of floor.

Then a most terrifying thing happened! The floor in front of them suddenly made a noise, moved, and sank swiftly down out of sight, into darkness! Fatty was so tremendously amazed that he couldn't even switch off his torch! He just stood there with it still shining, and in its light the boys saw the floor sink away below them. Another foot or two and they would have gone with it into blackness, goodness knows where!

Fatty snapped off his torch. Larry gripped him in fright. 'Fatty. What's happened? Did you see the floor go?'

'Yes. It's a movable floor, worked by machinery,' said Fatty. 'Gave me a scare to see it disappear like that, though! It hasn't gone down for nothing. Let's hide behind these big barrels and see if the floor comes back again.'

They hid behind the barrels for some time, getting cold and chilled. Nothing happened. Fatty flicked his torch quickly on and off again. The floor was still gone! A vast empty hole yawned below.

Fatty cautiously went to the edge, put on his torch and tried to light up the depth of blackness below him. A noise warned him to get back into hiding. He ran for his barrel.

A light, first dim and them brighter, now came up from the hole where the great floor had been. Noises came up from below too. Then voices shouted. Then came a curious whining sound—and the floor came up again, fitting into place! It really did behave like a lift that was nothing but a floor.

On the floor were three cars. None had any headlights on, only side-lamps.

Low voices spoke,

'All ready? Five minutes between each of you; You know what to do. Go now, Kenton.'

The great garage doors now rolled silently back. The first car rolled off the floor and went quietly out of the garage. It disappeared down the drive. When it came to the gate-keeper's lodge, it switched its headlights on and off once and waited. Peters came out, opened the gates quickly, the car slid out, and the gates closed again.

Five minutes later the three boys saw the second car go. Then after another five minutes the third one went. Then the garage doors were shut again, and the only man left in the garage whistled softly.

He went and stood on the floor, and waited. After a minute or two the floor slid downwards again, leaving the same yawning hole as before. Then there was a dead silence and complete darkness.

'Larry! Pip! Are you there?' came Fatty's whisper. 'We must do something or other now. We'll have to get down underground, I think. That's apparently where everything goes on. Are you game to?'

'Yes,' said both, in a whisper. Fatty switched on his torch in a corner and showed the others some strong coiled wire rope he had found, used for towing one car behind another.

'If we tie this to that beam, see—and let the rope drop down the hole—we can swarm down in one by one.'

It didn't take long to make the rope secure to the beam. The end was dropped into the hole by Pip. Then Fatty tested it. It held all right. He sat down on the floor and took hold of the rope.

'I'll wait for you at the rope's end,' he whispered. 'Follow me quickly.'

Down he went easily, as if he was performing on the ropes at school. Pip followed and then Larry. Soon they stood far down underground, in complete darkness. As they stood there they heard a noise of whirring and clattering some way off and a faint light came from that direction. Fatty saw the outline of a wide passage, and went down it, the others keeping close by him.

They followed the wide passage, which wound round and round rather like an enormous spiral stairway. 'We're going down into the bowels of the earth!' whispered Larry. 'Whatever's this curious winding passage, Fatty.'

'It's where cars come up to go on to that automatic floor,' said Fatty. 'Or go down! Ah—here we are!'

From their dark corner the boys now looked out into an enormous workshop. Machines whirred and clattered. There were cars everywhere! Two were being sprayed with blue cellulose paint. Another was being scraped. A fourth was almost in pieces. Others stood about with nobody working on them.

'What sort of place is this, Fatty?' asked Larry in a whisper, puzzled.

'I'm not absolutely sure,' said Fatty. 'But I rather think it's a receiving place for stolen cars. They are brought here in the dark, put on the moving floor, taken down here and completely altered so that nobody would ever know them again. Then they are sent above-ground again at night—and, I imagine sold for a colossal sum with faked log-books!'

'Whew!' said Larry. 'I heard my father saying the other day that the police were completely baffled over the amount of stolen cars disappearing lately. I bet this is where they come to. My word, Fatty—what a find!'

## 22   A STRANGE NIGHT

'I SAY, Fatty, look—who's that coming down those stairs at the end?' said Pip, suddenly. 'He must be the Boss. See the way the men straighten up and salute him.'

'It's Mr. Holland!' said Fatty. 'Oho, Mr. Holland, so this is your little hide-out! You knew far more about Harry's Folly than you wanted to admit. What business he must do in stolen cars!'

'I wonder how many of the men in his garage at Marlow know about this,' said Pip.

'None of them, I should imagine,' said Fatty. 'He keeps those garages of his as a very nice cover for himself. But this is his real line. My word, Inspector Jenks would like to know about this little nest of cars!'

The men had evidently had some kind of order to knock off work for a meal or drink, for one by one they left their jobs and disappeared into a farther room. Mr. Holland went with them.

The workshop was deserted. 'Now's our chance,' whispered Fatty. 'We must scoot to those stairs over there—the ones Mr Holland came down—and go up them. It's our only chance of finding Ern.'

They ran quietly to the stairs, and were up them long before the men returned to the workshop. The stairway was spiral, like the ascending passage-way to the place where the movable floor was. But this passage-way was very narrow and much steeper. The boys panted a little as they went. At the top of the stairs was a wide landing. Doors opened off it. Another flight of steps led upwards.

'Queer place!' said Fatty. 'Must have been used in the war for something very hush-hush, as I said before.

Something very secret must have been made down in that vast workshop—goodness knows what. Bombs perhaps ! '

The boys looked round at all the closed doors, fearing that one might open suddenly and somebody come out and challenge them. Fatty looked up the next flight of steps. 'I suppose those lead to the ground floor of the mansion, ' he said. 'Well—what shall we do ? Try these doors, or go up the stairs ? '

At that very moment there came a familiar sound—a rather forlorn, hollow cough.

' Ern ! ' said Pip at once. ' I'd know that cough anywhere. It's so like Goon's. Ern is in one of these rooms ! '

' That one, I think, ' said Fatty and went quietly to a door opposite. He cautiously turned the handle—but the door would not open. Then Fatty saw that the door was bolted—and probably locked too, for the key was on his side of the door.

He unbolted the door carefully. He unlocked it. He pushed it open and looked in. Ern was lying on a bed, a pencil in his hand, his portry note-book beside him. He was muttering something to himself.

' Ern ! ' said Fatty.

Ern sat up so suddenly that his note-book flew to the floor. He gazed at the three boys in astonishment that changed to the utmost delight. He threw himself off the bed and ran to them. He flung his arms round Fatty.

' Fatty ! I knew you'd come ! I knew you'd follow the clues I threw out of the car. Fatty, the kidnappers got me ! Oooh, I've had the most awful time trying to tell them I don't know anything at all. They keep saying I'm you, Fatty ! They're all potty. '

' Sh ! ' said Fatty. ' Are you quite all right, Ern ? They haven't hurt you, have they ? '

' No, ' said Ern. ' But they don't give me much food. And they said they'd starve me to-morrow if I don't answer their questions properly. But I don't know the answers. Fatty, let's go!'

'Larry—go to the door and keep watch,' ordered Fatty. 'Tell me at once if there's any sound of somebody coming up that spiral stairway. At once, mind!'

He turned back to Ern, who was now almost in tears with excitement. 'Listen, Ern—can you do something really brave?'

'Coo! I don't know,' said Ern, doubtfully.

'Well, listen,' said Fatty. 'We're right in the very middle of a great big mystery here—and I want to get to the police and tell them about it before the men are warned that somebody knows their secret. Now, Ern—if we take you away with us to-night, the men will know their game is up, for they'll find you gone and know that some one has rescued you. So will you stay here, locked up, all night long, in order to let the men think everything is all right—and wait till the police come in the morning?'

'I can't do that,' said Ern, almost crying. 'You don't know what it's like, to be a prisoner like this and not know what's going to happen to you. I can't even think of any portry.'

'Aren't you brave enough to do this one thing?' said Fatty, sadly. 'I did want to think well of you, Ern.'

Ern stared at Fatty, who looked back at him solemnly.

'All right,' said Ern. 'I'll do it, see! I'll do it for *you*, Fatty, because you're a wonder, you are! But I don't feel brave about it. I feel all of a tremble.'

'When you feel afraid to do a thing and yet do it, that's *real* bravery,' said Fatty. 'You're a hero, Ern!'

Ern was so bucked at these words that he now felt he would have stayed locked up for a week if necessary! He beamed at Fatty.

'Did Bets tell you about the wonderful pome I wrote in my sleep?' he asked anxiously. 'You should see it,

Fatty. Lovaduck, I feel so proud when I remember it. It's the best pome I ever wrote. I don't know when I've felt so pleased about anything. I feel reel proud of myself. '

Now was the time for Fatty to confess to Ern that he had played a trick on him and written out the poem in Ern's own handwriting—but Fatty, looking at Ern's proud face, simply hadn't the heart to tell him. Ern would be so bitterly disappointed! Let him think it was his own poem, if he was so proud of it. Fatty felt so embarrassed about the whole thing that he almost blushed. Whatever had possessed him to play such an idiotic trick on Ern?

' Sssssst! ' suddenly came warningly from Larry and Pip. Fatty gave Ern a pat on the back, murmured, ' Good fellow, see you to-morrow! ' melted out of the room, closed, locked and bolted the door in an amazingly deft and silent way, and then pulled Larry and Pip up the farther flight of stairs.

They had no sooner got up than Mr. Holland appeared at the top of the spiral stairway. He went into one of the rooms. The three boys did not dare to go down again.

' Better go on up to the top of these stairs and see where we are, ' whispered Fatty. So up they went. They soon found themselves on the ground floor of the great mansion. Fatty flicked on his torch. The boys shivered.

Cobwebs hung everywhere. Dust rose from the floor as they trod over it. A musty, sour smell hung over everything.

Fatty looked at his watch. ' Do you know it's almost one o'clock! ' he said, his whisper echoing round the room mysteriously. ' Let's get out of here somehow and go and give the warning to Inspector Jenks. '

But they could not get out! Shutters closed the windows on the outside, so even if the boys could have unfastened a window they could not have undone the shutters. Every outside door they tried was locked, but without a key! It was just like a nightmare, wandering through the dark, dusty house, unable to get out anywhere.

' This is frightful, ' said Fatty at last. ' I've never felt so completely done in my life. There's nowhere we can get out at all ! '

' Well—we shall have to see if we can go back the way we came, ' said Larry. ' We can't go through that enormous workshop whilst the men are at work there. We'll have to wait till they go for a meal again. Come on, let's go down the stairs to Ern's landing and see if any one is there. '

They went silently down. The landing was empty. No sound came from Ern's room. He was not asleep though. He was awake, feeling very solemn and exultant. He was being a hero, being really brave for Fatty's sake. Ern felt thrilled—and hoped intensely that Mr. Holland wouldn't come and badger him again with questions he couldn't answer. Suppose he asked him if any of the others had been there that night ? Ern lost himself in dreadful thoughts of what might happen to him if Mr. Holland tried to worm a lot of things out of him, thinking Ern was hiding something from him. He felt anything but a hero then.

The boys crept down the spiral stairway. Work was in full swing again in the workshop. Mr. Holland stood with his hands in his pockets talking to another man. Nobody could see the boys because they were in such a dark corner.

For two hours the tired boys watched. Then Pip fell suddenly asleep on the stairway, his head rolling on Fatty's shoulder.

' We'll take turns at watching, ' said Fatty. ' You sleep too, Larry. I'll wake you if any one comes this way. '

So two of them slept and Fatty kept watch. At half-past three he awoke Larry, who kept watch while he slept. Still the work in the great place below them went on at full

*In that minute the boys slipped out of the lorry*

speed. Half-past five came and Pip was awakened and told to keep watch. He was fresh after his four hour's sleep and looked with interest at everything going on. Nobody came near their corner.

It seemed as if there would be no chance at all of getting out. When Fatty awoke suddenly at seven o'clock, he felt worried. Time was getting on. They couldn't stay here much longer.

A big lorry was suddenly backed almost into their corner. The boys all retired a little way up the stairway in a hurry. Then an idea came to Fatty.

'That lorry's going out! It seems quite finished. If we get into the back, we might slip out with the lorry unseen. We've got to get out *some*how!'

The others were quite willing. When the man who had backed the lorry into their corner had got down to speak to Mr. Holland a little way off, the three boys climbed quietly into the back of the lorry. To their relief there was a partition between the driver's cabin and the back of the van, so that nobody could see them from the driver's seat. There were some old papers and sacks in the lorry. The boys covered themselves with these.

The man came back to the lorry. He started up the engine. So did two drivers of other cars. They were ready to go out. They had come in a week or two before— stolen, all of them—now they had been repainted, touched up, altered beyond even the owner's recognition—and were ready to go out and be sold again, with false log-books.

The lorry went slowly up the winding stone passage, up and up and up, following the other cars. They came to the movable floor and ran on to it. A minute's wait and the floor went upwards like a lift!

One by one, at five minute intervals, the cars ran silently out of the garage. In the last one, the lorry, lay the three hidden boys. The lorry-driver flashed his headlights on and off once, and waited for the gates to open at the end of the drive. In that minute the three boys slipped out of the lorry!

They waited in the shadow of the trees till the gates were closed and everything was quiet. Then they went to the wall. ' Have to feel our way round till we come to the ladder, ' whispered Fatty. ' Fat lot of good my marking the trees as I did. Come on ! We'll soon find the ladder—and then up we'll go and away home. '

## 23   INSPECTOR JENKS TAKES OVER

MEANTIME Mr. Goon had been sitting up all night long, expecting and hoping the telephone bell would ring to say that Fatty had found Ern.

But it didn't ring until eight o'clock the next morning, when an anxious Mrs. Hilton telephoned to say that Pip was missing! He hadn't been at home all night. Bets was in a dreadful state of worry and had told her mother such extraordinary things that nobody could make anything of them.

Then Larry and Daisy's father rang. Larry was missing! They couldn't get anything out of Daisy at all except that Fatty was in charge and everything was all right.

'Daisy says that Fatty has gone out to solve a mystery, but that Larry and Pip have gone to rescue your nephew. Mr. Goon, do you know anything about this at all?'

Well, Mr. Goon did. But what he knew was going to be very difficult to explain to angry and alarmed parents. He hummed and hawed, and then, at a banging on his door, hurriedly put down the receiver to answer the door, hoping against hope that it was Fatty with good news.

But it wasn't. It was Mr. Trotteville! Fatty was missing—hadn't been in his bed all night! Mr. Trotteville had tried to ring up Mr. Goon repeatedly but his telephone appeared to be engaged every time. Did Mr. Goon know anything about where Fatty had gone?

What with Ern being gone for two days and now three more boys missing, Mr. Goon began to feel he really couldn't stand any more. He telephoned to the Inspector.

'Sir, I'm sorry to worry you so early in the morning—but there's all kinds of things happening here, sir, and I

was wondering if you could come over, ' said the agitated
voice of Mr. Goon.

' What sort of things, Goon ? ' asked the Inspector.
' Chimneys on fire or lost dogs or something ? Can't you
manage them yourself ? '

' No, sir. Yes, sir. I mean, sir, it's nothing like that at all,
sir, ' said Mr. Goon, desperately. ' My nephew's
disappeared, sir—and Master Trotteville went to find
him—and now he's gone too, sir, and so have Master
Larry and Master Pip. I don't know if it's the robbers or
the kidnappers have taken them, sir. '

The Inspector listened to this astounding information
in surprise. ' I'll be right over, Goon, ' he said, and hung
up the receiver. He ordered his shining black car, got in
and drove over to Peterswood, wondering what Master
Frederick Trotteville was up to now. Inspector Jenks had
a feeling that if he could put his finger on Master
Trotteville he would soon get to the bottom of everything.

He drove to Mr. Goon's house and found him in a state
of collapse. ' Oh, sir, I'm so glad you've come, ' stuttered
Mr. Goon, leading the Inspector by mistake into the
kitchen and then out again into the parlour.

' Pull yourself together, Goon, ' said the Inspector,
severely. ' What's happened, man ? '

' Well, it all began when my young nephew, Ern, came
to stay with me, ' began Mr. Goon. ' I warned the others,
sir, not to lead him into no mysteries—you know what
that young limb of a Frederick Trotteville is, sir, for
getting into trouble—and the first thing I know is that
there's a mystery up on Christmas Hill, sir—two gangs
there—one robbers and one kidnappers. '

' Most extraordinary, Goon, ' said the Inspector.
' Go on. '

' Well, sir, I went up to inspect one night—and sure
enough there were lights flashing by the hundred all

round me—red, blue and green, sir—a most amazing sight. '

' Quite a firework show ! ' said the Inspector.

' Then sir, there were awful noises—like cows bellowing, sir, and hens clucking, and cats mewing and—and well, the most peculiar noises you ever heard, sir. '

The Inspector eyed Mr. Goon sharply. He had a sort of feeling that if cows suddenly mooed on deserted hills, and hens clucked and cats mewed, there might possibly be some boy there having a fine old game with Mr. Goon. And that boy's name would be Fatty.

' Then, sir, ' said Mr. Goon, warming up, ' a great hefty giant of a man flung himself on me, sir—got me right down on my face, he did. He hit me and almost knocked me out. I had to fight for my life, sir. But I fought him off, and gave him a fearful trouncing. He'll bear the marks to his dying day. '

' And you caught him handcuffed him and brought him back with you, ' suggested the Inspector.

' No, sir. He got away, ' said Mr. Goon, sadly. ' Well, then, sir, I heard as how a robbery had been committed and the loot, sir, was to be hidden in the old mill. '

' And how did you hear that ? ' asked the Inspector with interest. ' And why not inform me ? '

' I heard it from my young nephew, sir, ' said Mr. Goon. ' He got it from Master Frederick. '

' I see, ' said the Inspector, beginning to understand quite a lot of things. That scamp of a Fatty ! He had led poor Mr. Goon properly astray this time. Inspector Jenks regretfully decided that he would have to give Fatty a good ticking-off.

' Then, sir, my nephew disappeared. He just went out and never came back. Two days ago that was. '

The Inspector asked the question that Mr. Goon had been dreading.

'Was the boy in any trouble?'

'Well—a bit,' admitted Mr. Goon. 'He—er—he wrote an extremely rude pome about me, sir—and I corrected him.'

'In what way?' asked the Inspector.

'I just gave him one or two strokes with a cane, sir,' said Mr. Goon. 'But I'm sure that's not what made him run away, sir—if he's run away. He's very fond of me, sir, and he's my favourite nephew.'

'H'm,' sid the Inspector, doubting all this very much. 'What next?'

'Well, sir, Master Frederick told me he thought he knew where Ern was, and if I'd wait till night, he'd probably bring him back again. So I waited up all last night, sir, but Master Frederick didn't come back—and now all the parents of those kids have rung up or come to see me to complain that their boys are missing!'

'This sounds rather serious to me,' said the Inspector. 'Are you sure you've told me everything, Goon?'

'Well—everything that's any use,' said Mr. Goon, hastily. 'I went up after the loot, sir, but I couldn't find it.'

'I wonder where in the world those four boys are!' said Inspector Jenks. 'I can't quite see where to begin looking for them. Or what to do. Where *can* they be?'

At that very moment three of the boys were staggering home! They had found their rope-ladder, climbed up over the wall, and dropped down the other side. They had lost their way, and wandered about for some time before they got back to the cart-track they knew. They were so tired that they hardly knew what they were doing.

By now it was getting light. Thankfully Fatty, Larry and Pip stumbled along the banks of the little stream. What miles it seemed! At last they came to the bridge and made their way into the village.

'Better go to Goon first and tell him Ern's all right,' said Fatty. 'I'll telephone the Inspector from there. Gosh, I'm tired!'

To the Inspector's astonishment, as he stood looking out of the window, he suddenly saw Fatty, Larry and Pip walking like very tired old men up the street.

'Look, Goon!' he said. 'Here are three of them. But no Ern!'

Mr. Goon groaned dismally. The three boys walked up his front path and knocked at the door. Fatty gaped with surprise and pleasure when the Inspector opened the door to him. 'Oh sir! This is lovely! You're just the person I wanted to see,' he said, and shook hands warmly.

'You're not fit to stand, any of you,' said the Inspector, looking at the dirty, tired-out boys. 'Goon, put on some milk for cocoa for these three. They could do with something. Then ring up their parents and tell them they are safe. Get on with it, now!'

Goon hurried to do as he was told. No Ern! Oh, what had happened to him? He felt that if only Ern would come back he would never never again say a cross word to him. Never!

Fatty and the others sank into chairs. Pip's eyes began to close.

'I'll take you all back in my car,' said the Inspector. 'You can tell me your story later. I already know about this, er—rather incredible mystery on Christmas Hill, Frederick—with flashing lights, mysterious noises, and the rest.'

'Oh that!' said Fatty. 'That's nothing, sir. That wasn't a mystery at all.'

'So I gathered,' said the Inspector. 'Ah, here is the cocoa. Thanks, Goon. Now ring up those boys' people, will you?'

'Sir, may I ask just one question first?' pleaded Mr. Goon. 'It's about Ern. Is he all right?'

'Oh, Ern. Yes, he's quite all right as far as I know,' said Fatty, taking a deep drink of the cocoa. 'Gosh, I've burnt my mouth.'

'Drink up the cocoa, and then get into my car,' said Inspector Jenks, alarmed at the pale, worn-out faces of the three boys. Pip was fast asleep.

'Good gracious, sir! I've got a story that will keep you busy for the rest of the day!' said Fatty, feeling better for the cocoa. He took another drink.

'Don't let Mr. Goon telephone to our people, sir,' he said. 'You'll want the phone yourself in another couple of minutes! I've got a first-class mystery for you, sir! All ready to hand you on a plate!'

# 24 A NEAT MYSTERY—AND A NEAT ENDING!

MR. GOON came into the room, his eyes bulging. 'What do you mean? A first-class mystery! Haven't you just said that mystery up on Christmas Hill wasn't one at all? And what about those lights then, and those noises, and that giant of a fellow that nearly killed me? What about *them*?'

'Oh those!' said Fatty. 'Larry and Pip flashed the lights. I made the noises. And I pounced on you in the ditch, thinking you were Ern.'

Mr. Goon collapsed like a pricked balloon. 'Frederick must have been very strong if he seemed like giant to you,' said the Inspector to Mr. Goon with a laugh.

'And the gangs, of course, were all our make-up, just to play a trick on Ern,' said Fatty. 'It wasn't our fault if Mr. Goon believed everything too. We didn't think he'd be as silly as Ern.'

Mr. Goon went red to the ears, but he said nothing.

'We threw down a lot of clues for Ern,' said Fatty, 'and made a story up about some loot that was hidden in the old mill. We meant Ern to go and look, but instead of that poor Ern got a caning, and was locked up in his bedroom—and Mr. Goon went to find the loot instead. But it wasn't there, of course.'

Mr. Goon wanted to sink down through the floor, but he couldn't. He sat there looking very unhappy indeed. That pestering boy!

'Well, Inspector, what began the *real* mystery was this,' said Fatty, taking another drink. 'Ern went off to Christmas Hill, as he thought—but he lost his way, and

saw one or two queer things over at Bourne Wood. And
that set us thinking. '

' Go on, ' said the Inspector. 'So you did a bit of
detecting ? '

' Yes, sir, ' said Fatty, modestly. ' We soon knew there
was something fishy going on at Harry's Folly, sir—the
building in the middle of Bourne Wood. We went to see
the caretaker—the man at the lodge called Peters—and
we made a few inquiries about a man called Holland, who
seemed a pretty queer customer ... '

' Holland? ' said the Inspector, sitting up straight. ' What
do you know about him ? '

' Quite a lot, now, ' said Fatty, with a grin. ' Why, do
you know him too, sir ? '

' We've been suspicious of him for a long time, ' said
the Inspector. ' But there was never anything we could
put our finger on. Lived quietly with an old aunt in
Peterswood, gave to the churches around—all that kind
of thing—and yet his name cropped up here and there in
queer circumstances. Well—go on ... '

' I disguised myself as Ern one day and went over to
Holland's garage to make inquiries—and he must have
recognized my name, sir—as being—er—well, a bit of a
detective, sir—and so, when he saw Ern wandering
around alone in a lonely lane, he kidnapped him—
thinking he was me, sir. '

' I see, ' aid the Inspector. Mr. Goon sat and looked as
if he really couldn't believe his ears !

' Ern was clever, sir, ' said Fatty. ' He threw a whole lot
of clues out of the car—pretended he was feeling sick, or
something, I should think—and Mr. Goon here picked
them up and gave them to me. '

Mr. Goon gulped. The Inspector looked at him. ' Very
kind of Goon. I suppose he knew you would make good
use of them. '

'Yes, sir. Actually he thought we'd put the clues there ourselves to fool him. As if we'd do a thing like that, sir!'

'Well, I wouldn't put it past you,' said the Inspector. 'But go on. We're wasting time.'

'I did a bit of deduction, sir, and thought Ern must have been kidnapped and was probably taken to Harry's Folly. So I and Larry and Pip set off to rescue him last night. We got in, sir, rope-ladder and all that—and found the house deserted. But in the garage, sir—my word!'

Goon and the Inspector were listening hard now. Pip was still fast asleep in his chair.

'There was a movable floor there, sir, that sank right down. It takes cars. They go down on it like a lift and then run slowly down a winding passage deep underground. And there's a workshop there, sir—with heaps of cars being repainted and done over ...'

The Inspector whistled. 'My word! So *that's* where it is! We've been looking for that workshop for a long long time, Frederick. You remember, Goon, I reported it to you two years ago and asked you to keep a lookout in your district, as we had information it was somewhere here. And there it was, all the time, right under your nose! Well done, Frederick, my boy!'

'We found Ern, sir, and he said he'd stay in his locked room all night long, so that his escape wouldn't raise the alarm. It would give us a chance to get back here and warn you, sir, so that perhaps you could catch the whole gang at work.'

'Very brave of the boy,' said the Inspector, approvingly. 'Good work! I hope you agree with me, Goon?'

'Yes, sir,' mumbled Goon, marvelling at the idea of Ern appearing suddenly as a hero.

'So we left him there, and had a hard job getting out unseen,' said Fatty. 'Went out in one of their own lorries in the end! And here we are!'

' A very fine job of work, Frederick, ' said the Inspector, getting up. ' And now, as you so wisely said, I shall have to have the use of the phone for a few minutes. '

Inspector Jenks went to the telephone and dialled rapidly. Larry and Fatty listened raptly. Pip still slept peacefully on. Mr. Goon looked gloomily at his hands. Always that boy came out on top. And Ern a hero, too! It wasn't possible that any one could have such bad luck as Mr. Goon!

Inspector Jenks spoke rapidly and to the point. Fatty listened in glee. Six police cars! Whew, what a round-up! He dug Larry in the ribs and they both grinned at one another.

The Inspector stopped telephoning. ' Now I'm going to take you all home, ' he said. ' It will be a few minutes before the police cars come along. Wake Pip up, and we'll get cracking. '

' Look here, Inspector, I'm going with you to Harry's Folly, aren't I? ' said Fatty, in alarm. ' You wouldn't be so mean as to leave me out of the end of it, would you? After all, I've done all the dirty work so far, and so have Larry and Pip. '

' All right. You can come with me if you want to— in *my* car, ' said the Inspector. ' But I may as well tell you that you won't be in the thick of it—only a sightseer! Now do wake that boy up and bring him along. '

Larry and Fatty half-carried the sleepy Pip to the Inspector's car. Then, with a roar, the engine started up and the powerful car sprang forward. Pip was deposited at his house with a few words of explanation. He sat down in a chair and again went off to sleep, in spite of Bets' frantic questions.

Then to Larry's home, where poor Larry was ordered to stay behind. Then to Fatty's own home, where a half-mad Buster hurled himself at Fatty as if he had been away for a year.

'Frederick is safe,' said the Inspector to Fatty's surprised parents. 'Bit of a marvel, as usual. Do you mind if I borrow him for a time? All news when I see you again.'

And Fatty was whipped away again in the car, with a very happy Buster on his knee, licking the underneath of his master's chin till it dripped.

Six other police cars joined them, and went slowly along the narrow cart-track to Harry's Folly. Peters, the gate-keeper, was terrified when he say the posse of blue-coated figures at the gate. He opened without a word, and was captured immediately, pale and trembling, looking quite different from the surly, bad-tempered fellow the five children had encountered some days before.

Fatty remained behind with the Inspector in his car, shaking with excitement. What was happening?

Plenty was happening. The raid was a complete and utter surprise. Every man down below in the workshop was rounded up—and Mr. Holland was discovered asleep in one of the bedrooms near Ern's!

Ern was not asleep. He was waiting and waiting. He didn't feel he could be a hero much longer. He was so terribly hungry, for one thing!

He was so glad to see Fatty, when he was led to the car by one of the policemen that he could hardly keep from hugging him.

'So this is Ern,' said the Inspector, and to the boy's enormous delight and surprise, he shook hands with him very warmly. 'Quite a hero, I hear—and a bit of a poet too. I must read that poem you wrote about your uncle, Ern. I'm sure it's very very good.'

Ern blushed. 'Oh, sir. Thank you, sir! I couldn't show it to you, sir. My uncle wouldn't like me to.'

The Inspector's car moved off, with the others following in a close line. 'A very good haul, Frederick,' said Inspector Jenks. 'A neat little mystery, and a neat ending. Thanks very much, my boy. Make haste and grow up! I want a right-hand man, you know!'

Fatty went red with pleasure, 'Right, sir, I'll do my best to grow up as soon as I can!'

They arrived at Mr. Goon's. Ern got out. He looked miserable all of a sudden.

'Come on in, Ern,' aid the Inspector, pulling him indoors. 'Goon! Here's Ern back again. Quite a hero! And I hear he's written a very fine poem about you. Shall we hear it?'

'Well ...' said Goon, going scarlet, 'it's, it's not very *polite*, sir ...'

'It's all right, Uncle, I won't read it,' said Ern, taking pity on his uncle. 'I'll tear it up, see?'

'You're a good boy, Ern,' said Mr. Goon. 'I'm right-down glad to see you back. I've got some bacon and eggs ready to cook for you. Like that?'

'Lovaduck!' said Ern, his face beaming. 'I could eat a horse. I'm that hungry.'

'Good-bye, Ern,' said Fatty. 'See you later.'

He drove off with the Inspector, who was taking him home to report on the exciting happenings. 'That poem of Ern's,' said the Inspector, neatly turning in at Fatty's drive. 'I'm sorry I didn't have the pleasure of reading it, after all.'

'Yes,' said Fatty, yawning. 'Spitty.'

'What?' said the Inspector, in surprise.

'Spitty,' said Fatty. 'SwatIsaid.' He slumped down against the Inspector's arm, and his eyes closed. He was fast asleep!

The Inspector left him there asleep, and went in to have a talk with Fatty's parents. What he said about Fatty should have made both his ears burn! But they didn't, because Fatty was lost in dreams that came crowding into his mind, thick and fast.

Flashing lights—movable floors—Christmas Hill—dark dire deeds—clues in plenty—spiral stairways—a dark dark house—and there was Ern, crowned with laurel leaves, a hero! He was just going to recite a marvellous poem.

'Lovaduck!' said Fatty, and woke up.